DATE DUE

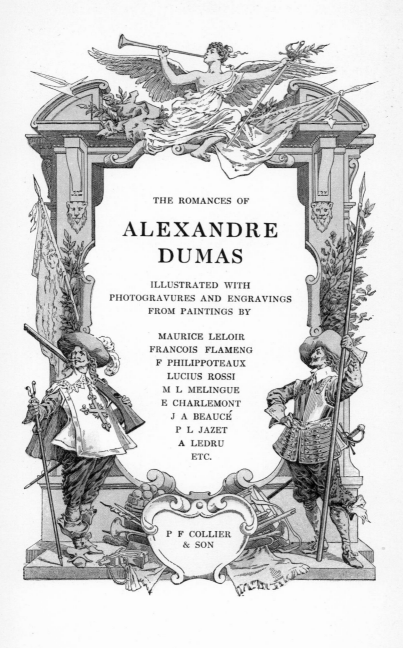

THE ROMANCES OF

ALEXANDRE DUMAS

ILLUSTRATED WITH
PHOTOGRAVURES AND ENGRAVINGS
FROM PAINTINGS BY

MAURICE LELOIR
FRANCOIS FLAMENG
F PHILIPPOTEAUX
LUCIUS ROSSI
M L MELINGUE
E CHARLEMONT
J A BEAUCÉ
P L JAZET
A LEDRU
ETC.

P F COLLIER
& SON

THE TWO DIANAS

VOLUME TWO

ILLUSTRATED

NEW YORK

P. F COLLIER & SON

PUBLISHERS

103581

CONTENTS

THE TWO DIANAS

CHAPTER I

LOVE SHARED

THEN Diana threw herself into the arms of Gabriel.

"And I must thank and bless you also, my Gabriel," said she. "My last thought before I fainted was to invoke my guardian angel, and you came. Oh, how I thank you!"

"Ah, Diana," said he, "how I have suffered since I saw you last, and how long it is since that!"

"And what of me, then?" she cried.

Then they began recounting, with a superfluity of details the reverse of dramatic, it must be acknowledged, all they had done and felt during an absence each had found so difficult to bear.

Calais, the Duke de Guise, the conqueror, and the conquered, all were forgotten. All the rumors and all the passions that surrounded the lovers did not affect them. Lost in their world of love and rapture, they no longer heard, they no longer saw, the world beyond them.

The soul that has encountered so many griefs and so many terrors is, in some sort, weakened and enfeebled by suffering, and, although strong against sorrow, cannot resist happiness.

In the soothing atmosphere of pure emotions, Diana and Gabriel willingly abandoned themselves to the gentle influence of that serenity and joy to which they had been hitherto unaccustomed.

To the scene of violent passion we have described succeeded another at once like and different.

"How good it is to be near you, my love!" said Diana. "Instead of the presence of that impious man whom I hated and who frightened me, what delight your reassuring and dear presence affords me!"

"And," said Gabriel, "since our infancy, when we were happy without knowing it, I do not remember, during my isolated and agitated life, a moment to be compared with this."

For a time they were silent, absorbed in mutual adoration. Diana resumed:

"Come and sit close to me, Gabriel. Would you believe it? Even in captivity, I have dreamed and almost foreseen the moment that united us in such an unhoped-for fashion. I had a surety that you would be my deliverer, and that in my last extremity God would bring you, my knight, to save me."

"And as to me, Diana, the thought of you," said Gabriel, "at once attracted me like a magnet and guided me like a light. Shall I confess it to you and to my conscience? Although other powerful motives might have urged me on, I should never have conceived the idea of taking Calais, never accomplished it by such rash methods, if you had not been here a prisoner; if an instinctive knowledge of the perils you ran had not inspired and encouraged me. Except for the hope of succoring you, except for another sacred interest that forms the object of my life, Calais would still be in the power of the English. God grant that I may not be punished for having wished and done good through purely interested motives!"

The Viscount d'Exmès thought for a moment of the scene in the Rue St. Jacques, of the self-denial of Ambroise Paré, and of the austere belief of the admiral that Heaven wishes pure hands for pure causes.

But the beloved voice of Diana reassured him, when it cried—

"God punish you, Gabriel! God punish you for having been great and generous!"

"Who knows?" said he, questioning Heaven with eyes that had in them a gloomy presentiment.

"I know," replied Diana, with her charming smile.

She was so enchanting when she said so that Gabriel, struck with her glorious beauty, and forgetting all other thoughts, could not help exclaiming—

"Diana, you are beautiful as an angel!"

"And you valiant as a hero, Gabriel!" she replied.

They were seated near each other. Their hands by chance met and clasped. Night was beginning to fall.

Diana, blushing to the temples, rose and took some steps across the chamber.

"You are leaving me, you are flying from me, Diana," said Gabriel, sadly.

"Oh, no!" she returned quickly, going up to him. "With you, it is different; I am not afraid, my dear Gabriel."

Diana was wrong. The danger was different; but it was still danger, and the friend was not less, perhaps, to be feared than the enemy.

"Well and good," said Gabriel, taking the soft little white hand she abandoned to him anew; "well and good, let us be happy for a little, after suffering so much. Let us unburden our souls and let them rest in confidence and joy."

"True," replied Diana; "I feel so happy by your side, Gabriel. Let us forget for a moment the world and the tumult around us; let us enjoy this delicious hour. God, I believe, will permit us to do so without trouble and without fear. You are right; else why have we suffered so?"

With a graceful movement familiar to her from childhood, she laid her charming head upon Gabriel's shoulder. Her great velvet eyes softly closed, and her hair touched the lips of the ardent young man.

It was he now who rose shuddering and confused.

"Well?" said Diana, opening her astonished and languishing eyes.

He fell on his knees before her, quite pale, and flung his arms around her.

"Diana, I love you! I love you!" he cried from the depths of his heart.

"And I love you, Gabriel!" answered Diana, courageously, and as if obeying an irresistible instinct of her heart.

How their faces approached, how their lips united, how in that kiss their souls mingled, God alone knows; for it is certain they did not know themselves.

But suddenly Gabriel, who felt his soul stagger under the confusing weight of so much happiness, tore himself from the arms of Diana.

"Diana, let me fly!" he cried in accents of terror.

"Fly! and why?" she asked, surprised.

"Diana! Diana! if you were my sister!" returned Gabriel, beside himself.

"Your sister!" repeated Diana, thunderstruck.

Gabriel stopped, astonished and to some extent stunned by his own words, and, passing his hand over his burning brow, he asked in a loud voice:

"What, then, have I said?"

"What have you said, indeed?" returned Diana. "Are those terrible words of yours to be taken literally? What is the solution of this frightful mystery? Good heavens! am I really your sister?"

"My sister? did I confess you were my sister?" said Gabriel.

"Ah, then it is true!" cried Diana, trembling.

"No, it is not, it cannot be true. I do not know; who can know? And, besides, I ought not to have told you all this. It is a secret of life and death I had sworn to keep. Ah, merciful Heaven! I preserved my coolness and my reason in suffering and misfortune; must the first drop of happiness that touches my lips intoxicate me even to madness, even to forgetfulness of my oaths?"

"Gabriel," returned Madame de Castro, gravely, "God

knows it is not a vain curiosity that leads me on. But you have said either too much or too little for my repose. It is necessary to finish now."

"Impossible! impossible!" cried Gabriel, with a sort of dismay.

"And why impossible?" said Diana. "Something assures me that those secrets belong to me as much as to you, and that you have not the right to hide them from me."

"You are right," replied Gabriel; "and you have certainly as much claim to bear these sorrows as I have. But since the burden crushes me alone, do not ask me to share it with you."

"Yes, I demand and wish it, I insist on sharing your troubles," rejoined Diana; "and, in addition to all this, I implore you, Gabriel, my friend, do not refuse me."

"But I have taken an oath to the king," said Gabriel, anxiously.

"You have taken an oath?" returned Diana. "Well, keep that oath loyally with regard to strangers and even toward friends: you will act rightly in doing so. But since I, by your own confession, have the same interest in this mystery as you, can you, ought you, to observe a pernicious silence? No, Gabriel, if you feel any pity for me. My anxiety upon this subject has already sufficiently tortured my heart. In this respect, if not, alas! in the other accidents of your life, I am in some sort your second self. Do you perjure yourself when you think of your secret in the solitude of your conscience? Do you believe that my soul, profound and sincere, and ripened by so many trials, cannot as well as yours guard jealously the secret confided to it, whether that secret be one of joy or sorrow—a secret, too, which is mine as well as yours."

The tender and caressing words flowed on, touching the fibres of the young man's heart, as if it were some responsive instrument.

"And then, Gabriel, since fate forbids us to be joined in

love and happiness, how have you the courage to refuse the only fellowship allowed us, that of sorrow? Shall we, at least, not suffer less if we suffer together? Would it not be a grievous thing if the only bond that unites us should keep us apart?"

And, feeling that Gabriel, though half conquered, still hesitated—

"Moreover, take care!" continued Diana; "if you persist in your silence, why should I not use that language which just now, I know not why, caused you such anguish and terror—language which you once taught my lips and my heart? The woman who is your betrothed in the sight of Heaven can, in all chastity, lay her head on your shoulder, and her lips on your brow, as I do now—"

But Gabriel, heart-broken, again released himself from Diana with a shudder.

"No, Diana, have mercy on my reason, I supplicate you!" he cried. "You would know absolutely, then, my terrible secret? Well, to escape a possible crime, I will tell it to you! Yes, Diana, it is necessary to take literally the words I let fall in my anguish a moment ago. Diana, you are perhaps the daughter of Count Montgommery, my father! you are perhaps my sister!"

"Holy Virgin!" murmured Madame de Castro, crushed by this revelation.

"But how can this be?" she asked.

"I should have wished," he said, "that your calm, pure life had never known this history, full as it is of terror and of crime. But, alas! I feel too well that my own strength is not a sufficient shield against my love. You must help me against yourself, Diana, and I am going to tell you everything."

"I listen to you with dismay, but with attention," answered Diana.

Gabriel then related everything: how his father had loved Madame de Poitiers, and, in the opinion of all the court, had appeared to be loved in return; how the dauphin,

to-day the king, had been his rival; how the Count de Montgommery had disappeared, and how Aloyse had succeeded
in learning, and had revealed to his son, what had become
of him. This was all his nurse knew, and, as Madame de
Poitiers refused to speak, Count Montgommery alone, if he
were still alive, could tell the secret of Diana's birth.

When Gabriel had finished his gloomy narrative—

"It is frightful!" cried Diana. "Whatever be the issue,
my friend, our destiny must be miserable in the end. If I
am the daughter of Count de Montgommery, you are my
brother, Gabriel; if I am the daughter of the king, you are
the justly angered enemy of my father. In any case, we are
separated."

"No, Diana," replied Gabriel, "our misfortune is not
quite hopeless. Since I have begun by telling you everything, I am going to finish. And, indeed, I feel that you
have been right: this confidence has relieved me, and
my secret has, after all, only left my heart to enter into
yours."

Gabriel then informed Diana of the strange and dangerous compact he had concluded with Henry the Second,
and the solemn promise of the king to restore liberty to
Count Montgommery, if his son, after defending St. Quentin against the Spaniards, should take Calais from the
English.

Now Calais became a French city an hour ago; and
Gabriel might, without vanity, believe that he had largely
contributed to this glorious result.

As he spoke, hope dispelled gradually the sadness that
overshadowed Diana's countenance, as the dawn dispels
the darkness.

When Gabriel had finished, she remained a moment in
pensive meditation; then, offering him her hand—

"My poor Gabriel," said she, firmly, "there will be for
us in the future, as there has been in the past, much to
think of and much to suffer. But let us not dwell upon
that, my friend. We must not become weak and enfeebled.

For my part, I will try to prove myself strong and courageous, like you, and with you. The essential thing at present
is to act and solve the riddle of our lives in some fashion
or other. Our sorrow is, I think, near its end. You have
kept, and more than kept, your engagement with the king.
The king will keep his, I hope, to you. It is upon that
hope we must henceforth concentrate all our feelings and
all our thoughts. What do you intend doing now?"

"The Duke de Guise," replied Gabriel, "has been my
illustrious confidant and associate in all I have done here.
I know that, without him, I could have done nothing. But
he knows he could have done nothing without me. It is he,
and he alone, who can and should attest to the king the part
I had in this new conquest. I have the more reason to expect this act of justice from him that he has a second time
within the last few days solemnly promised to bear witness
in my behalf. Now, I am going immediately to recall to
M. de Guise his promise, to ask a letter for his Majesty,
and, as my presence here is no longer necessary, to set out
at once for Paris."

As Gabriel was still speaking with animation, and Diana
was listening, her eyes bright with hope, the door opened,
and Jean Peuquoy appeared, dejected and alarmed.

"Well! what is the matter?" asked Gabriel, anxiously.
"Is Martin Guerre worse?"

"No, M. le Vicomte; Martin Guerre has been trans-
ported to our house, and visited by Master Ambroise Paré.
Although the amputation of the leg is necessary, Master
Paré is certain that your brave servant will survive the
operation."

"Glorious news! Master Paré is doubtless still with
him?" said Gabriel.

"Monseigneur," sadly replied Jean Peuquoy, "he has
been obliged to leave him in order to attend another patient
of greater importance and in greater danger."

"Who is it?" asked Gabriel, changing color—"Marshal
Strozzi? M. de Nevers?"

"M. de Guise, who is dying at this moment," answered Jean Peuquoy.

Gabriel and Diana uttered a cry of grief at the same time.

"And I said we were nearing the end of our sorrows!" replied Madame de Castro, after a silence of some time. "Oh, my God! my God!"

"Do not call upon God, madame!" said Gabriel, with a melancholy smile. "God is just, and justly punishes my selfishness. I took Calais for the sake of my father; and Thou, O God, hast willed that I should take it for the sake of France!"

CHAPTER II

THE BALAFRÉ

NEVERTHELESS, all hope was not dead for Gabriel and Diana, for the Duke de Guise still breathed. The wretched cling eagerly to the most uncertain chances, just as the shipwrecked clutch at any floating fragment. Viscount d'Exmès then left Diana with the view of seeing for himself the extent of the fresh misfortune that had fallen upon them, at the very moment their evil fortune seemed about to relax its rigors.

Jean Peuquoy, who accompanied him, related on the way all that had taken place.

Lord Derby, summoned by the mutinous burghers to surrender before the hour fixed by Lord Wentworth, had sent a flag of truce to the Duke de Guise to treat of capitulation.

However, the combat still lasted at several points, rendered more implacable in its last efforts by the anger of the conquered and the impatience of the conquerors.

Francis de Lorraine, as intrepid a soldier as he was an able general, was always in the thickest and hottest of the fight.

The calamity occurred at a breach already half carried, on the other side of a ditch entirely filled up.

The Duke de Guise, a mark for the weapons aimed at him from every direction, was on horseback, tranquilly encouraging his men by word and example.

Suddenly he perceived, above the breach, the white flag of truce.

A proud smile flitted over his noble visage; for it was the final consecration of his victory he beheld coming toward him.

"Halt!" he cried, in the midst of the tumult, to those around him. "Calais surrenders. Down with your arms!"

He raised the visor of his casque, and rode a few yards forward, his eyes riveted on that flag, the emblem of triumph and peace.

Night, however, was coming on, and the tumult did not cease.

An English soldier, who probably, on account of the uproar, had not seen the flag nor heard the Duke de Guise, seized the rein of his horse, making the animal rear; and as the duke, who in his preoccupation did not perceive that anything was the matter, was giving the spurs to his horse, the man struck him on the head with his lance.

"They could not tell me what part of his face was wounded; but it is certain that the wound is terrible. The lance was broken, and the iron has remained in the flesh. The duke did not utter a word, and fell forward upon the pommel of his saddle. The Englishman who dealt this disastrous blow was cut in pieces by the maddened French soldiers. But, alas! that did not save M. de Guise. He was borne away like one dead. He has not recovered consciousness since."

"So that even Calais is not in our hands?" asked Gabriel.

"Oh, yes," replied Jean Peuquoy. "M. de Nevers received the flag of truce, and, like a master, imposed most stringent conditions. But the gain of such a city will hardly compensate France for the loss of such a hero."

"Great God! you already regard him as dead?" said Gabriel, with a shudder.

"Alas, alas!" was the weaver's sole answer, as he shook his head.

"And where are you leading me so fast? You know, then, where they have carried him?"

"Into the guard-house of the Chateau-Neuf; the man who brought the fatal news told Master Ambroise Paré. Master Paré wished to run there at once; Pierre showed him the way, and I came to tell you the news. I had a feeling that it had special importance for you, and that in this crisis you would have doubtless something to do."

"I have as much reason to grieve as others, and more than others," said Viscount d'Exmès. "But," he added, "as far as the night allows me to distinguish objects, it would seem we are drawing near."

"Yes; that's the Chateau-Neuf," said Jean Peuquoy.

An immense crowd of citizens and soldiers, anxious and murmuring, blocked up the approaches to the guard-house into which the Duke de Guise had been carried. Questions, conjectures, and criticisms were circulating through these restless groups, as when a breath of wind stirs the responsive shadows of the forest.

Viscount d'Exmès and Jean Peuquoy had much difficulty in piercing this crowd and reaching the steps of the guard-house, the entrance to which was defended by a strong detachment of pikemen and halberdiers. Some of them held flaming torches, which cast a reddish glare over the moving masses of the people.

Gabriel started when he perceived, by this uncertain light, Ambroise Paré, standing at the bottom of the steps, gloomy and motionless, with eyebrows contracted, pressing his arms convulsively against his heaving breast. Tears of grief and indignation were shining in his fine eyes.

Behind him stood Pierre Peuquoy, as gloomy and as downcast as he.

"You here, Master Paré!" cried Gabriel. "But what are you doing here? If there is a breath of life in M. de Guise, your place is by his side!"

"Ah! there is no need to tell me that, M. d'Exmès," said he, as soon as he recognized Gabriel. "Say so to those stupid guards, if you have any authority over them."

"What! do they refuse to let you pass?" asked Gabriel.

"They won't hear a word from me," replied Ambroise Paré. "O God! to think that so precious a life should depend on such miserable fatalities!"

"But you must enter!" said Gabriel. "They must have gone the wrong way about it."

"We first entreated," interposed Peuquoy, "and then threatened. Our prayers were answered with laughter, our threats with blows. Master Paré, who tried to force a passage, was violently driven back, and wounded by a halberd, I think."

"It is quite simple," replied Paré, bitterly. "I have neither collar nor spurs of gold; I have only a keen glance and a sure hand."

"Wait; I'll see that you enter," said Gabriel. He advanced to the steps, but a pikeman, while bowing respectfully, barred his passage.

"Excuse me," he said deferentially; "we have received orders to let no one pass."

"Rascal!" returned Gabriel, still restraining himself, "do your orders affect Viscount d'Exmès, Captain of his Majesty's Guards, and friend of M. de Guise? Where is your leader? I want to speak to him."

"Monseigneur, he guards the inner door," replied the pikeman, more humbly than ever.

"I am going to him," replied M. d'Exmès, imperiously. "Come, Master Paré."

"Monseigneur, pass, since you insist," said the soldier; "but this man cannot pass."

"And why?" asked Gabriel. "Why cannot the surgeon attend the wounded?"

"All the surgeons, doctors, and quacks," answered the pikeman, "at least, all recognized and patented, have been summoned. There is not a single one lacking, I have been told."

"Ah! that is the very thing that frightens me!" said Ambroise Paré, with ironical disdain.

"That one there has no license in his pocket," continued

the soldier. "He has saved a good many in the camp, it is true; but he was not made for dukes."

"A truce to words!" cried Gabriel, stamping his foot impatiently. "I order Master Paré to come with me."

"Impossible, M. le Vicomte."

"I have said, I order, rascal!"

"But, monseigneur, my orders force me to disobey you."

"Ah!" cried Ambroise, sorrowfully, "the duke is perhaps dying during this ridiculous dispute."

This cry would have scattered all the hesitations of Gabriel, if the impetuous young man had felt any at such a moment.

"Do you wish me to treat you, then, as I treated the English!" he shouted to the halberdiers. "So much the worse for you, then! After all, the life of M. de Guise is worth twenty such lives as yours! We will see if your pikes dare to touch my sword."

The blade leaped from the scabbard like a flash of lightning, and, dragging Master Paré after him, he ascended the steps of the guard-house with uplifted sword.

His attitude and look was so menacing, there was so much serene strength in the demeanor of the surgeon, and, besides, the person and wishes of a gentleman had at that time such prestige, that the submissive guards stood aside and lowered their weapons, subjugated less by the sword than by the name of Viscount d'Exmès.

"Ah! let them pass!" cried a voice in the crowd. "They look as if they were sent by God to save the Duke de Guise!"

Gabriel and Paré reached the door of the guard-house without further obstacle.

The lieutenant of the soldiers and three or four soldiers were stationed in the narrow vestibule leading to the principal hall.

Viscount d'Exmès said to him briefly, and in a tone that admitted no reply—

"I am bringing a new surgeon to monseigneur."

The lieutenant bowed, and let him pass without making any objection.

Gabriel and Paré entered.

The attention of all was too deeply engrossed by the harrowing spectacle before them to permit them to notice the new-comers.

The sight that met the latter was truly terrible and heartrending.

On a camp-bed, in the middle of the hall, lay the Duke de Guise, motionless and unconscious, his face covered with blood.

That face was pierced through and through; the iron of the lance, after entering the cheek under the right eye, had penetrated as far as the nape of the neck beneath the left ear, and the fragment, broken off, projected half a foot from the head. The wound was horrible to behold.

Around the bed were ten or twelve surgeons, standing appalled amid the general desolation.

But they were not acting; they were only looking on and speaking.

At the moment when Gabriel entered with Ambroise Paré, one of them was saying, in a loud voice—

"So, after having consulted, we have found ourselves under the painful necessity of concluding that the Duke de Guise is mortally wounded; for, to have any chance of saving him, the fragment of the lance must be pulled out of the wound, and to do so would be to kill monseigneur at once."

"Then you prefer to let him die!" said Ambroise Paré, boldly, from behind the first row of the spectators—Ambroise Paré, who, from a distance, had judged at a single glance that the condition of the sufferer was almost hopeless.

The surgeon who had spoken raised his head to find out who was the audacious interrupter, and, not seeing him, resumed—

"Who is the foolhardy person who would dare to lay his impious hands upon that august visage, and risk, without any chance of success, hastening the death of such a hero?"

"I!" said Ambroise Paré, advancing, with head erect, into the midst of the surgeons. And, not troubling himself on account of the comments of those about him, and the murmurs of astonishment his appearance excited, he leaned over the duke to examine the wound more closely.

"Ah! it is Master Ambroise Paré!" retorted the surgeon-in-chief, disdainfully, as he recognized the madman who had ventured to differ from him. "Master Ambroise Paré," he added, "forgets he has not the honor of being numbered among the surgeons of the Duke de Guise."

"Say, rather, that I am his only surgeon, since his ordinary surgeons abandon him," answered Ambroise. "Moreover, M. de Guise, a few days ago, having seen me perform an operation, was good enough to say, very seriously if not officially, that he claimed my services whenever there was need of them. M. d'Exmès, who was present, will testify to that."

"I affirm that what you say is true," said Gabriel.

Ambroise Paré had already returned to the apparently lifeless body of the duke, and was examining the wound anew.

"Well," asked the surgeon-in-chief, with an ironical smile, "do you still persist, after your diagnosis, in extracting the iron?"

"I persist," said Paré, resolutely.

"And what marvellous instrument do you intend to use?"

"My hands," said he.

"I protest firmly," cried the surgeon, furiously, "against any such profanation of the illustrious sufferer's last agony."

"And we join you in your protest," shouted all the other surgeons.

"Have you any method of saving the prince's life?" rejoined Ambroise.

"No, for it is impossible," said they all.

"He is, then, mine," said Ambroise, stretching his hand over the body, as if to take possession.

"Then we retire," replied the surgeon-in-chief, who, with his *confrères*, made a movement as if to withdraw.

"But what are you going to do?" Ambroise was asked from all quarters.

"The Duke de Guise is apparently dead; I am going to treat him as if he were really dead," answered Ambroise.

So saying, he took off his doublet and tucked up his sleeves.

"To make such experiments on monseigneur, as if *in anima vili!*" said a scandalized old practitioner, clasping his hands.

"Yes!" replied Ambroise Paré, without turning his eyes from the patient; "I am going to treat him, not as a man, not even as an *anima vilis*, but as a thing. Look."

He boldly planted his foot on the breast of the duke.

A murmur of doubt, terror, and menace ran through the assembly.

"Take care, master!" said M. de Nevers, touching him on the shoulder; "take care! If you fail, I cannot answer for the anger of the friends and servants of the duke."

"Indeed!" said Ambroise, with a sad smile, turning round.

"You risk your head!" exclaimed another.

"Be it so!" he said, lifting his eyes to heaven with a melancholy seriousness; "I risk my head for his. But, at least," he added, proudly, "do not disturb me while doing so!"

All stood aside with a sort of respect for the supremacy of genius.

In the solemn silence that ensued nothing was heard but the labored breathings of the spectators.

Ambroise Paré placed his left knee upon the breast of the duke; then, leaning over, he took the wood of the lance in the tips of his fingers and shook it, first gently, but gradually with more force.

The duke started as if in horrible torture.

All the affrighted spectators turned equally pale.

Ambroise Paré paused for a second, as if struck with terror. An agonizing perspiration bedewed his forehead; but he returned to his work almost immediately.

At the end of a minute—a minute longer than an hour—the iron was extracted.

Ambroise Paré quickly flung it from him, and bent over the gaping wound.

When he rose a flash of joy illuminated his visage; but soon, resuming his usual seriousness, he fell on his knees, and poured out his thanks to God, while tears of joy slowly rolled down his cheeks.

It was a sublime moment. Without the great surgeon speaking, every one knew there was hope now. The servants of the duke wept warm tears; others kissed the skirts of his coat.

But all were silent; they awaited his first words.

At last, in a grave, though moved voice, he said—

"I answer now for the life of Monseigneur de Guise."

And, in fact, an hour after the Duke de Guise had recovered consciousness, and even speech.

Ambroise Paré finished bandaging the wound, and Gabriel was standing beside the bed to which the surgeon had had his illustrious patient carried.

"So, Gabriel," said the duke, "I not only owe you the possession of Calais, but also my life, since you have brought Ambroise Paré to me, almost by force."

"Yes, monseigneur," returned Ambroise, "without the aid of M. d'Exmès I could not have even come near you."

"Oh, my two saviors!" exclaimed Francis de Guise.

"Do not speak so much, monseigneur, I beg you," rejoined the surgeon.

"Well, well, I am silent. But allow me one word; only a single question."

"What is it, monseigneur?"

"Do you think, Master Paré, that the effects of this horrible wound will injure me in mind or body?"

"Not the slightest danger of that, monseigneur," said Ambroise. "But it will, I fear, leave a scar—a *balafré*—"

"A scar!" cried the duke. "Oh, that's nothing! A scar is an ornament to a soldier. It would not at all displease me if I were known by the sobriquet of the *Balafré*."

We know that both his contemporaries and posterity have been of the opinion of the Duke de Guise, who, from that time forward, as well as his son after him, has been surnamed the Balafré by his contemporaries and by history.

CHAPTER III

A PARTIAL DÉNOUEMENT

W E HAVE now reached the 8th of January, the morrow of the day when Gabriel d'Exmès restored to the King of France Calais, one of his fairest cities, lost to him for so long, and his greatest captain, the Duke de Guise, who was on the brink of the grave.

But it is no longer our intention to deal with questions involving the fate of nations, but rather with the interests of ordinary citizens and with family life. From the breach before Calais and the sick bed of Francis de Lorraine, we pass to the lower hall in the house of the Peuquoys.

It was there that Jean Peuquoy had caused Martin Guerre to be carried, in order that he might be as little fatigued as possible; and it was there where Ambroise Paré, the evening before, had, with his usual success, performed on the brave squire the amputation he judged necessary.

So what until now was only hope became certainty. Martin Guerre, it is true, would lose a leg, but Martin Guerre would live.

To depict the regret, or rather the remorse, of Pierre Peuquoy, when he learned the truth, would be impossible. That stern but honest and loyal soul could never pardon himself his cruel mistake. The worthy armorer conjured Martin again and again to accept all that he possessed— his heart and arm, his goods and his life.

But we know that Martin Guerre did not wait for this

expression of repentance to pardon Pierre Peuquoy, and even approve of his action.

They were, therefore, on the best of terms, and the reader will not be astonished to learn that a domestic council, similar to that we have brought to his notice during the bombardment, was held in the presence of Martin Guerre.

M. d'Exmès, who was to set out the same evening for Paris, was also present at their deliberations—deliberations less painful, after all, for his brave allies of Fort Risbank than those which had occurred before.

In fact, the reparation the honor of the Peuquoys demanded was not entirely impossible. The true Martin Guerre was married; but nothing proved that such was the case with the seducer of Babette. The question was, then, how to find the culprit.

Consequently, the countenance of Pierre Peuquoy expressed more serenity and calmness. That of Jean, on the contrary, was sad, and Babette seemed utterly cast down.

Gabriel observed them all in silence; and Martin Guerre, stretched on his bed of suffering, was disheartened at the thought that he could do nothing for his new friends except furnish some very vague and uncertain information as to the personality of his Sosia.

Pierre and Jean Peuquoy had just returned from seeing the Duke de Guise. The latter had refused to delay longer giving thanks to the brave burgher patriots for the successful and glorious part they had played in securing the surrender of the city; Gabriel had escorted them to his bedside on his express demand.

Pierre Peuquoy related to Babette, with pride and delight, the details of their reception.

"Yes, sister," said he; "when M. d'Exmès recounted to the duke our co-operation in all this, in terms far too flattering and exaggerated, that great man deigned to testify his satisfaction, both to Jean and me, with a gracious kindness the memory of which shall never leave me were I to live a

nundred years. But he particularly gladdened and touched
me when he expressed a desire to do us some service in his
turn, and asked how he could be useful to us. You know
me, Babette; I cared for nothing on my own account. But
are you aware what service I intend to ask of him?"

"No, really, brother," murmured Babette.

"Well, sister," said he, "as soon as we have found the
man who has so unworthily deceived you—and that we
shall find him you may rest assured—I shall ask M. de
Guise to aid me with his credit in restoring our honor. Of
ourselves, we are neither strong nor rich enough. And
such support may, perhaps, be necessary for us, in order
to obtain justice."

"And if, even with this support, justice fails you,
cousin?" asked Jean.

"Thanks to this arm," said Pierre, energetically, "vengeance, at least, will not fail me! And yet!" he continued,
looking timidly in the direction of Martin Guerre, "I must
admit that violence has not succeeded very well with me so
far, either."

He was silent and pensive for a minute. When he recovered from his revery, he perceived, with surprise, that
Babette was weeping.

"What ails you, sister?" he asked.

"Ah! I am very unhappy!" cried Babette, sobbing.

"Unhappy! and why? The future, it seems to me,
looks bright enough."

"It is growing dark, on the contrary," she answered.

"No, all will be well; do not be uneasy," said Pierre
Peuquoy. "Between a pleasant reparation and a terrible
chastisement he will not hesitate. Your lover will soon
return, and you will be his wife—"

"And if I refuse him for a husband?" cried Babette.

Jean Peuquoy could not restrain a movement of joy,
which did not escape Gabriel.

"Refuse him?" answered Pierre, in amazement. "But
you loved him!"

"I loved," said Babette, "the man who was suffering, who seemed to love me, who showed me respect and affection. But the deceiver, the liar, who stole the words, the name, and perhaps the very clothes of another, to surprise one poor heart, ah! him I hate and despise!"

"But still, if he married you?" asked Pierre Peuquoy.

"He would marry me," said Babette, "because forced to do so, or because he might thereby obtain the favor of the Duke de Guise. He would give me his name through fear or through cupidity. No, no! I do not want him now, any longer!"

"Babette," replied Pierre Peuquoy, severely, "you have not the right to say, 'I do not want him.'"

"Oh, my dear brother, for pity's sake! do not ask me to marry a man whom you yourself called a wretch and a coward," cried Babette, in tears.

"Babette, think that your forehead is branded with dishonor."

"I prefer to blush for my love for a moment than to blush for my husband all my life."

"Babette, think that your child will be without a father."

"Better for him, I fancy, to lose a father who would detest him than a mother who will adore him. Now, if his mother marry this man, she will certainly die of shame and sorrow."

"So, Babette, you refuse to listen to my remonstrances and prayers?"

"Give me your affection and your pity, brother, I implore you."

"Well, then," said Pierre Peuquoy, "my pity and my affection will answer you with pain indeed, but with firmness. As it is above all necessary, Babette, that you live esteemed by others and by yourself, as I should prefer to see you unhappy rather than dishonored, because, being dishonored, you would be twice unhappy, I, your brother, and the head of your family, understand me well, insist that you marry, if he consent, the man who has ruined you, and who alone can restore to you the honor you have lost. Both law and religion arm me with an authority I shall, I warn you, use if necessary, in order to force you to do what I consider your duty toward God, your family, and yourself."

"You are condemning me to death, brother," said Babette, in an altered voice. "It is well; I am resigned, since it is my destiny and my punishment, and since no one intercedes for me."

She looked while speaking at Gabriel and Jean Peuquoy, both silent, the one because he wished to observe, the other because he suffered.

But at this direct appeal of Babette, Jean could contain himself no longer, and, addressing her, but turning to his cousin, he said in an ironical tone not at all characteristic of him—

"Whom do you wish to intercede for you, Babette? Is not what your brother exacts from you altogether just and wise? His views are, in truth, admirable. He has chiefly at heart the honor of the family and yours; and to safeguard that honor, what does he do? He compels you to marry a forger. It is marvellous. It is true that once this wretch has entered the family, he will dishonor it by his conduct. It is certain that M. d'Exmès, here present, will not fail to call him to a severe account, in the name of Martin Guerre, for his infamous impersonation, and that the consequence may be your appearance, Babette, before the judges, as the wife of this abominable stealer of another's name. But what does it matter? You will not the less belong to him by the most legitimate title; your child will not the less be the lawful and recognized son of the false Martin Guerre. You will perhaps die of the shame of being his wife. But your reputation as a young girl will remain intact in the eyes of all."

Jean Peuquoy expressed himself with a warmth and indignation that struck Babette herself with surprise.

"I do not recognize you, Jean," said Pierre, in astonishment.

"It is because I am calm and moderate," returned Jean, "that I have a clearer view of the position you would make for us to-day."

"Do you believe, then, that I should accept the infamy of my brother-in-law more quietly than the dishonor of my sister? No; if I discover the seducer of Babette, I am in hopes his deception will have harmed only ourselves and Babette. In that case, I reckon on the good-will of Martin Guerre to desist from a complaint that would affect the innocent as well as the guilty."

"Oh," said Martin Guerre, from his bed, "I am not vindictive, and do not wish the death of the sinner. Let him pay his debt to you, and I cry quits, as far as I am concerned."

"That is all very fine for the past," returned Jean Peuquoy, not at all enchanted by Martin's clemency. "But the future? Who will answer for the future?"

"I will look out for that," said Pierre. "Babette's husband shall be ever under my eye, and he must act like an honest man and walk straight, or—"

"You will execute justice upon him yourself, will you not?" interrupted Jean. "It will have been full time. Meanwhile, Babette will not have been the less sacrificed."

"But, Jean," retorted Pierre, somewhat impatiently, "if the position is difficult, I endure it; I have not made it. Have you, who talk so much, found any other way out of it?"

"Yes, undoubtedly there is another way out of it," said Jean Peuquoy.

"What is it?" asked Pierre and Babette together; Pierre, it must be acknowledged, with as much eagerness as his sister.

Viscount d'Exmès still kept silence, but listened with renewed attention.

"Well," said Jean Peuquoy, "could not an honest man

be found who, touched rather than frightened by the misfortune of Babette, would consent to give her his name?"

Pierre shook his head incredulously.

"There is no hope of such a thing," said he. "The man who would shut his eyes in the circumstances would have to be either a lover or a base wretch. In any case, we should be obliged to share our family secrets with those who were strangers, or with those who were indifferent; and although M. d'Exmès and Martin are our devoted friends, I regret already that circumstances should have revealed a secret that should have never left the family."

Jean Peuquoy resumed with an emotion he tried vainly to dissemble—

"I would not propose a base wretch for the husband of Babette; but is not your other alternative, Pierre, equally admissible? If some one loved my cousin, if events had made him cognizant of the fault, but also of the repentance, and if he had determined, in order to insure himself a peaceful and happy future, to forget a past which Babette will most certainly efface by her virtues? If such were the case, what would you say, Pierre? what would you say, Babette?"

"Oh, that could not be; it is a dream!" cried Babette, whose eyes nevertheless were illuminated by a ray of hope.

"Do you know such a man?" said Pierre, rather peremptorily; "or is it merely a supposition, a dream on your part, as Babette says?"

At this question, Jean Peuquoy hesitated and showed evident signs of agitation.

He did not remark the silent and deep attention with which Gabriel was following all his movements. He was entirely absorbed in observing Babette, who, with eyes cast down and throbbing heart, appeared to be swayed by an emotion the honest weaver, little experienced in such matters, knew not how to interpret.

He did not augur from it a significance favorable to his

wishes; for it was in a very piteous tone he replied to the direct question of Pierre.

"Alas, cousin! it is only too probable all I said was but a dream. To make this dream a reality, it would not be enough that Babette should be loved, it would be necessary that she, on her part, should love also a little; otherwise, she would be unhappy. Now, the man who desired to purchase his happiness from Babette at the price of oblivion would probably be neither young nor handsome, nor, in a word, lovable. It is therefore not likely that Babette herself would consent to become his wife, and that is why all I have said was perhaps only a dream."

"Yes, it was a dream," returned Babette, sadly; "but not, cousin, for the reasons you mention. The man who would be generous enough to save me by such devotion, though he were old and withered and morose, would, in my eyes, be young; for his action would display a freshness of soul not always found in a youth of twenty. He would in my eyes be handsome, for such good and charitable thoughts needs must leave a stamp of nobility on his countenance; he would, in fine, in my eyes be lovable, for he would have given the greatest proof of love a woman can receive. My duty and delight, then, would be to love him all my life and with all my heart, and it would be very easy. But what is impossible and improbable, cousin, is to find such self-denial as you imagine for the sake of a poor girl like me, without beauty and without honor. There are perhaps men great enough and merciful enough to conceive the idea of such a sacrifice for a moment, and that is much. But on reflection, they would hesitate, they would recoil at last, and I should sink again from hope into despair. And these are the reasons, my excellent cousin, why what you have said was only a dream."

"And what if it were the truth?" said Gabriel, suddenly rising.

"How? What do you say?" cried Babette, utterly bewildered.

"I say," replied Gabriel, "that this generous and devoted man exists."

"You know him?" asked Pierre, with emotion.

"I know him," answered the young man, smiling. "He loves you indeed, Babette, but with a love equally paternal and tender—a love that desires to protect as well as to pardon. Therefore, you can accept without reserve a sacrifice in which there is no disdain, and which is inspired only by the gentlest pity and the sincerest devotion. Besides, you will give as much as you receive, Babette: you will receive honor, but you will give happiness; for he who loves you is alone and isolated in the world, without enjoyment, without interests, without a future, and you will bring him all this, and if you accept him, you will make him as happy to-day as he will make you happy in the near future. Is it not true, Jean Peuquoy?"

"But—M. le Vicomte—I do not know—" stammered Jean Peuquoy, trembling like a leaf.

"Yes, Jean," continued Gabriel, still smiling; "you do not know perhaps one thing: it is that Babette, too, has a profound esteem, a feeling of perfect gratitude and a sacred tenderness for him who loves her. Babette, if she has not divined, has, at least, had a vague presentiment of this love, and it has at first raised her in her own eyes, then touched her, then made her happy. It is since that time that she has conceived such a violent aversion for the scoundrel who deceived her. That is why she implored her brother on her knees not to unite her to him whom through a mistaken feeling she had believed she loved, and whom she execrates to-day as much as she loves him who would save her. Am I right, Babette?"

"In truth—monseigneur—I do not know," said Babette, pale as a ghost.

"The one doesn't know, and the other doesn't know," retorted Gabriel. "What, Jean! what, Babette! neither of you know anything of your own consciences? You are ignorant of your own feelings? Come, now, that's impossible. It is not I who reveal to you, Babette, that Jean loves you. You suspected before I did, Jean, that you were loved by Babette."

"Can it be!" cried Pierre Peuquoy, in an ecstasy; "no, it would be too much joy."

"Well, look at them," said Gabriel to Pierre. Babette and Jean were gazing upon each other, still irresolute and half incredulous.

And then Jean read in the eyes of Babette such fervent gratitude, and Babette read in the eyes of Jean such piteous entreaty, that they were suddenly convinced and resolved.

Without knowing how it happened, they found themselves in each other's arms.

Pierre Peuquoy, in his delight, had not strength to utter a word, but he grasped Jean's hand with a force that was more eloquent than all the languages in the world.

As for Martin Guerre, he sat up in bed, in spite of the danger, and with tears of joy rolling down his cheeks, clapped his hands enthusiastically at this unexpected dénouement.

When these first transports were somewhat calmed—

"Now all is arranged," said Gabriel. "Jean Peuquoy will marry Babette as speedily as possible; and before taking up their residence with their brother, they will come to my house in Paris, and be my guests for some months Thus the secret of Babette, sad cause of this happy marriage, will be buried in the five loyal hearts of those here present. There is a sixth person who might betray this secret. But should he learn the fate of Babette, which is doubtful, I answer for it he will not trouble you long You can, therefore, my dear, good friends, live henceforth in contentment and peace, and trust the future in all security."

"My noble and generous guest!" said Pierre Peuquoy, kissing Gabriel's hand.

"It is to you alone we owe our happiness," said Jean, "just as it is to you the king owes Calais."

"And on each day, morning and evening," said Babette, "we will offer up our prayers to God for our savior."

"Yes, Babette, yes," returned Gabriel, affected; "I thank you for that thought. Pray to God that your savior may now be able to save himself."

CHAPTER IV

HAPPY OMENS

"OH," was Babette's answer to the melancholy doubt of Gabriel, "do you not succeed in all you undertake; in the defence of St. Quentin and the taking of Calais, as well as in bringing about the marriage of poor Babette?"

"Yes, it is true," replied Gabriel, with a sad smile; "God is willing that the most invincible and terrible obstacles in my path should vanish from before me as if by enchantment. But, alas! my dear child, that is no proof that I shall attain the object of all my desires."

"Don't be downcast," said Jean Peuquoy, "you have made too many happy not to be happy yourself at last."

"I accept the omen, Jean," replied Gabriel; "and nothing can be to me of better augury than to leave my friends in Calais in the enjoyment of peace and contentment. But you know I must now leave you—who knows? perhaps, for sorrow and tears. Let us at least take care that there are no anxious hearts behind us, and let us settle everything in which we are interested." Thereupon, the date of the marriage was fixed—a ceremony at which Gabriel, to his great regret, could not be present—then the day of Jean and Babette's departure for Paris.

"It may be," said Gabriel, sadly, "that you will not find me at my hotel to receive you. This anticipation will, I hope, not be realized, but still I may perhaps be forced to absent myself from Paris and the court for a time. But let that not prevent you from coming. Aloyse, my good nurse, will receive you in my place as well as I could do myself. When you are with her, think sometimes of your absent host."

As for Martin Guerre, he was compelled, in spite of his protests, to remain at Calais. Ambroise Paré had declared that his convalescence would be long, and would require the greatest attention and watchfulness. His vexation was of no avail; he had to be resigned.

"But as soon as you are well, my trusty friend," said Viscount d'Exmès to him, "return to Paris also; and whatever happens to me, I'll keep my promise, don't fear, and free you from your singular persecutor. I am now doubly pledged to do so."

"Oh, monseigneur, think of yourself and not of me," said Martin Guerre.

"Every debt should be paid," returned Gabriel. "But, adieu, my good friends. It is now the hour when I must return to the Duke de Guise. I have asked of him in your presence certain favors which he will grant, I think, if I have done him good service during these late events."

But the Peuquoys would not accept this as the last farewell of Gabriel. They would wait for him at three o'clock at the Paris gate, so that they might take leave of him anew and see him once more.

Martin Guerre alone had now to bid farewell to his master, not without regret and sorrow. But Gabriel consoled him somewhat, speaking to him in that winning, kindly fashion which was one of his charms.

A quarter of an hour after, Viscount d'Exmès was introduced to the Duke de Guise.

"So there you are at last, my ambitious friend!" said Francis de Lorraine, laughing, when he saw him enter.

"All my ambition has been to second you the best I could, monseigneur," said Gabriel.

"Oh, in that respect you have not been particularly ambitious," replied the Balafré. (We may now give him this name, or, to speak more correctly, this title.) "I call you ambitious," he continued gayly, "on account of the numerous and exorbitant requests you have addressed to me, and which, in truth, I do not know very well how I can satisfy."

"I have, in effect, measured them by your generosity rather than by my merits, monseigneur," said Gabriel.

"So you have a fine opinion of my generosity," retorted the duke, with gentle raillery. "I am going to ask your decision on the matter, M. de Vaudemont," said he to a nobleman seated near him who was paying him a visit. "Yes; you shall tell me whether it is permitted to present such paltry requests to a prince."

"Consider then that I have spoken thoughtlessly," said Gabriel, "and that I have only measured my requests by my merits rather than by your generosity."

"Falsely answered again!" returned the duke; "for your merits are a hundred times greater than my power. Now listen for a moment to the incredible favors the Viscount d'Exmès demands of me, M. de Vaudemont."

"My decision is given in advance," said the Marquis de Vaudemont; "and it is that the favors demanded by M. d'Exmès will always be beneath his merits and your generosity. However, let us see what they are."

"In the first place," resumed the Duke de Guise, "M. d'Exmès requests me to lead to Paris, and employ on my own account, the little band which he had himself recruited. He reserves only four men to form his suite when in the city. And the heroes he lends me, under color of recommending them to me, M. de Vaudemont, are none other than those incarnate demons who, together with himself, scaled, as if they were Titans, the impregnable fort of Risbank. Well, which of us two renders the other a service here—M. d'Exmès or I?"

"M. d'Exmès, certainly," said the Marquis de Vaudemont.

"And, faith, I accept the obligation. Your eight braves shall not spoil for want of occupation, Gabriel," returned the Duke de Guise, gayly. "As soon as I am on my legs,

I'll lead them with me to Ham; for I will not leave these Englishmen an inch of territory in France. Malemort himself, the eternally wounded, will be there also. Master Paré has promised he shall be cured in less time than I.''

"You will make him very happy, monseigneur," said Gabriel.

"There now," said the Balafré, "a first favor granted, and that without too much effort on my part. As to the second, M. d'Exmès reminds me that Madame de Castro, the king's daughter, whom you know, M. de Vaudemont, is here, having been held as a prisoner by the English. In the midst of the cares that engross me, M. d'Exmès demands that I afford to this lady of royal blood the protection and honors that are due to her. In this, does or does not M. d'Exmès render me a service?"

"He does, undoubtedly," replied the Marquis de Vaudemont.

"The second point is then settled," said the Duke de Guise. "My orders are already given; and although I pass for an indifferent courtier, I know too well my duties to the ladies to actually forget the attentions exacted by the person and rank of Madame de Castro, who will be escorted to Paris, at whatever time she chooses, by a suitable train of attendants."

Gabriel expressed his thanks merely by a profound inclination, fearing that, if he spoke, others might learn the deep interest and importance this promise had for him.

"Thirdly," resumed the duke, "Lord Wentworth, the late English governor of this city, was made prisoner by M. d'Exmès. In the capitulation granted to Lord Derby, we agreed to hold him to ransom; but M. d'Exmès, to whom prisoner and ransom belong, permits us to show ourselves still more generous. He asks me, in fact, to authorize him to let Lord Wentworth return to England without paying anything whatever. Will not this action do great honor to French courtesy beyond the Straits, and does not M. d'Exmès in this also render us a true service?"

"According to the noble fashion in which you describe, monseigneur, he certainly does," replied M. de Vaudemont.

"You may be satisfied then, Gabriel," said the duke; "M. de Thermes has gone, on your part and on mine, to deliver Lord Wentworth and restore him his sword. He can depart whenever he desires."

"I thank you, monseigneur," said Gabriel; "but do not believe me so magnanimous. I am only making a return for the courteous treatment I received from Lord Wentworth when I was his prisoner, and at the same time giving him a lesson in honesty which he will comprehend; there is a tacit allusion and reproof in my action which he will comprehend also."

"You more than anybody have the right to be rigid on a subject of the kind," said the duke, gravely.

"Now, monseigneur," continued Gabriel, who saw with uneasiness that his chief concern was passed over in silence by the duke, "permit me to remind you of what you promised to me in my tent, on the eve of the capture of Fort Risbank."

"Wait a little, oh impatient youth!" said the Balafré. "After the three eminent services I have rendered you, and which M. de Vaudemont has verified, I have the right to demand one of you in return. I ask you, therefore, to set out at once for Paris and present to the king the keys of Calais—"

"Oh, monseigneur!" cried Gabriel, in a transport of gratitude.

"That will not give you too much trouble, I fancy," retorted Francis de Lorraine. "You have, besides, grown rather accustomed to such messages—you who were charged with a similar errand in connection with the flags taken in our Italian campaign."

"Ah, you double your favors by the gracious manner in which you grant them!" returned the delighted Gabriel.

"Moreover," continued the duke, "you will hand this

copy of the capitulation to his Majesty, and also this letter announcing our success, which I have written entirely with my own hand, despite the orders of Master Paré. But," he added with a significant look, "no one would have been able to render you justice, I am sure, with as much authority as I, and to have justice rendered to you as well. Now you will be satisfied with me, I hope, and consequently satisfied with the king. Stay, my friend, here is your letter, and here are the keys. I have no need to recommend you to be careful of them."

"And I, monseigneur, have no need of saying I am yours for life or death," said Gabriel, in a voice trembling with emotion.

He took the carved wooden casket and the sealed letter the Duke de Guise handed him. They were the precious talismans that would perhaps unlock the dungeon of his father and open a path to his own happiness.

"I shall not detain you any longer," replied the duke; "you are probably in a hurry to start, and, as for myself, I feel, after this morning's excitement, a fatigue which orders me to take a few hours' repose even more imperiously than Master Paré."

"Adieu, monseigneur, then, and accept my thanks a second time," returned Viscount d'Exmès.

At this moment, M. de Thermes, whom the duke had sent to Lord Wentworth, entered in a state of consternation.

"Ah," said the duke, when he perceived him, "our ambassador to the conqueror will not start without again seeing our ambassador to the conquered. But what is the matter, Thermes? You seem to be quite disturbed."

"And I am, monseigneur," said M. de Thermes.

"What has happened?" demanded the Balafré. "Has Lord Wentworth—"

"Lord Wentworth, to whom, in obedience to your orders, I announced his freedom and delivered up his sword, coldly and silently accepted this favor. I left, astonished at his reserve, when loud cries called me back. The first use Lord Wentworth made of his liberty was to pass the sword I restored to him through his body. He died immediately, and I saw only his corpse.''

''Ah,'' cried the duke, ''it was despair at his defeat that drove him to this extremity! Do you not think so, Gabriel? It is a real misfortune.''

''No, monseigneur,'' replied Gabriel, with melancholy gravity. ''Lord Wentworth did not die because he was conquered.''

''But what was the cause of his death, then ?'' asked the Balafré.

''Allow me to keep silence on the subject, monseigneur,'' answered Viscount d'Exmès. ''I would have kept this secret if Lord Wentworth had lived; I will keep it now that he is dead. However,'' continued Gabriel, lowering his voice, ''in presence of this proud departure from life, I may confide to you, monseigneur, that in his place I should have acted as he has done. Yes; Lord Wentworth has done well. For though he had not to blush before me, the conscience of a gentleman is so importunate a witness that it ought to be silenced at all hazards, and when a man has the honor to belong to the nobility of a noble country, there are faults so fatal that they can only be redeemed by death.''

''I understand you, Gabriel,'' said the Duke de Guise. ''All we have to do now is to pay him the last honors.''

''He is now worthy of them,'' replied Gabriel; ''and, while bitterly deploring this end—an end rendered necessary—I am glad, nevertheless, that it is in my power to esteem and regret, now that I am leaving, the man whose guest I was in this city.''

When he had, after some moments, taken leave of the Duke de Guise, with the renewed expression of his gratitude, Gabriel went straight to the hotel of the late governor, where Madame de Castro was still staying.

He had not seen Diana since the evening before; but she had very quickly learned, as well as all Calais, of the fortu-

nate intervention of Ambroise Paré and the safety of the
Duke de Guise. Gabriel found her calm and courageous.

Lovers are superstitious, and the serenity of his beloved
did Gabriel good.

Diana was naturally better pleased when he told her
what had occurred between Francis de Guise and himself,
and showed the casket and letters he had won at the price
of so many perils.

However, even in the midst of her joy, she felt a Christian regret for the sad end of Lord Wentworth, who had, it
was true, insulted her for an hour, but had respected and
protected her for three months.

"May God forgive him as I forgive him!" said she.

Gabriel spoke then of Martin Guerre, of the Peuquoys,
of the protection promised her by M. de Guise, of everything, in fact, connected with her.

He would have liked to find a thousand other subjects of
conversation as an excuse for remaining, and yet the object
that called him to Paris controlled his mind imperiously.
He wished to leave and to remain. He was at once happy
and restless.

"You are leaving, Gabriel? So much the better for a
hundred reasons!" said Diana. "I had not the courage
to speak to you of this departure, and, by not deferring
it, you will give me the greatest proof of your affection.
Go, my friend, that I may have the less time to wait
and to suffer. Go, that our fate may the more quickly
be decided."

May God bless you for that fine courage which sup-
ports mine!" replied Gabriel.

"Yes, I felt just now, while listening to you," returned
Diana, "as you must feel, while speaking to me, a certain
vague embarrassment. We talked of a hundred things, and
did not dare to approach the only question that concerns
our hearts and our lives. But, since you are leaving in a
few minutes, we may return to the only subject that interests us."

"You read with the same glance my soul and yours," exclaimed Gabriel.

"Listen to me, then," said Diana. "In addition to the letter you bear to the king from the Duke de Guise, you will hand another to his Majesty from me. I wrote it last night, and here it is. I relate in it how you have delivered and saved me. Thus, it will be plain to him and to all that you have restored to the King of France his city, and to the father his daughter. I speak in this way; for I hope that the affection of Henry the Second for me is not grounded on a mistake, and that I have a good right to call him my father."

"Dear Diana," cried Gabriel, "would that what you say may turn out true!"

"I envy you, Gabriel; you will lift the veil of our future before I shall. However, I will soon follow you to Paris, my friend. Since M. de Guise is so well disposed toward me, I shall ask his permission to set out to-morrow; and although I must necessarily travel more slowly than you, you will not reach Paris more than a few days in advance of me."

"Yes, come quick; your presence will bring me good fortune, I am sure of it."

"In any case, I will not be entirely absent from you. I wish you to have some one with you who may now and then recall me to your memory. Since you are forced to leave here your faithful squire Martin Guerre, take with you the French page Lord Wentworth placed near me. André is only a boy; he is hardly seventeen, and his disposition is perhaps even more youthful than his age. But he is devoted, loyal, and may be of service to you. Accept him, then, from me. Among the rough companions who attend you, he will be a more loving and gentle servant, whom I shall rejoice to know is by your side."

"Oh, thanks for this delicate attention," said Gabriel. "But you know I am leaving in a few moments—"

"André has been notified," said Diana. "If you knew

how proud he is of belonging to you! He must be now ready, and I have only to give him some final instructions. While you are bidding farewell to the Peuquoys, André will be on his way to join you before you leave Calais."

"I accept joyfully. I shall have, at least, some one to speak of you to," replied Gabriel.

"I thought of that, too," said Madame de Castro, blushing a little. "And now, adieu," she continued quickly; "we must say adieu."

"No, no," returned Gabriel; "not adieu, but *au revoir!*"

"Alas!" said Diana, "when shall we see each other again, and, above all, in what circumstances? If the enigma of our destiny have an unfortunate solution, would it not be better if that time never came?"

"Oh, do not say that, Diana!" cried Gabriel; "do not say that! Besides, who, except me, can tell you of the result, fatal or otherwise?"

"Ah, God!" replied Diana, with a shudder, "be it fatal or be it the reverse, it seems to me that, hearing it from your lips, I must die either of sorrow or of joy!"

"Yet how else can you learn?"

"Wait a minute," said Madame de Castro.

She drew a gold ring from her finger, and took from a drawer the nun's veil she had worn in the Benedictine convent of St. Quentin.

"Listen, Gabriel," said she, solemnly. "As everything will probably be decided before my return, send André to meet me outside of Paris. If God is on our side, he will hand this ring to the Viscountess de Montgommery. If our hope fails, he will, on the contrary, hand this nun's veil to Sister Bénie."

"Oh, let me fall at your feet and worship you as an angel!" exclaimed the young man, his soul stirred to its depths by this affecting evidence of love.

"No, Gabriel, no; rise," returned Diana. "Let us be firm and dignified in presence of the designs of God. Imprint a chaste and fraternal kiss upon my brow, as I imprint one on yours, endowing you with what faith and energy I can."

Silently did they exchange this sacred and sorrowful kiss.

"And now, my friend," returned Diana, "let us separate, not with an adieu, since you dread the word, but with an *au revoir*, either in this world or the next!"

"*Au revoir! au revoir!*" murmured Gabriel.

He strained Diana to his breast in a mute embrace; he looked upon her with an earnest longing, as if he might find in her beautiful eyes the strength of which he had such need.

At last she made him a sad but expressive sign, and he let her go; and, placing the ring on his finger and the veil in his bosom, he said, in a stifled voice, once more:

"*Au revoir*, Diana!"

"Gabriel, *au revoir!*" answered Diana, with a hopeful gesture.

Gabriel fled from the scene like one whose reason had been affected.

Half an hour afterward Viscount d'Exmès, who had become somewhat calmer, rode out of that city of Calais he had just restored to France. He was attended by the young page André, and by four of his volunteers.

One of these was Ambrosio, who was very glad to get to Paris, where he expected to dispose advantageously of some delicate articles of English merchandise in the neighborhood of the court.

Another was Pilletrousse, who feared temptation and a return to his former habits if he stayed in a conquered city of which he was one of the conquerors.

As to Yvonnet, he had not found, in that provincial Calais, a single tailor worthy of confidence, and his costume had been too much damaged by all it went through to be any longer presentable. It could be replaced suitably only at Paris.

The fourth was Lactance. He had asked leave to accompany his master, as he wished to see his confessor and ascertain whether his exploits had not outstripped his penances, and whether the assets of his austerities equalled the liabilities of his feats of arms.

Pierre and Jean Peuquoy, as well as Babette, insisted on following, on foot, the five cavaliers as far as the Paris gate.

There it was necessary to separate. Gabriel, after warmly pressing the hands of his friends, bade them a last farewell; and they, with tears in their eyes, sent after him a thousand good wishes and a thousand blessings.

But the Peuquoys soon lost sight of the little band, which started at a trot, and disappeared at the turn of the road. The worthy burghers returned, with sad hearts, to Martin Guerre.

As to Gabriel, he felt grave, but not sad.

He hoped!

He had once before quitted Calais to seek at Paris the solution of his destiny. But at that time circumstances were much less favorable: he was anxious about Martin Guerre, anxious about Babette and the Peuquoys, anxious about Diana, whom he was leaving a prisoner in the hands of Lord Wentworth. In fine, his vague presentiments of the future had nothing consoling; for he had, after all, only prolonged the resistance of a city; but this city was not the less lost to the country. Was that a service great enough for so great a reward?

To-day he was not leaving behind any cause for dejection. His wounded friends, his commander, and his squire were pronounced out of danger, and Ambroise Paré answered for their recovery; Babette Peuquoy would marry a man who loved her, and whom she loved in turn, and her honor and happiness were henceforth assured. Madame de Castro was free, and treated like a queen in a French city, and would be setting out on the next day to join Gabriel in Paris.

In fine, our hero had struggled so vigorously with Fortune that he might hope he had conquered her: the enterprise he had brought to a successful issue by furnishing the idea and the means of taking Calais was one of those that are not discussed or cheapened. The key of France restored to the King of France! Such a feat excused the extremest ambition, and his ambition was so just and sacred!

He hoped! The persuasive and sweet encouragement of Diana was still resounding in his ear, as well as the last prayers of the Peuquoys; Gabriel saw around him André, who reminded him of his beloved, and the valiant soldiers who escorted him. In front of him, firmly tied to the pommel of his saddle, he beheld the casket which contained the keys of Calais; he touched, in his doublet, the precious capitulation, and the still more precious letters of Madame de Castro and the Duke de Guise. The gold ring of Diana shone on his little finger. What present and eloquent pledges these of happiness!

A blue and cloudless sky seemed also to speak of hope. The air, keen but pure, made the blood circulate warm, in his veins. The thousand sounds of country life had, in the twilight, a character of serenity and peace; and the sun, which was setting in purple splendor on the left of Gabriel, presented the most consoling spectacle to his eyes and to his thoughts. It was impossible to start for a desired goal under happier auspices!

We are about to see what was the result.

CHAPTER V

A QUATRAIN

ON THE evening of the 12th of January, 1558, there was at the Louvre, in the apartments of Queen Catherine, one of those receptions of which we have already spoken, and which assembled around the king all the princes and gentlemen of the realm.

This one was particularly brilliant and animated, although, on account of the war, the Duke de Guise and a considerable part of the nobility were in the north.

There were present among the women, besides Catherine, queen *de jure*, Madame Diana de Poitiers, queen *de facto*, the young queen-dauphiness, Mary Stuart, and the melancholy Princess Elizabeth, who was about to become Queen of Spain, and whose beauty, already so much admired, was to be a source of misery to her in the future.

Among the men was the present head of the House of Bourbon, Antoine of Navarre, nominal king thereof, sent by his high-spirited wife, Jeanne d'Albret, to the Court of France, to try to regain, through the mediation of Henry the Second, the lands of Navarre which Spain had confiscated.

But Antoine of Navarre had already shown himself favorable to the Calvinists, and was badly looked upon by a court that burned heretics.

His brother, Louis of Bourbon, Prince de Condé, was there also; he knew how to make himself respected, if not loved. He was a much more decided Calvinist than his brother, and was generally considered the secret leader of the rebels. He enjoyed a good deal of popularity, for he was a bold rider, and handled sword and dagger equally well, although he was of small stature, and his shoulders were somewhat out of proportion. Moreover, he was a very gay gallant, and passionately fond of women. A popular song spoke of him as follows:

> "That little man so gay and pretty,
> Is always merry, always witty,
> And greets his girl with kisses warm;
> God save the little man from harm!"

Around the King of Navarre and the Prince de Condé were naturally grouped the gentlemen who openly or secretly favored the Reformation—Admiral de Coligny, La Renaudie, and the Baron de Castelnau, who had recently arrived from La Touraine, his native province, and was now presented at court for the first time.

The assembly was therefore numerous and distinguished, in spite of those who were absent. But in the midst of the noise, agitation, and joy, two men remained distracted, serious, and almost sad.

These men, whose sadness was excited by very opposite motives, were the king and Constable de Montmorency.

The person of Henry the Second was in the Louvre, but his thoughts were at Calais.

For three weeks, ever since the departure of the Duke de Guise, he had been pondering, night and day, on that hazardous expedition which might drive the English from France, but might also gravely compromise the fortunes of the realm.

Henry more than once reproached himself with having permitted the Duke de Guise to undertake so rash an enterprise.

If it failed, what a shame in the eyes of Europe! how many efforts would be needed to repair such a check! The calamity of St. Laurent would be nothing beside this. The constable had suffered a defeat; Francis de Lorraine had gone in search of one.

The king, who for three days had no news of the besieging army, was, then, engrossed by the darkest forebodings, and was hardly listening to the encouraging assurances of the Cardinal de Lorraine, who was standing beside the king and trying to revive his hopes.

Diana de Poitiers took keen notice of the gloomy temper of her royal lover; but, as she saw M. de Montmorency in another direction, looking quite as morose, it was to him she went.

It was the siege of Calais that was also troubling the constable, but, as we have said, for a different reason.

A success would, in fact, raise the Duke de Guise to the first rank, and reduce the constable to the second. The safety of France would be the ruin of this miserable constable! His selfishness, it must be admitted, had always surpassed his patriotism.

So he received, in the worst of tempers, the beautiful favorite, who advanced smilingly toward him.

"What is the matter with my old warrior to-day?" she asked, in her most caressing voice.

"Ah! so you, too, mock me, madame!" said Montmorency, bitterly.

"I mock you, my friend! You do not know what you are saying."

"I do know what you are saying," snarled the old veteran, in reply. "You call me your old warrior. Old? Yes; I am no longer a dandy of twenty. Warrior? No. You see I am thought good for nothing except to show myself on parade in the Louvre, with a sword by my side."

"Do not speak thus," said the favorite, with a tender look. "Are you not always *the constable?*"

"What does a constable amount to when there is a lieutenant-general of the kingdom?"

"This last title passes away with the events that have created it. Yours, attached, without possible revocation, to the first military dignity of the realm, can only pass away with yourself."

"And I have already passed away; in fact, I am dead," answered the constable, with a bitter smile.

"Why do you say so, my friend?" returned Madame de Poitiers. "You have not ceased to be powerful and quite as formidable to the public enemy as you are to your own private enemies here."

"Let us talk seriously, and not try to deceive each other with words."

"If I deceive you, it is because I deceive myself. Give me proofs of the truth, and I shall not only acknowledge my error, but repair it as well as I can."

"Well, then, you talk of the public enemy trembling before me; your words are, no doubt, consoling. But, in fact, whom do they send against that enemy? A general younger and doubtless more successful than I! a general who is pretty sure to make his success a help to his private interests some day or other."

"Surely you have no reason to believe the Duke de Guise will succeed?" asked Diana, with artful flattery.

"His failure would be a frightful disaster for France, which I should bitterly deplore for the sake of my country," said the constable, hypocritically; "but his success would be a still more frightful disaster, I am afraid, for my king."

"You believe, then, the ambition of M. de Guise—?"

"I have sounded it, and it is deep," replied the envious courtier. "If, through some unforeseen accident, there should be a change of sovereigns, have you thought, Diana, of the influence this ambition might exercise over the mind of a young and inexperienced king, especially when supported by Mary Stuart? My devotion to your interests has completely alienated Queen Catherine. The Guises would be more sovereign than the sovereign himself."

"Such a misfortune is, thank God! very improbable, and very remote," returned Diana, who could not help thinking that her sexagenarian constable was predicting quite too complacently the death of a king of forty.

"There are against us other chances, nearer and al ıost as terrible," rejoined the constable, shaking his head gravely.

"And what are they, my friend?"

"Have you lost your memory, Diana? or are you pretending ignorance as to the man who has gone to Calais with the Duke de Guise—the man who has, to all appearance, given him the idea of this rash enterprise; the man who will return triumphant with him if he triumphs, and obtain perhaps a part of the honor of the victory?"

"Are you speaking of Viscount d'Exmès?" asked Diana.

"And of whom else? If you have forgotten his extravagant promise, be sure he remembers it! Much more —luck is so singular!—he is quite capable of keeping it, and coming here to demand that the king fulfil his."

"Impossible!" cried Diana.

"What do you deem impossible, madame—that M. d'Exmès should keep his word? or that the king should keep his?"

"The two alternatives are equally mad and absurd, and the second more so than the first."

"If, however, the first were realized, the second would have to follow; the king is weak on points of honor, and, priding himself, as he does, on his chivalrous loyalty, would not be at all unlikely to deliver his secret and ours to our enemies."

"Oh, I tell you again, this is but an insensate dream!" cried Diana, who nevertheless turned pale.

"But, Diana, if you touched this dream with your hands and saw it with your eyes, what would you do?"

"I do not know, my good constable; it would be necessary to think deeply, to search keenly, and to act boldly. Anything rather than such an extremity! If the king abandoned us, we should do without him, and sure, in advance, that he dare not disavow us after the event, we should use all our power and all our personal credit."

"Ah! that is what I expected from you, madame: our power, our personal credit! Speak of yours, madame! but, as to mine, it is so low that, in truth, I regard it as dead. My private enemies, whom you pitied so strongly just now, might well amuse themselves at my expense. There is not a gentleman in this court who has not more power than this wretched constable. See you how few come near me! the reason is quite simple. Who cares to pay court to a fallen courtier? It will be safer, then, for you, madame, not to count any longer upon the support of an old disgraced servant, who is without friends, or influence, or even money."

"Without money?" repeated Diana, rather incredulously.

"Yes, *pâsque Dieu!* madame, without money!" said the constable, angrily, a second time; "and that is perhaps, at my age, and after my services, the most painful thing of all. The last war ruined me; my ransom, and the ransoms of some of my people, exhausted all my pecuniary resources. Well do they who forsake me know this! One of these days I shall be forced to go begging through the streets, like one Belisarius, a Carthaginian general, I think, that my nephew, the admiral, talks about."

"What, constable, have you no more friends?" returned Diana, smiling at the erudition and rapacity of her old lover.

"No, I have no friends any longer, I tell you," answered the constable. He added, with the most affecting pathos, "The unfortunate never have!"

"I will prove the contrary," said Diana. "I see now the cause of your savage temper at present. Why did you not tell me about all this at first? You have lost confidence in me, then? That is bad. No matter. The vengeance I intend taking on you will be friendly. Say, did not the king levy a new tax last week?"

"Yes, my dear Diana," replied the constable, who at once became quite sweet-tempered; "a very just tax, and heavy enough to pay the expenses of the war."

"That is all I want to know. I'll show you now that a woman is quite able to repair the wrong done by fortune to a man of such merit as you. Henry appears also to be in anything but a good temper. No matter! I am going to talk with him; and after I'm done, you'll have to acknowledge that I am a good friend and a faithful ally."

"Ah! Diana is as good as she is beautiful! I will proclaim as much from this moment," said Montmorency, gallantly.

"But you, on your side, will not abandon me when I have renewed the source of your influence and favor, eh! my old lion? and you will no longer speak to your closest friend of your impotence against her enemies and yours?"

"Why, my dear Diana, is not all my being at your service, and all my acts as well? and if I am sometimes grieved at the loss of my influence, is it not because I dread to be less able to serve my beauteous sovereign and mistress?"

"Good!" returned Diana, with her most charming smile.

She offered her white and royal hand to the bearded lips of her venerable adorer, who tenderly kissed it; then, giving him a last reassuring glance, she stepped briskly to the side of the king.

The Cardinal de Lorraine was still with the king, attending to the interests of his brother, and using his best eloquence to infuse hope into Henry as to the issue of the daring expedition of Calais.

But Henry was listening with more attention to his anxious fears than to the consoling words of the cardinal. It was at this moment that Madame Diana advanced toward them.

"I'll wager, monseigneur, that your Eminence is saying some evil to the king of poor M. de Montmorency," she said quickly.

"Oh, madame," returned Charles de Lorraine, stunned by this unexpected attack, "his Majesty will bear me wit-

ness that the constable's name has not even been mentioned
during the conversation.''

"It is true," said the king, carelessly.

"Another method of disparaging him!" retored Diana.

"But if I can neither speak nor be silent about the constable, what am I to do, madame, pray ?''

"You might say some good of him."

"Be it so, then!" answered the crafty cardinal. "I will
say, in that case, for the commands of beauty have always
found me obedient and submissive, that M. de Montmorency
is a great warrior, that he has won the battle of St. Laurent,
and restored the fortunes of France, and that at this moment
he is gloriously taking the offensive against our enemies,
and attempting a memorable achievement under the walls
of Calais.''

"Calais! Calais! ah, who will give me news of Calais?''
murmured the king, who, in the war of words between minister and favorite, had heard only the name of the city.

"You have an admirable and Christian method of prais-
ing, M. le Cardinal, and I compliment you on your caustic
charity!" retorted Diana.

"In truth, madame, I do not see what other eulogy I
could pass on this 'poor constable,' as you styled him just
now,'' answered Charles de Lorraine.

"You do not try to see, M. le Cardinal," returned Diana.
"Could you not, for instance, render justice to the constable's zeal in organizing at Paris all the means of defence
that were left, and collecting the few troops still remaining
in France, while others were risking and compromising the
real strength of the country in adventurous expeditions?''

"Oh, indeed!" said the cardinal.

"Might it not also be added," continued Diana, "that
if fortune has not favored the magnificent enterprises of
the constable, if luck has declared against him, he is at
least free from all personal ambition, he has no cause at
heart except that of the country, and to that cause he has
sacrificed everything—his life, which he was the first to

expose; his liberty, which he was so long deprived of; and his fortune, of which there is nothing left at the present moment."

"You don't say so!" said Charles de Lorraine, with an assumed air of astonishment.

"Yes, your Eminence," insisted Diana; "M. de Montmorency is ruined, that you may be certain of."

"Ruined! really?" said the cardinal.

"And so completely ruined," continued the impudent favorite, "that I have come now to ask his Majesty to assist him in his distress."

And as the king, still preoccupied, did not answer—

"Yes, sire," said Diana, addressing him directly, "I conjure you to come to the aid of your faithful servant, whom the payment of a heavy ransom and the expenses of a war waged for the service of your Majesty have deprived of his last resources. Are you listening to me, sire?"

"Madame, excuse me," said Henry; "I cannot attend to the matter this evening. You know well that my mind is entirely taken up with the thought of a possible disaster at Calais."

"That is just the reason," replied Diana, "why your Majesty ought, in my opinion, to countenance and favor the man who is already planning how the effects of that disaster, should it fall upon France, may be lessened."

"But we are as badly in want of money as the constable," said the king.

"And the new tax that has just been levied?" asked Diana.

"That money," said the cardinal, "is destined for the payment and support of the troops."

"Then surely the leader of the troops should receive the larger share of it?" returned Diana.

"But that leader is at Calais," answered the cardinal.

"No; he is at Paris, in the Louvre," said Diana.

"You think, then, he ought to be rewarded for having been beaten, madame?"

"Even that is better, M. le Cardinal, than to encourage madness."

"Enough!" interrupted the king. "Do you not see that this quarrel wearies and offends me? Do you know, madame, do you know, M. de Lorraine, the quatrain I have just found in my prayer-book?"

"A quatrain?" repeated Diana and Charles in unison.

"If I have a good memory," said Henry, "it runs as follows:

> "Sire, if you let yourself be too much governed,
> And kneaded, melted, this and that way turned,
> As Charles and Diana both alike require, 'tis *cire* (wax)
> You are, and surely no more *sire*."

Diana was not at all disconcerted.

"A rather neat play upon words!" said she; "but it attributes to me a far greater influence with your Majesty than, alas! I can lay claim to."

"Ah! madame," returned the king, "you ought not to abuse this influence, for the very reason that you know you have it."

"Have I it really, sire?" said Diana, in a gentle voice. "Then your Majesty grants me what I ask for the constable?"

"Be it so!" said the king, tired out with her importunity. "Now you will leave me, I think, to my anxieties and forebodings."

The cardinal, in presence of such weakness, could only raise his eyes to heaven. Diana, on the other hand, darted a triumphant look at him.

"Thanks, your Majesty," said she, "I withdraw in obedience to your commands; but banish all trouble and fear, sire! victory loves those who are generous, and I believe you will conquer."

"I accept the omen, Diana," replied Henry; "but with what transports should I receive the tidings of it! For some time I have no longer slept, I have no longer existed. My God! how limited is the power of kings! Not to have any means of knowing what is now passing at Calais! No matter what you say, monseigneur, this silence of your brother fills me with dismay! Ah! some news from Calais! Great God! who will bring me news from Calais?''

At this moment the usher on duty entered, and, bowing quickly before the king, announced, in a loud voice—

''A messenger of M. de Guise, from Calais, solicits the favor of being admitted to your Majesty's presence.''

''A messenger from Calais!'' repeated the king, rising, with eyes sparkling, and hardly able to restrain himself.

''At last!'' said the cardinal, trembling with fear and joy.

''Introduce the messenger of M. de Guise; introduce him at once,'' returned the king, quickly.

It goes without saying that all conversation was hushed, all hearts throbbed, and all eyes were directed toward the door.

Gabriel entered in the midst of a stillness that resembled the silence of the dead.

CHAPTER VI

VISCOUNT DE MONTGOMMERY

GABRIEL was followed, as at the time of his return from Italy, by four of his volunteers—Ambrosio, Lactance, Yvonnet and Pilletrousse—who carried the English flags, but stopped outside the threshold of the door.

The young man himself held, with both hands, a velvet cushion, on which lay two letters and the key of the city.

At this sight the face of Henry the Second expressed a singular mixture of joy and terror.

He believed he comprehended the happy message, but the stern messenger troubled him.

"Viscount d'Exmès!" he murmured, as Gabriel slowly approached him.

Madame de Poitiers and the constable, too, exchanged looks of alarm, and stammered in a low voice—

"Viscount d'Exmès!"

But Gabriel knelt on one knee, solemnly and gravely, before the king, and said, in a firm voice—

"Sire, here are the keys of the city of Calais, which, after a siege of seven days and three furious assaults, the English have delivered to the Duke de Guise, and which the Duke de Guise has hastened to deliver to your Majesty through me."

"Is Calais ours?" asked the king, although he had heard perfectly.

"Calais is yours, sire," repeated Gabriel.

"*Vive le roi!*" cried all those present, with one voice, with the exception, perhaps, of Constable de Montmorency.

Henry the Second, who had now no thought for anything except that all his fears were scattered, and that this was indeed a brilliant triumph for his arms, saluted the excited assembly with radiant countenance.

"Thanks, gentlemen, thanks!" said he; "I accept, in the name of France, these acclamations. But they ought not to be addressed to me alone: it is just that the larger share of them should be given to the valiant leader of the enterprise, my noble cousin, M. de Guise."

Murmurs of approbation ran from lip to lip; but the time had not yet come for any one to venture crying in presence of the king, "*Vive le Duc de Guise!*"

"And, in the absence of our dear cousin," continued Henry, "we are happy to be able, at least, to address our thanks and congratulations to you who represent him here, M. le Cardinal de Lorraine, and to you whom he has charged with this glorious commission, M. le Vicomte d'Exmès."

"Sire," said Gabriel, respectfully, but boldly, "excuse me; I am no longer called Viscount d'Exmès now."

"How is that?" asked Henry, frowning.

"Sire," continued Gabriel, "from the day Calais was taken I have believed I might assume my true name and title, Viscount de Montgommery."

At this name, which had not been uttered aloud at court for so many years, there was something like an explosion of astonishment in the assemblage. This young man called himself Viscount de Montgommery; then his father, the Count de Montgommery, was still alive! After so long a disappearance, what meant the return of this name so famous once upon a time?

The king could not hear these unspoken criticisms, but he had no difficulty in divining them. He turned ghastly pale, and his lips trembled with impatience and anger.

Madame de Poitiers shuddered also; and the constable, in his corner, lost his sullen impassiveness, and his eyes gleamed with a vague, uncertain light.

"What is this you say, monsieur?" returned the king, in a voice he controlled with difficulty. "What is this name you dare to assume? and whence the cause of such temerity?"

"This name is mine, sire," answered Gabriel, calmly, "and that which your Majesty believes temerity is only self-confidence."

It was evident that Gabriel had resolved by one bold stroke to take a course that would be irrevocable, to risk all in order to win all, and to cut off from the king as well as from himself all possibility of hesitation or retreat.

Henry understood this well, but he dreaded that his own anger might get the better of him; and, in order to at least put off the outbreak he feared, he continued—

"Your personal affairs can be discussed later, monsieur; do not forget, however, that you are the messenger of M. de Guise at present, and you have not yet, as far as I can see, fulfilled your mission."

"Your Majesty is right," said Gabriel, with a profound bow. "It remains, then, for me to present to you, sire, the flags conquered from the English. There they are. Moreover, M. de Guise has himself written this letter to the king."

He tendered on the cushion the letter of the Balafré. The king took it, broke the seal, tore open the envelope, and, handing the letter to the Cardinal de Lorraine, said—

"Be yours, M. le Cardinal, the joy of reading aloud your brother's letter. It is not addressed to the king, but to France."

"What, sire!" said the cardinal; "your Majesty wishes—"

"I desire, M. le Cardinal, that you accept this honor which is due to you."

Charles de Lorraine bowed, took respectfully the letter

from the king's hand, unfolded it, and read as follows in the midst of the deepest silence:

"SIRE—Calais is in our power; we have taken from the English in a week a city which cost them a year's siege two hundred years ago.

"Guines and Ham, the two points still possessed by them in France, cannot hold out very long; I venture to promise your Majesty that before a fortnight our hereditary enemies will be finally expelled from the entire kingdom.

"I thought it my duty to treat the conquered generously. They have surrendered their artillery and all their munitions of war; but the capitulation to which I agreed gives such of the inhabitants as desire it the right to retire to England with their goods. It would perhaps have been dangerous also to leave, in a city so lately occupied, such a pregnant source of rebellion.

"The number of our dead and wounded is inconsiderable, thanks to the rapidity with which the place was carried.

"I lack time and leisure to give your Majesty fuller details at present. Having been myself severely wounded—"

Here the cardinal turned pale and stopped.

"What, our cousin wounded!" cried the king, with assumed anxiety.

"Your Majesty and his Eminence need not be alarmed," said Gabriel. "This wound, thank God, will have no serious consequences. At the present moment, all that can remain of it is a scar on the face and the surname of the Balafré."

Having read some lines in advance, the cardinal was convinced that Gabriel spoke the truth, and, recovering his calmness, he continued to read:

"Having been myself severely wounded, on the very day of our entrance into Calais, I was saved by the marvellous skill of a young surgeon named Ambroise Paré; but I am still very weak, and consequently have to deny myself the pleasure of writing at length to your Majesty.

"You can learn the other details from the gentleman

who will bring along with this letter the keys of the city and the English flags, and of whom it is necessary I speak to your Majesty before finishing.

"For all the honor of this marvellous capture of Calais by no means belongs to me. I and my brave soldiers have tried to contribute to it with all our might; but we owe the first idea of it, the means of execution, and even the success to the bearer of this letter, M. d'Exmès—"

"It appears, monsieur," interrupted the king, addressing Gabriel, "that our cousin did not know you under your new name."

"Sire," said Gabriel, "I should dare to take it for the first time only in presence of your Majesty."

On a sign from the king, the cardinal continued—

"I confess I had not even a thought of this bold stroke when M. d'Exmès came to me in the Louvre, explained his sublime plan, banished my doubts, and scattered my hesitations, and, in fine, was the moving cause of an unheard-of feat of arms enough of itself to glorify a reign.

"But that is not all: the risk of such a daring expedition was not to be lightly encountered; it was necessary that the dream of heroism should be ratified by the counsel of experience. M. d'Exmès supplied Marshal Strozzi with the means of introducing himself under a disguise into Calais, and verifying the chances of attack and defence. Moreover, he gave us an exact and detailed plan of the ramparts and fortified posts, so that we advanced toward Calais as confidently as if the walls were made of glass.

"Under the walls of the city and in the assaults on Fort Nieullay and the Vieux-Chateau, the Viscount d'Exmès, at the head of a little band, levied at his own expense, performed prodigies of valor. But there he was only the equal of a number of our fearless captains, who, I believe, cannot be surpassed. I shall not dwell, therefore, upon the marks of courage he exhibited on all occasions, but examine only the actions which are peculiar and personal to him.

"Fort Risbank was itself protected by the sea, and at the same time afforded free and easy entrance to any troops, however numerous, England might choose to send to the aid of the city. Should it remain in the hands of the enemy, we were crushed, ruined. Our gigantic enterprise would fail amid the mockery of Europe. Yet how get possession of a tower which the ocean defended? This miracle Viscount d'Exmès performed. Alone with his volunteers in a boat during the night, aided by an understanding he had with certain persons in the city, he was able, after a venturesome voyage and a frightful escalade, to plant the French flag upon that impregnable fort."

Here, in spite of the king's presence, a murmur of admiration which nothing could repress interrupted the reader for a moment; it was the language of the hearts of that illustrious and valiant assembly, and its expression could not be resisted.

The attitude of Gabriel standing with downcast eyes, calm, dignified, and modest, a few paces from the king, added to the impression caused by the narrative of the chivalrous exploit, and charmed equally young women and old soldiers.

The king, too, was moved, and the look he fixed on the young hero of the epic adventure grew softer.

But Madame de Poitiers bit her white lips, and M. de Montmorency knit his shaggy brows.

After this short interruption the cardinal read on:

"Fort Risbank won, the city was ours. The English vessels dared not even attempt a useless assault. Three days afterward, we entered triumphantly into Calais, again seconded by a happy diversion made by the allies of Viscount d'Exmès in the place, and by an energetic sortie of the viscount himself.

"It was in this last struggle, sire, I received the terrible wound which nearly cost me my life, and, if it is permitted to recall a personal service after so many public services, I will add that it was also M. d'Exmès who led to my bedside, almost by force, the surgeon who saved me, Ambroise Paré."

"Oh, monsieur!" said Charles de Lorraine, interrupting himself, "it is now for me to thank you, which I do from the bottom of my heart."

And he read on, now with more emotion and warmth, as if it was his brother himself who was speaking—

"Ordinarily the honor of great achievements like this, sire, is wholly attributed to the leader under whom they have been performed. M. d'Exmès, as modest as he is great, would be the first to consent that his name should disappear in presence of mine. Nevertheless, I thought it only just to inform your Majesty that the young man who will hand you this letter has been the head and arm of our enterprise, and that without him Calais, at the moment I write, would still be English. M. d'Exmès has asked me to declare the facts, if I was willing, to the king and to the king only. I do so most gladly and most gratefully.

"My duty was to give M. d'Exmès this glorious certificate. The rest is in your hands, sire. You have a prerogative which I neither am able nor willing to usurp. There are few presents that can pay for a frontier city reconquered and the integrity of a realm assured.

"It appears, however, your Majesty has, M. d'Exmès tells me, a prize worthy of his achievement. I believe so, sire. But in fact, only a king, and a great king, can adequately reward such a royal exploit.

"In conclusion, I pray to God, sire, to give your Majesty a long life and a happy reign.

"And am of your Majesty,

"The most humble and obedient servant and subject,

"FRANCIS DE LORRAINE."

"At Calais, this 8th day of January, 1558."

When Charles de Lorraine had finished the letter and handed it back to the king, the movement of approbation which expressed the restrained congratulation of the whole court was manifested anew, and made the heart of Gabriel beat, for he was violently moved under an appearance of tranquillity. If respect had not imposed silence upon enthusiasm, loud applause would have undoubtedly greeted the young conqueror.

The king instinctively felt and to a certain extent shared the general enthusiasm, and could not help saying to Gabriel, as if he were the interpreter of the unexpressed wishes of all:

"It is well, monsieur! what you have done is glorious! I only wish, as M. de Guise implies, that it may be really possible for me to grant you a reward worthy of you and worthy of myself."

"Sire," replied Gabriel, "I only desire one thing, and your Majesty knows what it is."

Then, on a gesture of the king, he hastened to continue: "But, pardon me, my mission is not yet entirely fulfilled, sire."

"What is there further?" said the king.

"A letter, sire, from Madame de Castro to your Majesty."

"From Madame de Castro?" repeated the king, quickly.

With a rapid and impulsive movement, he rose from his chair, descended two steps of the royal dais, and took the letter of Diana, saying, at the same time, in a low voice:

"Truly, monsieur, you not only restore the king his daughter, but the father his child. I have contracted a twofold debt toward you. But let us see the letter."

And as the court, still motionless and mute, was respectfully awaiting the orders f the king, Henry, embarrassed by this attentive silence, said in a loud voice:

"Gentlemen, I do not wish to restrain the expression of your joy. I have nothing more to tell you. The rest is a private matter between myself and the messenger of our cousin of Guise. You have then only to discuss the happy news and congratulate one another on it, and you are free to do so, gentlemen."

The royal permission was quickly accepted. Groups were formed for conversation; and soon nothing was heard save the indistinct and confused hum which is the result of a hundred scattered discussions in a crowd.

Madame de Poitiers and the constable alone watched the king and Gabriel. An eloquent glance interchanged communicated their mutual fears, and Diana insensibly drew near her royal lover.

Henry did not notice the envious couple. He was entirely engrossed by the letter of his daughter.

"Dear Diana! my poor, dear Diana!" he murmured, deeply affected.

And when he had finished reading, carried away by his kingly nature, which was certainly generous and loyal in its first spontaneous impulses, he said to Gabriel in a voice that was almost loud:

"Madame de Castro also recommends her liberator to me, and it is justice. She tells me you have not only restored her to liberty, but also, as it appears, saved her honor."

"Oh, I have only done my duty, sire," said Gabriel.

"It is, therefore, my turn now to do mine," returned Henry, quickly. "It is for you to speak at present, monsieur. What can we do for you, *M. le Vicomte de Montgommery?*"

CHAPTER VII

JOY AND ANGUISH

M LE VICOMTE DE MONTGOMMERY! At that name, which, uttered by the king, contained more than a promise, Gabriel was thrilled with happiness.

Henry was evidently about to pardon.

"He is weakening!" whispered Madame de Poitiers to the constable, who had approached her.

"Let us wait our turn," answered M. de Montmorency, not in the least disconcerted.

"Sire," said Gabriel, more strongly moved, according to his nature, by hope than by fear, "I have no need to inform your Majesty of the favor I expect from your gracious kindness and clemency, and also, to some extent, from your justice. What your Majesty exacted from me, 1 hope I have performed. Will your Majesty also deign to do what I asked? Have you forgotten your promise, or are you graciously pleased to keep it?"

"Yes, monsieur, I will keep it on the conditions of silence agreed upon," replied Henry, without hesitation.

"As to these conditions, I pledge my honor anew that they shall be exactly and rigorously fulfilled," said Viscount d'Exmès.

"Approach, then, monsieur," returned the king.

Gabriel approached. The Cardinal de Lorraine discreetly stood aside. But Madame de Poitiers, who was seated quite close to Henry, did not stir, and could easily hear all he said, although he spoke in a low voice to Gabriel.

However, this sort of surveillance, it must be acknowledged, had no effect on the determination of the king, who continued firmly:

"M. le Vicomte de Montgommery, you are a valiant man whom I esteem and honor. When you have what you ask for and what you have so richly merited, we shall not certainly hold ourselves discharged from our obligations toward you. But now take this ring. To-morrow morning, at eight o'clock, present it to the governor of the Chatelet. He will be informed of your coming, and will surrender to you immediately the object of your holy and sublime ambition."

Gabriel, who felt his knees sinking under him with joy, could no longer control himself, and fell at the feet of the king.

"Ah, sire!" said he, his breast overflowing with happiness and his eyes wet with sweet tears, "all the determination and energy I think I have given some proofs of, are for the rest of my life at the service of my devotion to your Majesty, as they would have been at the service of my hatred, I confess, had your Majesty said, No!"

"Indeed?" said the king, similing graciously.

"Yes, sire, I confess it, and you must understand, since you have pardoned; yes, I would have pursued your Majesty and your Majesty's children, as I will now defend and love you in them. Sire, in the presence of God, who sooner or later punishes all perjuries, I promise to keep my oath of fidelity, as I would have kept my oath of vengeance."

"Come, come, rise up," said the king, still smiling. "Calm yourself, and to restore your self-control, give us some details of this unhoped-for recovery of Calais, for sure I am, I shall never be tired of speaking of it, and hearing it spoken of by others."

Henry the Second kept Gabriel with him over an hour, questioning and listening, and making him repeat the same details over and over again, without ever seeming tired.

Then he had to give way to the ladies, who were eager to question the young hero in turn.

And, in the first place, the Cardinal de Lorraine, who

did not know much of the antecedents of Gabriel, and looked on him as the protégé of his brother, insisted on himself presenting him to the queen.

The presence of the court forced Catherine de Médicis to congratulate the man who had gained such a brilliant victory for the king. But she did so with marked coldness and haughtiness, and the severe and disdainful look of her gray eye belied the words her lips had to utter against the wish of her heart.

Gabriel, while addressing to Catherine his respectful thanks, felt his soul somewhat frozen by her deceitful compliments; recalling the past, he thought he discerned a secret irony and a hidden menace in them.

After saluting Catherine de Médicis, he turned to withdraw, and then believed he found the cause of the sad presentiment he experienced. He saw with alarm that Diana de Poitiers was close by the king and speaking in an undertone to him with her wicked, sardonic smile. The more Henry the Second seemed to be defending himself, the more she appeared to be insisting.

She then called the constable, who spoke also for a long time with considerable vivacity.

Gabriel saw all this from a distance. He did not lose a single gesture of his enemies, and he suffered martyrdom.

But at the moment his heart was thus rent, the young man was gayly approached and questioned by the young queen-dauphiness, Mary Stuart, who overwhelmed him with compliments and inquiries.

Gabriel, in spite of his anxiety, answered as best he could.

"It was magnificent!" said Mary to him enthusiastically; "was it not, my gentle dauphin?" she added, turning to her young husband, who joined his own eulogies to those of his wife.

"To deserve such gracious words, what would not one do?" said Gabriel, whose eyes never quitted the group of the king, Diana, and the constable.

"When I used to feel drawn to you by a certain unde-finable sympathy," continued Mary Stuart, with her usual grace, "my heart doubtless warned me that you would lend your aid in achieving this marvellous enterprise for the glory of my dear uncle of Guise. Ah, but I should wish to have the power of the king in order to reward you in my turn! A woman, however, has, alas! neither titles nor honors at her disposal."

"Oh, in truth, I have all I wish for in the world!" said Gabriel. "The king no longer answers; he only listens," said he to himself.

"All the same," returned Mary Stuart, "if I had the power, I should, I fancy, inspire you with wishes, that I might have the pleasure of granting them. But at present all I have is this bouquet of violets, which the gardener of Les Tournelles lately sent me, because they are rare after the late frosts. Well, M. d'Exmès, with the permission of Monseigneur le Dauphin, I give them to you as a souvenir of this day. Do you accept them ?"

"Oh, madame!" cried Gabriel, respectfully kissing the hand that offered them.

"Flowers," continued Mary Stuart, dreamily, "are a per-fume for joy and a consolation for sorrow. I may some day be very unfortunate. I shall never be entirely so, as long as I am left flowers. It is well understood, M. d'Exmès, that to you, happy and triumphant, I offer them as a per-fume."

"Who knows?" said Gabriel, shaking his head sadly, "who knows but that the man you call happy and trium-phant may not have need of them as consolation ?"

His eyes, while he spoke, were all the time riveted on the king, who seemed to be reflecting, and giving way before the representations, more and more pressing, of Madame de Poitiers and the constable.

Gabriel trembled as he thought that assuredly the favor-ite had heard the king's promise, and that the conversation undoubtedly turned on his father and himself.

The young queen-dauphiness retired, gently bantering Gabriel on his absent-mindedness.

Admiral Coligny accosted him immediately after, and also cordially congratulated Gabriel on the brilliant manner in which he had sustained and surpassed at Calais the glory won at St. Quentin.

Never was the young man more favored by fortune and more worthy of envy than at the moment he was enduring the most unheard-of anguish.

"You are as successful," said the admiral, "in winning victories as in lessening the consequences of defeats. I feel proud of anticipating your glory, and I have only one regret, that of not participating in this noble feat of arms, which reflects such distinction on you and such renown on France."

"You will easily find other opportunities, M. l'Amiral," said Gabriel.

"I rather doubt it," replied Coligny, with some sadness. "God only grant that if we meet upon a field of battle, it be not on opposite sides."

"Heaven forbid!" said Gabriel, earnestly. "But what do you understand by these words, M. l'Amiral?"

"Four of the religion were burned alive last month," said Coligny. "The Reformers, who are every day growing in numbers and power, will become weary of these odious and unjust persecutions. On that day, the two parties that divide France will be changed into two armies."

"Well?" asked Gabriel.

"Well, M. d'Exmès, in spite of our walk down the Rue St. Jacques, you kept your freedom and only pledged yourself in certain contingencies. At present, you are apparently in such high favor that you are not very likely to be found in the ranks of the heretics, as they are called."

"I think you are mistaken," said Gabriel, whose eyes never left the king. "I have reason, on the contrary, for thinking, M. l'Amiral, that I may be marching with the oppressed against the oppressors."

"What is it you say, Gabriel?" asked the admiral. "You turn pale; your voice changes; pray, what is the matter with you?"

"Nothing, nothing, M. l'Amiral. But I must leave you. *Au revoir!* and may we soon meet again!"

Gabriel had just noticed a gesture of acquiescence on the part of the king; M. de Montmorency at once took his leave, darting a look of triumph upon Diana.

A few moments after, the reception was brought to a close; and Gabriel, while making his obeisance to the king before his departure, ventured to say—

"Sire, until to-morrow."

"Until to-morrow, monsieur," answered the king.

But Henry did not look Gabriel in the face while speaking; he turned his eyes away. He did not smile, but Madame de Poitiers's face was wreathed in smiles.

Gabriel, whom every one believed to be radiant with hope and joy, retired with sorrow and dismay in his heart.

He spent all the evening wandering around the Chatelet.

He recovered a little courage when he saw that M. de Montmorency did not come out from it.

Then he touched the royal ring upon his finger, and re-called those formal words of Henry the Second, which did not admit of doubt and could not conceal a snare: "The object of your holy and sublime ambition shall be restored to you!"

For all that, this night which separated Gabriel from the decisive moment was to appear longer to him than a whole year

CHAPTER VIII

PRECAUTIONS

WHAT Gabriel felt and suffered during these fatal hours, God alone knew; for, on his return home, he did not care to say anything either to his servants or even to Aloyse; and from that moment began his concentrated and, in some sort, dumb life—a life wholly consecrated to action, sparing of words, continued afterward as rigorously as if he had taken a vow of silence to himself.

Thus, his deceived hopes, his energetic resolutions, his plans of love and vengeance, all that Gabriel, during this night of waiting, felt or dreamed or solemnly swore to achieve—all remained a profound secret between his impenetrable soul and his Creator.

He could not appear at the Chatelet before eight with the ring which the king had presented to him, and which was to open every door, not only to himself, but to his father.

Until six in the morning he remained alone in his chamber, refusing to see any one.

At six, he descended clad and equipped as if for a long journey. He had already, the evening before, asked his nurse for all the gold she could collect.

The people of his household eagerly surrounded him, offering their services. The four volunteers he had brought from Calais especially placed themselves at his disposal; but he thanked them warmly, and dismissed them, keeping with him only the page André, his last recruit, and his nurse Aloyse.

"My good Aloyse," said he to the latter, "I am daily expecting two guests, two friends from Calais, Jean Peuquoy and his wife Babette. It may happen, Aloyse, that I am not here to receive them. But, in my absence, and, above all, on account of my absence, I beg you, Aloyse, to receive and treat them as if they were my brother and sister. Babette knows you, because she has heard me a hundred times speak of you. She will have in you the confidence of a daughter. I conjure you, then, in the name of the affection you bear me, to show her the tenderness and indulgence of a mother."

"I promise, monseigneur," said the good nurse, simply; "and you know that, in my case, these two words are all that's needed. Do not be uneasy about your guests. They shall want nothing that can comfort soul and body."

"Thanks, Aloyse," said Gabriel, pressing her hand. "And now as to you, André," he continued, addressing the page given him by Madame de Castro. "I have certain final commissions of a very grave nature which I wish to intrust to some one on whom I can depend; and it is you, André, who must fulfil them, because you take the place of my faithful Martin Guerre."

"I am at your orders, monseigneur," said André.

"Listen attentively," resumed Gabriel. "I leave this house in an hour, alone. If I return soon, you will have nothing to do, or rather I shall give you new orders. But it is possible that I may not return, at least that I may not return to-day, nor to-morrow, nor for a long time."

The nurse raised her arms to heaven in consternation André interrupted his master.

"Pardon, monseigneur! you say that you may not return for a long time?"

"Yes, André."

"And I do not accompany you; and I shall not see you again, perhaps, for a long time?" returned André, who at this news appeared at once sad and embarrassed.

"Undoubtedly it may be so," said Gabriel.

"But," said the page, "before my departure, Madame de Castro intrusted me with a letter, a message for monseigneur—"

"And you have not given me this letter?" asked Gabriel, quickly.

"Excuse me, monseigneur," replied André; "I was to give it to you only when, after returning from the Louvre, I should see you very sad or very much angered. Then only, said Madame Diana to me, give M. d'Exmès this letter, which contains a warning or a consolation for him."

"Oh, give it to me; give it at once!" cried Gabriel. "Advice and comfort could not arrive at a more seasonable moment."

André drew from his doublet a letter carefully wrapped up, and handed it to his new master. Gabriel hastily broke the seal, and retired to the window to read it.

The contents of the letter were as follows:

My friend, among the dreams and tortures of this last night, that is perhaps to separate us forever, the most cruel thought that has torn my heart is this:

It may be that the grand and dreadful duty you are about to accomplish so courageously may bring you into conflict with the king. It may be the unforeseen issue of your struggle may force you to hate him and urge you to punish him.

Gabriel, I do not yet know if he is my father, but I know that he has until now cherished me as his child. The mere anticipation of your vengeance makes me shudder at this moment; the accomplishment of your vengeance would kill me.

And yet the duty I owe to my birth should perhaps constrain me to think as you do; perhaps I shall have to avenge him who may be my father on him who has been my father—frightful extremity!

But while doubt and darkness still hover above this terrible question, while I am still ignorant on which side ought my hatred to take its stand, and on which side my love, Gabriel, I conjure you—and if you love me you will obey me—respect the person of the king.

I am reasoning now, if not without emotion, at least without passion; and it seems to me it is not the part of men, but of God, to punish men.

Therefore, my friend, whatever occurs, do not wrest from the hands of God the right of punishing, even though it be to punish a criminal.

If he whom I have named until now my father is guilty, and, being a man, he may be, do not be his judge, still less his executioner. Do not disturb yourself. The Lord will have all debts paid to Himself, and will inflict a more terrible vengeance than you could do yourself.

But unless the Lord make you the involuntary instrument, nay, in a certain sense, the predestined instrument, of this pitiless justice, unless He make use of your hand, in spite of yourself, unless you deal the blow without seeing and without wishing, do not pass sentence yourself, and, above all, do not carry out yourself the sentence you may have passed.

Do this for love of me, my friend. Mercy! it is the last prayer and the last cry to you from

DIANA DE CASTRO.

Gabriel read this letter twice; but, during these two readings, André and the nurse could discover on his pale countenance no other sign than the sad smile which had now become his peculiar characteristic.

When he had folded Diana's letter and concealed it in his bosom, he continued for some time silent and thoughtful, his head sinking on his breast.

Then awaking, so to speak, from his revery, "It is well," said he, aloud; "the orders I gave you, André, still continue, as I told you; and if I do not return at once, whether you hear anything concerning me, or do not hear mention made of me at all, finally, no matter what may happen, or may not happen, pay close attention to my words: this is what you must do."

"I am listening, monseigneur," said André, "and will obey you to the letter; for I love you and am devoted to you."

"Madame de Castro," returned Gabriel, "will be in

Paris in a few days. Manage to get information of her return as speedily as possible."

"That is easy, monseigneur."

"Go to meet her if you can, and place this sealed packet in her hands. Be very careful not to mislay it, André, although it contains nothing of value for anybody else—a woman's veil, nothing more. No matter, you will hand this veil to her yourself, and you will say to her—"

"What shall I say to her, monseigneur?" asked André, seeing that his master hesitated.

"No, say nothing," replied Gabriel, "except that she is free, and that I release her from all her promises, even from that of which the veil is the pledge."

"Is that all?" inquired the page.

"That is all," said Gabriel. "Still, if there be no longer any mention made of me, and if you should see Madame de Castro somewhat troubled, you might add— But what would be the use? Add nothing, André. Ask her, if you like, to take you into her service. If not, return here, and wait until I come back."

"What do you mean, monseigneur? Surely, you will come back!" exclaimed the nurse, with tears in her eyes. "You do not really mean what you said, that we shall no longer hear any mention made of you?"

"Perhaps it will be better so, my good mother, better if my name be buried for a time in oblivion," returned Gabriel. "In that case, hope and expect my return."

"Hope, when you have vanished from the sight of all, and even of your poor nurse! Ah, that is hard to bear!" said Aloyse.

"But who told you I should vanish?" answered Gabriel. "We have no mortgage on the future. And, in truth, Aloyse, although I am taking certain precautions, I have the strongest belief that I shall embrace you in the near future with all the affection of my heart; for Providence is a tender mother to him who implores her aid. And did I not, in the beginning, tell André that all my orders were useless and annulled, in the almost certain contingency of my return to-day?"

"Ah! may God bless you for these comforting words!" exclaimed Aloyse, with emotion.

"And you have no other orders to give us during this absence, which may God shorten!" said André.

"Wait," said Gabriel, struck by a sudden recollection; and, sitting down at a table, he wrote the following letter to Coligny:

MONSIEUR L'AMIRAL.—I intend to have myself instructed in your religion, and you may number me from this forward as one of your community.

Whether the determining motive of my conversion be faith, your persuasive eloquence, or some other reason, I devote not the less to your cause, and that beyond recall, as well as to your oppressed religion, my heart, my life, and my sword.

Your very humble companion and good friend,
                          GABRIEL DE MONTGOMMERY.

"Deliver this also, if I do not return," said Gabriel, giving André this letter, sealed. "And now, my friends, I must bid you farewell and leave you. The hour has come—"

Half an hour afterward Gabriel was knocking, with trembling hand, at the gate of the Châtelet.

CHAPTER IX

A PRISONER AU SECRET

M. DE SALVOISON, the governor of the Châtelet who had received Gabriel on his first visit, had recently died, and the present governor was named M. de Sazerac.

It was into his presence the young man was conducted. The iron hand of anxiety had taken such a rough grip of poor Gabriel's throat that he could not articulate a single word. But he silently presented to the governor the ring the king had given him.

M. de Sazerac bowed gravely.

"I was expecting you, monsieur," said he to Gabriel. "I received the order concerning you an hour ago. I am, as soon as I see that ring, and without asking for any other explanation, to surrender to you the nameless prisoner detained for so many years in the Châtelet, under the appellation of Number 21. Am I right, monsieur?"

"Yes, yes, monsieur," quickly replied Gabriel, to whom hope had restored his voice. "And this order, M. le Gouverneur—?"

"I am quite ready to obey, monsieur."

"O God! you are sure, M. le Gouverneur?" said Gabriel, trembling from head to foot.

"Yes, undoubtedly," replied M. de Sazerac, in a tone wherein an indifferent person would have discovered a certain sadness and bitterness.

But Gabriel was too much agitated, too much overwhelmed with joy.

"Ah! it is, then, quite true!" he cried. "I do not dream. My eyes are open. My foolish terrors, on the contrary, were dreams. You will restore me my prisoner, monsieur? Oh, I thank thee, my God! I thank thee, also, my king! But let us hasten, I beg you, monsieur."

And he took two or three steps in advance of M. de Sazerac. But his strength, so capable of enduring suffering, was enfeebled by joy. He was forced to stop for a moment. His heart beat so rapidly and so violently that he felt as if choking.

Poor human nature could not respond to so many accumulated emotions.

The almost unexpected realization of hopes that had loomed so far in the distance, the aim of a whole life; the final and successful achievement of superhuman efforts; gratitude toward a just God and a loyal king; filial love at last satisfied; another love, still more ardent, to be at last determined—all these feelings, called into existence and excited at the same time, made the heart of Gabriel overflow.

But amid all these unutterable emotions, amid all this insensate happiness, the feeling that stood out, perhaps, most distinctly, took the form of a hymn of thanksgiving to Henry the Second—the source of this intoxication of joy.

And Gabriel repeated, in his grateful heart, the oath to devote his life to this loyal king and to his children. How could he have for a moment doubted this great and excellent sovereign!

However, at last shaking off his delirium—

"Excuse me, monsieur," he said to the governor of the Chatelet, who was standing near him. "Excuse this weakness, which has for a time overwhelmed me. Joy, you see, is sometimes hard to bear!"

"Oh, do not excuse yourself, monsieur, I beg!" replied the governor, in a deep voice.

Gabriel, this time struck by the tone in which M. de Sazerac spoke, raised his eyes.

It was impossible to encounter a face more benevolent, more open, and more honest. Everything in this governor of a prison denoted sincerity and goodness.

Yet, strange to say! the feeling painted on the countenance of this worthy man at present, while he was remarking the excessive joy of Gabriel, was sincere compassion.

Gabriel caught this singular expression, and, seized by a sinister presentiment, he suddenly turned pale.

But such was his nature that this vague fear, which for a moment broke in upon his happiness, served only to render his valiant spirit more resolute still; and, drawing up his lofty figure to its full height, he said to the governor—

"Let us go on, monsieur. I am ready and strong now."

Thereupon Viscount d'Exmès and M. de Sazerac descended into the prisons, preceded by a servant carrying a torch.

At each step Gabriel recalled his sombre recollections, and recognized at the turns of the corridors and stairs the gloomy walls he had already seen, and the dismal impressions he had felt there formerly, without being able to account for them.

When they reached the iron door of the dungeon, where he had visited, with so strange an aching at the heart, the wasted and dumb prisoner, he did not hesitate a second, and stopped short.

"He is there," said he, his heart weighed down by anxiety.

But M. de Sazerac shook his head sadly.

"No," he returned; "he is not there at present."

"How! not there at present!" cried Gabriel. "Do you intend to mock me, monsieur?"

"Oh, monsieur," said the governor, in a tone of mild reproach.

Cold drops of perspiration stood on the forehead of Gabriel.

"Pardon me!" he returned; "but what is the meaning of these words? Oh, speak, and speak quickly!"

"Since yesterday evening, it is my painful mission to inform you of the fact, the prisoner *au secret* confined in this cell has been transferred to the floor beneath."

"Ah!" said Gabriel, astounded; "and why, pray?"

"You know, I believe, he was warned, monsieur, that if he attempted to utter anything whatever, though it were the slightest cry, the merest name, and even though he were questioned, he was to be transferred to another dungeon, deeper still, more dreadful, and more deadly than that in which he was."

"I know that," said Gabriel, in so low a tone that the governor did not hear him.

"Once before, monsieur, the prisoner had ventured to come in collision with that regulation, and then he was thrown into this prison—surely a cruel one enough!—which is before you, and where you have seen him yourself. I have been told, monsieur, that you were then informed of his condemnation to the silence he was doomed to suffer while yet alive."

"Yes, yes!" said Gabriel, wild with impatience. "And then, monsieur?"

"Well," answered M. de Sazerac, sadly, "yesterday evening, a little before the closing of the outer gates, a man came to the Chatelet—a powerful man, whose name I must conceal."

"No matter; go on!" said Garbiel.

"This man," continued the governor, "ordered me to introduce him into the dungeon of Number 21. I alone accompanied him. He addressed the prisoner, and did not get any reply. I was hoping the old man would come out triumphantly from this trial; for during half an hour he was obstinately silent, notwithstanding all the insults and provocations he had to face."

Gabriel heaved a profound sigh, and raised his eyes to heaven, but without uttering a word, in order not to interrupt the dismal narrative of the governor.

"Unfortunately," returned the latter, "at last something

was whispered in his ear which caused him to sit up, and tears started from his stony eyes! He spoke, monsieur! I have been authorized to relate all this to you, in order that you might the better believe my word as a gentleman when I add: the prisoner spoke. Alas! I must affirm, on my honor, that I myself heard him."

"And then?" asked Gabriel, in a broken voice.

"And then," replied M. de Sazerac, "I was immediately required, in spite of my representations and my prayers, to fulfil the barbarous duty my office imposes upon me, to obey an authority superior to mine, which, in case I refused, would have soon found more docile servants, and to convey the prisoner to the dungeon placed beneath this one."

"The dungeon beneath this one!" cried Gabriel. "Ah, let us run thither quickly, since I am bringing him freedom at last!"

The governor sadly shook his head; but Gabriel did not see this sign; he was already running impetuously down the slippery, dilapidated steps of the stone staircase that led to the lowest depths of the dismal prison.

M. de Sazerac, after taking the torch from the hands of the servant, dismissed him with a gesture, and, covering his mouth with his handkerchief, followed Gabriel.

At every step in the descent, the air became more impure and suffocating.

When they had reached the bottom of the stairs, they could hardly breathe; and it was easy to understand that the only creatures capable of living more than a few minutes in such an atmosphere of death were the unclean creatures they were crushing under their feet—an act of itself sufficient to create horror and loathing.

But Gabriel was not thinking of all this. He took from the trembling hand of the governor the rusty key the latter offered him, and, opening the heavy, worm-eaten door, he rushed into the dungeon.

By the glare of the torch could be seen, stretched on a sort of dung-heap of straw, a body.

Gabriel threw himself upon this body, raised it, shook it, and cried—

"My father!"

M. de Sazerac trembled with terror at this cry.

The arms and head of the old man fell back inert after the movement imparted to them by Gabriel.

CHAPTER X

COUNT DE MONTGOMMERY

GABRIEL, still on his knees, merely raised his pale and perplexed face, and gazed around with eyes that had a sinister calmness; he looked like one who was questioning and reflecting. But this calmness frightened M. de Sazerac more than any outcries or any sobs could have done.

Then, as if struck by an idea, Gabriel quickly placed his hand upon the heart of the dead body.

He listened, keeping his hand there for one or two minutes.

"Nothing!" he then said, in a voice gentle and equable, but rendered terrible by its very gentleness; "nothing! the heart no longer beats, but the place is still warm."

"What a vigorous constitution!" murmured the governor; "he might have lived for a long time still."

Meanwhile the eyes of the corpse were open; Gabriel bent over it, and tenderly closed them. Then he kissed reverently those poor worn eyes that had been wet with so many bitter tears.

"Monsieur," said the governor, who wished, at all risks, to distract his mind from this frightful contemplation, "if the dead man was dear to you—"

"If he was dear to me, monsieur!" interrupted Gabriel. "Yes, indeed! he was my father!"

"Well, monsieur, if you should wish to render him the last honors, you are permitted to take him away from here."

"Ah! indeed?" returned Gabriel, with the same fearful calmness. "How exceedingly just is this man, and how punctiliously he keeps his word to me! Know, M. le Gouverneur, that he swore before God to give me back my father. He does so; behold him! I am obliged to acknowledge he did not promise to give him back to me alive."

And he burst into a peal of strident laughter.

"Come, courage!" returned M. de Sazerac; "it is now time to bid adieu to him for whom you mourn."

"I am doing so, as you see, monsieur," answered Gabriel.

"Yes, but what I mean is that you must leave this. The air we are breathing was not made for living lungs; and a longer stay in this foul atmosphere might be dangerous."

"We have the proof of that before our eyes," said Gabriel, pointing to the body.

"Come away! come away at once!" cried the governor, seizing the young man by the arm, and trying to drag him outside.

"Yes, yes," answered Gabriel. "But," he added beseechingly, "for mercy's sake, let me stay a moment longer!"

M. de Sazerac made a gesture of acquiescence, and moved to the door, where the air was less poisonous and heavy.

As for Gabriel, he remained on his knees beside the corpse; with head bent and hands limp and relaxed, he remained for some moments motionless, silently praying or pondering.

What was he saying to his dead father? Did he ask of those lips, too soon, alas! touched by the fingers of death, the key to the enigma he was trying to solve? Did he swear he would avenge this sacred victim in this world, while waiting until God should avenge him in the next? Was he seeking in these disfigured features some trace of what his father, now seen for the second time, had once been—something that might indicate what a sweet and happy life he might have spent under his protection and love? In fine, was he thinking of the past or of the future, of men or of God, of justice or of forgiveness?

But this gloomy dialogue between a dead father and a living son remained so far a secret between Gabriel and his Creator.

Four or five minutes had slipped by.

The two men whom filial affection and humanity had severally led under these deadly vaults could hardly breathe.

"I must now entreat you, monsieur," said the honest governor, "to leave. It is impossible to stay here any longer."

"I am ready," said Gabriel; "quite ready now."

He took the icy hand of his father and kissed it; he bent over his discolored and damp forehead, and kissed it also.

Yet he never shed a tear. He could not.

"*Au revoir !*" cried he; "*au revoir !*"

He rose, still calm and firm in attitude, if not in heart, in appearance, if not in soul.

He sent his father a last look, a last kiss, and followed M. de Sazerac slowly and gravely.

After passing to the upper floor, he asked to see again the cold, dark cell in which the prisoner had left behind him so many sorrowful years and thoughts, and into which Gabriel had already entered, vainly thinking to embrace his father there.

In it he spent some minutes of mute meditation and of eager, hopeless curiosity.

When he ascended with the governor into light and life, M. de Sazerac, who conducted him into his own apartment, shivered when he saw the light.

But he did not dare to tell the young man that white patches silvered here and there his chestnut hair.

After a pause he only said, in a voice trembling with emotion—

"Can I do anything for you now, monsieur? Ask, and I shall be happy to grant any request that does not conflic* with my duties."

"Monsieur," answered Gabriel, "you have told me that I should be permitted to render the last honors to the dead. This evening certain men sent by me will come here; and if you will be kind enough to have the body placed in a coffin, and allow them to carry this coffin away, they shall deposit the prisoner in the family vault."

"Enough, monsieur," replied M. de Sazerac. "I must, however, warn you that there is a certain condition to be imposed, if I comply with your demand."

"What is it, monsieur?" asked Gabriel, coldly.

"You must, in conformity with a promise you have given, create no scandal on this occasion."

"I will also keep that promise," returned Gabriel. "My men will come in the night, and, without knowing the nature of what they are doing, will simply carry the body to the Rue des Jardins St. Paul, and place it in the vaults of the Counts de—"

"Excuse me, monsieur," quickly interrupted the governor of the Châtelet; "I did not know the name of the prisoner, and I neither desire nor ought to know it. My duty and loyalty force me to be silent on many points; you are bound to observe at least the same reserve in my regard."

"But I have nothing to hide," proudly answered Gabriel. "Only the guilty need concealment."

"And you belong to the number of the unfortunate," said the governor. "Is it not really better so?"

"Besides, monsieur," continued Gabriel, "what you have seen, I have guessed, and what it is I can tell you. Listen a moment as to the powerful man who came here yesterday evening, and spoke to the prisoner, in order to force the prisoner to speak; I know well by what means he forced

him to break silence—that silence upon which depended
the remainder of a life he had almost rescued from his
executioners. '

"What, monsieur! you knew?" said M. de Sazerac,
astonished.

"Undoubtedly," returned Gabriel, "the powerful man
said to the old man: 'Your son is alive!' or, 'Your son
has covered himself with glory!' or 'Your son is about
to deliver you!' He spoke to him of his son, the
wretch!"

The governor could not help letting his surprise be
seen by his attitude.

"And at the name of his son," continued Gabriel, "the
unhappy father, who had till then controlled himself in
presence of his deadliest enemy, could not master a feeling
of joy, and, dumb through hate, a cry escaped him through
love. Say, is that not true, monsieur?"

The governor bent his head without answering.

"It is true, since you do not deny it," resumed Gabriel.
"You see clearly it was useless to try to conceal from me
what the powerful man said to the poor prisoner! And it
was equally useless to pass over this man's name in silence.
Shall I tell it to you?"

"Monsieur! monsieur!" cried M. de Sazerac, anxiously; "we are alone, it is true. Still, take care! Are you
not afraid?"

"I told you," said Gabriel, "that I have nothing to
fear! This man, then, is the constable, the Duke de Montmorency, monsieur! The executioner cannot always wear
his mask."

"Oh, monsieur!" interrupted the governor, casting a
terrified glance around him.

"As to the name of the prisoner," continued Gabriel,
quietly, "and as to my name, you are at liberty to ignore
them both; but nothing prevents me from telling them to
you. For that matter, you may have met me before, and
you may meet me again. Moreover, you have been kind

to me in these last terrible moments; and, should you hear my name mentioned, and you may hear of it some months hence, it is as well you should know that the man whose name is in men's mouths is your grateful friend from this day forth."

"And I shall be happy to learn," answered M. de Sazerac, "that fate has not always been so cruel toward you as it is at present."

"Oh, I have nothing more to do with these matters," said Gabriel, gravely. "But, in any case, it is right you should know my name; and that name, since the death of my father to-night in this prison, is Count de Montgommery."

The governor of the Châtelet seemed turned to stone, and could not utter a word.

"So now farewell, monsieur," continued Gabriel; "farewell and thanks. May God keep you!"

He saluted M. de Sazerac, and passed out of the Châtelet with a firm step. But when he was in the air outside, and in the full light of day, he halted a moment, dazed and tottering. Life bewildered him after leaving that hell.

As the wayfarers, however, began to notice him with surprise, he collected his strength, and was soon at a distance from the fatal place.

It was to a deserted corner of the Grève that he first directed his steps. He took his tablets, and wrote as follows to his nurse:

My good Aloyse—Do not wait for me. I shall not return to-day. I must be alone for some time, alone to think and act and watch; but do not be anxious on my account. I shall surely see you again.

On this night, see that all in the hotel retire early. You alone must remain up and admit four men who will knock at the great gate a little late in the evening when the street is deserted.

You will yourself conduct these four men, laden with a sad and precious burden, to the family vault.

You will show them the open tomb in which they are to inter him whom they carry. You will watch religiously over these funeral preparations. Then, when they are terminated, you will give to each of these men four gold crowns, conduct them back noiselessly, and return to kneel and pray, as you would for your master and father.

I, too, shall pray at the same hour, but far from here; it is necessary. I feel that the sight of this tomb would drive me to violent and imprudent extremities. I have need rather to seek counsel from solitude and from God.

Au revoir, my good Aloyse; *au revoir*. Remind André of what concerns Madame de Castro, and do not forget about my guests, Jean and Babette Peuquoy. *Au revoir*, and may God keep you!   GABRIEL DE M.

After writing this letter Gabriel sought and found four men of the people—four workmen.

He gave to each of them four gold crowns in advance, and promised them the same amount after. To earn this sum, one of them was to carry a letter to its address immediately; then all four were to present themselves at the Châtelet in the evening, a little before ten o'clock, receive a coffin from the hands of M. de Sazerac, the governor, and carry it secretly and silently to the hotel in the Rue des Jardins St. Paul, to which the letter was addressed.

The poor workmen were profuse in their thanks to Gabriel; and, on leaving him, quite joyful at their good luck, they promised they would scrupulously carry out his orders.

"Well, this at least makes four men happy," said Gabriel to himself, with a sort of melancholy satisfaction.

He then followed the road leading out of Paris. It led him past the Louvre. Muffled up in his cloak, he stopped for a time, with folded arms, to gaze upon the royal château.

"You and I must settle accounts now!" he murmured, with a look of defiance.

He went on his way; and, as he walked, he repeated from memory the horoscope Master Nostradamus had for-

merly drawn up for the Count de Montgommery, and
which, by a strange coincidence, seemed to suit his son
equally well, according to the laws of astrology.

> En joûte, en amour, cettuy touchera
> Le front du roy,
> Et cornes ou bien trou sanglant mettra
> Au front du roy;
> Mais le veuille ou non, toujours blessera
> Le front du roy;
> Enfin l'aimera, puis las! le tuera
> Dame du roy.

Gabriel thought this singular prediction had been accomplished in every point with regard to his father. In
fact, the Count de Montgommery, who, when a young
man, had, in sport, struck King Francis the First on the
head with a burning brand, had afterward become the rival
of King Henry in love, and had been killed the evening
before by that same lady of the king, who had loved him.

And until now Gabriel also had been loved by a queen
—by Catherine de Médicis.

Was he to follow his destiny even to the end? Was his
vengeance or his lot to be to vanquish and slay the king
en joûte?

If this thing should happen, little it mattered to Gabriel
whether the *dame du roi* who loved him killed him sooner
or later.

CHAPTER XI

THE ERRANT GENTLEMAN

POOR Aloyse, accustomed to waiting of old, to solitude and to sorrow, spent, once again, two or three never-ending hours, seated before the window, looking for her dear young master's return.

When the workman, whom Gabriel charged with the letter, knocked at the door, it was Aloyse who ran to open it. News at last!

Terrible news! Aloyse, when she read the first lines, felt as if there was a mist before her eyes, and, to hide her emotion, had to return quickly to her chamber, where she finished, not without difficulty, reading the fatal letter, her eyes full of tears.

Still, hers was a strong nature and a valiant soul. She recovered her composure, dried her tears, and went out to say to the messenger—

"It is well. This evening. I shall expect you and your companions."

The page André questioned her anxiously; but she put off all reply until the morrow. Until then, she had enough to think of and enough to do.

When evening came she sent the people of the household to bed early.

"The master will certainly not return to-night," she said to them.

But when she was alone, she thought—

"Yes, the master will return! But, alas! not the young master, but the old; not the living, but the dead. For what corpse should I have been ordered to place in the vault of the Montgommerys, except that of the Count de Montgommery himself? O my noble lord! you for whom my poor Perrot died! you have come, then, to join that faithful servant! But have you carried your secret with you to the tomb? O mystery of mysteries! Everywhere mystery and terror! No matter! without understanding, or knowing, and, alas! without hoping, I shall obey. It is my duty, and I will do it, O my God!''

And the sorrowful revery of Aloyse ended in an ardent prayer. It is the custom of the human soul, when the weight of life becomes too heavy, to take refuge in the bosom of God.

About twelve, when the streets were entirely deserted, a heavy knock was heard at the great gate.

Aloyse started, and turned pale. But, collecting all her courage, she went, with a torch in her hand, and opened it for the men who bore their dismal burden.

She received with a profound and respectful salutation the master who thus returned to his home after so long an absence. Then she said to the bearers—

"Follow me, and make as little noise as possible. I am going to show you the way.''

And, walking in front of them with the light, she conducted them to the sepulchral vault.

When there, the men laid down the coffin in one of the open tombs, and replaced the marble lid; then these poor men, whom suffering had rendered reverential in presence of death, doffed their caps, knelt down, and said a short prayer for the soul of the unknown deceased. When they arose, the nurse conducted them back in silence, and, upon the threshold of the door, slipped into the hand of one of them the sum promised by Gabriel. They passed out like dumb shadows, not uttering a single word.

As to Aloyse, she descended again to the tomb, and passed the rest of the night on her knees, praying and weeping.

The next morning André found her pale but calm, and she simply said to him impressively—

"My child, we must always hope, but we must no longer wait for M. le Vicomte d'Exmès. You ought, therefore, to think of executing the commissions with which he has charged you, in case he did not return immediately.'

"That is enough," said the page, sadly. "I shall start then to-day, and try to meet Madame de Castro."

"In the name of your absent master, I thank you for your zeal, André," said Aloyse.

The boy did what he said, and set out the same day.

He made inquiries along the road as to the whereabout of the noble traveller; but he did not find her until he reached Amiens.

Diana de Castro had then just arrived in that city, with the escort which the Duke de Guise had given to the daughter of Henry the Second. She was resting for a few hours in the house of the governor, M. de Thuré.

As soon as Diana perceived the page she changed color; but, controlling herself, she made him a sign to follow her into the neighboring room, and, when they were alone, said:

"Well, André, what brings you here?"

"Only this, madame," he replied, handing her the folded veil.

"Ah! it is not the ring!" cried Diana.

It was all she could think of at first. Then she recovered her presence of mind a little, and, smitten with that greedy curiosity which impels the unhappy to sound the very depths of their misery, she asked—

"Has not M. d'Exmès charged you with any letter for me?"

"No, madame."

"But surely you must have at least some verbal message for me?"

"Alas!" replied the page, shaking his head, "all that M. d'Exmès said was that he released you from all your promises, even from that of which the veil is the pledge; he added nothing further.''

"But what were the circumstances that influenced him in sending you to me? Did you give him my letter? What did he say after reading it? What did he say when he intrusted you with this one? Speak, André; you are devoted and faithful. The interest of my life is perhaps involved in your answers, and the slightest clew may guide and reassure me in the darkness that surrounds me.''

"Madame," said André, "I will tell you all I know; but what I know is very little.''

"No matter; speak, for Heaven's sake!" cried Madame de Castro.

André thereupon related, omitting nothing, for Gabriel had not ordered him to conceal anything from Diana, all the directions given by his master, before starting, to himself and Aloyse, under the idea that his absence might be prolonged. He spoke of the young man's hesitation and anguish. After reading Diana's letter Gabriel seemed at first desirous of speaking; then he kept silence, only letting a few vague words escape him. André told, as he promised, everything. Not a word was forgotten, nor broken sentence, nor even his master's silence, when that silence was significant. But, as he had said, he knew very little, and his narrative only increased Diana's doubts and uncertainties.

She looked sadly at the black veil, his only message, the true symbol of her destiny. She seemed to be questioning it; to be taking counsel with it.

"In any case," said she to herself, "one of two things must have happened: either Gabriel knows that he is my brother, or he has lost all hope and all means of penetrating the fatal secret. I have to choose between these two misfortunes. Yes; the thing is certain, and there is no illusion wherewith I might beguile myself now. But should not Gabriel have spared me these cruel doubts? He releases me from my word; why? Why not confide to me what he intends doing, and what is going to become of him? Ah! his silence frightens me more than his anger or his threats could have done!"

And Diana then considered whether she should follow out her first intention, and enter, never to leave it this time, some convent in Paris or the provinces, or whether it was not rather her duty to return to court, try to see Gabriel again, wrest from him the truth as to his past actions and future designs, and watch over the threatened life of the king, her father— Her father? but was Henry the Second her father? and was she not, perhaps, an impious and guilty daughter in interfering with the vengeance that wished to strike and punish the king? Terrible extremity!

But Diana was a woman—a tender and generous woman. She said to herself that, whatever might happen, revenge might be regretted, forgiveness never; and, carried away by the natural bent of her upright soul, she decided to return to Paris, and, until she had reassuring news of Gabriel and his plans, to stay by the king as his protection and safeguard. Who knows but that Gabriel, too, might have need of her intervention? When she had saved both of those she loved, it would be time to seek a refuge in the bosom of God.

This resolution adopted, our brave Diana hesitated no longer, and continued her journey to Paris. She arrived there three days afterward, and entered the Louvre, Henry the Second receiving her with the utmost joy and with all the tenderness of a father.

But she could not help receiving these evidences of affection with sadness and coldness; and the king, who remembered Diana's liking for Gabriel, sometimes felt embarrassed and somewhat subdued in the presence of his daughter. She reminded him of things he would have preferred to forget.

Consequently, he no longer spoke of the marriage he had planned between her and Francis de Montmorency. On this subject her mind was at rest.

But she had enough of other cares. Neither at the Hôtel de Montgommery, nor at the Louvre, nor in any other quarter, could she obtain positive information as to the movements of Viscount d'Exmès.

The young man had, in fact, disappeared. Days, weeks, entire months slipped by; but no tidings came to Diana, directly or indirectly, of the fate of Gabriel.

Some persons, however, fancied they had met him, had looked upon his moody and dejected face, although none had spoken to him; the troubled soul they had taken for Gabriel had always avoided them, always fled at their approach. Moreover, all differed as to the place through which they had seen the Viscount d'Exmès pass; some said St. Germain, some Fontainebleau, some at Vincennes, and some Paris. What reliance could be placed upon so many contradictory reports!

And yet many of them were correct enough. Gabriel, hurried onward by a terrible memory, and an idea still more terrible, never remained a day in the same place. An uncontrollable desire of movement and action banished him from every spot he came to almost as soon as he reached it. On foot or on horseback, in town or in the country, he had to go on incessantly, pale and sinister-looking, like Orestes of old pursued by the Furies.

Besides, he never entered a house unless necessity constrained him, but was always found wandering beneath the open sky.

Once, nevertheless, Master Ambroise Paré, who, after his wounded patients were on the road to recovery and there was a partial cessation of hostilities in the North, had returned to Paris, was surprised by a visit from his old acquaintance, Viscount d'Exmès. The illustrious surgeon received him with deference and cordiality as a gentleman and a friend.

Gabriel, like a man just returned from a foreign land, questioned him on matters which were familiar to every one else.

Thus, after being informed that Martin Guerre was quite recovered and at this moment on his way to Paris, he made inquiries as to the condition of the Duke de Guise and the army. All was going on well with both. The Balafré was before Thionville; Marshal de Thermes had taken Dunkirk, Gaspard de Tavannes had made himself master of Guines and the Pays d'Oie. There remained not an inch of territory to the English in all the realm; so Francis de Lorraine had kept his oath.

Gabriel listened gravely and apparently coldly to this good news.

"I thank you, master," was his answer, "I am glad to know that, for France at least, our work at Calais has not been quite without result. Still, my chief motive in visiting you was not to learn these things. Master, before admiring your skill at the bedside of the wounded, certain words I heard from you in the little house in the Rue St. Jacques exercised a great influence over me. I have come, then, to converse with you upon those religious subjects of which you have so profound a knowledge. You have, I presume, finally embraced the cause of the Reformation?"

"Yes, M. d'Exmès," firmly replied Ambroise; "the correspondence which the great Calvin has deigned to open with me has banished my last doubts and my last scruples. I am now one of his most convinced followers."

"Well, then, master," said Gabriel, "would you be kind enough to give a neophyte of good-will the benefit of your discernment and penetration? It is of myself I am speaking. Would you strengthen my weak faith, just as you would set a broken limb?"

"It is my duty to give relief to the souls of my fellow-creatures as well as to their bodies, whenever I can, M. d'Exmès," replied Ambroise; "and I am entirely at your service."

They talked for more than two hours, Ambroise Paré ardent and eloquent, Gabriel calm, sad, and docile.

Then Gabriel rose, and, pressing the surgeon's hand, said—

"Thanks; this conversation has done me great good. The time has not yet come, unfortunately, when I can declare for the Reformation. In the interest of the religion itself, I must wait. Otherwise, my conversion might expose your sacred cause some day or other to persecution, or at least to calumny. I know what I am saying. But I now comprehend that your party is walking in the right path; and you may believe that, from this moment, I am with you in heart, if not openly. Adieu, Master Ambroise, we shall meet again."

And Gabriel, without further explanation, saluted the philosophic surgeon and took his leave.

Early in the month following, May, 1558, he reappeared for the first time since his mysterious departure in the hotel in the Rue des Jardins St. Paul.

There he learned of some new incidents. Martin Guerre had returned a fortnight before, and Jean Peuquoy and his wife had been Gabriel's guests for three months.

But God had not wished that the devotion of Jean should be without limit, or the fault of Babette without expiation. A few days previously, she had given birth prematurely to a dead child.

The poor mother wept much, but she bowed her head in presence of a sorrow which her repentance enabled her to offer as an atonement; and just as Jean Peuquoy had generously offered his sacrifice to her, so she offered in turn her resignation to him. Moreover, the tender sympathy of her husband and the motherly encouragement of Aloyse did not fail eventually to console the gentle sufferer. The good-natured commiseration of Martin Guerre had also its effect.

One evening, as the four happened to be in friendly conversation, the door opened; and, to their great surprise and still greater joy, the master of the house, Viscount d'Exmès, entered with a slow step and grave air.

There was the same cry from all, and Gabriel was at once surrounded by his two guests, his squire, and his nurse.

The first transports calmed, Aloyse was about to question him whom, indeed, she called her lord, but whom in her inmost heart she named her child always.

What had become of him during this long absence? What did he intend doing now? Would he at last stay with those who loved him?

But Gabriel laid a finger upon his lips, and, with a look sad but firm, imposed silence on her tender anxiety.

It was evident he would not or could not give any explanation as to his past or his future.

On the other hand, he asked Jean and Babette Peuquoy many things bearing on themselves. Had they wanted for anything? Had they news lately of their worthy brother Pierre, who was still in Calais?

He showed the sincerest pity for Babette, and tried to console her also, as far as he could console a mother who is weeping the loss of a child.

So Gabriel passed the rest of the day in the midst of his friends and retainers, kind and affectionate to all, but never attempting to shake off the black melancholy that seemed to enfold him.

As to Martin Guerre, whose eyes never for a moment left the master he had at last found again, Gabriel spoke to him, his inquiries displaying the strong interest he felt in his faithful squire. But, during the entire day, he never said a word relating to the promise he had formerly given, and seemed to have forgotten the obligation he undertook to punish the wretch who, by robbing poor Martin of name and honor, had so long persecuted him.

Martin Guerre, however, was too respectful and unselfish to remind the Viscount d'Exmès of either promise or obligation.

But when evening came, Gabriel rose, and in a tone that admitted of neither reply nor contradiction, said—

"I must now leave."

Then, turning to Martin Guerre, he added—

"My good Martin, I have not forgotten you during my wanderings, and without making myself known, I have made a close investigation into your business. I think I am on the track of a discovery in which you are interested; for I have always remembered the pledge I took in your regard."

"Oh, monseigneur!" cried the squire, equally happy and confused.

"Yes," returned Gabriel; "I repeat that I have gathered sufficient evidence to lead me to believe I am now on the right road. But you must help me, my friend. You will start, some time this week, for your native village; but do not go there at once. Be at Lyons a month from to-day. I will join you there at that time, and we will then settle on some plan for acting together in the matter."

"I will obey you, monseigneur," said Martin Guerre. "But shall I not see you before then?"

"No, no; I must be alone henceforth," answered Gabriel, with energy. "I am leaving again, and do not attempt to detain me; to do so would merely cause me useless affliction. Adieu, my good friends. Martin, remember; be at Lyons a month from now."

"I will be there, monseigneur," said the squire.

Gabriel took a cordial farewell of Jean and Babette Peuquoy, pressed the hands of Aloyse tenderly in his own, and, without appearing to notice the sorrow of his affectionate nurse, left once more to resume the wandering life to which he seemed to have condemned himself.

CHAPTER XII

IN WHICH ARNOLD DU THILL IS FOUND AGAIN

SIX weeks after, on the 15th of June, 1558, on the threshold of the handsomest house in the village of Artigues, the front of which was hidden by a green vine, a rustic domestic picture might have been witnessed, simple and somewhat vulgar indeed, but not lacking a certain interest.

A man who, to judge by his dusty boots, had come from a long journey, was seated upon a wooden bench, and holding out these same boots to a kneeling woman busily engaged in unlacing them.

The man was frowning; the woman was smiling.

"Will you never have done, Bertrande?" said the man, harshly. "Your awkwardness and slowness are driving me wild."

"There! it is finished now," said the woman, gently.

"Finished now? hum!" growled the pretended Martin Guerre. "Where are my other shoes? I wager you never brought them, you idiotic female. I suppose I must go barefoot for two minutes at the least."

Bertrande ran into the house, and in less than two minutes brought out a pair of shoes which she hastened to buckle on her master and lord.

The reader without doubt recognizes these two characters. The one was Arnold du Thill, imperious and brutal as ever; the other was Bertrande de Rolles, now exceedingly meek and reasonable.

"Where is my glass of hydromel?" returned Martin, in the same gruff tone.

"It is quite ready," said Bertrande, timidly, "and I am going to fetch it."

"Always delay!" exclaimed the other, stamping his foot impatiently. "Come, be alive, or if you don't—"

An expressive gesture completed the sentence.

Bertrande passed out and returned with the quickness of lightning. Martin took the glass from her hand, and tossed it off at a draught with evident satisfaction. "That's not bad," he condescended to say to his wife as he handed back the empty goblet.

"My poor dear, are you warm?" she ventured to say, wiping the forehead of her surly spouse with her handkerchief. "Stay; put on your hat for fear of cold. You are very tired, are you not?"

"Ah," returned Martin Guerre, still grumbling, "isn't it necessary to conform to the foolish customs of this foolish country, and on every anniversary of our marriage invite personally a heap of hungry relatives from all the surrounding villages? I had, faith, forgotten this stupid custom, and if you had not reminded me of it yesterday— Well, my tramp is over, and in two hours all our relatives will be here, and they'll bring their ravenous jaws with them, too."

"Thanks, my love," said Bertrande; "you are quite right, it is an absurd custom, but it is also an imperious custom, to which we must conform, if we would not be looked upon as proud and disdainful."

"Finely reasoned," returned Martin, ironically. "And have you been working also, lazybones? Have you spread the table in the orchard?"

"Yes, Martin, as you ordered."

"You have invited the judge, have you?" asked the tender husband.

"Yes, Martin; and he said he would be present if he possibly could."

"If he possibly could!" cried Martin, wrathfully. "I don't want that at all; he must come. You must have made a muddle of your invitation. You knew I wanted to get on the soft side of the judge, but you do everything to annoy me. His presence alone could reconcile me to this idiotic anniversary and the useless expense it entails."

"Idiotic anniversary! the anniversary of our marriage!" exclaimed Bertrande, with tears in her eyes. "Ah, Martin, you are now a learned man; you have seen much and travelled much, and may despise the old prejudices of the country. But no matter! This anniversary reminds me of the time when you were less severe and more tender to your poor wife."

"Yes," said Martin, with a grin; "and when my wife was less gentle and considerate of a shrew, when she sometimes so far forgot herself as to—"

"Oh, Martin! Martin! do not recall these memories which make me blush, and which I can hardly now believe real."

"And when I think I was so stupid as to endure— Ah, let us leave that aside; my character has changed considerably, and yours also, I must acknowledge. As you say, Bertrande, I have since then travelled a good deal. Your bad temper, if it has forced me to roam through the world, has also been the means of gaining me experience; and when I came back here last year, I was able to settle things in their natural order. For this purpose, I brought with me another Martin, called Martin Stick. So now everything is as it should be, and there is no more united couple."

"Quite true, thanks be to God!" said Bertrande.

"Betrande!"

"Martin!"

"You go at once," said he, in a tone that admitted of no reply, "to the Judge of Artigues. You will renew your entreaties, and not stop until you have his formal promise to be present at our banquet; and mind, if he does not come, you, and you alone, pay the penalty. Go, Bertrande, and return quickly."

"I'll be back immediately," said Bertrande, disappearing on the instant.

Arnold du Thill looked after her for a moment with a satisfied expression. Then, being alone, he stretched himself lazily on his wooden bench, drinking in the air and winking his eyes with the selfish and disdainful beatitude of a happy man who has nothing to fear and nothing to desire.

He did not see a traveller, who, supported by a stick, was walking painfully on the highway, which was deserted, as this was the hottest hour of the day, and who, on perceiving Arnold, stopped in front of him.

"Excuse me, monsieur," said the stranger. "Be so kind as to tell me if there is an inn in this village where I could rest and dine."

"No," said Martin, without disturbing himself. "You'll have to go to Rieux, two leagues from here, if you want to find a hotel."

"Two leagues more!" cried the traveller, "and I utterly worn out! I would willingly give a pistole to find food and lodging at once."

"A pistole!" said Arnold, rising, for he was as greedy after money as ever. "Well, my good man, we can give you a bed in a corner; and as to dinner, we have to-day an anniversary dinner at which a guest more or less will not count. Does that suit you, eh?"

"Of course," said the traveller. "Didn't I tell you I am dying of hunger and fatigue?"

"Well, then, the thing is settled; you remain for a pistole," replied Arnold.

"Here it is in advance," said the man.

In standing up to take it, Arnold at the same time removed the hat, which covered his eyes and face.

The stranger for the first time saw his features, and started back in surprise.

"My nephew!" he cried, "Arnold du Thill."

Arnold looked at him and turned pale, but, recovering himself immediately, he said—

"Your nephew? I do not recognize you. Who are you?"

"You do not recognize me, Arnold?" returned the man. "You do not recognize your old uncle by the mother's side, Carbon Barreau, to whom you have been such a trouble, as, indeed, you have been to all your family."

"You don't say so!" said Arnold, with an insolent laugh.

"What! do you deny me and deny yourself?" exclaimed Carbon Barreau. "Say, were you not the death of your mother, my sister, a poor widow you abandoned at Sagias ten years ago? Ah, you do not recognize me, you hard-hearted wretch, but I recognize you!"

"I don't at all know what you mean," retorted Arnold, impudently, not a whit disconcerted. "My name is not Arnold, but Martin Guerre. I do not belong to Sagias, but to Artigues. The old people of the country knew me when I was born, and would prove it; and if you wish to get laughed at, you have only to repeat what you have just said in presence of Bertrande de Rolles, my wife, and all my relatives."

"Your wife, your relatives!" cried Carbon Barreau, astounded. "Pardon me; can I have been mistaken? But no, it is impossible. Such a resemblance—"

"At the end of ten years would be difficult to establish," interrupted Arnold. "Nonsense! you are bleareyed, my good man. You are about to see my real uncles and my real relatives in a few moments."

"Well, then," returned Carbon Barreau, who was beginning to be convinced, "you can certainly boast of being the exact counterpart of my nephew Arnold du Thill."

"So you say," retorted Arnold, with a grin. "I have not boasted of it so far."

"Oh, when I said that you could boast of it," rejoined

the goodman, "I did not mean that there was any cause for pride in resembling such a rascal. I must acknowledge, although he was one of my family, that my nephew was one of the most awful scoundrels that ever existed. And, now I think of it, it is very unlikely he is still alive. He must have been hanged long since, the wretch!"

"You think so?" said Arnold, with some bitterness.

"I am certain of it, M. Martin Guerre," said Carbon Barreau, confidently. "My speaking in this way of the villain does not annoy you, I hope, since you are not he?"

"Oh, it is nothing to me," replied Arnold, anything but satisfied notwithstanding.

"Ah, monsieur!" said the uncle, who had an old man's talkativeness, "how often have I congratulated myself, when I saw his poor mother in tears, on having remained a bachelor, and never having had children, who might, like that ruffian, have dishonored my name and ruined my life."

"Stay, this is worth thinking of," said Arnold to himself. "Uncle Carbon has no children; that is to say, no heirs."

"What are you thinking of, Master Martin?" asked the traveller.

"I am thinking," answered Arnold, sweetly, "that, your statement to the contrary, you would like to have a son to-day, or, in default of a son, even that wicked nephew, for whom you feel so little regret, but who would surely be an object of family affection, and to whom you might leave your property after you."

"My property?" said Carbon Barreau.

"Yes, your property," returned Arnold du Thill. "A man who is so free with his pistoles cannot be poor; and this Arnold who resembles me would be your heir, I suppose. *Pardieu!* I rather regret that I am not he."

"Arnold du Thill would, in fact, be my heir, if he were not hanged," answered Carbon Barreau, gravely. "But he would not derive great profit from his inheritance. I have offered you a pistole at present for food and lodging, because I am exhausted with hunger and weariness. That, unfortunately, does not hinder my purse from being very light—too light, alas!"

"Hum!" muttered Arnold, incredulously.

"You do not believe me, Master Martin Guerre? That is just as you like. It is not the less true that I am on my way to Lyons, where the president of the parliament, in which I was an usher for twenty years, offers me a home and support for the remainder of my days. He sent me twenty-five pistoles to pay my debts and defray the expense of the journey, the generous man; but what is left of that is all I possess. And so my property would be too trifling for Arnold du Thill to claim it, if he were still alive. That is why—"

"Ah, hold your tongue, babbler!" interrupted Arnold, brutally, very much discontented at what he heard. "Do you think I have nothing better to do than listen to your gabble? Here, give me the pistole, and enter the house, if you like. You will dine in an hour, sleep afterward, and we shall be quits. No need at all that I should be bothered with your twaddle in addition."

"But it was you who asked me," said Carbon Barreau.

"Are you going to enter, my good fellow, or are you not? I see two of my guests, and I must leave you for them. Enter; I treat you without ceremony, and do not escort you."

"I can easily see that," said Carbon Barreau.

And he entered the house, grumbling at these sudden changes of temper in his host.

Three hours after, the guests, of whom the number was complete, were still seated at table under the elms, and the Judge of Artigues, whose favor Arnold was so anxious to win, occupied the place of honor.

Good wines and pleasant gossip went the rounds. The young people spoke of the future, and the old of the past;

and Uncle Carbon Barreau was able to convince himself that his host was really called Martin Guerre, and was known and treated by all the inhabitants of Artigues as one of themselves.

"Do you remember, cousin Martin," said one, "that Augustinian monk, Brother Chrysostom, who taught us both to read?"

"I remember," said Arnold.

"Do you remember, cousin Martin," said another, "that guns were first fired in this country at your wedding, as a sign of rejoicing?"

"Yes, I remember," replied Arnold.

And, as if to revive his memories, he embraced his wife, seated beside him, proud and happy.

"Since you have such a good memory, my master," said a loud and firm voice behind the guests, addressing Arnold du Thill—"and since you remember so many things, you will, perhaps, also remember me."

CHAPTER XIII

JUSTICE PUZZLED

THE person who had spoken in such an imperious tone cast aside the brown cloak in which he was muffled, and took off the wide-brimmed hat that concealed his features. The guests of Arnold du Thill, who had turned round on hearing him, were then able to see a young cavalier, lofty in bearing and rich in dress.

At some distance, a servant was holding the reins of the two horses that had brought them.

All rose respectfully, much surprised and very curious.

As for Arnold du Thill, he became as pale as if he were dead. "M. le Vicomte d'Exmès!" he murmured, quite scared.

"Ha!" resumed Gabriel, in a voice of thunder, addressing him, "so you recognize me, do you?"

Arnold, after a moment's hesitation, had calculated his chances and chosen his course.

"Of course," said he, in a voice he tried to render firm—"of course, I recognize M. le Vicomte d'Exmès, because I sometimes saw him in the Louvre and elsewhere at the time I was in the service of M. de Montmorency. But I cannot believe that monseigneur can recognize me, a humble and obscure servant of the constable."

"You forget," said Gabriel, "that you have also been in mine."

"Who—I?" cried Arnold, feigning the most profound astonishment. "Oh, excuse me, monseigneur; you are surely mistaken."

"I am so certain that I am not mistaken," returned Gabriel, calmly, "that I insist on the Judge of Artigues, here present, having you arrested and imprisoned. Is that plain?"

There was a movement of terror among the spectators. The judge approached, very much astonished. Arnold alone preserved his coolness.

"May I at least know of what crime I am accused?" asked he.

"I accuse you," answered Gabriel, firmly, "of iniquitously personating my squire, Martin Guerre, of wickedly and traitorously stealing his name, his house, and his wife, by the aid of a resemblance so perfect that it passes imagination."

At this accusation, so clearly formulated, the guests regarded one another with stupefaction.

"What does this mean?" they murmured. "Martin Guerre is not Martin Guerre! What diabolical sorcery is there under all this?" Several of these good people made the sign of the cross, and whispered to themselves the formulas used in exorcism. Most turned their eyes upon their host in terror.

Arnold du Thill saw the time was come to strike a decisive blow if he was to gain over these wavering people to his side. He turned to her he called his wife.

"Bertrande!" cried he. "Am I, or am I not, your husband?"

Poor Bertrande, frightened, gasping, had so far not uttered a word, but looked, with staring eyes, now at Gabriel, now at her supposed husband.

But at the imperious tone and threatening gesture of Arnold du Thill, she no longer hesitated; she threw herself into his arms with entire assurance.

"Dear Martin Guerre!" she exclaimed.

At these words the charm was broken, and the offensive murmurs turned against Gabriel.

"Monsieur," said Arnold, triumphantly, "in presence of

the testimony of my wife and of all my relations, do you still persist in your strange accusation?''

"I do," said Gabriel, quietly.

"A moment!" cried Carbon Barreau, interfering. "I knew well, my host, that I was not blear-eyed. Since there is somewhere another individual who resembles this one in every particular, I affirm that one of the two is my nephew, Arnold du Thill, like myself a native of Sagias."

"Ah, this assistance is providential, and comes just at the right moment!" said Gabriel. "Master," he added, turning to the old man, "do you, then, recognize your nephew in this man?"

"In truth," answered Carbon Barreau, "I cannot distinguish whether it is he or the other one; but I would take my oath beforehand that, if there is imposture anywhere, my nephew has a hand in it, for he had a knack at that sort of thing."

"You hear, M. le Juge?" said Gabriel. "Whoever is guilty, the crime is no longer doubtful."

"But where, pray, is the fellow who, in order to cheat me, claims that he has been cheated?" cried Arnold du Thill, audaciously. "Are you not going to confront me with him? Is he in hiding? Let him show himself and be judged himself."

"Martin Guerre, my squire," said Gabriel, "has, in obedience to my orders, already given himself up to the authorities at Rieux. M. le Juge, I am the Viscount de Montgommery, ex-captain of his Majesty's Guards. The accused has recognized me. I, as his accuser, summon you to have him arrested and imprisoned. When they are both in the hands of justice, I hope to be able to prove on which side is truth and on which imposture."

"The case is clear, monseigneur," said the puzzled judge. "Let Martin Guerre be taken to prison."

"I surrender at once and of my own will, strong as I am in my innocence," cried Arnold. "My good and dear friends," he added, addressing the crowd, whom he thought it wise to win over, "I count on your loyal testimony to help me in this extremity. All of you who have known me recognize me, do you not?"

"Yes, yes; keep up your courage, Martin," said all the friends and relatives, touched by this appeal.

As for Bertrande, she adopted the wisest course, and fainted.

Eight days after, the trial was opened before the tribunal of Rieux. A curious and difficult case assuredly. It well deserved to become as celebrated as it is even in our days, after three hundred years.

If Gabriel had not been mixed up with it a little, it is probable that these worthy Rieux judges, to whom the affair was referred, would never have been able to solve the riddle.

What Gabriel asked above all was that the two oppo· nents should not be brought face to face until a new order, under any pretext. They were interrogated and confronted with witnesses separately, and Martin, as well as Arnold du Thill, had to submit to the most rigorous seclusion.

Martin Guerre, wrapped in a cloak, was brought face to face with his wife, Carbon Barreau, all his friends and rela· tives, one after another.

All recognized him. It was his very face, his very self. No room for deception.

But all recognized equally Arnold du Thill as Martin when he was in turn presented to them.

How, in fact, distinguish between two Sosias so exactly alike as Martin Guerre and Arnold du Thill?

"It would bother the very devil himself," said Carbon Barreau, altogether at sea as to which was his real nephew.

But in presence of this marvellous and unheard-of freak of nature, Gabriel and the judges had hold of one clew. This was, in default of material differences, contradictions in fact and the contrariety of dispositions shown by the two men.

In telling the incidents of their early life, each related

the same facts, recalled the same dates, quoted the same names with an accuracy that had something frightful in it.

In support of his assertions, moreover, Arnold adduced Bertrande's letters, certain family papers, and the ring blessed on the occasion of his marriage. But Martin explained how Arnold, after having had him hanged at Noyon, could have stolen his papers and his wedding-ring.

Then the perplexity of the judges was always the same, their uncertainty always as great. Appearances and proofs were as clear and as eloquent on one side as on the other; the allegations of the two accused seemed equally sincere.

Formal proofs and the clearest evidence were needed for the disentanglement of such an intricate problem. These Gabriel promised to find and furnish.

First, he demanded that the presiding judge should put this question again to Martin Guerre and Arnold du Thill, both being still interrogated apart—

"Where did you spend your time from when you were twelve till you were sixteen?"

Immediate answer of the two accused examined separately:

"At St. Sebastian in Biscay, with my cousin Sanxi."

Sanxi was present, summoned as a witness, and swore that such was the case.

Gabriel approached him and whispered a word in his ear.

Sanxi laughed, and questioned Arnold in the Basque tongue. Arnold turned pale, and did not say a word.

"What?" exclaimed Gabriel; "after passing four years at St. Sebastian, you do not understand the dialect of the country?"

"I have forgotten it," stammered Arnold.

Martin Guerre, submitted to the same test in his turn, chatted in Basque for a quarter of an hour, to the great delight of his cousin, and the perfect edification of spectators and judges.

This first test, which was beginning to throw some light on the subject, was followed by another which, although it was borrowed from the Odyssey, was not the less significant on that account.

The inhabitants of Artigues, who were of Martin Guerre's age, recalled with admiration and some jealousy his skill at tennis.

But ever since his return the false Martin had always refused to play, under the pretext of a wound in his right hand.

The true Martin, on the contrary, held his own against the best players in the country, in presence of the judges, and took evident pleasure in doing so.

He even played seated, all the time muffled up in his cloak. His second had only to bring him the balls, which he threw with marvellous dexterity.

From that moment, the public sympathy—an important element on this occasion—was with Martin; that is, a rare thing enough, on the side of the right.

A last queer incident completed the ruin of Arnold du Thill in the mind of the judges.

The two accused were absolutely of the same height; on the watch for the slightest clew, Gabriel had thought he noticed that the foot of the brave squire, his only foot, also, was much smaller than the foot of Arnold du Thill.

The old shoemaker of Artigues appeared before the tribunal, and brought his old and new measurements with him.

"Yes," said the worthy cobbler; "formerly I used to take Martin's measure for nines, and I was quite astonished when, after his return, I had to take them for twelves; but I thought it was the effect of his long journeys."

The true Martin Guerre then proudly held out to the shoemaker the only foot Providence had left him, doubtless for the greater triumph of the truth. The simple old fellow, after measuring, acknowledged and proclaimed that this was the authentic foot he had made boots for of yore, and that, in spite of its long journeyings and double duty, it had remained pretty much the same.

From that moment the belief in Martin's innocence and Arnold's guilt was universal.

But these material proofs were not enough. Gabriel wished to adduce moral evidence also.

He produced the peasant to whom Arnold du Thill had given the strange commission to announce at Paris the hanging of Martin Guerre at Noyon. The good man related artlessly his surprise at finding in the Rue des Jardins St. Paul the person he thought he had seen travelling on the road to Lyons. It was this circumstance that had inspired Gabriel with the first suspicion of the truth.

Then Bertrande de Rolles was examined again.

Poor Bertrande, in spite of the change of opinion, was always on the side of him who made himself feared.

Questioned, however, as to whether she had not observed a difference in her husband's character since his return—

"Oh, yes, certainly," she said. "There has been quite a change since his return, but the change has been to his advantage," she hastened to add.

And when she was urged to explain clearly—

"Formerly," said Bertrande, naïvely, "Martin was weaker and milder than a sheep, and let me lead him and even beat him, to that degree that I was sometimes ashamed of it. But he has come back a man and a master. He has shown me in a way that did not allow any reply that I was quite wrong at that time, and that my duty as a wife was to obey his commands and his cudgel. Now he orders and I serve; he raises his hand and I bend my head. It is from his travels he has brought back his lordly ways; and ever since his return we have changed parts, as was, indeed, right and proper. Now that I have become used to them, I am very well satisfied."

Other inhabitants of Artigues proved that the old Martin Guerre had been always inoffensive, pious, and good-natured, while the new one was aggressive, impious, and quarrelsome. Like the shoemaker and Bertrande, they had attributed these changes to his travels.

Count Gabriel de Montgommery then spoke, amid the respectful silence of judges and spectators.

He related through what strange circumstances he had had the two Martin Guerres in his service, how long it had taken him to find any explanation of the variations in character and temper of his double squire, and what events had finally put him on the track.

Gabriel told everything, in fact—the terrors of Martin and the treacheries of Arnold du Thill; the virtues of the one and the crimes of the other. He made the dark and puzzling story plain and evident to all eyes, and concluded with demanding the punishment of the guilty and the rehabilitation of the innocent.

The justice of that time was less complaisant and less favorable to the accused than it is in our days. Consequently, Arnold du Thill was still ignorant of the overwhelming charges made and proved against him. He had, indeed, seen with considerable dread that the tests of the Basque language and the game of tennis turned to his confusion; but he thought that, after all, the excuses he gave were sufficient. But he knew nothing of the evidence of the old shoemaker, nor could he learn whether Martin Guerre, whom his jailers never let him see, had got clear of all these questions and difficulties with more success than himself.

Gabriel, moved by a sentiment of equity and generosity, had required that Arnold du Thill should be present when his case was summed up, and might, if he thought fit, reply to the charges. Martin had nothing to do with this, and remained in prison. But Arnold was taken from it and brought to court, so that he might be judged after hearing both sides, and so he did not lose a word of the convincing narrative of Gabriel.

Nevertheless, when Viscount d'Exmès had finished, Arnold du Thill, without allowing himself to be intimidated or discouraged, rose tranquilly and asked permission to defend himself. The tribunal would have refused, but Gabriel supported him, and he was heard.

He spoke admirably. The astute rascal had really great natural eloquence, combined with a most clever and crafty mind.

Gabriel had specially exerted himself to shed light on the darksome adventures of the two Martins. Arnold did his best to entangle all the threads again, and to bring the minds of his judges a second time into a state of salutary confusion. He acknowledged that he himself understood nothing of all these perplexing events which involved two lives severally. It was not his part to explain all these enigmas by which it was sought to embarrass him. He had only to answer for his own life and justify his own actions. This he was ready to do.

He then gave a logical and connected history of his acts and movements from his childhood up to the present day. He appealed to his friends and relatives, reminding them of circumstances they themselves had forgotten, laughing at certain recollections, weeping at others.

He could not, it is true, speak Basque, nor play at tennis; but then every one had not a good memory for languages, and he showed the scar in his hand. Though his opponent should satisfy his judges on these two points, nothing was easier, for that matter, than to learn a *patois* and become skilled in a game by practice.

Finally, Count de Montgommery, evidently deceived by some schemer, accused him of stealing from his squire the papers which established his condition and personality; but did he bring forward any proof of this?

As to the peasant, who could affirm that he was not a tool of the so-called Martin?

As to the ransom money, which Martin Guerre had stolen from Count de Montgommery, he had, in fact, returned to Artigues with a much larger sum than that mentioned by the count, and he explained the origin of this money by exhibiting the certificate of the most high and mighty lord the Constable Duke de Montmorency.

Arnold du Thill, in his peroration, used the renowned

name of the constable with infinite address, and held it up constantly before the dazzled eyes of the judges. He begged that they should at once send a messenger to his illustrious master, and learn what he thought of him. He was sure his character would come out stainless and unblemished from any such inquiry.

In short, the discourse of the crafty rascal was so able and wily, he expressed himself with such warmth, and impudence is sometimes so like innocence, that Gabriel saw the judges were again uncertain and undecided.

The time had come, therefore, to strike a decisive blow, and Gabriel determined to do so, though with reluctance.

He whispered a word in the president's ear, and the latter ordered Arnold du Thill to be led back to prison, and Martin Guerre to be brought into court.

Arnold

CHAPTER XIV

WHEREIN ARNOLD SHOWS HIMSELF TOO CLEVER BY HALF

A RNOLD DU THILL was not immediately led back to the dungeon he occupied in the *conciergerie* of Rieux. He was conducted to a yard bordering on the court, where he was left for some moments.

It was possible, he was told, that after the examination of his adversary the judges might find it necessary to put some further questions to him. Left to his reflections, the wily reprobate began to congratulate himself on the effect he had evidently produced by his clever and impudent discourse. Worthy Martin Guerre, despite the justice of his cause, would certainly find it rather difficult to be so persuasive.

In any case, Arnold had gained time. But, on a closer view of things, he could not dissemble the fact that this was all he had gained. The truth he had so audaciously perverted would at last break out in all directions. Would M. de Montmorency himself, whose testimony he had dared to invoke, venture to cover by his authority the proven misdeeds of his spy? It was very doubtful.

In effect, the conclusion of Arnold du Thill's meditations, pleasant enough in the beginning, led him to exchange hope for anxiety, and after a more careful consideration he said to himself that his position was anything but reassuring.

He had become very much disheartened, indeed, when his jailer came to take him back to prison.

The tribunal, then, did not see any further necessity for

examining him after the explanations of Martin Guerre—
a new source of anxiety!

However, this did not prevent him from noticing—he
noticed everything—that the jailer who guarded him now
was not the one to whom he was accustomed.

Why this change? Were they taking renewed precautions against his escape? Were they trying to make him
speak? Arnold du Thill made a vow that he would be on
his guard, and was dumb during the entire way.

But here a fresh subject of astonishment confronted him:
the prison into which his new keeper conducted him was not
the one he had before occupied!

This one had a grated window and a tall chimney-piece,
both lacking in the other.

Nevertheless, everything attested the recent presence of
a prisoner: bits of bread, still fresh, a half-emptied pitcher
of water, a bed of straw, and a partially open trunk, in
which might be seen a man's clothes.

Arnold du Thill, accustomed to self-restraint, did not
manifest any surprise; but, as soon as he was sure he was
alone, he ran to the trunk and began rummaging it.

It contained nothing but clothes; there was no indica-
tion of anything else. But Arnold thought he could remember the color and form of these same clothes, especially
of two brown cloth jackets, and a pair of yellow knitted
hose, which, neither in shade nor cut, were at all common.

"Oh," said Arnold to himself, "that would be queer,
surely!"

When it was near nightfall, the new jailer entered.

"Ho, there, Master Martin Guerre!" said he, striking
the shoulder of the meditative Arnold, in such a way as to
prove that, if the prisoner did not know his jailer, the jailer
knew his prisoner very well.

"What is the matter, pray?" asked Arnold of this very
familiar jailer.

"Why, my dear boy," returned the man, "things are
beginning to look up for you more and more. Do you know

who has got leave from the judges and now asks leave of
yourself to have the pleasure of talking a few moments with
you?"

"Faith, no," said Arnold, "how could I? Who can it
be?"

"Your wife, my good fellow, Bertrande de Rolles in
person, who, no doubt, is at last beginning to see on which
side the right is. But, if I was in your place, I'd never
think of receiving her."

"And why?"

"Why? Because she has so long refused to acknowl
edge you; that's why! It's rather late for her to be open
ing her eyes to the truth, when to-morrow at the latest the
decision of the court will proclaim it publicly and officially!
You agree with me, don't you? I have your leave to send
away this ungrateful hussy of yours much quicker than she
came?"

The jailer took a step toward the door; but Arnold du
Thill stopped him with a gesture.

"No, no," he said; "do not send her away. On the
contrary, I wish to see her. As Bertrande de Rolles has
obtained permission from the judges, oblige me, my dear
friend, by bringing her in."

"Hum!" muttered the jailer; "always the same, always
good-hearted and merciful! If you let your wife get the
upper hand over you she had formerly, do you fancy you
run no risk? Well, that's your affair."

The jailer retired, shrugging his shoulders compas-
sionately.

Two minutes after he returned with Bertrande de Rolles.
It was becoming darker and darker every moment.

"I leave you alone," said the jailer; "but I will come
for Bertrande before it is quite nightfall: such are my
orders. You have scarcely a quarter of an hour before
you; profit by it to quarrel or become reconciled, just as
you choose."

And he passed out again.

Bertrande de Rolles advanced, downcast and ashamed, to the false Martin Guerre, who remained seated and silent, waiting for her to approach him and speak.

"Oh, Martin," said she at last, in a weak and timid voice, when she was near him—"Martin, can you ever pardon me?"

Her eyes were wet with tears, and her limbs trembled.

"Pardon you for what?" returned Arnold du Thill, who did not care to pledge himself.

"For my gross mistake," said Bertrande. "I have been very much in fault not to recognize you. Still, was it not natural, after all, that I should be mistaken, since it seems that at times you were mistaken yourself? So it was necessary, I confess, that, before I could see my error, the whole country, M. le Comte de Montgommery, and justice, which is never baffled, had to prove to me that you were my true husband, and the other only a deceiver and impostor."

"Look here," returned Arnold, "which is the real impostor? The man brought here by M. de Montgommery, or the man found in possession of the goods and chattels of Martin Guerre?"

"Why, the other one, of course! the fellow who deceived me; the man I called my husband a week ago, blind idiot that I have been!"

"Ah! the matter has been settled at last, has it?" asked Arnold, with emotion.

"Good heavens! yes, Martin," answered the agitated Bertrande. "The judges and your worthy lord and master have just proved to me that they have no longer a doubt, and that you are the real Martin Guerre, my dear, good husband."

"Is it so, really?" said Arnold, turning pale.

"Thereupon," continued Bertrande, "they told me I should do well to ask your pardon, and become reconciled to you before they gave their decision, and I have asked and obtained leave to see you—"

She paused, but, seeing her pretended husband did not answer, she resumed—

"It is but too certain, my dear Martin, that I have acted very culpably in your regard. But I beg you to consider that I have done so involuntarily; the Blessed Virgin and the Child Jesus be my witnesses that such is the case! My first fault was not to have discovered and unmasked the fraud of this Arnold du Thill. But how could I imagine there could be two men so alike in the world, and that the good God could amuse himself in making two men so exactly of the same pattern! Same in features and in form, but not, it is true, in character and heart; and it was this difference that opened my eyes, I acknowledge. But what was there to put me on my guard? Arnold du Thill talked to me about the past just as you might have done. He had your ring and your papers. No friend, no relative, suspected him. I accepted him in entire good faith. I attributed the change in your temper to the experience you had gained in your travels through the world. Consider, my dear, that it was you, under the name of this stranger, whom I loved, and to whom I joyfully submitted. Consider this, and you must pardon me a mistake that has made me commit, unwillingly and unknowingly, great God! a sin for which I will pass the rest of my life in asking forgiveness from Heaven and from you."

Bertrande de Rolles again paused, to see whether Martin Guerre would not speak to her and encourage her a little. But he preserved an obstinate silence, and poor Bertrande, almost broken-hearted, resumed—

"Although it is impossible, Martin, that you can feel any enmity toward me on account of my first involuntary fault, my second, unhappily, surely deserves all your reproaches and all your anger. When you were no longer there I might, indeed, take another for you, innocently; but when you were present, and it was in my power to draw comparisons, I ought to have recognized you at once. Yet reflect whether, even in this case, there be not some excuse

for my conduct. In the first place, Arnold du Thill was, as
you said, in possession of the title and name that belonged
to you, and I naturally shrank from admitting a supposition
that would presume me guilty. In the second place, I was
hardly allowed to see you or speak to you. When we were
confronted you had not on your ordinary clothes, and were
muffled up in a long cloak that concealed your figure and
shape from me. Since then I have been almost as much a
prisoner as Arnold du Thill and yourself, and have seldom
seen you both at the same time, except at court, where you
were always considerably separated from each other. Before this frightful resemblance, what means had I of ascer-
taining the truth? I decided, almost at hazard, in favor of
him I had so lately called my husband. Be not angry with
me, I beseech you. The judges to-day assure me that I
have been deceived, and that they have proof of the fact.
So now I return to you penitent and ashamed, trusting
solely to your good heart and to your love of other days.
Have I made a mistake, also, in counting upon your indulgence?"

After this almost direct question, Bertrande was again
silent; but the false Martin never spoke.

Clearly, in thus abandoning Arnold du Thill, Bertrande
was adopting a singular method of softening him; but she
was perfectly sincere, and rushed with increasing eagerness
on the path she believed the true one, in order to reach the
heart she wished to touch.

"As to myself," she resumed, in a humble tone, "you
will find me very much changed in disposition. I am no
longer the disdainful, angry, capricious woman that made
you suffer so much. The ill-usage I have received from
that infamous Arnold, which indeed ought of itself to have
unmasked him, has at least had the good effect of bending
and taming me, and you may expect to find me, in future,
as compliant and docile as you yourself are gentle and kind
—for you will be gentle and kind to me in the future as you
have been in the past, will you not? You will prove that

now by forgiving me, and I shall thus recognize you by your heart, as I have already recognized you by your features.''

"Then you do recognize me now?" said Arnold du Thill at last.

"Oh, yes," answered Bertrande; "and what I most blame myself for is to have waited for the sentences and decisions of judges."

"You recognize me?" returned Arnold, with emphasis. "You recognize that I am not that plotter who, even last week, audaciously styled himself your husband, but your true and legitimate husband, Martin Guerre, whom you have not seen for so many years? Look at me. You recognize me as your first and only spouse?"

"Undoubtedly," said Bertrande.

"And by what marks do you recognize me, come now?" asked Arnold.

"Alas!" was the naïve answer, "by marks that have nothing at all to do with your person, I confess. If you and Arnold du Thill were placed side by side, and you were dressed like him, the resemblance would be so perfect that I should not distinguish one from the other even now. I recognize you for my true husband because I was told I should be led to my true husband, because you are in this prison, and not in Arnold's, because you receive me with the severity I merit, while Arnold would be trying to abuse and cajole me—"

"Infamous Arnold!" cried Arnold, in an austere tone. "And you, oh woman, so weak and easily deluded!—"

"Yes, scold me," answered Bertrande; "I prefer your reproaches to your silence. When you have said all that is in your heart—I know you—you are indulgent and tender, you will be softened, you will pardon me!"

"Well, well, Bertrande," said Arnold, in a gentler voice, "don't despair; we'll see, we'll see!"

"Ah!" cried Bertrande, "what did I say! Yes, you are my own, my true Martin Guerre!"

She threw herself at his feet, bathed in tears; for she had not the slightest doubt she was speaking to her husband. And Arnold du Thill, who was observing her distrustfully, could not conceive the least suspicion. The evidences of joy and repentance she exhibited were indisputable.

"It's all right!" growled Arnold to himself; "but you'll pay me for this some day, traitress!"

Meanwhile, he appeared to be carried away by a tender impulse there was no resisting.

"I have no courage, and I feel as if I was yielding," said he, wiping away a tear that was not there.

And, as if in spite of himself, he slightly touched the forehead of the repentant woman with his lips.

"What happiness!" exclaimed Bertrande; "he has almost taken me back to his love!"

At this moment the door opened, and the jailer appeared again.

"So you're reconciled, are you?" said he, peevishly, when he saw the two fictitious spouses in their sentimental attitudes. "I was sure of it from the first. What a poor creature you are, Martin!"

"What! do you rate him for his goodness as if it were a crime?" retorted Bertrande.

"Ha! ha! oh, this is as it ought to be now, isn't it?" said Arnold, smiling, with quite a fatherly air.

"Well, that is your concern; mine," replied the inflexible jailer, "is to obey orders: the time is up, and you cannot remain here a minute longer, my tearful beauty."

"What! leave him so soon!" said Bertrande.

"Can't be helped; you'll have time to see him to-morrow, and many a day after," answered the jailer.

"It is true, you'll be free to-morrow!" said Bertrande. "To-morrow, my love, we shall begin again the happy life of other days."

"Yes, put off your endearments, then, till to-morrow," answered the rough jailer. "At present, you must clear out."

Bertrande, for the last time, kissed the hand which Arnold du Thill royally extended to her, wafted him a last adieu, and passed out before the jailer.

As the latter was about to close the door, Arnold recalled him.

"Could I not have some light—a lamp?" he asked.

"Of course," said the jailer; "on this evening as on the others—at least, until nine o'clock, the curfew hour. Upon my conscience, your treatment is rather pleasanter than Arnold du Thill's! But, then, your master, Count de Montgommery, is so generous! We oblige you—to oblige him. In five minutes you'll have your candle, friend Martin."

In fact, a turnkey brought the light a few minutes afterward and retired, after recommending the prisoner to extinguish it at curfew.

As soon as Arnold du Thill was alone, he quickly stripped off the cloth garments he was wearing, and, no less quickly, endued himself in the famous brown jacket and yellow knitted hose he had discovered in the trunk of Martin Guerre.

Then he burned his old costume, piece after piece, in the flame of the candle, and mixed the ashes with the ashes on the hearth of the chimney.

It was done in less than an hour, and he was able to put out the light and stretch himself upon his virtuous couch, even before the curfew rang.

"Let us wait, now," he said to himself. "Clearly, I have been beaten before the judges; but it would be amusing if I should pluck from my defeat the means of my safety. Let us wait."

CHAPTER XV

HOW A CRIMINAL'S REQUISITION TURNED AGAINST HIMSELF

IT WILL be easily understood that Arnold du Thill slept but little that night. He lay extended on his litter of straw, with eyes wide open, very busy with calculating his chances, arranging his plans, and combining his resources. The project he had conceived, of finally substituting himself for poor Martin Guerre, was bold, undoubtedly; but its very boldness ought to give it a prospect of success.

When accident had served him so marvellously, why should he allow his own audacity to fail him now?

No; he soon decided on the part he was to play, being also determined to be guided by future incidents and unforeseen circumstances.

As soon as it was daylight he examined his costume, found that it was irreproachable, and practiced himself once more in the gestures and attitudes which he had formerly noticed were peculiar to Martin Guerre. The imitation was perfect, except that he slightly exaggerated the good-natured manner of his Sosia. It must be admitted that this abominable rascal would have made an excellent actor.

At eight in the morning the door of his prison turned on its hinges. Arnold du Thill restrained himself from starting, and tried to appear indifferent and tranquil.

The same jailer entered, introducing Count de Montgommery. "The devil! now for it!" said Arnold to himself. "I must have my wits about me!"

He waited anxiously for the first words from Gabriel's lips.

"Good-day, my poor Martin," said the visitor.

Arnold du Thill breathed. The count had looked him straight in the face when calling him Martin. The cross-play was beginning again. Arnold was saved!

"Good-day, my dear, kind master," said he to Gabriel, with an exuberant gratitude that was not entirely feigned, by any means.

And he ventured to add—

"Is there anything new, monseigneur?"

"Sentence will, in all likelihood, be pronounced this morning," said Gabriel.

"At last! God be praised!" cried Arnold. "I am anxious for the end, I confess. And there is no longer any doubt or fear of the result, is there, monseigneur? You are sure justice will triumph?"

"Well, I hope so," said Gabriel, regarding Arnold more fixedly than ever. "That wretch, Arnold du Thill, is now playing his last desperate card."

"Is it possible? And what might he be plotting now, monseigneur?" asked Arnold.

"Would you believe it?" said Gabriel; "the traitor is actually trying to mix things up worse than before."

"Can it be?" cried Arnold, raising his arms to heaven. "Great God, what fresh villany is he contriving?"

"Why, he dares to pretend that on yesterday the warders were deceived when the court rose, and conducted you to Arnold's prison, and Arnold to yours."

"It's incredible!" cried Arnold, with a fine gesture of astonishment and indignation. "And on what does the miserable fellow base such an impudent assertion?"

"On this. Like yourself, he was not at once conducted back yesterday to his dungeon. The judges, after retiring to deliberate, might possibly have required the presence of one or both of you. The guards therefore left him in the hall downstairs, and you in the courtyard. Now he swears that this has caused the mistake, for they had heretofore left you in the hall, and Martin in the courtyard. When the jailers went for their prisoners, then, they naturally confounded, he says, one with the other. Both of you have had the same guards; and these guards, being mere human machines, only know their prisoners, but have no opinions on their identity. It is on these wretched quibbles that he rests his new claim. And he is weeping, and crying, and begging to see me."

"And have you seen him, monseigneur?" asked Arnold, abruptly.

"Faith, no!" said Gabriel. "I am afraid of his twisting and turning. The fellow is quite capable of deluding and deceiving me again; he is such a clever and audacious coundrel!"

"Ah, monseigneur, you're not taking his part now, are you?" returned Arnold, with assumed discontent.

"Indeed I am not, Martin," said Gabriel. "But you must admit, yourself, that the fellow is full of resources; and if he had devoted the half of his ability to an honest career—"

"He is an infamous wretch!" interrupted Arnold, vehemently.

"How you do abuse him to-day!" returned Gabriel. "Still, I was thinking, as I came along, I confess, that, after all, he has killed nobody, and that, if he is condemned in a few hours, he will surely be hanged before a week; that the death penalty is too severe a punishment for his crimes, and that, in fine, we could, if you consented, petition for his pardon."

"His pardon!" repeated Arnold, apparently somewhat undecided.

"Yes; this requires some reflection, I know well. But come now, Martin, what do you say to it?"

Arnold du Thill, with his chin in one hand, and scratching his cheek with the other, pondered over the matter for some moments, without replying; then, like a man who had, with some hesitation, come to a resolution, he said resolutely—

"No, no! no pardon! No pardon for him, I say. That will be for the best."

"Why, Martin! I never thought you were so implacable!" returned Gabriel; "this is not like you; and, as late as yesterday, even, you pitied him, and expressed a hope he might be saved."

"Yesterday! yesterday!" grumbled Arnold; "yesterday he had not played me this last trick—a trick far more odious, in my opinion, than any of the others."

"That's true," said Gabriel. "So your decided opinion is that the culprit should die?"

"Good heavens! monseigneur," replied Arnold, with a sanctimonious air, "you know how foreign to my nature are all deeds of blood and vengeance. I am heartbroken under the necessity of adopting such a course; but it is a necessity. His last astounding stroke of audacity proves him incorrigible. Imprison him, he will escape; exile him, he will return! And in either case, there I am! uneasy, anxious, every moment expecting to see him come back and upset my life again, as he has done before. My friends and my wife will never be really certain that I am I. There will be everlasting suspicion. There will always be new quarrels and fresh complications; so that I shall never be able to say I am my own master. I must, therefore, monseigneur, do violence to my temper, though with sadness and despair. The rest of my days will doubtless be clouded by sorrow, for having caused the death of a man; but it cannot be helped! This imposture of to-day banishes my last scruples. Let Arnold du Thill die! That he should do so grieves me, but I am resigned!"

"Well, be it so!" said Gabriel; "he shall die. That is to say, he shall die if he is condemned. For, after all, there has been no decision yet."

"What? it is not certain, then?' exclaimed Arnold.

"Not certain, but probable," replied Gabriel. "Tha

infernally clever rascal, Arnold, addressed such a subtle and persuasive discourse to the judges that there's no knowing.''

"Idiot that I was!" thought Arnold.

"While you, Martin," continued Gabriel, "you who have now proved to me with such admirable eloquence and composure the necessity of Arnold's death—you were not able yesterday, you will remember, when in presence of the court, to discover a single argument, a single fact that would help along the truth. You were confused and almost dumb, in spite of my entreaties. And, though you were informed of the nature of your opponent's pleadings, you had not a word to say in reply."

"Because, monseigneur," replied Arnold, "while I am at my ease in your presence, I always feel embarrassed before these judges. Besides, I must confess, I relied entirely on the justice of my cause, and I thought its very justice would plead for me better than I could do for myself. But it seems these law people, after all, don't care for justice alone. Evidently they want words. Ah! if I had to begin over again, and if they would hear me a second time!"

"Well, what would you do, Martin?"

"Oh! I would gain a little confidence, and I would speak! I should not have much trouble in upsetting all the proofs and allegations of Arnold du Thill, I can tell you!"

"You would not find that so easy!" retorted Gabriel.

"Excuse me, monseigneur, I saw the weak points in his harness as plainly as he must have seen them himself; and, if I had been less timid, if words had not failed me, I would have said to the judges—"

"What would you have said to them? Come now, speak."

"What would I have said to them? The simplest thing in the world. Listen, monseigneur."

Thereupon Arnold du Thill set to work to refute his

discourse of the day before from beginning to end. He disentangled the incidents and misunderstandings arising from the double existence of Martin Guerre and Arnold with so much the more ease that it was his own hand that had done the entangling. There had been some points which Count de Montgommery could not explain to the judges, for the simple reason that he could not explain them to himself. Arnold du Thill made them as clear as daylight. He showed, in fine, to Gabriel the two destinies of the honest man and the rascal as plainly marked and distinct in their confusion as oil and water.

"So you have been making inquiries at Paris, have you not?" asked Gabriel.

"Undoubtedly, monseigneur," returned Arnold; "and I can furnish proofs of what I assert whenever they are wanted. I am not easily moved; but if I am driven into my last intrenchments I can make vigorous sorties."

"Still," said Gabriel, "Arnold du Thill has invoked the testimony of M. de Montmorency, and you do not reply to that."

"But I do, though, monseigneur. True, Arnold was in the service of the constable, but his was a disgraceful service. He must have been a kind of spy; and that fact explains how and why he attached himself to you in order to track and spy you. But such people are employed, not acknowledged. Think you M. de Montmorency would accept the responsibility of the acts and deeds of his creature? No, no! Arnold du Thill, though driven to the wall, would never really venture to address the constable, or, if he did so through despair, that is all he would get by it. M. de Montmorency would deny him. And now—"

Wherewith Arnold proceeded to demolish clearly and logically, bit by bit, the structure of imposture he had erected with such skill the day before.

Being gifted with such convincing eloquence and such persuasive clearness of expression, Arnold du Thill would, in our days, have been a most distinguished advocate. Unfortunately, he came into the world three hundred years too soon. Let us pity his shade!

"I think what I have just stated is irrefutable," he said to Gabriel, when he had finished. "What a pity the judges can no longer hear me, and have not heard me!"

"They have heard you," said Gabriel.

"How?"

"Look!"

The door of the dungeon opened, and Arnold, astounded and a little frightened, perceived the president of the tribunal and two of his judges standing, grave and motionless, upon the threshold.

"What does this mean?" he asked, turning to Gabriel.

"It means," replied M. de Montgommery, "that I was afraid the bashfulness of my poor Martin Guerre would hinder him from doing himself justice, and therefore have arranged that the judges, without his knowledge, should hear his *irrefutable* arguments, and they have done so."

"How fortunate!" cried Arnold, who breathed again. "I thank you a thousand times, monseigneur."

And, turning to the judges—

"Can I believe," said he, in a voice he tried to render timid, "and may I hope, that my words have really proved the justice of my cause to the enlightened men who are at this moment the masters of my fate?"

"Yes," said the president; "the proofs furnished to us have convinced us."

"Ah!" exclaimed Arnold du Thill, triumphantly.

"But," continued the president; "other proofs not less certain and conclusive have shown us that there was, yesterday, a mistake made in the removal of the two prisoners; that Martin Guerre was led, *Arnold du Thill*, into your prison, and you into Martin Guerre's."

"What! how?" stammered Arnold, thunderstruck,

"monseigneur, what do you say to this?" he asked, turning to Gabriel.

"I say that I was aware of it," returned Gabriel, severely. "I say that I was determined to prove out of your own mouth, *Arnold*, Martin's innocence and your guilt. You have forced me, you scoundrel, to play a part that is repugnant to me. But your insolence yesterday proved to me that when a person has to enter into a conflict with such as you, he has to employ their weapons, and that deceivers can only be conquered by deception. For that matter, you have left me nothing to do. You have been in such a hurry to betray your own cause that your very baseness has made you run to fall into the trap set for you."

"The trap set for me," repeated Arnold. "Oh, there was a trap, then? But, monseigneur, in any case, it is your own Martin you are forsaking, when you forsake me. Don't let any one delude you on that point, monseigneur."

"Do not persist, Arnold du Thill," said the president. "The mistake has been ordered and arranged by the tribunal. You are unmasked beyond any possible recall, I tell you."

"But since you agree there has been a mistake," replied the brazen-faced Arnold, "how do you know, M. le Président, that there has not been a mistake in the execution of your orders."

"The testimony of the guards and jailers," said the president.

"They are mistaken," answered Arnold; "I am Martin Guerre, the squire of M. de Montgommery; I will not let myself be condemned thus! Bring your prisoner and me face to face, and when we are side by side, dare to separate, to distinguish Arnold du Thill from Martin Guerre! the innocent from the guilty! As if the case was not confused enough before, you have added new difficulties. Your conscience will prevent you from getting out of the trouble in this fashion. I will cry to the end, in spite of everything, I am Martin Guerre! I challenge any one, be he who he may, to contradict me, and I defy you to bring forward any facts to rebut my evidence.''

The judges and Gabriel shook their heads, and smiled gravely and sadly in presence of such shameless and unspeakable persistency.

''Once more, Arnold du Thill,'' said the president, ''I declare there is no longer any confusion possible between you and Martin Guerre.''

''And why?'' asked Arnold; ''how do you recognize him? By what sign do you distinguish us?''

''You shall soon see, wretch!'' said Gabriel, indignantly.

He made a sign, and Martin Guerre appeared on the threshold of the prison.

Martin Guerre, without his cloak! Martin Guerre mutilated! Martin Guerre with a wooden leg!

''My brave squire, Martin Guerre,'' said Gabriel to Arnold, ''after escaping at Noyon from the gibbet, to which you had consigned him, did not, however, escape at Calais from a vengeance which was righteously directed against one of your infamies. Being taken for you, he was hurled into an abyss, and thereby lost a leg; but the loss of that leg, by the mysterious will of Providence, just even when it appears cruel, serves now to establish a difference between the persecutor and his victim. The judges here present no longer run any risk of error, and can now recognize the criminal by his shamelessness, and the just man by the misfortune he has innocently incurred.''

Arnold du Thill, pale, crushed, annihilated by the terrible words and scathing glances of Gabriel, no longer attempted to protest or deny: the sight of poor disabled Martin scattered all his falsehoods to the winds.

He sank heavily on the floor, limp and lifeless.

''I am lost!'' he murmured; ''lost!''

CHAPTER XVI

JUSTICE!

A ND lost Arnold du Thill, in fact, was. The tribunal immediately assembled for deliberation, and, at the end of a quarter of an hour, the accused was summoned to listen to the following decree, which we transcribe, textually, from the registers of the time:

"In virtue of the examination of Arnold du Thill, alias Sancette, alias Martin Guerre, prisoner at the *conciergerie* of Rieux;

"In virtue of the depositions of divers witnesses, Martin Guerre, Bertrande de Rolles, Carbon Barreau, etc., and notably M. le Comte de Montgommery;

"In virtue of the avowals of the accused himself, who, after vainly attempting to deny his crime, confessed it at last;

From which examinations, depositions, and avowals it appears,

"That the said Arnold du Thill is well and duly convicted of imposture, false assumption of name and surname, adultery, rape, sacrilege, larceny, and other crimes—

"The court has condemned and condemns the said Arnold du Thill:

"First, to make reparation in front of the church of Artigues, on his knees, in his shirt, bareheaded and barefooted, with a halter about his neck and a lighted torch of burning wax in his hand.

"Secondly, to ask pardon publicly of God, the king, and justice, and of the said Martin Guerre and Bertrande de Rolles, both married.

"And, this done, the said Arnold du Thill shall be delivered into the hands of the executioner, who shall conduct him through the streets and public places of the said town of Artigues, with the halter always around his neck, and bring him in front of the house of the said Martin Guerre.

"In order to be hanged and strangled there on a gallows erected for that purpose, and, afterward, his body to be burned.

"And, moreover, has discharged and discharges the said Martin Guerre and the said Bertrande de Rolles, and remands the said Arnold du Thill to the Judge of Artigues, who shall proceed to the execution of the present decree according to its form and tenor.

"Judicially pronounced at Rieux the twelfth day of July, 1558."

Arnold du Thill heard his sentence with a gloomy and sombre air. However, he confirmed his former confession, recognized the justice of his sentence, and showed some repentance.

"I implore," he said, "the clemency of God and the pardon of men, and I am disposed to suffer my punishment like a Christian."

Martin Guerre, who was present, gave a new proof of his identity by bursting into tears at the words, perhaps hypocritical, of his enemy.

He triumphed even over his usual timidity so far as to ask the president whether there was no means of obtaining mercy for Arnold du Thill, whom he forgave sincerely himself for the past.

But our honest Martin was told that the king alone had the right of pardoning, and that he would most assuredly refuse to show mercy to such an exceptional and outrageous crime, though they, the judges, were to ask for it.

"Yes," thought Gabriel; "the king would refuse pardon, would he? and still he might yet have need of pardon for himself! But he would be right to be inflexible. No pardon! no mercy! justice!"

Martin Guerre probably did not agree with his master; for so overpowering was his longing to pardon that he at once opened his arms to the contrite and repentant Bertrande de Rolles.

Bertrande had no need to repeat the prayers and prom·
ises which, in her last useful blunder, she had addressed to
the traitor, Arnold du Thill. Martin did not give her time
to deplore her errors anew. He cut her short with a big
kiss, and joyously and triumphantly conducted her into the
happy little cottage at Artigues, which he had not seen for
so long.

In front of this same house, which had at last re·
turned to its legitimate owner, Arnold du Thill suffered
the well-merited penalty of his crimes a week after his
sentence.

From twenty leagues around people flocked from every
direction to witness the execution; and the streets of the
shabby village of Artigues were more thronged on this occa·
sion than those of the capital.

The culprit, it must be said, showed a certain courage at
the last moment, and crowned a worthless existence by an
exemplary end.

When the executioner had cried thrice to the people,
according to custom, "Justice has been done!" while the
crowd was slowly retiring, silent and terrified, there was
inside the victim's house a man who wept, and a woman
who prayed—Martin Guerre and Bertrande de Rolles.

His natal air, the sight of the places where his youth had
glided by, the affection of relatives and old friends, and,
above all, the tender caresses of Bertrande soon banished
from Martin's face every trace of sorrow.

One evening, in this very month of July, he was seated
at his door, under his arbor, after a calm and happy day.
His wife was busy in the cottage with some household
cares; but Martin could hear her coming and going. He
was not, then, alone! and, gazing at the sun, setting in all
its splendor, he was looking forward to a day as pleasant
as that which had just slipped by.

He did not therefore see a horseman, who was noiselessly
approaching him on the left.

This horseman halted a moment, to observe, with a grave

smile, the silent, tranquil attitude of Martin. Then, without speaking, he extended his hand, and touched him on the shoulder.

Martin Guerre turned quickly, raised his hand to his hat, and rose.

"What! it is you, monseigneur!" said he, quite moved. "Forgive me; I did not see you coming."

"No excuses, my brave Martin," returned Gabriel (for it was he). "I have not come to trouble your tranquillity, but to make certain of it, on the contrary."

"Oh, as for that, you have only to look at me, monseigneur," said Martin.

"Just what I was doing, Martin," said Gabriel. "You are happy, then?"

"Oh, happier than the bird in the air or the fish in the water, monseigneur."

"That is natural enough," returned Gabriel; "you have found rest and plenty in your home."

"Yes," said Martin Guerre; "that, undoubtedly, is one of the causes of my contentment. I have perhaps seen enough of the world, enough of battles, fasted, and watched, and suffered enough in a hundred ways to give the right—don't you think so, monseigneur?—of taking a spell of recreation for a few days. As to the plenty," he added in a graver tone, "I have found the house rich; in fact, too rich. This money does not belong to me, and I won't touch it. It was Arnold du Thill who brought it, and I intend restoring it to whoever has a right to it. The largest part belongs to you, monseigneur, for it was the money intended for your ransom, and which he appropriated. This money has been put aside for you. As to the remainder, where Arnold got it is of little importance; these crowns must not soil my fingers. Master Carbon Barreau, like the honest man he is, is of the same opinion as I am, and having enough to live on, refuses the shameful inheritance of his nephew. After the expenses of the trial are defrayed, the rest will go to the poor."

"But then there won't be much left for you, my poor Martin, will there?" asked Gabriel.

"I beg your pardon, monseigneur," said the squire. "One does not serve a master as generous as you so long as I have done without something being left. I have brought back from Paris a neat little sum in my wallet. Besides, Bertrande's family had considerable property, and some of it has come her way. In short, after settling our debts and restoring what does not belong to us, we'll still be among the rich people of the country."

"Well, Martin," said Gabriel, "I hope you won't refuse, coming from me, what you might well refuse, coming from Arnold. I must beg you, my trusty follower, to accept, as a souvenir and a recompense, this sum which you say belongs to me."

"What, monseigneur!" replied Martin, with a gesture of protest; "a present of such importance for me!"

"Nonsense, man," said Gabriel; "do you think I can pretend to pay you for your devotion? Shall I not always be your debtor? Don't have any false pride with me, Martin, and let us talk no more about it; it is settled that you shall accept the little I offer less for your sake than for mine, in truth; for, as you have said, you don't require my money in order to live rich and respected in your country, and it will not add greatly to your happiness. You have not, I fancy, realized fully in your own mind in what this happiness consists; but it must arise, must it not, from your return to the scenes amid which you grew up from childhood to manhood?"

"What you say is true, monseigneur," said Martin Guerre. "I have felt perfectly contented ever since I came here, solely because I am here. I look with tender emotion upon houses, trees, and roads which a stranger would hardly notice. Certainly, I believe a man does not really breathe until he breathes the air he has inhaled the first day of his life!"

"And your friends, Martin?" asked Gabriel. "I came,

as I told you, Martin, to verify all your sources of happiness on my own account. Have you found your friends again?"

"Alas! monseigneur," said Martin; "some were dead. But still I have met a good number of the comrades of my young days, and they all love me as much as in the past. They, too, are still believers in my sincerity, friendship, and devotion. Faith! they are quite ashamed of having for a moment mistaken for me that Arnold du Thill who, it seems, gave them some samples of a disposition quite at variance with mine. Two or three of them had even quarrelled with the false Martin Guerre because of his bad conduct. You ought to see how proud and satisfied they are now! To make a long story short, they outstrip one another in overwhelming me with marks of esteem and affection, perhaps to make up for lost time; and since we are now discussing my reasons for being happy, that is a very sweet one, I assure you."

"I believe you, my good Martin, I believe you," said Gabriel. "Ah! but you say nothing of the love of your wife, while speaking of the affection of your other dear friends?"

"Oh, as to my wife—" answered Martin, scratching his ear, with an embarrassed air.

"Yes, your wife," said Gabriel, anxiously. "Eh! does Bertrande annoy you as much as formerly? Is she still ungrateful for your kindness, ungrateful for the good fortune that has restored her so tender and devoted a husband? Is her temper as bad as ever? What! Martin, is she going to make you miserable again with her shrewish and quarrelsome disposition, and force you to abandon home and friends once more?"

"Oh, quite the contrary, monseigneur," said Martin Guerre; "she only makes home and friends more delightful than ever. She devotes herself to my comfort; she caresses and kisses me. No more caprices or rebellions. It would be impossible to describe how sweet and good-

tempered she is. I no sooner open my lips than she runs.
She does not wait for me to express a wish; she antici-
pates it. It is wonderful. And as I am naturally neither
imperious nor tyrannical, but rather easy and good-natured,
our life is as sweet as honey, and there is no household
in the world more agreeable than ours."

"Why, I am delighted!" said Gabriel; "you almost
frightened me at first."

"Well," replied Martin Guerre, "that, monseigneur, is
because I feel, I must confess, a little embarrassed and
confused when this subject is on the *tapis*. The feeling
I discover in my heart, when I examine myself on the subject, is queer enough, and makes me somewhat ashamed.
But with you, monseigneur, I can express myself with all
sincerity and simplicity, can I not?"

"Most assuredly," said Gabriel.

Martin Guerre looked timidly around him, to see if any
one was listening, particularly his wife. Then, lowering
his voice, he said:

"Well, monseigneur, not only do I forgive that poor
Arnold du Thill, but I bless him. What a service he has
done me! He has turned a tigress into a lamb, a demon
into an angel. I inherit the happy results of his brutal
manners without having anything to reproach myself with.
To all henpecked and tormented husbands, and the number
of them, I am told, is large, I should like to give a Sosia—a
Sosia as persuasive as mine. Finally, monseigneur, though
Arnold du Thill has caused me considerable annoyance and
sorrow, are not all my troubles well compensated, and more
than compensated, by the pleasing effects of his energetic
system, which insure me domestic happiness and the tranquillity of my last days?"

"Certainly," said the young count, smiling.

"I am then right in blessing Arnold," concluded Martin,
gayly; "although I do so in secret, since I am now enjoying
the happy fruits of his collaboration. You know, monseigneur, I am something of a philosopher, and always look at

the good side of things. Now it must be acknowledged that, from every point of view, Arnold has done me far more good than evil. He has been for a while the husband of my wife; but he has restored her to me milder than a day in May. He has robbed me for a time of my friends and property; but, thanks to him, that property is increased and those friends are more devoted than ever. In fine, he has caused me to pass through some rough experiences both at Noyon and Calais, but my present life only seems the more agreeable on account of them. I have every reason to be grateful, then, to my good Arnold, and I am grateful."

"Yours is a grateful heart, truly," returned Gabriel.

"Oh, but," said Martin Guerre, becoming again serious, "it is not Arnold du Thill, a somewhat involuntary benefactor, to whom my thanks are due above and beyond all; it is you, monseigneur—you to whom I really owe everything, property, country, fortune, friends, and wife."

"Oh, we've had enough of that, Martin," said Gabriel. "What I am anxious about is that you should have all these good things. And you have them, have you not? Tell me again, Martin, are you happy?"

"Yes," answered Martin, "as happy as I have ever been."

"That's all I wanted to know," said Gabriel. "And now I can leave."

"What! leave?" cried Martin. "You are thinking of leaving already, monseigneur?"

"Yes, Martin; nothing keeps me here."

"Excuse me; you are right; but when do you go?"

"This evening."

"And you did not warn me!" cried Martin, "and I was forgetting—falling asleep, like the good-for-nothing fellow I am. But wait, wait, monseigneur; I shall not be long!"

"What do you mean?" said Gabriel.

"To prepare to go along with you, of course."

He rose up eagerly and quickly, and ran to the door of his house.

"Bertrande! Bertrande!" he called.

"Why are you calling your wife, Martin?" asked Gabriel.

"To pack my trunk and bid me good-by."

"But that is useless, Martin; you are not going with me."

"What! not going with you, monseigneur?"

"No; I am going away alone."

"And you will not come back?"

"Not for a long time at least."

"Then what fault have you to find with me?" asked Martin Guerre, sadly.

"Why, none, Martin; you are the most faithful and devoted of my servants."

"Yet it is natural that the servant should follow his master, the squire his knight, and yet you do not take me with you."

"I have three good reasons for that, Martin."

"Might I presume to ask you what they are?"

"In the first place, Martin, it would be a cruelty to tear you away from the happiness you have only just enjoyed and the rest you have so well earned."

"Oh, as to that, monseigneur, it is my duty to follow and serve you to the end, and I think I would give up paradise even for the pleasure of being by your side."

"Yes, but though I am grateful for your zeal, I cannot abuse it. In the second place, my brave Martin, the accident that befell you at Calais prevents you from being as serviceable to me as you have been in the past."

"It is true, monseigneur, that I can no longer, alas! fight by your side, nor ride with you. But in Paris, in Montgommery, in the camp even, there are still many things or a confidential nature which you might find it of advantage to confide to the poor cripple, and which he would acquit himself of as best he could."

"I know it, Martin, and so I should have the selfishness to accept but for a third reason."

"May I know it, monseigneur?"

"Yes," answered Gabriel, gravely and sadly; "but on condition, in the first place, that you do not ask any explanation of it, and, in the next, that you will be satisfied and no longer seek to follow me."

"It is, then, very serious and very imperative, monseigneur?"

"It is sad and unanswerable," said Gabriel, in a deep voice. "Until now my life has been all honor, and if I cared to have my name in the mouths of men would have been all glory. I believe, in effect, that I have rendered to France and its king immense services, and without speaking of St. Quentin and Calais, I have perhaps paid my debts to my country fully and nobly."

"Who knows it better than I, monseigneur?" said Martin Guerre.

"Yes, Martin; but just as the first part of my life has been loyal and noble and without any need of concealment, the rest of it will be gloomy and frightful, and will seek to hide itself in darkness. No doubt I shall display the same energy, but in support of a cause I cannot avow, and for an object I must not disclose. Till now, in a fair field, before God and before men, it has delighted me to win joyously the reward of valiant deeds. Henceforth, I must, in darkness and anguish, devote my life to the avenging of a crime. Once I fought; now I must punish. France's soldier has become God's executioner."

"Jesus!" cried Martin, clasping his hands.

"Moreover, I must do this sinister work alone—a work for the accomplishment of which I beg God to employ my arm and not my will, to make me a blind instrument and not a responsible mind. And since I ask and hope that my terrible duty may enlist only the half of my being, how can you wish, Martin, that I should take you as my associate in it?"

"You are right, monsiegneur, and I understand," said the squire, bending his head. "I thank you for giving me this explanation, although it saddens me; and I am resigned, as I promised I would be."

"And I, in my turn, thank you for this submission," said Gabriel; "you show your devotion here by not adding to the burden of responsibility I already bear."

"But can I do absolutely nothing for you, monseigneur, in the present circumstances?"

"You can pray to God for me, Martin; you can pray that He may spare me the necessity of undertaking a task which I shudder at approaching. Your heart, my friend, is pious, and your life honest and pure; your prayers may help me more than your arm."

"I will pray, monseigneur, I will pray, how ardently I have no need of telling you!"

"And now farewell, Martin," said Gabriel; "I must return to Paris to be ready and present on the day it pleases God to give me the signal. I have all my life defended the right and fought for justice. May the Lord remember it on the supreme day of which I speak! May He render justice to His servant as I have done to mine!"

And, with eyes raised to heaven, the noble young man repeated—

"Justice! justice!"

For six months, whenever Gabriel opened his eyes, it was to fix them on that heaven from which he demanded justice. When he shut them, it was to behold once more the gloomy prison of the Chatelet, gloomier still in his remembrance of it, and then his cry was, Vengeance!

Ten minutes later, he tore himself away with great difficulty from the tears and farewells of Martin Guerre and Bertrande de Rolles, who had been summoned by her husband.

"Farewell, farewell! dear Martin, faithful friend!" he said, freeing his hands almost by force from the hands of his squire, who kissed them, sobbing. "I must leave; adieu! We shall see each other again."

"Adieu, monseigneur, and may God keep you! Oh, God keep you!"

It was all that poor Martin, choked with emotion, could say.

And through his tears he beheld his master and bene-factor mount his horse and plunge into the darkness, which was beginning to grow thicker, and which soon concealed the gloomy rider from his gaze, as it had for a long time concealed that rider's life.

CHAPTER XVII

TWO LETTERS

AFTER the happy conclusion of this puzzling trial between the two Martin Guerres, Gabriel Montgommery
again disappeared for several months, and resumed
his wandering, uncertain, and mysterious existence. He
was met in twenty different places again. Still, he never
removed from the neighborhood of Paris and the court,
taking such a position in the shade that he could see everything without being seen.

He was watching events, but events were not arranging
themselves in accordance with his wishes. The soul of the
young man, wholly engrossed by one idea, did not yet get
a glimpse of the issue to which his just vengeance pointed.

The only fact of importance that occurred in the political
world during these months was the peace that followed the
treaty of Chateau-Cambrésis.

The Constable de Montmorency, jealous of the exploits
of the Duke de Guise and of the new claims his rival
was daily acquiring to the gratitude of the nation and the
favor of the sovereign, had at last wrested this treaty from
Henry the Second by the omnipotent influence of Diana
de Poitiers.

The treaty was signed on the 3d of April, 1559. Although concluded after a long course of victories, it was
but little advantageous to France.

She kept the Three Bishoprics, Metz, Toul, and Ver-
dun with their territories. She was to retain Calais for
eight years only, and then pay England eight hundred

thousand gold crowns if the city was not restored (but this key of France never was restored, nor were the eight hundred thousand crowns paid either). Finally France regained St. Quentin and Ham, and was to hold Turin and Pignerol in Piedmont provisionally.

But Philip the Second obtained in full sovereignty the strong places of Thionville, Marienbourg, and Hesdin. He was allowed to raze Thérouanne and Yvoy to the ground, to restore Bouillon to the bishop of Liège, Corsica to the Genoese, and the greater part of Savoy and Piedmont, conquered under Francis the First, to Emmanuel Philibert. Moreover, he arranged a marriage between himself and Elizabeth, the daughter of the king, and between the Duke of Savoy and Princess Marguerite. These were advantages so enormous that he could not have hoped for greater ones after his victory of St. Quentin.

The Duke de Guise ran up from the army in a perfect fury. He loudly accused, and not without reason, the constable of treason and the king of weakness in granting with a stroke of the pen more than the Spanish arms could have forced from him after thirty years of success.

But the evil was done, and the gloomy dissatisfaction of the Balafré availed nothing.

This state of things did not please Gabriel. His justice pursued the man in the king, and not the king in France. He wished to avenge himself with his country, not against her.

Still he noted mentally the resentment the Duke de Guise must have felt and must feel at seeing the sublime efforts of his genius nullified by the secret plots of intriguers.

In such circumstances, the wrath of a princely Coriolanus might serve the plans of Gabriel.

Besides, Francis de Lorraine was far from being the only discontented man in the realm.

One day, Gabriel met in the suburb of Pré-au-Clercs Baron de La Renaudie, whom he had not seen since the morning conference in the Rue St. Jacques.

In place of avoiding him, as was now Gabriel's custom whenever he met an acquaintance, he approached him.

These two men were born for mutual appreciation; they had many points of resemblance, notably in their energy and loyalty. Both were born for action, and both were passionate lovers of justice.

After the usual compliments—

"Well," said La Renaudie, resolutely, "I have seen Master Ambroise Paré; you belong to us now, do you not?"

"Virtually, yes; actually, no," answered Gabriel.

"And when may we expect you to belong to us virtually and openly?" said La Renaudie.

"I will not now make use of the selfish language which perhaps excited your indignation against me before," returned Gabriel. "I will, on the contrary, answer you: I will be yours when you have need of me, and I no longer have need of you."

"I call that generosity," returned La Renaudie. "As a gentleman, I admire you; as a man of party, I cannot imitate you. If you are waiting for the moment when we shall have need of all our friends, learn that that moment has now come."

"What is happening, pray?" asked Gabriel.

"A secret blow is being prepared against those of the religion," said La Renaudie. "They want to get rid once for all of the Protestants."

"What are your reasons for thinking so?"

"Oh, there is no attempt at concealment. Antoine Minard, president of the parliament, has said openly at a council held at St. Germain, 'a good blow must be struck, if we are not to fall into a sort of republic like that of the Swiss cantons.'"

"What! he uttered the word *republic?*" exclaimed Gabriel, in surprise. "But doubtless he exaggerated the danger, in order to exaggerate the remedy?"

"Not much," replied La Renaudie, lowering his voice.

"He exaggerated very little, to tell the truth. We too have changed somewhat since the time we met in Calvin's chamber. The theories of Ambroise Paré do not seem to us as rash to-day as they did then; and, besides, you see they are driving us to extremes."

"Then, perhaps," said Gabriel, eagerly, "I shall be one of you earlier than I expected."

"I hope so at least," returned La Renaudie.

"On what should I keep my attention fixed?" asked Gabriel.

"On the parliament," said La Renaudie, "for it is there the question will be debated. The evangelical members have a strong minority—Anne Dubourg, Henri Dufaur, Nicolas Duval, Eustache de la Porte, and a score of others. In answer to the harangues of those who insist on the prosecution of heretics, the partisans of Calvinism demand the meeting of a general council to settle religious affairs in accordance with the decrees of Constance and Bâle. They have right on their side; therefore it will be necessary to employ violence against them. But we are watching; do you watch also."

"Certainly," said Gabriel.

"Remain in your hotel at Paris, so that we may send for you in case of need."

"I will do so, though very reluctantly, provided you do not leave me to languish there too long. You have, it seems to me, written enough and talked enough; it is time now for you to act."

"My opinion also," said La Renaudie. "Be prepared, and be tranquil also."

They separated. Gabriel went his way, deep in thought.

In the ardor of his vengeance, was not his conscience taking a wrong direction? Why, he was actually on the brink of civil war.

But since events did not come to him, he must seek events.

That same day, Gabriel returned to his hotel in the Rue

des Jardins St. Paul. He met none except his faithful Aloyse. Martin Guerre was there no longer; André had stayed with Madame de Castro; Jean and Babette Peuquoy had returned to Calais, and from there had started for St. Quentin, the gates of which were opened to the patriotic weaver by the treaty of Chateau-Cambrésis.

The return of the master to his deserted house was, therefore, on this occasion sadder even than usual. But did not the motherly old nurse love him enough for all? It would be useless for us to try to depict the joy of the worthy woman when Gabriel told her he intended spending some time with her. He would live in the strictest retirement and the most absolute solitude; but still he would be with her and would go out very seldom. Aloyse would see him, would care for him. It was long since she had felt so happy.

Gabriel, as he gazed sadly upon that loving old face, envied her happiness. Alas! he could no longer share it. His life was henceforth for him a terrible enigma, the solution of which he at once desired and dreaded.

In such impatience and apprehension, over a month passed—a month of restlessness and lassitude.

In accordance with his promise to the nurse, he seldom left his hotel; but in the evening he would sometimes prowl around the Chatelet, and on his return would shut himself up for long hours in the vault where on a certain night unknown sextons had furtively deposited the body of his father.

Gabriel took a sombre pleasure in recalling the day of the outrage, and keeping his courage alive with his anger.

When he saw again the black walls of the Chatelet, and, above all, when he saw again the marble tomb in which the sufferings of a noble life had found their termination, the frightful morning on which he had closed the eyes of his murdered father came back to him in all its horror.

Then he clinched his hands, his hair stood on end, his

breast swelled, and his terrible meditations produced a fresh outburst of hatred.

Then he would regret that he had allowed his vengeance to depend on circumstances; waiting became insupportable to him.

What! while he was patiently waiting, the murderers were joyous and triumphant! the king was peacefully enthroned in his Louvre! the constable was growing rich on the misery of the people! Diana de Poitiers was revelling in her infamous loves!

That could not last. Since God's thunderbolts were sleeping, since suffering was powerless to give courage to the oppressed, Gabriel would do without God or men, or rather he would be the instrument of divine justice and of human anger.

Thereupon, carried away by an irresistible impulse, he would grasp the hilt of his sword and take a step as if to go out.

But his alarmed conscience recalled to him the letter of Diana de Castro—that letter written from Calais, in which his beloved begged him not to punish with his own hand, and unless he were an involuntary instrument, not to strike even the guilty.

Gabriel would read again this touching letter, and his sword fell back in the scabbard.

Full of compunction, he would decide to wait.

Gabriel, in fact, was one of those who act, not one of those who lead. His energy was admirable when he had with him an army, a party, or even a single great man. But neither his rank nor his nature was of a kind to permit him to accomplish extraordinary things by himself, even when they were good, still less when they were evil. He was neither a powerful prince nor a powerful genius. He wanted the ability as well as the will to take the initiative.

With Coligny and the Duke de Guise, he had executed deeds of superhuman grandeur. But now, as he had hinted to Martin Guerre, his occupation was changed; instead of an enemy to fight, he had a king to punish. And this time he had no one to aid him in his terrible work.

Nevertheless, he counted still upon these same men who had already lent him their power—upon Coligny the Protestant and Guise the ambitious.

A civil war in defence of religious truth, a revolt to bring about the triumphant usurpation of a great genius, such were the secret hopes of Gabriel. The death or deposition of Henry the Second, his punishment, would, in any case, be the consequence of either of these risings. Gabriel would show himself in the second rank as one who ought to be in the first. He would keep to the end the oath he had sworn to the king himself; he would attack the perjurer even in his children and grandchildren.

If Gabriel, ever accustomed to come too late, missed these two chances, he would have only to leave the matter in the hands of God.

But at first he did not seem likely to miss them. On the 13th of June, he received, almost at the same time, two letters.

The first was brought him about five in the afternoon by a mysterious man who would only hand the letter to himself alone, and then not until he had compared his features with the indications in an exact description.

The following is the letter:

FRIEND AND BROTHER—The hour has come; the persecutors have raised the mask. Let us bless God! Martyrdom leads to victory.

This evening at nine, search for a brown-colored door at No. 11 Place Maubert.

Strike three distinct strokes, separated by a regular interval. A man will open and say: "Do not enter; you would not see clearly." You will answer: "I bring my light with me." The man will conduct you to a staircase having seventeen steps, which you will ascend in the dark. At the top, another acolyte will approach you, saying: "What do you ask for?" You will answer: "That which is just." You will then be led into a deserted room, where some one will whisper the password in your ear: *Geneva.* You will answer with the countersign: *Glory.* Then you will be brought into the presence of those *who have need of you to-day.*

This evening, friend and brother. Burn this letter. Discretion and courage!   L. R.

Gabriel had a lighted lamp brought to him, burned the letter before the messenger, and only said these words—

"I will go."

The man saluted and withdrew.

"Well," said Gabriel, "the religionists are getting tired of waiting also."

Close upon eight, while he was still reflecting on the summons of La Renaudie, a page in the Lorraine livery was introduced by Aloyse.

The page was the bearer of a letter conceived in these terms:

Monsieur and dear Comrade—I have been six weeks in Paris, having returned from the army, where I had no longer anything to do.

I have been assured that you also must have been at home for some time. Why have I not seen you? In these days of forgetfulness and ingratitude, have you too forgotten me? No, I know you; the thing is impossible.

Come, then; I will be waiting for you to-morrow, if you wish, in my apartments at Les Tournelles at ten o'clock.

Come, if only that we may mutually console each other for what these people have done with our successes.

Your very affectionate friend,

Francis of Lorraine.

"I will go," said Gabriel simply to the page.

And when the boy had retired—

"Good!" said he; "the man of ambition is awaking also."

Nursing a double hope, he started a quarter of an hour afterward for the Place Maubert.

CHAPTER XVIII

A CONVENTICLE OF THE PROTESTANTS

THE house No. 11 Place Maubert, in which Gabriel was to meet La Renaudie, belonged to a lawyer named Trouillard. There had been for some time vague rumors among the people that it was a resort for heretics; and the chanting of psalms sometimes heard in the evening by the neighbors gave some authority to these dangerous reports. But they were only reports, and the police of the time had not taken any steps so far to ascertain their correctness.

Gabriel easily found the brown door, and, as he was directed to do in the letter, struck three regular blows on the door.

The door opened as if of itself; but a hand seized the hand of Gabriel in the darkness, and some one said—

"Do not enter; you would not see clearly."

"I bring my light with me," answered Gabriel, according to the formula.

"Enter, then," said the voice, "and follow the hand which guides you."

Gabriel obeyed, and went a few steps. Then he was released, and the voice said—

"Now go."

Gabriel felt his foot on the first step of a staircase. He counted seventeen steps and stopped.

"What do you ask for?" said another voice.

"That which is just," he answered.

A door opened at once before him, and he entered a room lighted by a dim light.

There was but one man in it. He approached Gabriel, and said in an undertone—

"*Geneva!*"

"*Glory!*" replied the young count, immediately.

The man then struck a bell; and La Renaudie, in person, entered through a secret door.

He went straight up to Gabriel, and pressed his hand affectionately.

"Do you know what passed in the parliament to-day?" he asked.

"No; I did not leave my house," answered Gabriel.

"You are going to learn it here, then," returned La Renaudie. "You have not pledged yourself to us; no matter, we will pledge ourselves to you. You shall know our plans, and calculate our strength. There shall be no secrecy as to the affairs of our party, as far as you are concerned; while, on the other hand, you are free to act alone, or with us, just as you wish. You have told me that you were one of us virtually; that is enough. I do not ask you even to pledge your word as a gentleman to reveal nothing of what you see or hear. Precaution in your case is useless."

"Thanks for your confidence," said Gabriel, with emotion. "You shall have no reason to regret it."

"Enter with me," said La Renaudie, "and remain by my side; I will tell you the names of such of our brethren as you may not recognize. You can judge for yourself of other matters. Come."

He took Gabriel by the hand, pressed the hidden spring of the secret door, and entered a long oblong hall, in which two hundred persons were gathered.

Some torches, scattered here and there, threw a faint light on the moving groups. Except a rough wooden pulpit for the minister or the speaker, there was no furniture, neither hangings nor benches.

The presence of a score of women explained, but, we

must say, by no means justified, the belief prevalent among
Catholics as to the nature of these nocturnal and secret conventicles of the Reformers.

No one remarked the entrance of Gabriel and his guide.
All eyes and all thoughts were fixed upon the man then
occupying the tribune—a religionist of sad countenance and
grave speech.

La Renaudie named him to Gabriel.

"It is Nicolas Duval, counsellor to the parliament," he
whispered. "He has just begun narrating what took place
to-day at the Augustins. Listen."

Gabriel listened.

"Our ordinary hall in the palace," continued the orator,
"being occupied by the festive preparations for the Princess
Elizabeth's marriage, we sat provisionally, for the first time,
at the Augustins, and I believe the strange appearance of
this hall foreshadowed in some vague sort of way the occur-
rence of some event equally strange.

"However, our president, Gilles Lemaître, opened the
session in the usual manner, and nothing seemed to justify
the apprehensions of a few among us.

"We resumed the discussion of the question submitted
on the preceding Wednesday. It was on the subject of
religious opinions. Antoine Fumée, Paul de Foix, and
Eustache de la Porte spoke successively in favor of toleration; and their eloquent and firm discourses evidently made
a lively impression on the majority.

"Eustache de la Porte had resumed his seat in the midst
of applause, and Henry Dufaur was beginning to speak, in
order to gain the support of those who were still hesitating,
when suddenly the great door opened, and the usher of parliament announced, in a loud voice: 'The king!'

"The president appeared not at all surprised, and descended hastily from his chair to meet the king. All the
councillors rose in disorder, some quite astounded, others
calm, as if they were expecting what happened. The king
entered, accompanied by the Cardinal de Lorraine and the

constable. 'I do not come to disturb your labors,' said he, 'but to second them.'

"And, after a few insignificant compliments, he concluded with these words:

"'We have made peace with Spain; but wicked heresies have taken advantage of the wars to introduce themselves into the kingdom; they must be extinguished, just as the war has been. Why have you not registered an edict against the Lutherans, which I submitted to you? I repeat, however, continue freely, in my presence, the deliberations already begun.'

"Henry Dufaur, who had been speaking, courageously resumed his discourse after these words of the king, pleaded the cause of liberty of conscience, and even added to his bold argument some melancholy and severe warnings in connection with the king's government.

"'You complain of disturbances?' he cried. 'Well, we know their author. We might answer in the words of Elias to Ahab: "It is thou who troublest Israel!"'

"Henry the Second bit his lips, and turned pale, but he kept silence.

"Then Dubourg rose, and compelled the king to listen to remonstrances still more direct and serious.

"'I feel,' said he, 'that there are certain crimes which ought to be mercilessly punished, sire; such as adultery, blasphemy and perjury. Yet every day these same crimes are treated with favor; licentiousness and guilty passion are to be seen everywhere. But of what are the men accused who are delivered over to the executioner? Of high treason? Never have they omitted the name of the prince in their prayers. Never have they contrived plot or treason. What! because they have discovered by the light of the Scriptures the great vices and scandalous faults of the Roman power, and have asked it to be restored to some sort of order, is that a license worthy of fire?'

"The king never stirred; but any one could see his anger, though kept under, was intense.

"The president, Gilles Lemaître, wished to basely flatter this dumb rancor.

" 'We have to deal with heretics, then!' he said, with assumed indignation. 'Let us get rid of them as the Albigenses were got rid of: Philip Augustus had six hundred of them burned in a single day.'

"This violent language did the good cause more service even than the moderate firmness of our people. It was becoming evident that the final result would be that opinions would be at least equally balanced.

"Henry the Second understood this, and resolved to end everything by a sudden act of violence.

" 'M. le Président is right,' said he. 'We must make an end of the heretics, no matter where they take refuge. And, to begin, M. le Connétable, arrest these two rebels immediately.' He pointed to Henry Dufaur and Anne Dubourg, and hurriedly left the hall, as if he could no longer control his wrath.

"I have no need to tell you, friends and brethren, that M. de Montmorency obeyed the king's orders. Dufaur and Dubourg were seized in full parliament, and we all remained in a state of consternation.

"Gilles Lemaître alone found courage to add—

" 'It is justice! May all be so punished who fail in respect to the royal majesty!'

"But, as if to give him the lie, guards again entered the sacred precincts of the law, and, in pursuance of other orders which they produced, arrested De Foix, Fumée, and De la Porte, who had spoken before the arrival of the king, and had confined themselves to a defence of religious toleration, without uttering the slightest reproach against the sovereign.

"It was therefore certain that it was not for their remonstrances to the king, but for their religious opinions, that five inviolable members of parliament had fallen, through an odious stratagem, under an accusation entailing a capital penalty."

Nicolas Duval was silent. Murmurs of grief and anger had interrupted the speaker a score of times, and grew more and more energetic as he narrated the events of that great and stormy session, which to us, at this distance, seems to belong to another assembly, and to have the appearance of having occurred two hundred and thirty years later.

Only two hundred and thirty years later it was not royalty, it was liberty that was to have the last word!

The minister, David, succeeded Duval in the pulpit.

"Brethren," said he, "before we deliberate, let us raise our hearts and voices to God in some goodly psalm, so that He may inspire us with His spirit and His truth."

"Psalm xl.!" cried several of the Reformed.

And all began chanting the said psalm.

It was a singular selection, if it was intended to restore calmness. It must be confessed it was much more a strain of menace than a hymn of prayer.

But indignation was at the moment overflowing all hearts; and all sang these strophes with such sincere emotion that the utter want of poetry was almost supplied by the animation and energy of the singers.

> O foolish men, you really have the heart
> To thus make war on Jesus Christ,
> And all to prop up Antichrist?
> And will you play the persecutor's part?
> O traitors outrageous,
> What you do's advantageous
> To the devil alone.
> And God's laws to man given
> To conceal ye have striven,
> As if God ye'd dethrone!

The last stanza was particularly significant:

> No longer try the preaching to prevent
> Of God's own word which comfort brings,
> That God who is the King of Kings!
> Or on your heads dire curses shall be sent,
> Which, o'er you extending,

Shall cause you, descending
To hell's blackest caves,
To suffer pangs painful
And agonies baneful.
Plunged in hell's hottest waves.

The psalm finished, as if this cry to God had already relieved their hearts, there was silence, and the assembly proceeded to deliberate.

La Renaudie spoke first, and proceeded to give an exact account of the present condition of their affairs.

"Brethren," said he, from his place, "we are confronted by an unheard-of deed, which overturns every idea of justice and equity. We have therefore to determine what ought to be the conduct of reformers in the present crisis. Shall we continue to suffer in patience, or shall we act? And, in that case, how shall we act? Such are the questions each ought to put to himself, and resolve, according to his conscience. You see that our persecutors speak of nothing less than a universal massacre, and insist on blotting us out from life as they would a badly written word from a book. Shall we wait meekly for the deadly stroke? Or, since justice and the law are violated even by those whose duty it is to protect them, shall we try to do ourselves justice, and substitute force for the law? It is for you, friends and brethren, to answer."

La Renaudie made a short pause, as if to let this formidable dilemma be plainly perceptible to all minds. Then he resumed, desirous at once to throw light on the conclusion and to hasten it—

"Two parties divide, we know, all those whom the cause of reform and truth ought to unite: there are among us the party of the nobility and the party of Geneva; but, in presence of the common danger and the common enemy, we should, it seems to me, have only one heart and one will. The members of both factions are equally invited to give their advice and suggest their remedies. The counsel offering the best chances of success, from whatever quarter it comes, ought to be universally adopted. And now, friends and brethren, speak in all confidence and in all freedom.''

There was a long period of hesitation after La Renaudie's speech.

What they who heard him wanted was not freedom, but confidence.

And, at first, in spite of the indignation wherewith all hearts were filled, royalty had then such a great prestige that the Reformers, novices in conspiracy, did not dare to express, at once frankly and unreservedly, their ideas on armed rebellion. They were resolute and devoted as a body, but individually they recoiled before the responsibility of the first attempt. All were perfectly willing to follow; none dared to lead.

Then, just as La Renaudie had given it to be understood, they distrusted one another; neither of the two parties knew where the other would lead it, and yet their aims were, in truth, too unlike to make the choice of words and leaders a matter of indifference to them.

In effect, the tendency of the party of Geneva was toward a republic, while that of the nobility simply desired a change of kings.

The elective forms of Calvinism, the principle of equality everywhere taught by the new church, led directly to a republican system, similar to that of the Swiss cantons. But the nobility did not wish to go so far, and would, in accordance with the advice of Queen Elizabeth of England, have deposed Henry the Second, and replaced him by a Calvinist king. The name of the Prince de Condé was whispered about in this connection.

Evidently it was hard to get two such opposing elements to unite for a common object.

Gabriel saw with regret that, after the discourse of La Renaudie, the two almost hostile camps measured each other with a distrustful eye, not caring, apparently, to draw any conclusions from premises so daringly placed before them.

A few minutes passed amid confused murmuring and painful indecision. La Renaudie was forced to ask himself whether by his too brusque sincerity he had not unknowingly destroyed the effect of the narrative of Nicolas Duval. But since he had entered on this path, he would risk all to win all; and, addressing a thin, shabby-looking little man, with thick eyebrows and bilious face, who was in a group near him, he said aloud—

"Well, Lignières, are you not going to speak to our brethren, and show them what is in your heart?"

"Be it so!" answered the little man, his gloomy features lighting up. "I will speak, but without yielding anything or extenuating anything."

"Of course you are among friends," replied La Renaudie.

While Lignières was ascending the pulpit, La Renaudie whispered to Gabriel—

"I am employing a dangerous method. This Lignières is a fanatic; whether sincere or not, I can't say. He goes to extremes and excites more repulsion than sympathy. But no matter! We must, at any risk, know where we stand, must we not?"

"Yes," said Gabriel; "so that truth may at last come forth from these locked hearts!"

"With his Genevese doctrines, Lignières will not let it fall asleep, you may be certain!" replied La Renaudie.

The orator opened his discourse *ex abrupto*.

"The law itself has just been condemned," said he. "What appeal is left us? An appeal to force and no other! You ask what ought to be done? If I do not answer this question, here is something shall answer for me."

He raised and pointed to a silver medal.

"This silver medal," he continued, "speaks more eloquently than any words of mine. For those who cannot see it, I will explain what it represents: it bears the image of a flaming sword that cuts a lily whose stalk is bending and falling. Beside it, the sceptre and crown are rolling in the dust."

Lignières added, as if afraid he might not be fully understood—

"Medals ordinarily serve to commemorate accomplished facts: may this serve as the prophecy of a fact to be accomplished! I will say no more."

He had said quite enough! He descended amid the applause of a small portion of the congregation and the murmurs of the larger number.

But the general attitude was that of silence and stupefaction.

"Ah!" said La Renaudie, in a low voice to Gabriel, "that chord does not vibrate very strongly among us. Let us see if there is another."

"M. le Baron de Castelnau," he said, in a loud tone, addressing an elegant and thoughtful-looking young man who was leaning against the wall, ten paces from him—"M. de Castelnau, have you nothing to say in your turn?"

"Perhaps I have nothing to say," replied the young man, "but I may have something to answer."

"We are listening," said La Renaudie.

"He belongs," whispered La Renaudie to Gabriel, "to the party of the gentlemen, and you must have seen him at the Louvre on the day you brought the news of the capture of Calais. Castelnau is frank, loyal, and brave. He will set up his flag as boldly as Lignières, and we shall see whether he is better received."

Castelnau took his stand on one of the steps of the pulpit, and spoke from there.

"I will begin," he said, "like the orators who have preceded me. We have been attacked with iniquity; let us defend ourselves with iniquity. Let us transfer to the open field, among coats of mail, the war they have begun in parliament, among their red robes! But I differ from M. de Lignières. I, too, have a medal to show you. Here it is. It is not his. At a distance it resembles the minted crowns you have in your purses. So it does in reality; but it also presents the effigy of a crowned king. Only instead of *Henricus II.*, *rex Galliæ*, the exergue bears the legend, *Ludovicus XIII.*, *rex Galliæ*. I have spoken.'' [1]

The Baron de Castelnau left his station proudly. The allusion to Prince Louis de Condé could not be mistaken. Those who had applauded Lignières murmured at his words, and those who had murmured applauded.

But the bulk of the congregation remained impassive and dumb between the two minorities.

"What do they want, then?" asked Gabriel of La Renaudie.

"I am afraid they want nothing!" replied the baron.

At this moment the lawyer, Des Avenelles, asked leave to speak.

"This is, I believe, their man," said La Renaudie. "Des Avenelles is my host when I am in Paris—a man honest and wise, but too prudent, too timid, even. Whatever he says will go down with them."

Des Avenelles, from the very beginning, proved the truth of the baron's remark.

"We have just," he said, "heard courageous and even audacious words. But has the moment really come to pronounce them? Are we not going a little too fast? An elevated goal has been pointed out to us, but as to the means of reaching it, not a word. These means can only be criminal. My soul, more than that of any of you, is tortured by the persecution we have to endure. But when we have so many prejudices to vanquish, is it necessary to add to them the odium of assassination? Yes, of assassination, for in no other way could you obtain the result you hope for."

Almost unanimous applause interrupted the speaker.

---

[1] These two curious and singular medals are to-day in the Cabinet des Médailles.

Des Avenelles continued:

"The king is in the full vigor and maturity of his age. To deprive him of his throne you must hurl him from it. What living man would undertake a deed of such violence? Kings are divine; God alone has any rights over them! Ah! but if some accident, if some unforeseen misfortune, nay, if the felonious deed of some individual should at the present moment strike the king, and place the guardianship of his successor in the hands of the insolent subjects who oppress us!—then it would be this guardianship and not royalty, the Guises and not Henry the Second, whom we would attack. Civil war would be laudable, and revolt sacred, and I would be the first to cry out, 'To arms!' "

This mixture of timidity and energy moved the assembly to admiration, and fresh marks of approbation rewarded the prudent courage of Des Avenelles.

"Ah!" said La Renaudie, in an undertone to Gabriel, "I regret now that I brought you; you will begin to pity us."

But Gabriel was thoughtfully saying to himself—

"No, I have no right to reproach them for their weakness; it resembles my own. Just as I was counting secretly upon them, it seems they were counting upon me."

"What do you intend doing?" cried La Renaudie to his triumphant host.

"To remain within the limits of the law, and wait!" answered the lawyer, resolutely. "Anne Dubourg, Henry Dufaur, and three of our friends in parliament have been arrested; but who says they will be condemned, or even accused? It is my opinion that violence on our side would only tend to call forth violence on the side of authority. And who knows but our very moderation may be the salvation of the victims? Let us display the calmness of strength and the dignity of a just cause. Let us put our persecutors in the wrong. Let us wait. When they see us firm and moderate, they will think twice before declaring war upon us; and I beg you also, friends and brethren, to think twice before entering on a course of reprisals."

Des Avenelles was silent, and the applause was renewed.

The lawyer, proud of his success, wished to verify his victory.

"Let those who think with me," he said, "raise their hands."

Almost every hand was raised, proving that Des Avenelles had voiced the feeling of the assembly.

"Now, then," said he, "our decision is—"

"To decide on nothing at all," interrupted Castelnau.

"To adjourn to a more favorable moment extreme measures," continued the lawyer, casting a furious look upon his interrupter.

The minister, David, proposed to intone a new psalm, asking God to deliver the poor prisoners.

"Come away," said La Renaudie to Gabriel. "All this makes me ashamed and indignant. These only know how to sing; their psalms are all that's seditious about them."

When they were in the street they walked along in silence, both absorbed in their thoughts.

At Notre-Dame bridge they separated, La Renaudie returning to the Faubourg St. Germain, and Gabriel to the Arsenal.

"Adieu, M. d'Exmès," said La Renaudie; "I am sorry to have made you lose your time. Still, this is not our last word, I assure you. The prince, Coligny, and our most thoughtful people were absent this evening."

"My time with you was not lost," said Gabriel. "You may be able to convince yourself of the fact before long."

"So much the better! so much the better!" returned La Renaudie. "Still, I doubt—"

"Do not doubt," said Gabriel. "I wanted to learn whether the Protestants were really beginning to lose patience. It is more useful to me than you can imagine to have learned that they are not yet weary."

CHAPTER XIX

ANOTHER TRIAL

THE discontent of the Reformers having failed him, there still remained for Gabriel another chance of help in his vengeance from the ambition of the Duke de Guise.

So, at ten o'clock on the next morning, he was punctual to the appointment which Francis de Lorraine had given him at Les Tournelles.

The young Count de Montgommery was evidently expected; for, on his arrival, he was shown into the presence of him who, thanks to Gabriel's daring, was now hailed as the conqueror of Calais.

The Balafré came eagerly forward to meet Gabriel, and pressed his hands affectionately in his own.

"So here you are at last, then, my forgetful friend," said he; "you have forced me to send for you, to pursue you into your retirement, and, if I had not done so, God knows when I should have seen you again! Now, why is this? Why have you not come near me since my return?"

"Monseigneur," replied Gabriel, in a low voice, "painful and absorbing preoccupations—"

"Ah! that was it! I was sure of it!" interrupted the Duke de Guise. "They have also broken the promise they made to you, have they not? They have deceived and tortured you—you, the savior of France! Oh, I suspected there was some infamy under all this! My brother, the Cardinal de Lorraine, when he saw you at the Louvre, and

neard you announced as Count de Montgommery, divined,
with his priestly finesse, that you were about to be the dupe
or victim of these people. Why did you not apply to him?
He might have been of assistance to you in my absence."

"I thank you, monseigneur," replied Gabriel, gravely;
"but you are mistaken, I assure you. Every promise they
made me they kept in the strictest fashion possible."

"Oh, but you say this in such a tone, my friend!"

"I say it as I feel it, monseigneur; but I repeat that I do
not complain, and that the promises upon which I reckoned
have been executed—to the letter. Do not speak of my
affairs, I entreat you. You know it is a subject that pleased
me but little ordinarily. To-day it is more painful to me
than ever. Please, monseigneur, I beg of you, do not per
sist in your kindly inquiries."

The duke was struck with the melancholy tone ot
Gabriel.

"Enough, my friend," he said; "after this, I shall be
afraid of touching, though unwittingly, some of your still
bleeding wounds, and I will never again question you upon
your private affairs."

"Thanks, monseigneur," returned Gabriel, with dignity,
though not without emotion.

"But at least be certain of this," said the Balafré, "that
in all places and at all seasons, no matter for what object,
my influence, my fortune, and my life are yours, Gabriel;
and that if I ever have the good fortune to discover that
you need me for anything, you have only to reach out your
hand to find mine."

"Thanks, monseigneur," repeated Gabriel.

"This being settled between us," said the Duke de
Guise, "what would you wish us to talk about, my good
friend?"

"Why, of yourself, monseigneur," replied Gabriel,
"your glory and plans—these are what interest me. These
are what made me run to you at your first call."

"My glory? my plans?" retorted Francis de Guise,

shaking his head. "For me too, alas! that would be a sad subject of conversation."

"Oh, monseigneur! what is this you are saying?" answered Gabriel.

"The truth, my friend. Yes, I confess I thought I had won some reputation. It seemed to me that my name was pronounced with a certain respect in France and a certain terror in Europe. And as this somewhat distinguished past rendered it a duty for me to concern myself with the future, I was arranging my projects in harmony with my fame, and was dreaming of great things for my country and myself. I would have attained them, too, if I am not greatly mistaken."

"Well, monseigneur?" asked Gabriel.

"Well!" returned the Duke de Guise, "during the six weeks since I have returned to court, I have ceased to believe in my glory and have renounced all my plans."

"And, my God! why?"

"Have you not seen the shameful treaty that has been the fruit of all our victories? If we had been forced to raise the siege of Calais; if the English had still in their power the gates of France; if, in fine, defeat at all points had demonstrated to us the insufficiency of our forces and the impossibility of continuing an unequal struggle—we could not have signed a more disadvantageous and dishonoring peace than that of Chateau-Cambrésis."

"It is true, monseigneur; and every one deplores that the fruit yielded by such a magnificent harvest should be so insignificant."

"Well, then, how can you expect me to sow any more for people who reap so badly? Besides, have they not forced me to inaction by this fine peace of theirs? My sword, you see, is condemned to remain in its scabbard for a long time. War being, at any cost, brought to an end everywhere, my glorious dreams are brought to an end with it; and, between ourselves, that was one of the things aimed at."

"But you are not less powerful even in your retirement,
monseigneur," said Gabriel. "The court respects you, the
people adore you, and the foreigner dreads you."

"Yes, I think I am loved at home and feared abroad;
but do not say, my friend, that I am respected at the Louvre.
While they were bringing to naught the assured results of
our successes in public, they were undermining my influence also in private. When I returned from yonder, whom
did I find in higher favor than ever? The vanquished
boaster of St. Laurent, that insolent rascal Montmorency,
whom I detest!"

"Certainly not more than I do!" murmured Gabriel.

"Is it not by him and for him that this peace which puts
us all to the blush has been concluded? Not content with
thus minimizing my efforts, he has known well how to take
care of his own interests in the treaty, and to have the
amount of his ransom after St. Laurent returned to him for
the third or fourth time, I believe. He speculates on his
defeat and shame."

"And does the Duke de Guise accept such a man as a
rival?" returned Gabriel, disdainfully.

"He shudders at the thought, my friend; but you see
well that this same rivalry is imposed upon him. You see
that this constable is protected by something stronger than
glory, by some one more powerful than the king himself.
You see well that my services can never equal those of
Madame de Poitiers, whom may the lightning wither!"

"Oh, would that God heard you!" murmured Gabriel.

"But what can this woman have done to the king?
Have you any idea, my friend?" continued the duke.
"The people speak of philters and sorceries; is there any
foundation for it? For my part, I imagine there is between
them a bond stronger than love? It cannot be passion
alone that unites them so closely; it must be crime. There
is, I would swear to it, remorse among their memories of
the past. They are more than lovers; they are accomplices."

The Count de Montgommery shivered from head to foot.

"Do you not agree with me, Gabriel?" demanded the Balafré.

"Yes, monseigneur," replied Gabriel, in a faint voice.

"And to cap the climax of my humiliation," continued the Duke de Guise, "do you know, my friend, the reward, in addition to the monstrous treaty of Chateau-Cambrésis, I found on my arrival in Paris? My summary dismissal from the dignity of Lieutenant-General of the realm. These extraordinary functions were useless in time of peace, I was told. And without notice, without thanks, this title was taken from me and flung aside, just as you fling aside a piece of furniture that is no longer good for anything."

"Is it possible? They showed you no more respect than that!" cried Gabriel, who wished to add fuel to the flame burning in that incensed scul.

"What is the use of respect for a superfluous servant?" said the Duke de Guise, grinding his teeth. "As to M. de Montmorency, it is quite another thing. He is and he remains constable. It is an honor that cannot be revoked, and which he has well merited by forty years of defeats. But, oh, by the cross of Lorraine! should a new war break out, if they come to beg and entreat and conjure me to save the country, I will send them back to their constable. Let him serve them, if he can. It is his business, and one of the duties of his office. As for myself, since they condemn me to idleness, I accept the sentence, and until better times I rest."

Gabriel, after a pause, answered gravely—

"This determination on your part, monseigneur, is annoying, and I deplore it, for I have actually come here with the intention of making you a proposition."

"Useless, useless, useless!" said the Balafré. "I have decided on my course. Besides, the peace, as you know well, deprives us of all chance of glory."

"Pardon me, monseigneur," urged Gabriel; "but it is the peace which renders my project feasible."

"Indeed!" said Francis, his curiosity excited. "Something daring, is it, like the siege of Calais?"

"Something far more daring, monseigneur."

"How can that be?" returned the duke, with astonishment. "I confess you excite my curiosity to the liveliest degree."

"You permit me to speak, then?" said Gabriel.

"Undoubtedly; nay, I entreat you to do so."

"We are quite alone here?"

"Quite alone; no living soul can hear us."

"Well, then, monseigneur," said Gabriel, resolutely, "this is what I wanted to say to you. This king and this constable wish to do without you; do you do without them. They have deprived you of the title of Lieutenant-General of France; do you seize it again."

"How? explain yourself!" said the Duke de Guise.

"Monseigneur, foreign nations dread you, the people adore you, the army is entirely yours. You are already more of a king in France than the king himself. Dare to speak as a master, and all will listen to you as subjects. Will Henry the Second be stronger in the Louvre than you in your camp? He who now speaks to you would be proud and happy to be the first to address you as your Majesty."

"Well, your scheme is daring enough, in all conscience, Gabriel," said the Duke de Guise.

But he did not look as if he were very much irritated. He smiled even under his assumed surprise.

"I propose this daring scheme to an extraordinary soul," returned Gabriel, firmly. "I speak for the good of France. It needs a great man for its king. Is it not disastrous that all your grand ideas of conquest and glory should be obstructed by the caprices of a courtesan and the jealousy of a favorite? If you were once free and master, where would your genius stop? You would renew the era of Charlemagne."

"You know the house of Lorraine is descended from him," said the Balafré, quickly.

"Let none deny it who has seen you in action," returned Gabriel. "Be in your turn a Hugh Capet for the Valois."

"Yes, but if I only turned out a Constable de Bourbon?" said the Duke de Guise.

"You calumniate yourself, monseigneur," said Gabriel. "The Constable de Bourbon called in the aid of foreigners, of enemies. You would use only the forces of the country."

"But where are these forces, which, according to you, I could dispose of?" asked the Balafré.

"Two parties offer them to you," replied Gabriel.

"Where are they, for, in truth, I am letting you speak as if the whole thing was not chimerical—where are these two parties?"

"The army of the Reformed. You might, at first, be a military chief," answered Gabriel.

"And usurper!"

"Say a conqueror. But, if you like it better, be the King of the Huguenots."

"And the Prince de Condé?" said the duke, smiling.

"He has a certain charm and a certain ability; but you nave greatness and renown. Do you believe that Calvin would hesitate between you both? Now, it may as well be confessed that the cooper's son of Noyon can do what he likes with his party. Say but the word, and to-morrow you have under your command thirty thousand sectaries."

"But I am a Catholic prince, Gabriel."

"The religion of men like you, monseigneur, is glory."

"I should have to quarrel with Rome."

"You would have a pretext to conquer her."

"My friend, my friend!" returned the duke, regarding Gabriel earnestly, "you must hate Henry the Second deeply."

"As much as I love you," replied the young man, with noble frankness.

"I prize your sincerity, Gabriel," rejoined the Balafré,

seriously; "and to show you I do so, I also will speak to you from my heart."

"And my heart will never reveal what you confide to it," said Gabriel.

"Listen, then," continued Francis de Lorraine. "I have already, I acknowledge, beheld in my dreams the goal you have shown me to-day. But you will doubtless agree, my friend, that when one sets out with such a goal in view, he ought at least to make sure of reaching it, and that to risk aiming at it prematurely is to insure losing it?"

"That is true," said Gabriel.

"Well, do you really believe that my ambition is ripe, and that the times are favorable? Such profound changes should be prepared long beforehand, and the people should be already quite prepared to accept them. Now, do you imagine that the people are at the present habituated to the idea of a change of dynasty?"

"They would become habituated to it," said Gabriel.

"I doubt it," replied the Duke de Guise. "I have commanded armies, I have defended Metz and taken Calais, I have been twice Lieutenant-General of the realm; but that is not enough. I have not yet approached close enough to royal power. There are malcontents. But parties do not make a people. Henry the Second is young, intelligent, and brave. He is the son of Francis the First. One should think a good deal before dreaming of dispossessing him."

"Then you hesitate, monseigneur?" said Gabriel.

"I do more, my friend; I refuse," replied the Balafré. "Ah, if to-morrow, by accident or disease, Henry the Second should suddenly die."

"He, too, is thinking of that," said Gabriel to himself. "Well, monseigneur," he said aloud, "if such an unforeseen event should happen, what would you do then?"

"Then," returned the Duke de Guise, "under a young, inexperienced king, entirely under my influence, I should in some sort become the regent of the kingdom. And if the queen-mother or the constable attempted to oppose me; if the Reformers revolted; if, in fine, the dangerous condition of the country required a firm hand at the helm—opportunities would spring up of themselves, and I should be almost necessary. Then I do not say but that your schemes might be welcome, and I would listen to you."

"But until then—until the death of the king, which is very unlikely for a long time?"

"I will resign myself, my friend. I will content myself with preparing for the future. And if the ideas sown in my brain only bear fruit for my son, it will be because God has wished it."

"That is your last word, monseigneur?"

"It is my last word; but I do not thank you the less, Gabriel, for having had confidence in my destiny."

"And I thank you, monseigneur, for having had confidence in my discretion."

"Yes," answered the duke; "it is understood that all thus passed between us is buried."

"And now," said Gabriel, rising, "I shall retire."

"What! already?" cried the Duke de Guise.

"Yes, monseigneur; I have learned what I wanted to learn. I shall remember your words. They are safely locked up in my heart; but I shall remember them. Excuse me; but I wanted to find out whether the royal ambition of the Duke de Guise was still sleeping. Adieu, monseigneur."

"*Au revoir*, my friend."

Gabriel left Les Tournelles sadder and more restless than when he entered it.

"Courage!" said he to himself. "The two human auxiliaries I counted upon have failed me. But God remains to me still."

CHAPTER XX

A DANGEROUS STEP

D IANA DE CASTRO was residing, in the midst of continual terrors and sorrows, at the Louvre. She too was waiting. But her forced inaction was perhaps more painful than the constant restlessness of Gabriel.

Every tie between them, however, was not severed. Her page André went each week to the Rue des Jardins St. Paul, and made inquiries of Aloyse.

The news he brought back to Diana was seldom reassuring. The young Count de Montgommery was always taciturn, always gloomy, and always disturbed. The nurse never spoke of him but with tear-dimmed eyes and pallid cheeks.

Diana hesitated long. At last, on one morning in June, she took a decisive resolution to have done with her fears once for all.

She wrapped herself in a very plain mantle, concealed her face under a veil, and before the inhabitants of the chateau were awake, left the Louvre, attended by André alone, and set out to visit Gabriel.

Since he avoided her, since he was silent, she would go to him.

A sister might well visit a brother. Was it not her duty to admonish and console him?

Unfortunately, all the courage Diana had expended in coming to this decision was rendered useless.

Gabriel also devoted the solitary hours of the morning to those wanderings in which he still passed a good deal of his time. When Diana knocked with trembling hand at the door of his hotel, he had already been gone more than half an hour.

Should she wait for him? No one knew when he would return. And too long an absence from the Louvre might expose Diana to calumny.

No matter! she would wait at least the time she had intended to devote to him.

She asked for Aloyse, for she longed to see her also and question her face to face.

André introduced his mistress into an unoccupied room, and ran to notify the nurse of her presence.

For years, ever since the happy days of Montgommery and Vimoutiers, Aloyse and Diana, the woman of the people and the daughter of the king, had not met.

But both their lives had been engrossed by the same thought; the same anxieties had filled their days with terrors and their nights with sleeplessness.

So when Aloyse, entering hastily, would have bowed humbly before Madame de Castro, Diana threw herself into her arms and embraced the good woman as of old, saying—

"Dear nurse!"

"What!" said Aloyse, moved to tears, "you still remember me then? you recognize me?"

"Not remember you! not recognize you!" returned Diana; "it would be like forgetting the house of Enguerrand; it would be like forgetting the chateau of Montgommery."

Then Aloyse contemplated Diana more earnestly, and, clasping her hands, cried, smiling and sighing at the same time—

"How beautiful you are!"

She smiled, for she had well loved the young girl who had become so great a lady; she sighed, for she understood all the misery of Gabriel.

Diana comprehended the look, at the same time sorrowful and fascinated, of Aloyse, and hurriedly said, with a slight blush—

"I did not come to speak of myself, nurse."

"It was of him, then?" said Aloyse.

"Of whom else could it be? I can open my heart to you. How unfortunate that I have not found him! I came for the purpose of consoling him while consoling myself. How is he?—very gloomy and disheartened, is he not? Why has he not been to see me at the Louvre? What does he say? What does he do? Speak, speak; I beg of you, nurse!"

"Alas, madame," replied the nurse, "you have good reason to believe him gloomy and disheartened. Figure to yourself—"

Diana interrupted the nurse.

"Stay, my good Aloyse," said she; "before you begin, I have one request to make. I would remain until to-morrow listening to you, you may well believe, and that without feeling wearied or perceiving the flight of time. Still, I must return to the Louvre without attracting notice to my absence. Promise me one thing: when I have been here an hour, whether he is back or not, warn me and send me away."

"But, madame," said Aloyse, "I am quite as capable of forgetting the hour as you, and I should no more grow tired of speaking than you of hearing."

"What is to be done, then? I have to fear your weakness as well as my own."

"The difficult task must be intrusted to another." said Aloyse.

"You are right. André!"

The page, who was in the neighboring room, promised to knock when an hour was past.

"And now," said Diana, sitting down by the nurse, "let us talk at our ease, and tranquilly, if not, alas! gayly."

But this conversation, whatever attraction it had for the

two sorrowful women, had many points of difficulty and bitterness.

In the first place, neither knew how far the other was acquainted with the terrible secrets of the house of Montgommery.

Moreover, there were, in whatever Aloyse knew of the past life of her master, many disturbing breaks which she was afraid to allude to. In what way could she explain his absences, his sudden returns, and his very silence?

At last, the nurse told Diana all she knew, or at least all she observed; and Diana no doubt found great pleasure in listening to the nurse's account of Gabriel—a pleasure, however, modified by the sad nature of the information she conveyed.

And, indeed, the revelations of Aloyse were less calculated to calm the anguish of Madame de Castro than to revive it, for this living witness of the sufferings and weakness of the young count brought vividly before her all the torments of that agitated life.

Diana became more and more persuaded that if she was to save the lives of those whom she loved, it was certainly time she should interfere.

However painful may be the interchange of confidences, an hour passes quickly. Diana and Aloyse started in astonishment when they heard André's knock at the door.

"What! already!" they both cried at the same time.

"No matter!" added Diana. "I am going to wait a quarter of an hour longer."

"Madame, take care!" said the nurse.

"You are right, nurse; I must and will leave now. One word only. In all you told me of Gabriel, you have omitted —at least so I thought—to mention whether he has spoken of me."

"Never, madame; I am sure of it."

"Oh, he acts rightly," said Diana, with a sigh.

"And he would do better still if he never thought of you any more."

"Then you believe he still thinks of me?" asked Madame de Castro, eagerly.

"I am only too sure of it, madame," said Aloyse.

"And yet he carefully avoids me; he avoids the Louvre."

"If he avoids the Louvre, madame," said Aloyse, shaking her head, "it cannot be because what he loves is there."

"I understand," said Diana, with a shudder; "it is because what he hates is there."

"Oh," said she aloud, "it is absolutely necessary that I see him, absolutely necessary."

"Shall I tell him you wish him to call on you in the Louvre?"

"No, no!" cried Diana in terror, "not in the Louvre! Let him not come to the Louvre! I will watch for another opportunity, as I have done this morning. I will surely come here again."

"But suppose he is out again? Name the day or the week. Can you fix on any time? If you do, he will be waiting for you."

"Alas! I am unfortunately the daughter of a king, and know not on what day or at what hour I may be free. But if it can be managed, I will send André in advance."

The page, at this moment, afraid he had not been heard, knocked a second time.

"Madame," he cried, "the streets and places about the Louvre are beginning to be filled."

"I am going; I am going!" replied Madame de Castro. "Well, we must separate, my good nurse," she said to Aloyse; "embrace me closely, just as when I was a child, you know, and happy."

And while Aloyse, unable to utter a word, was holding her clasped to her bosom, she whispered in her ear—

"Watch over him carefully."

"Yes, just as when he was a child and happy," said the nurse.

"Oh, more carefully still. In that time he did not need it so much."

Diana quitted the hotel before Gabriel returned.

Half an hour after, she was back in her apartments in the Louvre, without encountering any obstacle. But if the consequences of the risky step she had taken no longer alarmed her, she only felt the greater anguish on account of the unknown plans of Gabriel.

The presentiments of a loving woman are the surest and clearest of prophecies.

It was late in the day when Gabriel returned home. The heat was excessive; he was wearied in body, still more wearied in mind.

But when Aloyse uttered the name of Diana and told him of her visit, he recovered all his energies, and his pulses throbbed with renewed vigor.

"What did she want? What did she say? What has she done? Oh, why was I not there? But speak, tell me everything, Aloyse, all her words and gestures."

It was now his turn eagerly to question the nurse, and he hardly gave her time to reply.

"She wishes to see me!" he cried. "Has she anything to tell me? And she does not know when she can return? Oh, Aloyse, you know I cannot remain in such uncertainty! I shall start for the Louvre immediately."

"For the Louvre!" cried Aloyse, in dismay.

"Undoubtedly," answered Gabriel, calmly. "I am not banished from the Louvre, I presume; and the man who rescued Madame de Castro at Calais has surely the right to present his respects to her at Paris."

"Yes," said Aloyse, trembling; "but Madame de Castro has advised that you should not come to see her at the Louvre."

"Have I anything to fear there?" returned Gabriel, proudly. "If I have, the greater reason is there for my going."

"No," replied the nurse; "it is probably for herself that Madame de Castro is alarmed."

"Her reputation would have suffered more from such a secret and clandestine step, if it were discovered, than from a public visit in the full light of day, like that which I intend making to-day—nay, this very instant."

And he called for a change of clothes.

"But, monseigneur," said poor Aloyse, at the end of her resources, "you yourself have until now avoided the Louvre, as Madame de Castro remarked. You have not once attempted to see her since your return."

"I was not going to see Madame de Castro when she did not call me," said Gabriel. "When I had not any reason for going to the Louvre, I avoided it. But to-day, although my action may be ineffectual, something irresistible calls me thither, and Madame de Castro desires to see me. I have sworn, Aloyse, to let my own will slumber, but to be swayed by the destiny of God, and I shall go to the Louvre at once."

And so the visit of Diana was likely to produce a result the exact contrary of what she wished.

CHAPTER XXI

THE IMPRUDENCE OF PRECAUTION

GABRIEL entered the Louvre without opposition Since the taking of Calais, the name of the young Count de Montgommery had been mentioned too often for any one to think of refusing him entrance to the apartments of Madame de Castro.

Diana was at the moment alone with one of her women working at some embroidery. Often she let her hands fall, and her thoughts became busy with her morning's interview with Aloyse.

Suddenly André entered, looking quite scared.

"Madame, M. d'Exmès!" he announced. The lad had not yet given up the habit of so calling his former master.

"Who? M. d'Exmès here?" exclaimed Diana, astounded.

"Madame, he is just behind me," said the page. "Here he is."

Gabriel appeared on the threshold, controlling his emotion as best he could. He made a profound salutation to Madame de Castro, who at first did not reply to it, speechless from amazement.

But, with a gesture, she dismissed her page and her attendant.

When Gabriel and Diana were alone, they approached and clasped each other's hands.

They remained thus for some moments, each contemplating the other.

"You have been good enough to come to my house, Diana," said Gabriel, in a deep voice. "You wanted to see and speak to me. I have hastened to obey you."

"Did it require my visit to tell you, Gabriel, that I longed to see you, and did you not know it without that?"

"Diana," returned Gabriel, with a sad smile, "I have given elsewhere proofs of my courage; I can therefore say that I have been afraid to come to the Louvre."

"Afraid of whom?" asked Diana, who was afraid herself to put the question.

"Afraid of you! afraid of myself!" answered Gabriel.

"And this is why you have preferred to forget our old-time affection? I am speaking of the sacred and lawful aspect of that affection," she hastened to add.

"I should have preferred to forget everything, I confess, Diana, rather than return of my own accord into this Louvre. But, alas! I have not been able. And the proof—"

"The proof?"

"The proof is that I am looking for you always and everywhere; that, while dreading your presence, I would have given everything in the world for the chance of catching a glimpse of you in the distance. The proof is that when prowling around royal châteaux at Paris or Fontainebleau or St. Germain, instead of desiring what I was supposed to be watching for, it was your robe perceived among the trees or on some terrace, that I wished and longed to touch; the proof, in fine, is that you have only to take a step toward me, and duty, terror, and prudence are flung to the winds. So now I am at the Louvre, which I ought to fly! And I am answering all your questions. And I feel that all this is dangerous and insensate, and yet I do it. Diana, are the proofs sufficient?"

"Yes, yes, Gabriel," said Diana, trembling.

"Ah, how much wiser it would have been," continued Gabriel, "to have persisted in my resolution to see you no more, to fly if you called me, to be silent if you questioned me! Believe me, Diana, it would have been better for both of us. I knew what I was doing. I preferred that you should suffer anxiety rather than pain. Great God! why am I without strength to resist your voice, your eyes?"

Diana was beginning to understand that perhaps she had done wrong in trying to get rid of her mortal uncertainty. Every subject of conversation led to suffering; every question was a peril. Between these two beings whom God had created for happiness, there could only be distrust, danger, and misfortune, thanks to men.

But since Diana had challenged her fate, she was resolved to see the end of it. She would sound the bottom of the abyss on whose brink she had ventured, though there she found despair and death.

After a thoughtful silence, she therefore resumed—

"I had two reasons for seeking you, Gabriel: I had an explanation to give and an explanation to demand."

"Speak, Diana," returned Gabriel; "open my heart and rend it at your will. It is yours."

"I wanted, first, Gabriel, to tell you why, after receiving your message, I did not at once accept that veil which you sent me, and immediately enter a convent, as I told you was my intention at our last sad interview in Calais."

"Have I reproached you in the slightest degree on this subject, Diana?" said Gabriel. "I told you, through André, that I released you from your promise. It was not on my part a vain form, but a real intention."

"It was also a real intention on mine to become a nun, Gabriel, and be assured this intention continues."

"Why, Diana, renounce a world for which you were formed?"

"Do not let your conscience trouble you; it is not to obey the oath I have sworn to you, so much as to satisfy the secret desire of my soul, that I desire to abandon this world, which has been for me a world of suffering. I have need of peace and repose, and can only find them with God. Do not envy me this last refuge."

"Oh, yes, I do envy you!" said Gabriel.

"I have not accomplished my irrevocable design immediately, for one reason," continued Diana: "I wished to see that you complied with the request contained in my last letter; that you would not make yourself judge and executioner; that you would not anticipate God."

"Does one ever anticipate Him?" murmured Gabriel.

"I hoped, in fine, to be able to throw myself between those whom I love and who hate each other and perhaps prevent—who knows?—a misfortune or a crime. Are you angry with me for entertaining this idea, Gabriel?"

"Angry with angels for acting according to their nature, Diana! You have been generous, and that is easy to understand."

"Ah!" cried Madame de Castro, "how do I know I have been generous; or, at least, to what degree I have been generous? My pardon is a pardon given in darkness and uncertainty! And it is on this point I wish to question you, Gabriel, for I wish to know my destiny in all its horror."

"Diana! Diana! yours is a fatal curiosity!" said Gabriel.

"No matter!" replied Diana. "I will not remain a day longer in this horrible perplexity! Tell me, Gabriel, have you finally acquired the conviction that I am really your sister; or have you lost all hope of discovering the truth on this strange secret? Answer; I ask, I beg you to do so."

"I will answer," said Gabriel, sadly. "Diana, there is a Spanish proverb which says: 'Always prepare for the worst.' I have therefore accustomed myself since our separation always to regard you as my sister. But the truth is that I have not acquired any fresh proofs. Only, as you said, I have no longer any means nor any hopes of acquiring them."

"God in heaven!" cried Diana; "he who was to furnish these proofs was not alive, then, after your return from Calais?"

"He was, Diana."

"Then I see it all; they did not keep the sacred promise they made you. Still, did not some one tell me that the king received you with the greatest favor?"

"Oh, they kept their promise in the strictest fashion, Diana."

"Gabriel, with what a sinister expression you say that! Holy Mother of God! what frightful riddle do your words conceal?"

"You have insisted, Diana, and you shall know everything," said Gabriel. "You will have now to share with me my terrible secret. In fact, I shall be glad to learn what you think of my revelation, and whether you will persist, after hearing it, in your ideas of clemency, and whether, in that case, your face, your eyes, your gestures, do not give the lie to your words of pardon. Listen!"

"I listen and tremble, Gabriel," said Diana.

Then Gabriel, in a gasping and broken voice, related everything to Madame de Castro—the king's reception, the renewal of the promise, the apparent remonstrances of the constable and Madame de Poitiers, his night of anguish and fever, his second visit to the Chatelet, his descent into the hell of the pestiferous prison, the ghastly tale of M. de Sazerac—in fine, all!

Diana never interrupted, never stirred, never cried, dumb and rigid as a statue of stone, her eyes fixed in their orbit, her hair alone showing marks of the emotion that thrilled her.

There was a long pause when Gabriel had finished his dismal story. Diana wished to speak, but could not. The words stuck in her throat. Gabriel regarded her dismay and agitation with a sort of terrible joy. At last she was able to utter this cry—

"Mercy for the king!"

"Ah!" shouted Gabriel, "you ask mercy? You, too, then deem him to be a criminal! Mercy? ah! it is a sentence! Mercy! he deserves death, does he not?"

"Oh, I did not say that," replied Diana, bewildered.

"Yes, you have said it! You are of my opinion, I see, Diana. You think, you feel as I do. Only we draw different conclusions, according to our natures. The woman asks for mercy, and the man for justice!"

"Ah!" cried Diana, "how mad and imprudent it was of me to call you to the Louvre!"

At the same moment there was a gentle knock at the door.

"Who is there, and what is wanted?" said Madame de Castro.

André half opened the door.

"Excuse me, madame," said he, "a message from the king."

"From the king!" repeated Gabriel, and his eyes blazed.

"Madame, it is, I have been told, urgent."

"Give it, let me see, what can the king want with me? Go, André; if there is an answer, I will call you."

André passed out. Diana unsealed the letter, and read what follows, with increasing terror:

MY DEAR DIANA—They tell me you are at the Louvre. Do not leave it, I pray you, before I call on you. I am now at a session of the council, which will shortly adjourn. As soon as it does so, I shall go at once to your apartments. Expect me at any moment.

It is so long since I have seen you alone! I am sad, and I long to spend a short time in conversation with my beloved daughter. Good-by for the moment.   HENRY.

Diana, who had turned quite pale, crumpled the letter in her hand when she had read it.

What ought she to do?

Send Gabriel away immediately? But then he might encounter the king, who was likely to come at any instant?

Keep the young man with her? The king would discover him on entering!

To warn the king was to arouse suspicions; to warn Gabriel was to provoke his wrath by seeming to dread it.

A collision between these two men so hostile to each other seemed now inevitable; and it was she, Diana—she who would have saved them at the price of her blood—that would have caused this fatal meeting!

"What is the nature of the king's communication, Diana?" asked Gabriel, with an affected calmness which his trembling voice belied.

"Oh, nothing!" returned Diana. "A recommendation connected with the reception of this evening."

"I am in the way, perhaps, Diana," said Gabriel. "I shall retire."

"No, no! remain!" cried Diana, quickly. "Still, if you have any business abroad, I should not wish to detain you."

"This letter troubles you, Diana; I fear my presence inconveniences you, and will bid you farewell."

"You inconvenience me, my friend! How can you think of such a thing?" said Madame de Castro. "Was it not I who, in a certain fashion, sought you? Alas! very imprudently, I am afraid. I will see you again, but not here; at your hotel, rather. As soon as I am at liberty I will go to see you and resume this sweet but terrible conversation. You have my promise. Rely upon me. At present you were right, I confess. I am preoccupied and indisposed—I have a kind of fever—"

"I see it, Diana, and I leave you," said Gabriel, sadly.

"We shall see each other again soon, my friend," said she. "Now go, go!"

She walked with him to the door of the chamber. "If I detain him," she thought, "it is certain he will see the king; if he goes away at once, there is at least a chance that he may not meet him."

However, she still hesitated, still doubted and trembled.

"Pardon me; a last word, Gabriel," said she, displaying the utmost agitation on the threshold. "My God! your story has entirely crushed me!— I cannot collect my ideas— What was I about to ask of you? Ah! I know now. Just one word—a word of importance. You have not yet told me what you intended doing. I have cried for mercy, you for justice! How do you hope to obtain this justice?"

"I do not know so far," said Gabriel, with a gloomy air. "I leave it to God, to some unforeseen event, to opportunity."

"To opportunity!" repeated Diana, shuddering. "To opportunity? What do you mean by that? Oh, come back, come back! You must not leave, Gabriel, until you have explained the meaning of that word, opportunity. Stay, I conjure you."

And, taking his hand, she conducted him back into the chamber.

"Should he encounter the king outside," thought poor Diana, "they will meet as man to man—the king without his suite, and Gabriel with his sword by his side. At least, if I am by, I can rush between them, entreat the forbearance of Gabriel, and, if necessary, face the stroke myself. Gabriel must remain.

"I feel better," she said aloud. "Remain, Gabriel. Let us resume our conversation. Give me the explanation I am waiting for. I am much better."

"No, Diana; you are now more agitated than ever," replied Gabriel. "And do you know what idea has come into my mind, and what I judge to be the cause of your terror?"

"No, indeed, Gabriel. How could I know?"

"Well," said Gabriel, "just as your cry for mercy, a moment ago, was a confession that in your eyes the crime was patent, so your apprehensions at present prove that you consider its punishment would be legitimate. You are afraid I may avenge myself on the criminal; therefore you acknowledge my vengeance would be just. You retain me

here to prevent possible reprisals by which you are frightened, but at which you would not be astonished, is it not
so?—reprisals that, in fact, appear to you quite natural,
eh?"

Diana started, so keenly had the blow told.

Nevertheless, collecting all her energy, she said—

"Oh, Gabriel! how can you imagine I could conceive
such an idea? You, my Gabriel, a murderer! You deal
a treacherous blow to any one who could not defend himself! It is impossible! for it would be not only a crime,
it would be the act of a coward! You imagine that I am
detaining you? It is a mistake! Go! depart! I will open
the door for you. I am not at all disturbed, not on this
point, at least, thank Heaven! If anything troubles me,
it is not that, believe me. Leave me; leave the Louvre in
peace. I will return to your house to finish our conversation. Go, my friend, go. You see now whether I wish to
keep you!"

While thus speaking, she had led him into the ante-
chamber.

The page was there. Diana was much inclined to order
him to escort Gabriel beyond the Louvre; but this precaution, too, would have betrayed distrust.

She could not refrain, however, from making André a
sign, and whispering this question in his ear—

"Do you know, is the council over?"

"Not yet, madame," answered André, in an undertone.
"I have not seen any of the councillors leave the grand
chamber."

"Good-by, good-by, Gabriel," said Diana, aloud, with
affected sprightliness. "Good-by, my friend; you are almost forcing me to banish you, in order to prove that I do
not detain you. Farewell, we shall soon meet again."

Yes; we shall soon meet again," he answered, with
a melancholy smile, clasping her hands.

He passed out. She stood watching him until the last
door was closed behind him.

Then, returning to her chamber, she fell on her knees before her *prie-Dieu*, her eyes full of tears, her breast heaving.

"O my God!" she said, "watch, in the name of Jesus, over him who is perhaps my brother, over him who is perhaps my father. Preserve the two beings whom I most love from each other, O my God! Thou alone canst do it now!"

CHAPTER XXII

OPPORTUNITY

I N SPITE of the efforts she made to prevent it, or rather because of those efforts, what Madame de Castro had foreseen and feared was realized.

Gabriel had left her quite sad and disturbed. The fever of Diana had, in some sort, affected himself, clouding his eyes and confusing his thoughts.

He walked mechanically along the well-known corridors and down the staircases of the Louvre, without paying much attention to external objects.

Nevertheless, just as he was opening the door of the grand gallery, he remembered that, after his return from St. Quentin, it was there he met Mary Stuart, and that the intervention of the young queen-dauphiness had enabled him to reach the king, by whom he was so basely deceived a first time.

For it was not once only that he had been betrayed and outraged. His hopes had been extinguished again and again. After the first deception, he ought to have accustomed himself to expect these exaggerated and mean interpretations of the letter of a secret compact!

While he was revolving these irritating recollections, he opened the door and entered the gallery.

Suddenly he shuddered, recoiled a step, and stood like one turned to stone.

The door at the other end of the gallery had just opened. A man entered.

That man was Henry the Second—Henry, the author of, or, at least, the principal accomplice in those criminal deceptions that had forever ruined the life and soul of Gabriel!

The king was advancing alone, without arms and without attendants.

The offender and his victim were for the first time since the outrage face to face, alone, and separated by a distance of scarcely a hundred feet—a space that might be cleared in twenty seconds with twenty bounds.

We have said that Gabriel stopped short, rigid and impassive as a statue—as the statue of Vengeance or of Hatred!

The king also halted when he perceived so suddenly him whom for nearly a year he had seen only in his dreams.

These two men remained thus for nearly a minute without moving, as if fascinated by each other. In the hurricane of sensations and ideas that darkly whirled through Gabriel's brain, the bewildered young man knew not what course to choose, what resolution to adopt. He waited.

As to Henry, in spite of his proved courage, his feeling was one of terror!

However, no sooner did the idea that he was really afraid strike him, than he raised his head, banished the craven emotion, and determined on his action.

To call would have been to fear; to withdraw would have been to fly.

He advanced toward the door where Gabriel remained rooted.

But a superior force, a sort of irresistible and fatal spell, summoned him, impelled him toward the wan phantom that seemed to be waiting for him.

The enigma of his destiny was confusing him.

Gabriel saw, with a species of blind and instinctive satisfaction, the monarch approach him; but he was unable to disengage any thought from the darkness that enveloped his mind.

All he thought of doing was to place his hand on his sword.

When the king was but a few feet from Gabriel the fear which he had managed to chase away for a time resumed its possession of him, and held his heart as in a vise.

He said to himself vaguely that his last hour had come, and that it was just.

However, he continued to advance. His feet seemed to bear him on against his will, which was asleep. It is so that somnambulists walk.

When he was close to Gabriel, so close that he could hear him breathing and touch his hand, he raised his hand to his cap, in his singular agitation, and saluted him. Gabriel did not return the salute. He stood like a marble image, and his hand never left the hilt of his sword.

Gabriel, in his eyes, was no longer a subject, but a representative of God, before whom it is necessary to bow.

In the eyes of Gabriel, Henry was no longer a king, but a man who had slain his father, to whom his only duty was hatred.

However, he let him pass without doing or saying anything to him.

The king passed, never turning round, or seemingly astonished at this mark of disrespect.

When the door was shut between them, and the charm broken, each awoke, rubbed his eyes, and asked himself—

"Was it not a dream?"

Gabriel passed slowly out of the Louvre. He did not regret his lost opportunity; he did not repent that he had let it escape.

He experienced rather a feeling of confused joy.

"My prey comes to me now," he thought; "he is now prowling around my nets, and is drawing within reach of my spear."

He slept that night as he had not slept for a long time.

The king was not so easy in his mind. He entered the chamber of Diana, who was waiting for him. We can guess with what transports of joy she received him!

But Henry was distracted and restless. He did not dare to speak of Count de Montgommery. He believed that Gabriel must have been leaving the apartments of Diana when he encountered him. Better, he thought, not venture on that subject, so, although he had come with the intention of indulging in an outburst of confidence, he maintained, during the entire visit, an attitude of distrust and constraint.

Then he returned, gloomy and sad, dissatisfied with himself and with others. That night he slept not.

It seemed to him as if he had entered a labyrinth from which he never could escape alive.

"Yet," he said to himself, "I offered myself, in some sort, to-day, to his sword. It is, then, certain that he does not want to slay me!"

The king, if he wished to distract his thoughts, could not remain in Paris. During the days that followed the meeting between him and Count de Montgommery, he went successively to St. Germain, to Chambord, and to the château of Anet, where Diana de Poitiers was staying.

Toward the end of the month of June he was at Fontainebleau.

And everywhere he displayed the utmost activity.

He evidently was trying to forget his anxieties in noise and excitement.

The approaching fêtes to be given on the marriage of his daughter Elizabeth with King Philip the Second supplied a pretext for his feverish activity.

At Fontainebleau he wished to offer the Spanish ambassador the spectacle of a grand hunt in the forest. This hunt was fixed for the 23d of June.

The day promised to be hot and threatening, and the weather stormy.

Nevertheless, Henry did not countermand the orders given. A tempest was excitement.

He mounted his fleetest and most fiery steed, and engaged in the chase with a kind of fury.

There was a moment when, carried away by his own

ardor and that of his horse, he outstripped all his followers, lost sight of the hunt, and went astray in the forest.

Clouds were heaped up on one another in the sky; heavy rumblings were heard from afar. The storm was about to break.

Henry, leaning forward over his foaming steed, whose course he did not attempt to check, but which he rather urged forward with voice and spur, still dashed on, on, swifter than the wind, among the trees and stones. This giddy gallop pleased him, and he laughed aloud in his solitude.

For some moments he had forgotten everything.

Suddenly his horse reared in terror; a flash rent the clouds; and one of those white rocks which abound in the forest of Fontainebleau suddenly towered aloft, phantom-like, at the corner of a path.

The rolling of the thunder that followed increased the terror of the shy animal. He leaped forward, altogether scared. The sudden movement broke the rein near the bit. Henry was no longer master of his horse.

Then began a furious, terrible, insensate chase.

The horse, with mane erect, foaming flanks, and legs like steel, clove the air like an arrow.

The king, holding on by the neck to avoid falling, with hair on end and clothes tossed about by the wind, vainly snatched at the reins, which, in any case, would have been useless to him.

If any one had seen them pass thus in the tempest, he would have surely taken them for some infernal vision, and would have thought only of making the sign of the cross.

But nobody was there! not a living soul, not an inhabited cottage. That last chance of safety which the presence of his fellow offers to the man in peril, failed the crowned cavalier. Not a woodcutter, not a beggar, not a poacher, not a robber there, to save a king!

And the pouring rain, and the claps of thunder ever

drawing nearer, accelerated more and more the headlong gallop of the terrified steed.

Henry, with wandering eyes, tried vaguely to recognize the forest path along which he was taking his fatal course. He finally ascertained that he was in a certain clearing among the trees, and he shuddered.

The path led straight to the summit of a craggy rock, hanging perpendicularly over a deep gulf, an abyss!

The king tried to check his horse with hand and voice. In vain!

To let himself fall was to dash himself to pieces against some trunk or granite projection. Better adopt this desperate resource only when all else failed.

But, in any case, Henry felt that he was lost, and was already recommending his soul to God—that soul so filled with remorse and dismay.

He did not know exactly in what part of the path he was, and if the precipice was near or far. But he thought it must be near, and was about to throw himself off his horse, at all risks.

As he was casting a last look into the distance, he perceived, at the end of the path, a man on horseback, like himself, but standing under the shelter of an oak.

He was not able to recognize this man at a distance. Besides, a long cloak and a broad-brimmed hat concealed his features and his figure. But he was doubtless some gentleman who had missed his way in the forest.

Henry was now safe. The path was narrow; and the stranger had only to push his horse forward to bar the king's passage, or to stretch out his hand to arrest his course.

Nothing more easy; and even though there might be some danger in this, surely as soon as the man recognized the king he would have no hesitation in risking this danger to rescue his sovereign.

In less time than it takes to write these lines, the three or four hundred paces that separated Henry from his savior were cleared.

Henry, to warn him, uttered a cry of distress, waving his uplifted arm.

The man saw him, and made a movement. He was doubtless making ready. But a terrible thing occurred! the furious steed passed in front of the unknown horseman, and the latter made not the slightest effort to stop him.

Indeed, it seemed as if he fell back a little to avoid a possible shock.

The king uttered a second cry, no longer, this time, of appeal and entreaty, but of rage and despair.

And now he heard the iron hoofs of his horse striking on stone, and not on the turf.

He had reached the fatal rock.

He pronounced the name of God, removed his feet from the stirrups, at all hazards, and leaped to the ground.

The shock carried him fifteen paces away. But, by what looked like a real miracle, he fell on a mound of moss and grass, and did not suffer any damage. It was time; the abyss was within twenty feet of him.

As for his horse, astonished at no longer feeling its burden, it gradually slackened its pace, so that, when it was on the brink of the precipice, it had time to measure it, and by a natural instinct, fell back violently on its haunches, with eyes distended, nostrils smoking, and disordered mane.

But if the king had been still mounted, the momentum of the sudden halt would assuredly have hurled him into the chasm.

So, after a fervent prayer of thanks to God, who had so evidently protected him; after soothing and remounting his horse, Henry's first thought was to rush, full of anger, upon that man who, except for the divine intervention, would have basely left him to perish.

The stranger was in the same place, still motionless under the folds of his black mantle.

"Wretch!" cried the king, when he was near enough to make himself heard. "Did you not see my peril? Did you not recognize me, regicide? And ought you not to have saved any man from such a danger, even though he were not your king, since all you had to do was to stretch out your arm?"

The man did not stir, did not answer; he merely raised his head a little, which his broad felt hat had concealed from the eyes of Henry.

The king shuddered as he recognized the pallid and gloomy features of Gabriel. He ceased to speak, but muttered as he lowered his head—

"The Count de Montgommery! then I have nothing to say."

And, without another word, he set spurs to his horse, and galloped back into the forest.

"He would not kill me," he said to himself, seized with a deadly chill; "but it seems he would let me die."

When Gabriel was alone, he repeated with a ghastly smile—

"I feel my prey is coming, and the hour is drawing near."

CHAPTER XXIII

BETWEEN TWO DUTIES

THE marriage contracts of Elizabeth and Marguerite of France were to be signed on the 28th of June at the Louvre. The king returned on the 25th sadder and more absorbed than ever.

Since the last appearance of Gabriel especially, his life had become a torture. He avoided solitude, and was constantly in search of something to distract him from the gloomy thoughts by which he was, so to speak, possessed.

He had not, however, spoken of this second meeting to any one. Yet he was at once anxious and afraid to confide the whole matter to somebody who was faithful and devoted. He himself no longer knew what to think or on what to determine, and by dint of looking in the face the fatal thought which possessed him, his mind had become entirely confused.

He resolved to open his mind to Diana de Castro.

Diana had certainly seen Gabriel lately. It was undoubtedly from her apartments he was coming when the king saw him the first time. Diana was then, perhaps, acquainted with his projects. She could, she ought, either to reassure her father on this point or warn him. And Henry, in spite of all the bitter doubts by which he was constantly assailed, did not believe his fondly loved daughter either guilty of treason toward him or an accessory to it.

A secret instinct seemed to warn him that Diana was not less agitated than he.

Madame de Castro, in effect, if she was ignorant of the two strange encounters that had already occurred between the destinies of the king and Gabriel, was also ignorant as to what had become of the latter. André, whom she had sent several times to the hotel in the Rue des Jardins St. Paul, had not brought back any news. Gabriel had again disappeared from Paris. We have seen him on the track of the king at Fontainebleau.

On the afternoon of the 26th of June, Diana was musing alone in her chamber. One of her women entered hurriedly and announced the king.

Henry was grave, as usual. After the first compliments he immediately entered upon the subject, as if to get rid of his annoying anxieties as soon as possible.

"My dear Diana," he said, and his eyes were riveted on those of his daughter, "it is a long time since we have spoken together of Viscount d'Exmès, who lately took the title of Count de Montgommery. How long is it since you have seen him?"

At the name of Montgommery, Diana turned pale and shuddered; but, recovering herself as best she could, she answered—

"Monseigneur, I have seen M. d'Exmès only once since my return from Calais."

"Where have you seen him, Diana?" asked the king.

"Here in the Louvre, sire."

"A fortnight ago or thereabout, was it not?"

"Yes, sire, about a fortnight ago."

"I suspected as much," said the king.

He paused a moment to arrange his thoughts anew.

Diana regarded him with anxiety and fear, trying to guess the motive at the bottom of this unexpected question.

But the serious expression of her father seemed impenetrable.

"Sire, excuse me," she said, collecting all her courage; "may I venture to ask your Majesty why, after the long silence you have observed in regard to the man who at Calais saved me from infamy, you do me the honor to visit me to-day, expressly for the purpose, I imagine, of questioning me respecting him?"

"Do you wish to know why, Diana?" asked the king.

"Sire, I make so bold as to do so."

"Be it so, then; you shall know everything. I am anxious that this confidence of mine should also invite yours. You have often told me you loved me, my child?"

"I have said so and I repeat it," cried Diana; "I love you as my king, my benefactor, and my father."

"I can reveal everything to so tender and loyal a daughter. Listen attentively, then, Diana."

"I am listening with all my soul."

Henry then related his two meetings with Gabriel—the first in the gallery of the Louvre, the second in the forest of Fontainebleau. He told Diana of the young man's strange, rebellious attitude, how the first time he refused to salute the king and the second time to save him.

As Diana heard, she could not dissemble her sadness and dismay. The conflict she dreaded between Gabriel and the king had already been engaged in upon two occasions, and she had every reason to dread a renewal of it still more dangerous and terrible.

Henry, seemingly not noticing her emotion, concluded with these words—

"Are not those grave offences, Diana? They are almost crimes of high treason. And yet I have concealed these outrages from every one, and controlled my resentment, because this young man has had to suffer on account of me in the past, in spite of the glorious services he has rendered the realm, and for which he ought to have been better rewarded—"

And, fixing his penetrating eyes upon Diana, he continued—

"I know not, Diana, and I do not wish to know whether you are aware of the nature of the wrong I have done to

Viscount d'Exmès. I only wish you to know that my silence has been dictated by my sense of that wrong and my regret for it. But is not this silence also imprudent? Do not these outrages augur others more serious still? Ought I not, therefore, to protect myself against Viscount d'Exmès? These are the points, Diana, upon which I wanted to consult you."

"I thank you for your confidence, sire," answered Diana, sadly, her duties to two beings equally loved being placed in a sort of antagonism.

"This confidence is quite natural," said Henry. "Well?" he added, seeing she hesitated.

"Well!" answered Diana, with an effort, "I think your Majesty is right, and—you will act wisely—by paying some attention to M. d'Exmès."

"Do you think then that my life is in any danger?" said Henry.

"Oh, I do not say that, sire!" said Diana, quickly. "But as M. d'Exmès has been deeply wounded, there might be fear—"

Poor Diana stopped, trembling, her face bathed in perspiration. This kind of denunciation, forced from her by a species of moral constraint, was repugnant to her noble heart.

But Henry gave quite a different meaning to her suffering.

"I understand you, Diana," he said, rising and taking long strides up and down the room. "Yes; I anticipated as much. You see clearly that I ought to distrust this young man. To live with the sword of Damocles constantly hanging over my head is impossible; kings have different obligations from other gentlemen. I intend taking such measures as shall prevent any danger from M. d'Exmès."

And he took a step as if to leave; but Diana threw herself before him.

What! Gabriel was about to be accused, delivered up,

imprisoned, perhaps! And it was she, Diana, who had betrayed him! She could not endure this idea. After all, Gabriel's words had not been so menacing!

"Sire, one moment!" she cried. "You misunderstand me; I swear that you misunderstand me! I have not even remotely hinted that your doubly sacred head was in danger. Nothing I have ever learned from M. d'Exmès has given me the slightest grounds for supposing that he ever even thought of a crime. Great God! do you not know that, were it otherwise, I should have revealed everything to you?"

"I have no doubt as to that," said Henry, pausing. "But then what would you advise me to do, Diana?"

"I should simply advise you, sire, to avoid these unpleasant meetings, in which an injured subject might forget the respect due to his sovereign. But there is great difference between want of respect and regicide. Would it be worthy of you, sire, to repair one wrong by a second injustice?"

"Certainly such was not my intention," replied the king; "the proof of this is that I have been silent. And since you have dispelled my suspicions, Diana, since you answer for my safety before your conscience and your God, and since, in your opinion, I may be tranquil—"

"Tranquil!" interrupted Diana, with a shudder. "But I have not gone as far as that, sire. What a terrible responsibility you are forcing upon me! On the contrary, your Majesty ought to watch, to be on your guard."

"No," returned Henry; "I cannot be always in dread, always trembling. For two weeks I cannot be said to have lived. There must be an end of it. One of two things must happen: either, trusting in your word, I must quietly accept my lot and go through my life with all my thoughts for my kingdom and none for M. d'Exmès, or I must render the man who is my enemy incapable of doing me an injury, denounce his outrages to those who have the right to deal with them; and as I am too highly placed and too elevated in mind to defend myself, I shall leave the care of my person to those whose duty it is to protect it."

"Who are they, sire?" asked Diana.

"In the first place, M. de Montmorency, the constable, and the head of the army."

"M. de Montmorency!" repeated Diana, shuddering.

The abhorred name of Montmorency recalled to her mind all the misfortunes of Gabriel's father, his captivity and death. If Gabriel fell into the constable's hands, a similar fate was in store for him. He was lost!

Diana in her mind's eye saw him whom she so much loved plunged in a dungeon which no breath of air ever visited, dying there in a single night, or, more terrible still, after twenty years, and accusing with his last sigh God and men, and particularly Diana, who, on account of some vague, equivocal words, had basely surrendered him!

There was no proof that the vengeance of Gabriel was aimed at the king or could reach him, while it was certain that the rancor of Montmorency would not spare Gabriel.

Diana revolved all this in her mind in a few seconds, and when the king, putting the question directly to her, asked—

"Well, Diana, what advice do you give me? As you have a better idea than I have of the dangers I run, your word shall be my law. Ought I to occupy myself about M. d'Exmès, or ought I not?"

"Sire," said Diana, frightened by the tone in which these last words were spoken, "your conscience is a better adviser than I am. If any other than a man you had injured, sire, had shown you disrespect, or traitorously abandoned you when exposed to danger, you would not, I think, have asked my advice as to the proper punishment of the criminal. Some imperious motive must have constrained your Majesty to observe a silence which is equivalent to a pardon. Now I can see no reason why the same motive should not continue to influence you. For, in fact, if the idea of a crime had occurred to M. d'Exmès, he could never, I imagine, have met with two better opportunities than those offered to him in a deserted gallery of the Louvre and in the forest of Fontainebleau, on the edge of a precipice—"

"That is enough," said Henry; "it is all I wanted. You have banished a serious trouble from my soul, and I thank you for it, my child. Let us not speak of it any more. I can now think in all freedom of mind of the fêtes connected with our marriages. I hope they will be splendid. I hope you, too, will be splendid. Diana, do you hear?"

"Will your Majesty please pardon me? but it was my intention to ask you to excuse me from appearing at these festivals. I confess I should prefer remaining in my solitude."

"What, Diana! But are you aware that it will be a scene of quite royal magnificence? The sports and tournaments will be the finest ever seen, and I myself shall be one of the holders of the lists. What motive can induce you to keep away from these glorious spectacles, my dear daughter?"

"Sire," replied Diana, gravely, "I have to pray."

Some minutes afterward, the king took his leave, in great part relieved from his anxieties.

But these anxieties he had transferred to the heart of poor Diana.

CHAPTER XXIV

OMENS

THE king, now almost freed from the troubles that had saddened him, eagerly pressed forward the preparations for those magnificent fêtes which he desired to give to his good city of Paris, on the occasion of the two happy marriages, of his daughter Elizabeth with Philip II. and his sister Marguerite with the Duke of Savoy.

Happy marriages indeed! marriages well deserving to be celebrated with so much rejoicing! The poet of "Don Carlos" has told us so well how the first ended that there is no need for us to repeat the story. What the preliminaries of the second led to we are about to see.

The marriage contract of Emmanuel Philibert with Princess Marguerite was to be signed on the 28th of June.

Henry the Second announced that on this day and on the two days following there would be lists opened for tournaments and other chivalrous sports.

And under the pretext of doing greater honor to the couple, but in reality to satisfy his passionate love for jousting, the king declared he would himself be among the holders.

But on the morning of the 28th of June, the queen, who at that time seldom left her retirement, asked for an interview with the king.

Henry, of course, yielded at once to this demand of his queen and lady.

Catherine betrayed much emotion as she entered the king's apartment.

"My dear sire," she cried, "I conjure you not to quit the Louvre before the end of the present month of June."

"And why so, madame?" asked Henry, astonished at such an abrupt request.

"Because otherwise some misfortune is sure to happen to you," returned the Florentine.

"Who has told you so?" said the king.

"Your star, sire, observed by me and my Italian astrologer last night. It exhibited the most menacing signs of peril, and of deadly peril."

Catherine, it is as well to state, was at this time beginning to devote herself to the practice of magic and judicial astrology; and, if the memoirs of the time are to be believed, she was rarely deceived by them during the whole course of her life.

But Henry the Second was very incredulous with respect to the stars, and answered the queen with a laugh.

"Why, madame, if my star predicts danger, it will reach me here as well as outside."

"No, sire; it is under the sky and in the open air that danger awaits you," replied Catherine.

"Indeed? a storm, perhaps," said Henry.

"Sire, do not jest about these things," returned the queen. "The stars are the written word of God."

"Perhaps!" said Henry. "Still, you must agree that this divine writing is generally very obscure and confusing."

"How so, sire?"

"The erasures, I think, render the text unintelligible, so that each can read in it what he likes. You have seen, you say, madame, in this celestial parchment that my life is threatened if I leave the Louvre?"

"Yes, sire."

"Well, Forcatel saw something different last month. You esteem Forcatel, I believe, madame?"

"Yes, sire; he is a learned man, who can read where we can only spell."

"Learn, then, madame, that Forcatel has read for me in your stars this fine verse, which has only one defect, that of having no meaning—

"If this is not Mars, dread his image."

"In what does this prediction weaken the one I mention, sire?" asked Catherine.

"Wait, madame; I have my nativity somewhere or other, which was composed last year. Do you remember what it predicts for me?"

"Somewhat indistinctly, sire."

"According to this nativity, madame, it is written that I shall die in a duel—a rare and novel ending for a king, most assuredly. But a duel is not the image of Mars, but Mars himself, in my humble opinion."

"What do you conclude from that, sire?"

"Why, madame, that since all these predictions are contradictory, it is not safe to believe any of them. These lies upset one another, as is plain to be seen."

"And your Majesty will leave the Louvre on these days?" said Catherine.

"In any other circumstances, I should be happy to oblige your Majesty by remaining with you. But I have publicly promised and announced that I should go to these fêtes, and go I must."

"At least, sire, you will not go down into the lists," said Catherine.

"Here again my pledged word obliges me to refuse you, madame. But what danger is there in these sports? I am grateful to you from the bottom of my heart for your solicitude; however, let me assure you that such fears are chimerical, and that for me to give way would be to establish quite a false notion as to the danger of these gay and gentle tournaments, which I should certainly not like to see abolished on my account."

"Sire," returned Catherine, vanquished, "I am accustomed to yield to your wishes. I do so to-day, but with grief and terror in my heart."

"And you will come to Les Tournelles, will you not, madame," said the king, kissing Catherine's hand, "were it only to applaud my skill with the lance and convince yourself of the folly of your fears?"

"I will obey you to the end, sire," said the queen, retiring.

Catherine, with all the court except Madame de Castro, was present at this first tournament, in which the king tilted against all comers.

"Well, madame, you see the stars were wrong," he said with a smile in the evening.

Catherine shook her head sadly.

"Alas! the month of June is not over," she said.

But it was the same on the second day, the 29th; Henry never left the lists, and was as successful as he was daring.

"So the stars were mistaken to-day also, madame," he said to Catherine, as they were returning to the Louvre.

"Ah, sire!" cried Catherine, "I only dread the third day the more."

The last day of the tournament occurred on Friday, the 30th of June, and was to be the most brilliant and magnificent of the three, and bring the fêtes to a worthy close.

The four holders were—

The king, who wore the colors of Madame de Poitiers, white and black; the Duke de Guise, who wore white and crimson; Alfonzo of Este, Duke de Ferrara, who wore yellow and red; Jacques of Savoy, Duke de Nemours, who wore yellow and black.

"These four princes were," says Brantôme, "the four best men-at-arms that could be found, not only in France, but in any other country. So upon that day they did wonders, and none knew to whom to give the palm, although the king was one of the most skilful and excellent cavaliers in his kingdom."

The chances were, in fact, pretty even between these four adroit and renowned holders; and as the day advanced, course followed course, without any one being able to say to whom the honor of the tourney belonged.

Henry the Second was thoroughly excited, and indeed feverish. These sports and passes of arms were his element, and he was perhaps as proud of a victory in them as he would have been of one on a real field of battle.

However, evening was coming on, and the trumpets and clarions sounded the last course.

It was run by M. de Guise, and he accomplished it amid the loud applause of the ladies and the assembled throng.

Then the queen, who now at last breathed freely, arose.

It was the signal of departure.

"What! over?" exclaimed the king, excited and jealous. "Wait, ladies, wait; is it not my turn to run?"

M. de Vieilleville observed to the king that he had been the first to open the lists, that the four holders had furnished an equal number of courses, that the advantage was, it is true, equal, and no one had come off conqueror; but the lists were now closed, and the tournament ended.

"Nonsense!" retorted Henry, impatiently; "if the king is the first to enter, he ought to be the last to leave. I do not wish matters to end thus. And see, yonder are two lances still entire."

"But, sire," said M. de Vieilleville, "there are no assailants."

"Yes," returned the king. "But stay, do you not see that man who has always kept his visor lowered and has not yet run? Who is he, Vieilleville?"

"Sire, I do not know. I did not notice him."

"Ho there, monsieur!" said Henry; "you must break a lance with me, one last lance."

The man did not reply for some time. Then in a deep and grave voice, he said with emotion—

"Your Majesty will allow me to decline the honor."

"Allow you to decline it! No, monsieur; I cannot allow you to do so," he said, with a nervous and angry gesture.

Thereupon the unknown silently raised his visor.

And, for the third time during the fortnight, the king beheld the pale, dejected countenance of Gabriel de Montgommery.

CHAPTER XXV

THE FATAL TOURNEY

A T THE sight of that solemn and gloomy figure, the king felt a shudder of surprise, and perhaps of terror, run through all his veins.

But he did not wish to acknowledge to himself, still less to others, that first tremor, which he at once repressed. His soul reacted against his instinct; and just because he had experienced the sensation of fear for a moment, he showed himself brave and even rash.

Gabriel said a second time, slowly and gravely—

"I beg your Majesty not to insist."

"But I do insist, M. de Montgommery," returned the king.

Henry, whose eyes were dazed by so many contradictory emotions, believed he detected a shade of defiance in the words and tone of Gabriel. Frightened by a return of the strange agitation which Diana de Castro had for a moment banished, he bore up against his weakness and resolved to have done once for all with the cowardly anxieties which he deemed unworthy of a king, of Henry the Second, the child of France.

So he said to Gabriel, with almost exaggerated firmness—

"Make ready, monsieur, to run against me."

Gabriel, whose soul was at least as much disturbed as that of the king, bowed and did not answer.

At that moment, M. de Boissy, the grand equerry, approached, and said that the queen had begged him to entreat his Majesty not to run for the love of her.

"Tell the queen," replied Henry, "that it is precisely for love of her that I am about to run this course."

And, turning to M. de Vieilleville, he said—

"Come, Vieilleville, arm me at once."

In his preoccupation, he was asking M. de Vieilleville to render him a service which belonged to the office of the grand equerry, M. de Boissy.

M. de Vieilleville was surprised at this, and respectfully called the king's attention to it.

"You are right," said the king, striking his forehead. "I must be losing my senses."

He met the cold impassive gaze of Gabriel, and continued impatiently—

"Oh, yes! I know now. M. de Boissy had to return to the queen with my answer. I knew well what I did and said. Do you arm me, M. de Vieilleville."

"That being so, sire," replied M. de Vieilleville, "and since your Majesty absolutely insists on breaking the last lance, allow me to observe that it is my turn to run against you, and I demand my right. In fact, M. de Montgommery was not present at the opening of the lists, and entered only when he believed them closed."

"Very true, monsieur," said Gabriel, quickly; "and I withdraw in your favor."

But in the eagerness of Count de Montgommery to avoid a combat with him, the king persisted obstinately in fancying that he saw the contemptuous efforts of an enemy to impugn his courage and frighten him.

"No, no!" he answered, stamping the ground. "I wish to run against M. de Montgommery, and against no one else this time. We have had enough of delay! Arm me."

He met the grave, fixed look of the count with a proud and haughty glance, and bent his head in order that M. de Vieilleville might helm him.

Clearly his destiny was blinding him.

M. de Savoie then begged him to quit the field, in the name of Queen Catherine.

As the king did not even answer his remonstrances, he added in an undertone—

"Madame de Poitiers, sire, has also asked me to caution you secretly to be on your guard against him with whom you are going to tilt now."

At the name of Diana the king could not help starting; but he controlled himself.

"Is it that I am about to show fear in presence of my lady?" he said to himself.

And he still maintained the haughty silence of one who is importuned to change his mind, but determined not to do so.

M. de Vieilleville, however, while arming him, whispered in turn—

"Sire, I swear by the living God that for the last three nights I have dreamed that some misfortune would happen to you to-day, and that this last day of June would be fatal to you."[1]

But the king paid no attention to him: he was already armed, and seized his lance.

Gabriel took his and entered the lists.

The two combatants mounted their horses and rode to their positions.

There was in the crowd a strange, deep silence. Every eye was intent on the spectacle, and all held their breath.

The constable and Madame de Castro were, however, absent; so none had any idea, with the exception of Madame de Poitiers, that there was between the king and M. de Montgommery any cause of enmity or motive of vengeance. None foresaw that this mock combat was to have a bloody ending. The king, accustomed to these comparatively safe sports, had appeared in the arena a hundred times during the three days, and the conditions were then the same that presented themselves now.

---

[1] Memoirs of Vincent Carloix, secretary of M. de Vieilleville.

And yet in presence of this adversary, enshrouded in mystery until the very end, of his significant refusals to engage in the combat, and of the blind obstinacy of the king, a vague and unusual feeling of terror pervaded the spectators; and before this unknown danger they were silent and expectant. Why? Nobody could tell. But a stranger, arriving at that moment, would have said to himself, on scanning their features, "Some event of supreme importance is about to happen!"

There was terror in the air.

A remarkable circumstance gave an evident sign of the ominous feeling of the crowd.

During the whole time the ordinary courses lasted, the clarions and trumpets never failed to sound their deafening flourishes. They were the triumphant and joyous voice of the tourney, as it were.

But when the king and Gabriel entered the lists, the trumpets were all suddenly silent. Not a single one of them sounded a note; and during this unusual silence the general anxiety and horror redoubled, without any one being able to account for the feeling. The two champions felt even more than the spectators the extraordinary disquietude that seemed, so to speak, to fill the atmosphere.

Gabriel no longer thought, no longer saw, no longer lived, almost. He rode mechanically, and as if in a dream, doing instinctively what he had already done in such circumstances, but guided in some sort by a secret and potent will which assuredly was not his own.

The king was more passive and bewildered still. He had also before his eyes a kind of cloud, and looked as if he was acting and moving in a sort of phantasmagoria which was neither a reality nor a dream.

Sometimes, however, his mind was pierced as by a flash of lightning, and he saw clearly both the predictions the queen had made him aware of two days before, as well as those of his nativity and those of Forcatel. Suddenly, enlightened by some terrible gleam, he understood the sense and relation of those terrible auguries. A cold sweat bathed him from head to foot. For a moment he had decided to renounce the combat and abandon the lists. But, no! those thousands of eager eyes weighed upon him and nailed him to the spot.

Moreover, M. de Vieilleville had just given the signal.

The die was cast. Forward! and let the will of God be done!

The two horses started at a gallop, at that moment more intelligent and less blinded, perhaps, than their heavy riders, barbed in iron.

Gabriel and the king met in the midst of the arena. They advanced and broke their lances without any accident.

The terrible forebodings had, then, been wrong! There was a hoarse murmur of joy from the relieved hearts of the spectators. The queen raised a grateful look to heaven.

But they rejoiced too soon.

The cavaliers, in fact, were still in the lists. After reaching the extremity opposite that by which they had entered, they galloped back to their starting-points, and consequently met a second time.

What danger, however, was to be feared now? They would cross without touching.

But either through anxiety or designedly, or through misfortune—none but God can ever tell the reason—Gabriel, on returning, instead of throwing down the fragment of the lance left in his hand, as was the usage, kept it; and when the king bore down upon him afresh, he drove this fragment clean against Henry's visor.

The visor was broken by the violence of the blow and the fragment entered the king's eye, coming out at the ear.

Only half of the spectators who had risen to leave the lists saw the dreadful blow. But they raised a great cry, which warned the others.

Henry dropped the reins and threw his arms around the neck of his horse, and in this manner galloped round the ring till stopped by De Vieilleville and De Boissy.

"Ah! I am dead!" were the first words of the king. His next were: "Let no one trouble M. de Montgommery! —it is but just— I forgive him." And he fainted.

We will not describe the confusion that followed.

Catherine de Médicis was carried away fainting. The king was immediately borne to his chamber in Les Tournelles, without recovering consciousness even for a moment.

Gabriel dismounted, and remained standing against the barrier, motionless, as if turned to stone, dazed by the blow he had struck.

The last words of the king had been heard and repeated. No one, therefore, dared to interfere with him at the time; but men whispered around him, and looked at him askance with a sort of dread.

Coligny, who was present at the tournament, alone had courage to approach the young man, and, coming close to his left side, said in an undertone—

"This is a terrible accident, my friend! I know well it has been an accident. Our ideas and the discourses you have heard, as I have been told by La Renaudie, in the conventicle at the Place Maubert, have assuredly had nothing to do with this fatality! No matter! Although you can only be accused of an accident, be on your guard. I would advise you to disappear for a time; to leave Paris, and even France. Rely upon me always; *au revoir*."

"Thanks," replied Gabriel, without changing his attitude.

A sad and feeble smile was on his pale lips while the Protestant chief was speaking to him.

Coligny nodded and took his departure.

Some moments after, the Duke de Guise, who had just been making arrangements for the king's removal, advanced toward Gabriel after giving some orders.

He, too, came close to the young count, on his right, and said in his ear—

"A very unfortunate stroke, Gabriel! But you cannot

be blamed; you can only be pitied. But just consider! If any one had heard the conversation between us at Les Tournelles, what frightful conjectures might not the malevolent draw from this simple but very fatal mischance! All the same, I am powerful, and I am devoted to you, as you know. Do not show yourself for some days. But do not leave Paris; it would be useless. If any one dare to accuse you, you remember what I said to you: rely upon me everywhere and always, no matter in what difficulty you may be placed."

"Thanks, monseigneur," said Gabriel, in the same tone, and with the same melancholy smile.

Evidently the Duke de Guise and Coligny had, not a certain conviction, but a vague suspicion, that the accident they pretended to deplore was not quite an accident.

At bottom the Protestant and the ambitious warrior, without wishing to probe the matter too deeply, believed firmly, the latter that Gabriel had, at all risks, seized this opportunity of serving the interests of an admired protector; the former that the fanaticism of the young Huguenot had urged him to free the oppressed from their persecutor.

Both, therefore, believed themselves bound to address some kind words to their discreet and devoted auxiliary; and this was the reason why both approached him in turn, and this was the reason why Gabriel received their double error with that sad smile.

Meanwhile, the Duke de Guise had returned to the excited groups standing around. Gabriel at last looked around him, noticed the dismayed curiosity of which he was the object, sighed, and resolved to remove from the fatal spot.

He returned to his hotel in the Rue des Jardins St. Paul, undisturbed, and even unquestioned.

At Les Tournelles the king's chamber was closed to everybody except the queen, her children, and the surgeons, who had hastened to the aid of the royal sufferer.

When the King bore down upon him afresh, he drove this fragment clean against Henry's visor.

The Two Dianas, II
—p. 222

But Fernel and the other doctors soon saw that there was no longer any hope, and that they could not save Henry the Second.

Ambroise Paré was at Péronne. The Duke de Guise never thought of sending for him.

The king remained four days unconscious.

On the fifth he came to himself, and gave some orders, especially to hurry on the marriage of his sister.

He saw also the queen, and offered her some advice touching his children and the administration of the kingdom.

Then he was seized by fever and delirium, followed by the last agony.

At last, on the 10th of July, 1559, the day after his sister Marguerite, by his express will, had been married, amid tears and sobs, to the Duke of Savoy, Henry the Second expired, his agony having lasted eleven long days. The same day Madame de Castro went, or rather fled, to her old home, the Benedictine convent at St. Quentin, reopened after the peace of Chateau-Cambrésis.

CHAPTER XXVI

A NEW STATE OF AFFAIRS

FOR the favorite of a king, whether male or female, the true death is not death, but disgrace.

The son of Count de Montgommery would have exacted sufficient vengeance for the horrible death of his father from the constable and Diana de Poitiers, if, through his means, the two criminals fell from power into exile, from ostentatious magnificence into oblivion.

It was this result Gabriel was waiting for in the dull and gloomy solitude of his hotel, where he buried himself after the gloomy event of the 30th of June. It was not his own punishment he was in fear of, if Montmorency and his accomplice remained in power, it was their exoneration. And he waited.

During the eleven days of Henry the Second's agony the constable devoted all his exertions to the task of retaining his share in the government. He had written to the princes of the blood, exhorting them to take their place in the councils of the young king. He was especially urgent with Antony de Bourbon, King of Navarre, the nearest heir to the throne after the king's brothers. He recommended him to hasten, as the slightest delay would give strangers a superiority which it would be vain to think of depriving them of afterward. In fine, he sent courier after courier, aroused some, solicited others, and neglected nothing tending to the creation of a party capable of making head against the Guises.

Diana de Poitiers, in spite of her dejection, assisted him

with all her efforts; for her fortune also was attached to
that of her old lover.

In fact, when, on the 10th of July, 1559, the eldest of
Henry's sons was proclaimed king by the herald-at-arms,
under the name of Francis the Second, the young prince
was only sixteen, and, although the law declared that he
had attained his majority, his age, inexperience, and ill
health would condemn him to abandon for several years
the conduct of affairs to a minister who, under his name,
would be more powerful than himself.

Now who should be that minister, or rather that guardian? The Duke de Guise or the constable? Catherine
de Médicis or Antony de Bourbon?

This was the question waiting for an answer the day
after the death of Henry the Second.

On that day Francis the Second was to receive the deputies of the parliament. Whomsoever he should present to
them as his minister might, in all conscience, be hailed
by them as their true king.

Every claimant for the position was therefore on the
alert; and, on the morning of the 12th of July, Catherine
de Médicis and Francis de Lorraine went each separately to
visit the young king, on the pretext of condoling with him,
but in reality to influence him.

The widow of Henry the Second had even infringed for
this important object the etiquette which ordered her to
remain forty days in strict retirement.

Catherine de Médicis, neglected and not allowed any
influence by her husband, had felt during the last twelve
days within her the promptings of that vast and profound
ambition which filled the remainder of her life.

But since she could not be regent of a king who had
reached his majority, her only chance of reigning was
through a minister devoted to her interests.

The Constable de Montmorency could not be that minister; he had not a little contributed during the preceding
reign to deprive her of her legitimate influence, in order

to substitute for it that of Madame de Poitiers. The queen-mother had not forgiven him for his intrigues, and was, on the contrary, thinking of punishing him for his harsh and often barbarous conduct toward her.

Antony de Bourbon would have been a more docile instrument in her hands. But he belonged to the Reformed religion; and his wife, Jeanne d'Albret, was an ambitious woman also. Finally, his title of prince of the blood, joined to his actual power, might inspire him with dangerous aspirations.

Remained the Duke de Guise. But would Francis de Lorraine recognize with a good grace the moral authority of the queen-mother, or would he refuse her a share of his authority?

This was the point on which Catherine de Médicis would like to be assured. So she joyfully accepted the interview in presence of the king, which chance procured her on this decisive day between herself and Francis de Lorraine.

She would find or create opportunities of testing the Balafré and sounding his disposition in her regard.

But the Duke de Guise, on his side, was as able a politician as warrior, and he was carefully on his guard.

This prologue before the play took place at the Louvre, in the royal chamber in which Francis the Second had been installed the evening before, and had for actors only the queen-mother, the Balafré, the young king, and Mary Stuart.

Francis and his youthful queen, in presence of the cold and selfish ambitions of Catherine and the Duke de Guise, were but two charming children, artless and in love, whose confidence would belong to the first comer adroit enough to win their hearts.

They wept sincerely for the death of the king their father, and Catherine found them very sad and depressed.

"My son," said she to Francis, "it is well you should give tears to the memory of him whom you, above all,

ought to mourn. You know how deeply I share this bitter sorrow. However, you must consider that you have
not only the duties of a son to fulfil; you are a father
also, the father of your people. After granting the due
tribute of regret to the past, turn to the future. Remember you are a king, my son, or rather your Majesty, to
conform to a style of language which recalls your obligations and your rights."

"Alas, madame!" replied Francis the Second, "the
sceptre of France is a very heavy burden for the hands
of sixteen years to carry, and nothing had prepared me to
think that such a heavy weight was so soon to overwhelm
my inexperienced and inconsiderate youth."

"Sire," returned Catherine, "accept with resignation and
gratitude the charge which God imposes upon you; it will
be for those who surround you and love you to do their best
to lighten it, and to unite their efforts with yours in order
that you may support it worthily."

"Madame, I thank you," answered the young king, not
knowing what reply to make to these advances.

And he turned his eyes mechanically to the Duke de
Guise, as if to seek counsel from his wife's uncle. At his
first step in royalty, and even in his mother's presence,
the poor crowned boy was already feeling instinctively the
snares that lay in his path.

Then the Duke de Guise said without any hesitation—

"Yes, sire, your Majesty is right; thank, thank heartily
the queen for her good and encouraging words. But do not
content yourself with thanking her. Tell her boldly that,
among those whom you love and who love you, she holds
the first rank; and that, therefore, you have a right to count
on her effective maternal aid in the difficult task you have
been called upon to accomplish at such an early age."

"My uncle of Guise has been the faithful interpreter of
my thoughts, madame," said the young king, who was
quite delighted, to his mother; "and if, from fear of weakening them, I do not repeat his words, regard them, how-

ever, as said by myself, madame, and dearly loved mother, and deign to promise your precious support to my weakness.''

The queen-mother flashed on the Duke de Guise a glance of good-will and assent.

"Sire," she replied, "the little intelligence I possess is yours, and I shall be happy and proud every time you consult me. But I am only a woman, and you require a defender beside your throne who can wield a sword. The strong arm and virile energy needed, your Majesty will doubtless find among those whom alliance and kinship render your natural support."

So Catherine paid immediately her debt to the Duke de Guise for his friendly intervention.

There was between them a mutual compact ratified by a single glance, but which, it must be confessed, was not sincere on one side or the other, nor lasting either, as we shall soon see.

The young king understood his mother, and, encouraged by a look from Mary, offered his hand timidly to the Balafré.

With that grasp of the hand he made over to him the government of France.

Nevertheless, Catherine was disinclined to allow her son to pledge himself too soon, until at least the Duke de Guise had given her assured pledges of his good-will.

She therefore anticipated the young king, who was probably about to confirm by some formal promise his expression of confidence, and was the first to speak.

"In any case, before you have a minister, sire," said she, "your mother has, not a favor to ask of you, but a demand to make."

"Say rather an order to give me, madame," said Francis the Second. "Speak, I pray you."

"Well, then, my son!" returned Catherine, "there is question of a woman who has done me much evil, but France still more. It is not for us to blame the weaknesses of him who is now more sacred to us than ever. But your father is unfortunately no more, sire; it is not his will that rules in this chateau, and yet this woman, whom I do not wish even to name, dares to stay here still and inflict on me the insult of her presence to the end. During the long unconsciousness of the king, she was already told that it was not proper for her to remain at the Louvre. 'Is the king dead?' she asked. 'No; he still breathes.' 'Well, none but him has a right to give me an order.' And she has impudently remained."

The Duke de Guise respectfully interrupted the queen-mother, and hastened to say—

"Excuse me, madame; but I think I know his Majesty's intentions on the subject to which you allude."

And without further preliminary he struck a bell. A servant appeared.

"Inform Madame de Poitiers," he said, "that the king would speak with her at once."

The servant bowed, and retired to fulfil the order.

The young king did not appear at all astonished or disturbed at seeing his authority thus wrested from his hands without his permission. The fact was he was enchanted with everything that could lessen his responsibility and save him the trouble of ordering and acting.

Nevertheless, the Balafré wished to give the sanction of the royal consent to this step.

"I believe I am not presuming, sire," he resumed, "when I say that I know your Majesty's wishes in this connection?"

"Certainly not, dear uncle," answered Francis, eagerly. "Do as you like. I know in advance that what you do will be well done."

"And whatever you say is well said, darling," whispered Mary Stuart in his ear.

Francis blushed with satisfaction and pride. For a word, a look of admiration from his adored Mary, he would, to tell the truth, have compromised and bartered all the kingdoms in the world.

The queen-mother awaited with impatient curiosity the result of the Duke de Guise's action.

She thought it well to add, however, as much to fill up the silence as to mark her intention more emphatically—

"She whom you have summoned, sire, may well, it seems to me, abandon the Louvre to the only legitimate queen of the past, as well as to the charming queen of the present," she added, with a gracious bow to Mary Stuart. "Has not this fair and opulent dame for her refuge and consolation her magnificent royal chateau of Anet, more royal and magnificent, certainly, than my poor house of Chaumont-sur-Loire?"

The Duke de Guise did not answer, but he noted this hint in his mind.

He detested Diana de Poitiers, it must be confessed, quite as much as did Catherine de Médicis. It was Madame de Valentinois who, until now, had baffled with all her power the fortunes and the plans of the Balafré; it was she who would undoubtedly have relegated him to obscurity, if the lance of Gabriel had not destroyed, with the life of Henry the Second, the authority of the enchantress.

But the day of revenge had come at last for Francis de Lorraine, and he knew as well how to hate as to love.

At this moment, the usher announced with a loud voice—

"Madame la Duchesse de Valentinois."

Diana de Poitiers entered, evidently disturbed, but haughty withal.

CHAPTER XXVII

THE CONSEQUENCES OF GABRIEL'S VENGEANCE

MADAME DE VALENTINOIS bowed slightly to the young king, still more slightly to Catherine de Médicis and Mary Stuart, and did not seem to notice even the presence of the Duke de Guise.

"Sire," said she, "your Majesty has ordered me to appear before you—"

She paused. Francis the Second, at once irritated and embarrassed by the haughty demeanor of the ex-favorite, hesitated, blushed, and ended by saying—

"Our uncle of Guise has been good enough to undertake to make known our intentions to you, madame."

And he began to converse in an undertone with Mary Stuart.

Diana turned slowly to the Balafré, and, seeing the sly, mocking smile that was flickering on his lips, she tried to confront him with one of her most imperious, Juno-like glances, when Juno is wrathful.

But the Balafré was much less easy to intimidate than his royal nephew.

"Madame," said he to Diana, with a profound inclination, "the king has known the sincere sorrow caused you by the terrible misfortune which has stricken us all. He thanks you. His Majesty believes he will meet your dearest desire by permitting you to quit the court for some place of retirement. You can set out as soon as you judge it suitable; this evening, for example."

Diana kept back the tears of rage in her inflamed eyes.

"His Majesty in this gratifies my fondest wish," she replied. "What could I do here now? I have nothing so much at heart as to withdraw into my exile, monsieur, as speedily as possible. Do not be alarmed!"

"Everything, then, is for the best," said the Duke de Guise, playing with the tassels of his velvet mantle. "But, madame," said he, seriously, at the same time giving to his words the tone and significance of an order, "your chateau of Anet, which you obtained from the goodness of the late king, is perhaps too worldly a retreat, too open and gay for an afflicted recluse like yourself. Now her Majesty, Queen Catherine, offers you in exchange for it her chateau of Chaumont-sur-Loire, further from Paris and, therefore, more in harmony with your tastes and wants at present, I presume. It will be placed at your disposal as soon as you desire."

Madame de Poitiers well understood that this pretended exchange disguised an arbitrary confiscation. But what could she do? How could she resist? She had no longer either influence or power. All her friends of yesterday were her enemies to-day. It was necessary to yield, although she was furious. She yielded.

"I shall be happy," she said hoarsely, "to offer to the queen the magnificent domain I received from the generosity of her noble husband."

"I accept the reparation, madame," retorted Catherine, dryly, casting on Diana an icy look, and a grateful one upon the Duke de Guise.

It seemed as if it was he who was making her a present of Anet.

"The chateau of Chaumont-sur-Loire is yours, madame, and shall be placed in a state of readiness for the reception of its new proprietor at once.

"And there," resumed the Duke de Guise, opposing the fierce glances with which Diana was trying to wither him by a little innocent raillery—"and there, madame, you can tranquilly repose at your leisure after the fatigue caused you, I have been told, by your frequent correspondence, and by the interviews held by you, in concert with M. de Montmorency, during these last days—"

"I did not think," returned Diana, "I was serving badly him who was then king by conferring with the great statesman and soldier of his reign on matters connected with the welfare of the realm."

But in her eagerness to parry one sarcasm by another, Madame de Poitiers forgot that she was furnishing arms against herself, and recalling to the rancor of Catherine de Médicis the queen-mother's other enemy, the constable.

"It is true," said the implacable Florentine, "M. de Montmorency has filled with his glory and his works two entire reigns! and it is quite time, my son," she added, addressing the young king, "that you should assure to him the honorable retreat he has so laboriously earned."

"M. de Montmorency," returned Diana, bitterly, "expects, like me, this recompense for his long services! He was with me just now when his Majesty commanded my presence. He must be there now; I will join him and inform him of the kindly arrangements made in his regard. He will immediately present his thanks to his sovereign at the same time he takes leave of him. And he is a man, too; he is constable; he is one of the most puissant lords of the realm! Doubtless he will, sooner or later, prove better than by words his deep gratitude to a king so mindful of the past, and to the new advisers who co-operate so usefully for the advancement of those public interests which he wishes to see benefited."

"A threat!" said the Balafré to himself. "The viper, although crushed under the heel, shows signs of life. So much the better. I prefer that."

"The king is always ready to receive M. le Connétable," returned the queen-mother, pale with anger. "And if he has protests or observations to address to his Majesty, he can appear and do so. He will be listened to, and, as you say, madame, will have justice."

"I will send him," replied Madame de Poitiers, with an air of defiance.

She made her usual stately salutation to the king and two queens, and withdrew, with head erect, but with a heart that was broken, pride on her face and death in her soul.

If Gabriel could have seen her, he would have thought himself fully avenged.

Catherine de Médicis herself was satisfied with this humiliation, and did not persecute Diana further.

But the queen-mother had remarked with uneasiness that at the name of the constable the Duke de Guise was silent and did not again respond to the insolent challenge of Madame de Poitiers.

Was the Balafré afraid, then, of Montmorency, and did he intend to chaffer with him? Would he, if he thought it his interest, conclude an alliance with Catherine's old enemy?

It was important for the Florentine to know what she had to expect in this regard before she allowed the power to fall into the hands of Francis de Lorraine without an effort.

Then, to sound him and also to sound the king, she resumed, after the departure of Diana—

"Madame de Poitiers is very impertinent, and seems to place great confidence in her constable! In fact, it is certain, my son, that if you give M. de Montmorency any authority, he will share it with Madame Diana."

The Duke de Guise still kept silent.

"As for myself," pursued Catherine, "if I may offer an opinion to your Majesty, it is that you ought not to share your confidence among many, but select a single minister, whether that minister be M. de Montmorency or your uncle of Guise or your uncle of Bourbon. But it should be one or the other, and not all. There should be only one single will in the state, along with that of the king counselled by the small number of persons who have no interest but that of his prosperity and glory. Is that not your opinion, M. de Guise?"

"Yes, madame, if it is yours," replied the Duke de Guise, with an air of condescension.

"Ha! I guessed as much," said Catherine to herself. "He was thinking of winning the constable's support. But he must decide between him and me, and I don't believe there is any longer room for hesitation."

"It seems to me, M. de Guise," she continued aloud, "that you ought to share my opinion, so much the more that it is to your advantage; for, as the king well knows, it is neither the Constable de Montmorency nor Antony de Navarre whom I should like him to select as his adviser, and when I pronounce in favor of exclusion, it is not you whom I exclude."

"Madame," returned the duke, "believe that my deep and grateful devotion to you is not less exclusive."

The cunning politician emphasized these last words as if he had finally come to a resolution and sacrificed the constable to Catherine for good and all.

"Nothing could be better!" said Catherine. "When our parliamentary friends arrive, it is well that they should find among us this rare and touching unanimity of ideas and sentiments."

"It is I especially who rejoice at this harmony," cried the young king, clapping his hands. "With my mother as adviser and my uncle as minister, I am beginning to be reconciled to this royalty which frightened me so much at first."

"We will reign as one family," said Mary Stuart, gayly.

Catherine de Médicis and Francis de Lorraine smiled at the hopes, or rather illusions, of their young sovereigns. Both had for the moment what they desired—he, the certainty that the queen-mother would make no attempt to prevent the supreme authority from being invested in him; she, the belief that the minister would share this authority with her.

However, M. de Montmorency was announced. The constable, it must be admitted, was at first more dignified and calm than had been Diana de Poitiers. Undoubtedly he had been informed by her of the state of affairs, and was determined to fall with honor.

He bowed respectfully to Francis the Second, and was the first to speak.

"Sire," said he, "I suspected in advance that your father's and grandfather's old servant would enjoy but little favor with you. I do not complain of this sudden change of fortune, which I had anticipated. I retire without a murmur. If the King of France ever needs me, I shall be found at Chantilly, sire; and my goods, my children, as well as my life—all that I possess—will always be at your Majesty's service."

This moderation seemed to touch the young king, who, more embarrassed than ever, turned toward his mother in a kind of distress.

But the Duke de Guise, well knowing that any interference on his part would change the moderation of the old constable into anger, thereupon said, with affected and excessive politeness—

"Since M. de Montmorency is about to leave the court, he would do well, I fancy, before his departure, to hand over to his Majesty the royal seal confided to him by the late king, and of which we have need from to-day."

The Balafré was not disappointed. These simple words excited to the highest degree the ire of the jealous constable.

"Here is the seal!" said he, drawing it from his doublet. "I was about to surrender it to his Majesty without being asked; but his Majesty, I see, is surrounded by persons disposed to advise him to affront those who have a right to his gratitude."

"Of whom does M de Montmorency speak?" demanded Catherine, haughtily.

"Eh? I have spoken of those who surround his Maj-

esty, madame," retorted the constable, resuming his natural
peevishness and brutality.

But he had chosen his time badly, and Catherine was
only waiting for an opportunity to burst out.

She arose, and, losing all self-restraint, began reproaching the constable with the rough and scornful treatment she
had always met at his hands, his hostility to everything
Florentine, the preference he had publicly given to the mistress over the legitimate wife. She was not unaware that to
him were due all the humiliations suffered by the emigrants
who had followed her. She knew that, during the first
years of her marriage, Montmorency had dared to propose
to Henry the Second to repudiate her as barren; that afterward he had basely calumniated her.

Upon this, the constable, in a fury, for he was but little
accustomed to reproaches, replied by a sneering laugh which
was a fresh insult.

Meanwhile, the Duke de Guise had time to receive his
orders, given in a low tone, from Francis the Second, or
rather to dictate these orders; and, quietly raising his voice,
he overwhelmmed his rival, to the great satisfaction of
Catherine.

"M. le Connétable," said he, with his sarcastic politeness, "your friends and creatures who sat with you in the
council, Bochetel, L'Aubespine, and the others, notably his
Eminence the Keeper of the Seals, Jean Bertrandi, would
probably wish to imitate you in your desire for retirement.
The king charges you to thank them in his name. To-
morrow they will be entirely at liberty and their places
filled."

"It is well!" murmured Montmorency, between his
teeth.

"As to M. de Coligny, your nephew, who is at the
same time Governor of Picardy and the Ile-de-France,"
continued the Balafré, "the king considers that such a
double task is too heavy for one man, and is kind enough
to relieve M. l'Amiral from whichever of the governments

he chooses. You will have the goodness, will you not, to inform him of the fact?"

"As you wish!" returned the constable, with a snarl.

"As for yourself," continued the Duke de Guise, smoothly, "M. le Connétable—"

"Do you want also to take from me the constable's baton?" interrupted M. de Montmorency, bitterly.

"Oh," returned Francis de Lorraine, "you know well that is impossible, and that the office of constable does not resemble that of Lieutenant-General of the Kingdom; it is irrevocable. But is it not incompatible with that of grand master, with which you are equally invested? Such is the opinion of his Majesty, who desires you to resign this last charge, monsieur, and deigns to grant it to me, as I have no other."

"Better and better!" rejoined Montmorency, grinding his teeth. "Is that all, monsieur?"

"Yes, I think so," answered the Duke de Guise, taking his seat.

The constable felt it would be difficult to restrain his rage longer; that it would burst forth, perhaps, in spite of him; that he might speak disrespectfully to the king, and from a disgraced favorite become a rebel. He would not give this joy to his triumphant enemy. After an abrupt salutation to the king he was about to take his leave.

Then a thought seemed to strike him as he was passing out—

"Sire," said he to the young king, "only one last word, only one last duty to be fulfilled to the memory of your glorious father. He who dealt him a mortal blow, the author of the desolation of us all, has not, perhaps, been merely clumsy and thoughtless; I have at least ground for believing so, sire. In this fatal accident there has been, in my opinion, a criminal intention. The man whom I accuse believed, as I know, that he was injured by the king. Your Majesty will, I have no doubt, order a strict inquiry into the matter."

The Duke de Guise shuddered at this formal and dangerous accusation against Gabriel. But this time Catherine de Médicis charged herself with the duty of replying.

"Learn, monsieur," said she to the constable, "that your interference was not needed for the purpose of calling the attention of those to this deed to whom the royal existence so cruelly cut short was not less precious than to you. I, the widow of Henry the Second, cannot allow any person in the world to assume the initiative in such a task. Be tranquil, therefore, monsieur, you have been forestalled in your solicitude. You can retire without allowing yourself to be disturbed on this point."

"I have nothing to add, then," said the constable.

He was not allowed even to satisfy personally his bitter rancor against Count de Montgommery, and to pose as the denouncer of the culprit and the avenger of his master.

Suffocated with shame and anger, he withdrew in despair.

He started the same evening for his domain of Chantilly. On that day Madame de Valentinois also quitted the Louvre, where she had been more of a sovereign than the queen, for her gloomy and distant exile of Chaumont-sur-Loire. She never left it till her death.

As far as Diana de Poitiers was concerned, then, the vengeance of Gabriel was accomplished.

It is true that the ex-favorite was reserving a terrible retaliation for him who had hurled her from her greatness.

As for the constable, Gabriel had not done with him, and was to encounter him again on the day when he had regained his influence.

But let us not anticipate events, but hasten to the Louvre, where the deputies of the parliament have just been announced to Francis the Second.

CHAPTER XXVIII

CHANGE OF TEMPERATURE

IN ACCORDANCE with the aspiration expressed by Catherine de Médicis, the delegates from the parliament found the most perfect concord at the Louvre. Francis the Second, having his wife on his right hand and his mother on his left, presented the Duke de Guise to them as Lieutenant-General of the Kingdom, the Cardinal de Lorraine as superintendent of finance, and Francis Olivier as keeper of the seals. The Balafré was triumphant, the queen-mother smiled on his triumph, and everything was for the best. And no symptom of a misunderstanding seemed to trouble the fortunate beginnings of a reign that promised to be equally long and happy.

One of the councillors of the parliament doubtless thought that an idea of clemency would not be unwelcome amid all this happiness, and, when passing before the king, cried from the centre of a group—

"Mercy for Anne Dubourg!"

But this councillor forgot what a zealous Catholic the new minister was. The Balafré, according to his custom, feigned not to have heard correctly, and, without consulting either the king or queen-mother, he was so sure of their assent, he answered in a loud, firm voice—

"Yes, gentlemen, yes; the trial of Anne Dubourg and those accused along with him will be attended to and speedily terminated, rest assured!"

After which assurance the members of the parliament left the Louvre, pleased or downcast according to their several opinions, but all persuaded that never had their rulers been more united and better pleased with one another than were those they had just saluted.

And indeed, after their departure, the Duke de Guise saw still on the lips of Catherine de Médicis the smile which, every time she regarded him, seemed to be stereotyped there.

As for Francis the Second, he rose from his seat, utterly worn out with the protracted ceremonies he had gone through.

"We are at last free for to-day from all this business and formality," said he. "Could we not, mother and uncle, leave Paris for a time and spend the time of our mourning at Blois, for example, on the banks of that Loire which Mary loves so much? Say, could we not?"

"Oh, try and see if it can be managed!" added Mary Stuart. "Paris is so tiresome during these lovely summer days, and the country is so gay."

"M. de Guise will see to that," said Catherine de Médicis. "But to-day, my son, your task is not yet quite finished. Before letting you rest, I must ask you to give me an additional half-hour of your time, in order that you may fulfil a sacred duty."

"What is it, mother?" asked Francis.

"A duty incumbent on you as justiciary of the realm, sire," said Catherine—"a duty in which M. le Connétable imagined he had forestalled me. But the justice of a wife is prompter than that of a friend."

"What does she mean?" asked the Duke de Guise of himself in alarm.

"Sire," continued Catherine, "your august father has died a violent death. Is the man who struck him only unfortunate, or is he guilty? As for myself, I lean to the latter supposition. But in any case, the question, it seems to me, is worth the trouble of being examined. If we accept such an attack with indifference, without even taking the trouble of asking whether it was voluntary or not, what dangers must not all kings adventure, and you among the first, sire? An inquiry into what is styled the accident of the 30th of June is therefore necessary."

"But in that case," said the Balafré, "it would be necessary, in your opinion, to have M. de Montgommery immediately arrested on a charge of regicide?"

"M. de Montgommery has been arrested this morning," said Catherine.

"Arrested! and by whose order?" cried the Duke de Guise.

"On mine," returned the queen-mother. "No authority was yet constituted. I took this responsibility upon myself. M. de Montgommery might have taken flight at any moment, it was necessary to prevent him. He has been conducted to the Louvre without noise and without scandal. I insist, my son, that you question him."

Without waiting for permission, she struck a bell, as the Duke de Guise had done two hours before.

But this time the Balafré frowned. The storm was preparing.

"Bring in the prisoner," said Catherine when the usher appeared.

There was then an embarrassed silence. The king seemed undecided, Mary Stuart restless, the Duke de Guise dissatisfied.

The queen-mother alone affected an air of dignity and assurance.

The Duke de Guise merely uttered this simple remark—

"I think, if M. de Montgommery wanted to escape, he could easily have done so during the last fortnight."

Catherine had not time to answer, for at this moment Gabriel was led in.

He was pale, but calm. Early that morning, four armed men had come for him at his hotel, to the great dismay of Aloyse; he followed them without resistance, and since then was composedly awaiting what might happen.

When Gabriel entered with a firm step and tranquil de

meanor, the young king changed color, either from emotion at the sight of him who had slain his father, or terror at the thought of having to fulfil for the first time the office of justiciary of which his mother had just spoken—the most terrible of all the duties which the Lord has imposed on kings.

So it was in a voice that could scarcely be heard that he said to Catherine—

"Speak, madame; it is for you to speak."

Catherine availed herself of the permission immediately. She now believed that her influence with the king and the minister was all-powerful. She addressed, therefore, Gabriel in a haughty and authoritative tone—

"Monsieur," she said to him, "we have wished, before making any formal charge, to summon you to his Majesty's presence, and question you with our own lips, in order that there might be no necessity for offering you a reparation, if you are declared innocent, and that justice may be speedily rendered if you are found guilty. Extraordinary crimes demand extraordinary judges. Are you ready to answer, monsieur?"

"I am ready to hear you, madame," replied Gabriel.

Catherine was more irritated than persuaded by the composure of a man whom she had hated before he made her a widow, hated with the strength of all the love she had for a moment felt for him.

She continued, then, with offensive bitterness—

"Certain singular circumstances, monsieur, rise up against you and accuse you: your long absences from Paris; your voluntary exile from the court for nearly two years; your mysterious presence and attitude at the fatal tournament, even your refusal to enter the lists against the king. How came it that you, accustomed to these sports and passages at arms, omitted the ordinary and necessary precaution of throwing down the fragment of your lance when returning to meet the king? How do you explain this strange forgetfulness? Answer, then. What have you to say to all this?"

"Nothing, madame," replied Gabriel.

"Nothing!" exclaimed the queen-mother, astonished.

"Absolutely nothing."

"What! you confess? you acknowledge—?"

"I confess, I acknowledge nothing."

"Then you deny?"

"I deny nothing. I am silent."

Mary Stuart made a slight gesture of approval; Francis the Second listened and looked on eagerly; the Duke de Guise was mute and impassive.

Catherine went on, in a tone of increasing bitterness—

"Monsieur, beware! You would do better to try to defend and justify yourself: M. de Montmorency, who, if necessary, can be called as a witness, affirms that he is aware you had certain causes of complaint against the king—motives of personal animosity."

"What are they, madame?" said Gabriel. "Has he mentioned them?"

"Not yet; but doubtless he will do so."

"Well, let him mention them, if he dare!" answered Gabriel, with a proud and tranquil smile.

"So you refuse to speak?" insisted Catherine.

"I refuse."

"Do you not know that torture may get the better of your scornful silence?"

"I do not think so, madame."

"By acting as you do, you risk your life, I warn you."

"I will not defend it, madame; it is no longer worth the trouble."

"You have fully decided, monsieur? Not a word?"

"Not a word, madame," said Gabriel, shaking his head.

"You are right!" exclaimed Mary Stuart, as if carried away by an irresistible impulse. "This silence is noble and grand! it is the silence of a gentleman who disdains to repel suspicion because he does not imagine that suspicion can touch him. I say that this silence is the most eloquent of justifications!"

However, the old queen regarded the young one with a severe and wrathful countenance.

"Yes," resumed Mary Stuart; "it may be wrong to speak thus. So much the worse! I say what I think and feel. My heart will never allow my lips to be silent. My impressions and emotions must have a free course. My instinct is my policy. Now, that instinct cries to me that M. d'Exmès is incapable of the voluntary conception or execution of such a crime in cold blood; that he has been only the blind instrument of fatality; that he believes himself above any contrary supposition, and scorns to justify himself. This is what my instinct tells me, and I proclaim it aloud. Why not?"

The king gazed with love and delight on his *mignonne*, as he was in the habit of calling her; her eloquence charmed him, and her animation made her twenty times lovelier than usual.

As for Gabriel, he cried, in a voice deepened by emotion—

"Oh, thanks, madame! I thank you! And you do well, not for my sake, but for yours, to act thus."

"Ah! I know that!" returned Mary, with the most gracious accent conceivable.

"Well! have we done with these sentimental puerilities?" exclaimed the incensed Catherine.

"No, madame," retorted Mary, wounded in her self-esteem as a young wife and a young queen; "no! if you have done with these puerilities, we, who are young, thank God! we are only beginning. Is it not so, my gentle sire?" she added, turning lovingly to her husband.

The king did not answer, but touched with his lips the rosy fingers that were held out to him.

The anger of Catherine, until now restrained, burst forth. She had not been yet accustomed to treat as a king a son who was almost a child. Moreover, she be-

lieved herself strong in the support of the Duke de Guise,
who had not spoken, and who she did not know was a devoted protector, and, so to speak, a tacit accomplice of the
Count de Montgommery. She ventured, therefore, to give
free rein to her anger.

"Ah! so this is the situation!" she said, in a tone of
delicate sarcasm, to Mary. "I claim a right, and I am
derided. I demand, in all moderation, that the slayer of
Henry the Second be at least interrogated, and, when he
refuses to answer, his silence is approved, nay, applauded.
Well, since so matters stand, away with all cowardly reservations and half-measures! I proclaim myself, aloud, the
accuser of Count de Montgommery. Will the king refuse
justice to his mother, because she is his mother? The constable shall be heard, if need be, and Madame de Poitiers
also! The truth shall be shown; and if state secrets be
compromised in the affair, we will have a secret trial and
a secret condemnation. But the death of a king traitorously
assassinated in the presence of his people shall at least be
avenged."

During this outburst of the queen-mother, a sad and
resigned smile played on the lips of Gabriel.

He recalled the last two verses of the prediction of
Nostradamus:

> Enfin, l'aimera, puis las! le tuera
> Dame du roy.

Well! the prediction, correct so far, was to be fulfilled
to the end! Catherine would have him whom she had
loved, condemned and executed! Gabriel was expecting
as much; Gabriel was ready.

However, the Florentine, judging that pernaps she had
gone too far, paused a moment, and, turning in her most
gracious fashion to the Duke de Guise, who had never
spoken, she said—

"Have you nothing to say, M. de Guise? You are, of
course, of my opinion?"

"No, madame," returned the Balafré, slowly; "no, I am not of your opinion, I confess; and that is the reason I have said nothing."

"Ah! you too! you are against me!" rejoined Catherine, in a hoarse and menacing tone.

"I regret very much that such should be the case, madame," said the Duke de Guise. "You see that until now I have been with you, and have entered into your views in all that concerned the constable and Madame de Valentinois."

"Yes, because they were of service to yours," murmured Catherine. "I see it now when too late."

"But as to M. de Montgommery," tranquilly continued the Balafré, "I cannot conscientiously share your feelings. It seems to me impossible to render a brave and loyal gentleman responsible for an action that was quite fortuitous. A trial would be for him a triumph, and would cover his accusers with confusion. And as to the perils to which kings might be exposed, according to you, madame, by the exercise of a forbearance that prefers to believe in a misfortune rather than in a crime, I think, on the contrary, the danger would be to accustom the people to the idea that the lives of sovereigns are not as sacred and invulnerable in their eyes as they suppose—"

"These are lofty political maxims, no doubt," returned Catherine, with acrimony.

"I esteem them at least true and sensible, madame," added the Balafré; "and for all these reasons and others besides, I am of the opinion that what we have to do is to apologize to M. de Montgommery for his arbitrary arrest, which, fortunately, is a secret—fortunately for us as well as for him! and these apologies accepted, we shall have but to dismiss him, free, honorable and honored, as he was yesterday, as he will be to-morrow, and always. I have spoken."

"With marvellous force," sneered Catherine, and, addressing the young king abruptly, she demanded—

"Is this opinion also yours, my son?"

The attitude of Mary Stuart, who thanked the duke with a smile and a look, made it impossible for Francis the Second to hesitate.

"Yes, mother; the opinion of M. de Guise is also mine," said he.

"So you betray the memory of your father?" rejoined Catherine, in a deep and trembling voice.

"On the contrary, I respect it, madame," said Francis the Second. "Were not the first words of my father, after he was wounded, to the effect that M. de Montgommery should not be molested? And during his last agony did he not, in his lucid moments, reiterate this request, or rather this order? Madame, permit his son to obey him."

"And, in the meantime, you despise the sacred will of your mother!"

"Madame," said the Duke de Guise, "let me remind you of your own words, 'One single will in the State!'"

"But I have said, monsieur, that that of the minister should come after that of the king," cried Catherine.

"Yes, madame," returned Mary Stuart; "but you added that the will of the king should be enlightened by those whose sole interest was evidently that of his prosperity and glory. Now I presume no person has greater interest in his prosperity and glory than his wife. And I counsel him, as my uncle of Guise has done, to believe rather in the loyalty than in the perfidy of a tried and valiant subject, and not to inaugurate his reign by an injustice."

"And these are the suggestions which you obey, my son!" said Catherine.

"I obey the suggestions of my conscience, mother," replied the young king, with more firmness than might have been expected from him.

"Is this your last word, Francis?" returned Catherine. "Take care! If you refuse your mother the first request she addresses to you, if you are going to be an independent master for her and a docile instrument for others, you may reign alone with or without your faithful ministers! I will no longer busy myself with anything in connection with king or kingdom; I will withdraw from you the advantage of my experience and devotion; I will retire into my solitude, and abandon you, my son. Think well on this! think well on it!"

"We should deplore your retirement, but would manage to be resigned to the calamity," murmured Mary Stuart, in a low voice, heard by Francis alone.

But the fond and imprudent lover, like a faithful echo, repeated aloud—

"We should deplore your retirement, but would be resigned to it, madame."

"It is well!" was Catherine's only answer. And she added, in a low voice, pointing to Gabriel, "As for him, I shall find him again sooner or later."

"I know it, madame," replied the young man, who was still thinking of the prediction.

But Catherine did not hear him.

Filled with fury, she darted an ominous and terrible glance at the royal and charming young couple as well as at the Duke de Guise—a baleful glance, that foretold all the crimes that were to be the fruit of Catherine's ambition and all the sombre history of the last Valois kings!

After this withering look, she passed out without uttering a word.

CHAPTER XXIX

GUISE AND COLIGNY

AFTER the departure of Catherine there was a moment's silence. The young king appeared astonished at his own boldness. Mary, with the subtle intuition that love gives, dwelt, with some degree of terror, on the last menacing look of the queen-mother. But the Duke de Guise was secretly delighted at being rid in the first hour of his power of an ambitious and dangerous associate.

Gabriel, the cause of all the trouble, was the first to speak.

"Sire," said he, "and you, madame, and you also, monseigneur, I thank you for your kind and generous intentions with regard to an unhappy man whom even Heaven abandons. But, despite the profound gratitude with which my heart is filled, I must say that it is of little use to rescue from danger and death a life as sad and hopeless as mine—a life that is no longer of value to anybody, not even to myself. Surely I would not have entered into a contest for it with Madame Catherine, because it is henceforth worthless." He added sadly, in his own mind, "And because some day it may become a bane to others."

"Gabriel," returned the Duke de Guise, "your life has been a glorious and useful one in the past, and will be glorious and useful in the future. You are one of those energetic men so much needed by those who govern empires, and so rarely found by them."

"And, moreover," added the sweet, consoling voice of

Mary Stuart, "you have a noble heart, M. de Montgommery—a grand and noble heart. I have known you long, and Madame de Castro and I have often talked about you."

"In fine," said Francis the Second, "your previous services, monsieur, authorize me to reckon on your future services. The wars that have for a time ceased may break out again, and I do not wish that a moment of despair, whatever be its cause, should deprive the country of a defender as loyal and as valiant as you."

Gabriel heard these words of encouragement and hope with a sort of grave and melancholy surprise. He regarded in turn the lofty personages who addressed him, and seemed to be reflecting deeply.

"Well!" he answered, at last, "the unexpected kindness shown by you all to me, whom perhaps you ought to hate, has changed my heart and my destiny. To you, sire, to you, madame and monseigneur, shall be devoted the life which is, so to speak, your gift. I was not born wicked! Your good-will reaches to the bottom of my soul. I was made for devotion, for sacrifice—made to be the instrument of great ideas and great men. An instrument sometimes fortunate, sometimes fatal! Alas! God in His anger has proved this only too well! But let us not speak of the dismal past, since you deign to believe that I have still a future. This future, however, belongs not to me, but to you. To admire what you admire, and believe what you believe, is now my lot. I abdicate my own will. Let the beings and objects in which I have faith do with me whatever they please. My sword, my blood, my death—all that I have is theirs. I dedicate without reserve, without ever looking back, my arm to your genius, monseigneur, as I give my soul to religion."

He did not say which religion. But those who heard him were too devout Catholics for any thought of the Reformed religion to enter their minds for a moment.

The eloquent abnegation of the young count touched

them. Mary had tears in her eyes; the king congratulated himself on a firmness that had saved such a grateful heart. As to the Duke de Guise, he knew better than any one to what lengths this ardent virtue of sacrifice would lead Gabriel.

"Yes," said he, "my friend, I shall have need of you. I shall claim some day, in the name of France and the king, that brave sword you promise us now."

"It shall be ready, monseigneur, to-day, to-morrow, always!"

"Let it rest for some time in its scabbard," returned the Duke de Guise. "As his Majesty has told you, the times are, for the moment, peaceful; wars and factions have called for a truce. Rest for a while, then, and let the fatal rumors that have during these last days clung to your name have time to settle. Certainly no one who has any claim to be called a gentleman will think of reproaching you with your misfortune. But your true glory requires that this cruel notoriety should fade away. Later on, in a year or two, I will beg the king to grant you the office of captain of the Guards—an office of which you have never ceased to be worthy."

"Ah!" said Gabriel, "it is not honors I desire, but opportunities of being useful to the king of France—opportunities of fighting; I no longer dare to say, for fear of seeming ungrateful, opportunities of dying."

"Speak not thus, Gabriel," returned the Balafré. "Merely say that when the king calls upon you to march against his enemies you will be ready."

"I will, monseigneur; wherever I am, and wherever it may be necessary to go."

"It is well," said the duke; "that is all I ask of you."

"And I," said Francis the Second, "thank you for this promise—a promise you will not repent of, I give you my word."

"And I," added Mary Stuart, "assure you that our con

fidence in you will always be as great as your devotion to us, and that you shall be in our eyes one of those friends from whom nothing is concealed, and to whom nothing is refused.''

The young count, more moved than he wished to confess to himself, bent forward and kissed respectfully the hand which the queen offered him.

Then he clasped that of the Duke de Guise, and, when the king dismissed him with a friendly gesture, retired, henceforth pledged by an act of kindness to the son of him whom he had sworn to pursue even in his posterity.

When Gabriel returned home, he found Admiral de Coligny waiting for him.

Aloyse had informed the admiral, who was come to visit his comrade of St. Quentin, that her master had been summoned to the Louvre; she made him a sharer of her anxiety, and Coligny had decided to remain until the return of Count de Montgommery should reassure himself as well as the nurse.

He received Gabriel warmly, and questioned him on what had passed.

Gabriel, without entering into details, merely said that, after a simple explanation on his part touching the death of Henry the Second, he had been dismissed, uninjured in person and honor.

"It could not be otherwise," replied the admiral; "and all the nobility of France would have protested against a suspicion that would try to cast a blemish on one of its most illustrious representatives.''

"Let us dismiss the subject," said Gabriel, sadly and constrainedly. "I am glad to see you, M. l'Amiral. You knew I was at heart a member of your religion. I have told you so orally and also by letter. Since you think I shall not dishonor the cause in which I believe, I wish to abjure now, and am able to do so. Your discourses, those of Master Paré, books, and my own reflections have convinced me; I am yours.''

"The news is good, and comes at the right time," said the admiral.

"Still, I think that, in the interests of the religion, it might perhaps be good to keep my conversion secret for a time. As M. de Guise just now remarked to me, it is well that there should be as few rumors about me at present as possible. This delay, besides, will harmonize with the new duties I have to fulfil."

"We shall always be proud to name you publicly as a member of our sect," answered the admiral.

"But it rests with me to refuse or, at least, postpone this precious mark of your esteem," said Gabriel. "I only wish to give this pledge of my firm and heartfelt faith, and to be able to call myself, in my own mind, one of your brethren, both in intention and in deed."

"Nothing could be more satisfactory!" returned Coligny. "All I ask of you is to allow me to announce to the leaders of our sect this remarkable conquest finally gained by our ideas."

"Oh, I consent to that with all my heart," said Gabriel.

"For that matter," continued the admiral, "the Prince de Condé, La Renaudie, and the Baron de Castelnau are already acquainted with you, and appreciate you at your value."

"I am afraid, alas! that they exaggerate it; in any case, this value has much decreased."

"No, no!" replied Coligny; "they are right in prizing it. I, too, know you! Moreover," he went on, in a lower tone of voice, "we are likely before long to have an opportunity of testing your new zeal."

"Indeed?" asked Gabriel, surprised. "You know, M. l'Amiral, that you can count on me—with certain reservations, however, which I must communicate to you."

"Who hasn't them? But listen, Gabriel. I visit you to-day not only as a friend, but as a sectary. We have spoken of you to the prince and to La Renaudie. Even before you definitely belonged to us, we held you for an auxiliary of singular merit and of stainless probity. In fine, we were all agreed in considering you a man capable of serving us if he could, incapable of betraying us in any case."

"I may not have the first quality, but I certainly have the second," answered Gabriel. "You can always rely on my word, if not on my assistance."

"We have therefore resolved to have no secrets from you," said the admiral. "You will be treated as one of the leaders, initiated into all our plans, and will only have the responsibility of silence. You are not a man like others; and exceptional men must be dealt with exceptionally. You will remain free, and we alone shall be bound—"

"Such confidence—" Gabriel was replying.

"Pledges you, I repeat, only to discretion," said the admiral. "And to begin, know this: the projects which were revealed to you in the assembly at the Place Maubert, and which had to be postponed, are to-day practicable. The weakness of the young king, the insolence of the Guises, the determination to persecute us, which is no longer concealed—everything calls us to action, and we are going to act—"

"Excuse me," interrupted Gabriel; "I have told you, M. l'Amiral, that there are certain limits to my devotion. Before you proceed further in your confidences I ought to inform you that I can have nothing to do with the political phases of reform; at least as long as the present reign lasts. To propagate our ideas and our moral influence, I willingly offer my time, my fortune, and my life; but I have no right to regard the Reformation as aught else than a religious movement. Francis the Second, Mary Stuart, and the Duke de Guise have treated me nobly and generously. I no more intend betraying their confidence than I do yours. Allow me to concern myself with ideas, and not with actions. Demand my testimony when you will, but I reserve the independence of my sword."

M. de Coligny reflected a moment, then resumed:

"My words, Gabriel, were not vain words. You are and always shall be free. Go your own way, if that suits you. Act without us, or do not act at all. We shall not ask you for any reckoning. We know," he added, with a significant air, "that it is sometimes your custom not to seek either advisers or associates."

"What do you mean?" asked Gabriel, astonished.

"I know what I mean," returned the admiral. "For the moment you ask not to mingle in our conspiracies against the royal authority. Be it so. Our part will be confined to giving you information as to our movements and our plans. Follow us or stand aside, that concerns you, and you only. You will know always, either by letter or by messenger, when we need you, and then you shall do as you please. If you come, you shall be welcome. If you stay away, no one will reproach you. Such was the understanding entered into by the leaders of the party, even before you informed us of your position. You can accept these conditions, it seems to me."

"I accept them thankfully," said Gabriel.

During the night which followed, Gabriel, on his knees before the tomb of his father, in the funeral vault of the Montgommerys, spoke thus to the beloved dead:

"Yes, my father, I have sworn, undoubtedly, not only to punish your murderer during his own life, but to pursue him in his posterity. There is no doubt of this, O my father! But I did not foresee what has happened. Are there not duties more sacred even than obedience to an oath? What obligation can constrain you to strike an enemy who places the sword in your hand and bares his breast to receive the stroke? If you lived, my father, you would counsel me, I am sure, to defer my vengeance, and not to respond to confidence by treason. Pardon me, then, O my dead father, for doing that which, living, you would order me to do. Moreover, something tells me that my vengeance is not long suspended. You know in your

heavenly abode things of which we can only have a presentiment here below. But the pallor of this sickly king;
the frightful glance with which his mother menaced him; the
predictions, hitherto so exactly fulfilled, which declare that
my own life must be the prey of this woman's rancor; the
conspiracies already formed against this reign begun but
yesterday—all unite in proving that the boy of sixteen will
probably occupy the throne for a time even shorter than
the man of forty has occupied it; and that I shall soon, my
father, be able to resume my task and the fulfilment of my
oath of expiation under another son of Henry the Second."

CHAPTER XXX

REPORTS AND DENUNCIATIONS

SEVEN or eight months elapsed, and no event of importance occurred connected with the heroes of our story or with the heroes of history.

But still, during that space of time, events of importance were preparing.

To learn what they were, and that upon the best authority, we have only to transport ourselves, on the 25th of February, 1560, into the cabinet of M. le Lieutenant de Police, who for the nonce answered to the name of M. de Braguelonne.

On the 25th of February, 1560, then, M. de Braguelonne, nonchalantly seated in his great armchair of Cordova leather, was listening to the report of Master Arpion, one of his secretaries.

Master Arpion was reading as follows:

" 'To-day the famous robber, Gilles de Rose, was arrested in the grand hall of the palace, while cutting off a golden tassel from the girdle of a canon of the Ste. Chapelle.' "

"A canon of the Ste. Chapelle! Wonderful!" said M. de Braguelonne.

"And very impious!" returned Master Arpion.

"And very adroit," replied the lieutenant of police—"very adroit; for the canon is suspicious. I will tell you in a moment what must be done with this crafty thief. Continue."

" 'The ladies living in the huts in the Rue Grand-Heuleu,' " continued Arpion, " 'are in a state of open revolt.' "

"And why, in Heaven's name?"

"They maintain they have directly addressed a petition to our lord the king, asking to be allowed to retain their habitations; and, meanwhile, they have made the watch run for their lives."

"Funny, that!" said M. de Braguelonne, laughing. "That can be easily settled. Poor girls! anything else?"

Master Arpion resumed:

" 'The deputies of the Sorbonne, having visited the residence of the Princess de Condé at Paris, with the object of insisting that she should not eat flesh-meat during Lent, were received with much jeering and mockery by M. de Sechelles, who, among other insults, told them that he liked them as little as he did a boil on his nose; and that such calves as they made strange ambassadors.' "

"Ah! this is serious!" said the lieutenant of police, rising. "To refuse to abstain from meat, and insult the professors of the Sorbonne! That is going to swell the items in your account, Madame de Condé; and when we present the sum total— Arpion, is that all?"

"*Mon Dieu!* yes, for to-day. But monsieur has not told me what I'm to do with Gilles de Rose?"

"I'll tell you: take him and the nimblest pickpockets and cut-purses you can find in his prison, and send these adroit rascals to Blois, where they are getting up fêtes for his Majesty, and let them show the court some of their best tricks."

"But what if they have the best of the joke and keep the objects stolen?"

"Then have them hanged."

At this moment an usher entered, and announced:

"M. le Grand Inquisiteur of the Faith."

There was no need to tell M. Arpion to withdraw. He saluted respectfully, and was gone.

In fact, the man who entered was an important and formidable personage.

To his ordinary titles of Doctor of the Sorbonne and Canon de Noyons he added the fine extraordinary title of Grand Inquisitor of the Faith in France. So, to have a name as sonorous as his title, he called himself Démocharès, although his real name was Antoine de Mouchy. The people had baptized his emissaries *mouchards*.

"Well! M. le Lieutenant de Police?" asked the grand inquisitor.

"Well! M. le Grand Inquisiteur?" returned the lieutenant of police.

"Anything new in Paris?"

"I was just about to ask you the same question."

"That means there is nothing!" returned Démocharès, with a profound sigh. "Ah! the times are hard! Nothing stirring; not the least little plot! What cowards these Huguenots are! Our trade is going to the bad, M. de Braguelonne!"

"No, no!" replied M. de Braguelonne, firmly. "Governments pass; the police remains."

"And yet," said M. de Mouchy, bitterly, "see what has come of your descent on the Reformers in the Rue des Marais. By surprising them at their supper, we hoped to catch them eating pork instead of the paschal lamb, as you had announced; and all the result of that fine expedition has been a poor larded chicken. Is that the kind of thing that can do credit to your organization, M. le Lieutenant?"

"Oh, one can't always succeed," said M. de Braguelonne, nettled. "You have not, I fancy, been more successful yourself with that lawyer in the Place Maubert—Troulliard, I think, was the fellow's name—have you? And yet you expected marvels."

"I confess as much," answered Démocharès, piteously.

"You thought you could prove as clear as daylight that Trouillard had wound up a frightful carousal by delivering his two daughters to his Huguenot friends, and your well-

paid witnesses—ha! ha!—suddenly retract and give you
the lie."

"The traitors!" murmured De Mouchy.

"Moreover," continued the lieutenant, "I have received
the reports of the surgeons and matrons; they showed
clearly that the virtue of the two young girls had not
been subjected to any trial."

"It's an infamy," growled Démocharès.

"No, a failure, M. le Grand Inquisiteur—a failure!" retorted Braguelonne, complacently.

"Ah! if the thing has failed," cried the inquisitor, impatiently, "it has been your fault!"

"What! my fault?" returned the lieutenant, astounded.

"Yes, undoubtedly. You are satisfied with reports and
retractions and such nonsense! Why did you pay any attention to these denials and obstacles? You should have
set about the prosecution all the same, and boldly accused
these heretics, just as if nothing had occurred."

"What! without proofs?"

"Yes; and have them condemned, too."

"Without crimes?"

"Yes; and have them hanged."

"Without judges?"

"Yes; I'll repeat it a hundred times for you, if you
like! yes, without proofs or crimes or judges! Do you think
you deserve any praise for getting people hanged who are
guilty?"

"But don't you see what furious outcries would be raised
against us in such a case?" said M. de Braguelonne.

"Ah! that is just what I expected from you!" returned
Démocharès, triumphantly. "That is the cornerstone of
all my system, monsieur. In fact, what is the cause of the
outcries you speak of? Plots. What do those plots lead
to? Revolts. And what do revolts prove? The evident
utility of our functions."

"From that point of view, certainly," said M. de Braguelonne.

"Monsieur," interrupted Démocharès, authoritatively, "let this principle be well grounded in your mind: To reap a harvest of crimes, the seed must first be sown. Persecution is our strength."

"Well," said the lieutenant, "it seems to me that we have had a fair share of persecution since the beginning of this reign. It would be difficult to provoke and arouse more discontent than exists at present; and that of every kind."

"Tush! What has been done, after all?" rejoined the inquisitor, with some disdain.

"Do you reckon the attacks, visits, and robberies to which the Huguenots, innocent or guilty, are every day exposed, nothing?"

"By my faith, I do," said Démocharès. "The patience and calmness with which they bear them show that these vexations are very trifling."

"And is the punishment of Anne Dubourg, the nephew of a chancellor, burned alive two months ago on the Place de Grève, nothing?"

"Not much, anyway," returned De Mouchy, a man evidently hard to please. "What came of it all? The assassination of President Minard and a pretended conspiracy, of which a trace cannot be found. That was not enough to make much noise, you see!"

"But what do you think of the last edict?" asked M. de Braguelonne—"the last edict, which is not only an attack on the Huguenots, but on all the nobility of the kingdom? As for me, I have told M. le Cardinal himself that I thought the measure rather bold."

"What!" said Démocharès; "are you speaking of the ordinance suppressing pensions?"

"No, indeed; but of the one enjoining suitors, whether nobles or clowns, to quit the court within twenty-four hours under pain of being hanged. You must agree that to threaten gentlemen with the halter is rather harsh, not to say revolting."

"Yes; the thing does not want boldness," said Démocharès, with a smile of satisfaction. "Fifty years ago such an ordinance would have stirred up a revolt among the entire nobility of the realm. But to-day, you see, they have not acted; they have only cried. Not a man of them has moved."

"There you are mistaken, M. le Grand Inquisiteur," said Braguelonne, lowering his voice; "if they do not move at Paris, they are making some stir in the provinces, believe me."

"Ha!" returned De Mouchy, eagerly; "you have news, then?"

"Not yet; but I am expecting some every moment."

"And from where?"

"From the Loire."

"You have agents there?"

"Only one; but he is a good one."

"Only one! Risky that," said Démocharès, with a self-sufficient air.

"I prefer to pay one who is safe and reliable as much as I might have to pay twenty stupid rascals. It is my way, I assure you."

"Yes; but who can answer for this man?"

"First, his head; and next, his past services."

"No matter; it is risky!"

Master Arpion entered softly while M. de Braguelonne was still speaking, and whispered in his master's ear.

"Ah!" cried the lieutenant, triumphantly. "Very well! Arpion, introduce Lignières immediately. Yes, although M. de Mouchy is present. Is he not to some extent one of us?"

Arpion bowed and passed out.

"Lignières is the very man of whom I was speaking," said Braguelonne, rubbing his hands. "You must hear him. He is just from Nantes. There are no secrets between us, are there? and I am glad to have a chance of proving that my method is as good as another."

Here Master Arpion opened the door for M. Lignières.

It was the lean, dark, wretched-looking little man we have already seen at the Protestant assembly in the Place Maubert; the same who had so boldly exhibited the republican medal and talked of cutting down lilies and trampling crowns under foot.

We see then that if the name of *agent provocateur* was unknown at the period, the thing itself was already in a flourishing condition.

CHAPTER XXXI

A SPY

LIGNIÈRES at first cast a cold, distrustful look upon Démocharès on entering; and, after bowing to M. de Braguelonne, remained prudently silent and impassive, waiting to be questioned.

"I am charmed to see you, M. Lignières," said M. de Braguelonne. "You can speak without fear before the Grand Inquisitor of the Faith in France."

"Oh, certainly!" exclaimed Lignières, eagerly. "If I had known I was in the presence of the illustrious Démocharès, believe me, monseigneur, I should not have so hesitated."

"Very well," returned De Mouchy, nodding, with an air of approval, flattered evidently by the respectful deference of the spy.

"It's all right. Speak, M. Lignières, and speak quickly!" said the lieutenant.

"But," insinuated Lignières, "perhaps M. de Mouchy is not perfectly informed as to what took place at the last conventicle but one of the Protestants at La Ferté?"

"I do not, in fact, know much about it," said Démocharès.

"With your permission, then," added Lignières, "I am going to give a brief summary of the grave facts I have recently collected; it will make matters clearer and better connected."

M. de Braguelonne by a nod gave the assent which Lignières waited for. This little delay harmonized ill with the lieutenant's impatience, but flattered his pride, as it was likely to convince the grand inquisitor not only of the superior capacity, but of the extraordinary eloquence of his chosen agents. And assuredly Démocharès was both surprised and charmed, like a clever connoisseur who meets with an instrument more perfect and irreproachable than any he has hitherto utilized.

Lignières, excited by such high approval, did his best to show himself worthy of it, and was, in truth, very fine.

"The first assembly at La Ferté was really of very little moment," said he. "The things done and said there were utterly wanting in spirit. In vain did I propose to overthrow his Majesty, and establish a constitution similar to that of the Swiss cantons. I was echoed only by insults. All these people could be prevailed upon to do for the time was to draw up a petition to the king, asking him to put a stop to the persecution of the Reformers, to dismiss the Guises, form a ministry of the princes of the blood, and convoke the States-General. A poor result enough, this simple petition! However, there was some plotting and some organizing. That was not altogether unimportant. Then they discussed the nomination of the leaders. As long as this had relation to the secondary leaders of districts, there was no trouble. But when they came to the supreme head of the conspiracy, there was the rub! M. de Coligny and the Prince de Condé refused through their agents the dangerous honor which was about to be conferred upon them. It was better, said their representatives, to choose a leader of humbler rank, so that the movement might have clearly the aspect of being of a popular character. A nice pretext for the idiots! They were, however, satisfied with it; and, after a great deal of discussion, they elected Godefroid de Barry, Seigneur de la Renaudie."

"La Renaudie!" repeated Démocharès. "Yes, he is, in fact, one of the most ardent among the ringleaders of those heretics. I know him to be a determined and energetic man."

"You will know him soon as a Catiline!" said Lignières.

"Oh, oh!" returned the lieutenant of police; "it seems to me that is a little too strong."

"You will see," answered the spy—"you will see whether it is a little too strong or not! I now come to our second assembly, which was held at Nantes, on the 5th of the present month of February."

"Ah!" cried Démocharès and Braguelonne together.

And both approached Lignières with greedy curiosity.

"They did not then confine themselves to mere words!" said Lignières, with an important air. "Listen! Shall I give your lordships the details and proofs at length; or shall I hasten on to facts?" added the rascal, as if he wished to prolong as much as possible the kind of ownership he had, for the moment, of these two souls.

"The facts! the facts!" cried the lieutenant, impatiently.

"Here they are, then; and they will send a shudder through you. After some unimportant preliminary speeches, La Renaudie rose and spoke substantially as follows: 'Last year, when the Queen of Scotland wished to have the ministers tried at Stirling, all their parishioners determined to follow them to that city; and, although they were without arms, this great movement intimidated the regent, and made her abandon the violent measures she was meditating. I propose that we do the same in France; and that a great body of those of our religion march on Blois, where the king is now residing, and appear unarmed before his Majesty, at the same time presenting a petition in which he will be implored to revoke the edicts of persecution and grant the free exercise of their religion to our brethren; and, since their nocturnal and secret assemblies have been calumniated, to allow them to assemble in temples, under the eye of authority.' "

"Well, well! always the same thing!" interrupted Démocharès, in a disappointed tone. "Peaceful and respectful manifestations that end in nothing! Petitions! protests! supplications! Is this the terrible news you had to announce to me, Master Lignières?"

"Wait! wait!" said Lignières. "You can well understand that, like you, ay, more than you, I scoffed at this innocent proposal of La Renaudie. 'What had been the end,' I said, 'and what was to be the end of all these aimless schemes?' Others spoke in the same sense. Thereupon, La Renaudie, greatly delighted, disclosed his real purpose and betrayed the audacious project that lay under his apparently innocent plan."

"What is this innocent plan, pray?" asked Démocharès, in the tone of a man not to be surprised at trifles.

"It is well worth the trouble, I imagine, of an effort being made to baffle it," rejoined Lignières. "While the attention of the court is distracted by this crowd of timid and unarmed petitioners approaching the throne as suppliants, five hundred horse and a thousand foot—you understand, messieurs, fifteen hundred men chosen from among the most resolute gentlemen devoted to the Reformation and to the princes—are to meet in different provinces, advance silently on Blois by different routes, penetrate into the city by fair means or foul, carry off the king, the queen-mother, and M. de Guise, bring the last two to trial, and put the princes of the blood in their place, until the States-General decide as to the form of the administration in future. That is the plot, messieurs. What do you think of it? Is it mere childish nonsense? Shall it be passed over unnoticed? Am I good for nothing or useful for something?"

He paused triumphant. The grand inquisitor and the lieutenant of police looked at each other with considerable surprise and alarm. There was a long silence, filled up, however, with reflections of a very varied character on their part.

"By the Mass, it is admirable, I confess!" cried Démocharès at last.

"Say rather, frightful," retorted the lieutenant.

"That is to be seen," answered the grand inquisitor, shaking his head arrogantly.

"Oh," said M. de Braguelonne, "we know only the designs which this La Renaudie avows. But it is easy guessing that he has other ones in view, that the Guises will defend themselves, nay, allow themselves to be cut in pieces rather than that he should succeed, and that, if his Majesty intrusts the power to the Prince de Condé, he will do so because he has been subjected to violence."

"But then, we are forewarned!" returned Démocharès. "All that these miserable rascals do against us will turn against themselves, and they will be caught in their own snares. I wager that M. le Cardinal is delighted, and will pay liberally for such a chance of ridding himself of his enemies."

"God grant that he may be delighted to the end!" said M. de Braguelonne.

And addressing Lignières, who had now become a man to be treated with respect—a man of importance, nay, an invaluable man—he said:

"As for you, M. le Marquis" (the wretch was really a marquis), "you have rendered one of the greatest of services to his Majesty and to the State. You may be sure of being worthily rewarded for it."

"Yes, faith!" added Démocharès, "like the saints, you deserve the best candle going, and you have all my esteem. Accept, M. de Braguelonne, my sincere compliments on the ability of the persons you employ. As for M. de Lignières, he has in truth the very highest claims to my respect."

"It is a very agreeable return for what little I have done," said Lignières, with a modest bow.

"You know we are not ungrateful, M. de Lignières," returned M. de Braguelonne. "But let us see. You have not told us everything, have you? Have they fixed on the date or the place of meeting?"

"They are to assemble at Blois on the 15th of March," answered Lignières.

"The 15th of March! Just think of it!" exclaimed the lieutenant. "We have not twenty days before us. And M. le Cardinal at Blois! Two days before we can warn him and receive his orders! What a responsibility!"

"But what a triumph at the end!" said Démocharès.

"See here, M. de Lignières, have you the names of the leaders?" continued M. de Braguelonne.

"Yes, in writing," answered the spy.

"The man is unique!" exclaimed Démocharès. "This almost reconciles me to humanity."

Lignières undid a portion of the lining of his doublet, drew from it a scrap of paper, unfolded it, and read in a loud voice:

"List of the leaders and of the provinces they are to direct:

"Castelnau de Chalosses—Gascony.
"Mazères—Béarn.
"Du Mesnil—Périgord.
"Maillé de Brézé—Poitou.
"La Chesnaye—Maine.
"Sainte-Mari—Normandy.
"Cocqueville—Picardy.
"De Ferrières-Maligny—Ile-de-France and Champagne.
"Chateauvieux—Provence," etc.

"You can read and meditate on this list at your leisure, monsieur," said Lignières, handing the treacherous document to the Lieutenant of Police.

"It is civil war organized," rejoined M. de Braguelonne.

"And note well," added Lignières, "that while these bands are marching on Blois, other chiefs in the several provinces are holding themselves in readiness to repress any movement in favor of MM. de Guise."

"Capital! We'll have them all in one vast net, as it were," cried Démocharès, rubbing his hands. "Eh, what a downcast look you have, M. de Braguelonne! I declare that, although at first astounded, I should be very sorry, for my part, if all this was not to take place."

"But do you not see how little time we have?" said the lieutenant. "In truth, my good Lignières, I would not for the world address the slightest reproach, but surely you might have given me notice of this since the 15th of February."

"How could I?" said Lignières. "I have had to execute more than twenty commissions for La Renaudie between Nantes and Paris. Besides, I had to gather valuable information. To neglect or put off these commissions would have been to excite suspicion; to write you a letter or send a messenger would have been to compromise our secrets."

"You are right," returned M. de Braguelonne, "always right! Let us not speak, then, of what is done, but of what is to be done. You have said nothing of the Prince de Condé? Was he not with you at Nantes?"

"He was," replied Lignières. "But before coming to a decision, he desired to see Chaudieu and the English ambassador, and he said he would accompany La Renaudie to Paris with this object."

"He is coming to Paris, then? and La Renaudie also?"

"Better than that; they are here already."

"And where do they lodge?" asked the lieutenant, eagerly.

"I do not really know. I have asked, as if it was not a matter of much interest, where I could communicate with the prince, if necessary; but was informed that I could do so indirectly. Doubtless La Renaudie did not wish to compromise the prince."

"That is annoying, certainly. We should have been able to follow their tracks to the end."

At this moment Arpion entered again, with his soft and mysterious tread.

"What is the matter, Arpion?" said M. de Braguelonne, impatiently. "What the devil, man, don't you know we are engaged upon important business?"

"I should not have interrupted you, except on business equally important."

"Well, well, what is it? Speak quickly and speak aloud. We have no secrets here."

"A man named Pierre des Avenelles—" said Arpion.

De Braguelonne, Démocharès and Lignières interrupted him with one and the same cry—

"Pierre des Avenelles!"

"It is that lawyer in the Rue des Marmousets who ordinarily lodges the Reformers at Paris," said Démocharès.

"And in the house upon which I have had my eyes for a long time," continued De Braguelonne. "But the good man is artful and cautious, and always baffles my vigilance."

"He wants to speak to monseigneur immediately," said the secretary. "He looked to me like a man out of his wits."

"He can know nothing," said Lignières, quickly and jealously. "Besides," he added disdainfully, "he is an honest man."

"That is to be seen; that is to be seen!" returned the grand inquisitor (that was a favorite phrase with him).

"Arpion," said the lieutenant, "show this man in at once."

"At once, monseigneur," replied Arpion, as he left.

"Excuse me, my dear marquis," continued De Braguelonne, addressing Lignières. "This man knows you, and seeing you unexpectedly might confuse him. Moreover, neither you nor I care that he should learn you are one of us. Be good enough, then, to take a seat in Arpion's cabinet during our interview; it is yonder at the bottom of the passage. I will have you recalled the moment we are through. As for you, M. le Grand Inquisiteur, pray remain; your imposing presence can only be useful to us."

"As you wish. I will remain to be at your service," said Démocharès, well pleased.

"And I will retire," added Lignières. "But remember what I told you, M. le Lieutenant de Police. You won't get much out of this fellow. A poor, weak creature; a feeble-minded, honest idiot. A paltry fellow, a paltry fellow, monseigneur."

"We'll do the best we can. But go, go, my dear Lignières. Here is our man."

Lignières had, in fact, barely time to escape. A man entered, quite pale and shaken with a nervous trembling, led in and almost carried by Master Arpion.

It was Pierre des Avenelles, the lawyer, whom we saw for the first time with Lignières at the conventicle in the Place Maubert, and who, if our readers remember, had the success of the evening, with his discourse so bravely timid.

CHAPTER XXXII

AN INFORMER

WHEN we meet him again, on the present occasion, he is anything but brave and altogether timid.

After bowing down to the ground before Démocharès and Braguelonne, he said in a trembling voice—

"I am doubtless in the presence of M. le Lieutenant de Police."

"And of M. le Grand Inquisiteur de la Foi," added M. de Braguelonne, pointing to De Mouchy.

"Oh, Jesus!" cried poor Des Avenelles, turning still paler, if that were possible. "Messeigneurs, you see before you a great criminal, one of the greatest. May I hope for pardon? I do not know. Can a sincere confession extenuate my faults? It is for you in your clemency to answer."

M. de Braguelonne saw at once the kind of man he had to deal with.

"To confess is not enough," he said in a stern voice; "there must also be reparation."

"Oh, I will make it, if I can, monseigneur," answered Des Avenelles.

"Yes; but to do so," continued the lieutenant, "you must render us a service—you must give us some valuable information."

"I will try," he said in a stifled voice.

"That will be difficult," returned De Braguelonne, carelessly, "for we know everything."

"What! you know?"

"Everything, I tell you. In the predicament into which you have got yourself, your tardy repentance will do little to save your head, I warn you."

"My head, great Heaven! my head in danger! Still, as I have come—"

"Too late!" said the inflexible Braguelonne. "You can no longer be of any use to us, and we know beforehand all you could tell us."

"Perhaps," returned Des Avenelles; "but, excuse me, monseigneur, what do you know?"

"In the first place, you are one of those infernal heretics!" interrupted Démocharès, in a thundering voice.

"Alas, alas, it is only too true!" replied Des Avenelles. "Yes; I am of the religion. Why? I know not really. But I will abjure, monseigneur, if you grant me my life. There are too many perils in preaching; I shall return to Mass."

"That is not all," said Démocharès; "you lodge Huguenots in your house."

"Only one has been discovered during all the visitations, only one," returned the lawyer, quickly.

"Yes," said M. de Braguelonne; "but you have probably some secret exit, some concealed passage, some unknown mode of communication with the outside. However, we are going one of these days to demolish your house from top to bottom, and you may be sure it will deliver its secret to us then."

"I will deliver it to you myself, monseigneur; I have sometimes received and entertained the Huguenots. They pay well, and lawsuits bring in so little. One must live. But this shall not happen again, and after I abjure not a Huguenot will ever think of coming to knock at my door."

"You have also," observed Démocharès, "often spoken in Protestant conventicles."

"I am a lawyer," said Des Avenelles, piteously. "But

I have always spoken in favor of moderation. You must know this, since you know everything."

And, growing bold enough to lift his eyes to the faces of the two sinister personages before him, he continued —

"But, pardon me, I think you do not know everything. For you speak of me and are silent about the general affairs of the party, although, in fact, of far greater importance. I see, then, with pleasure that you are still ignorant of many things."

"There's where you're mistaken," rejoined the lieutenant, "and we are going to prove to you quite the contrary."

Démocharès made a sign to him to take care.

"I understand, M. le Grand Inquisiteur," said Braguelonne to him. "But there is no imprudence in showing our hand to this person; for it will be long before he leaves this spot."

"How! long before I leave here?" cried Pierre des Avenelles, in dismay.

"Undoubtedly," said M. de Braguelonne, calmly. "Do you think that, under the pretence of making revelations, you can quietly take notes of our position, learn all we know, and carry that knowledge to your accomplices? That is by no means the case, my dear monsieur, and you are from this moment our prisoner."

"Prisoner!" repeated Des Avenelles, entirely prostrated.

Then, after reflecting, he came to a decision. It will be recollected that the good man had the courage of cowardice in the highest degree.

"Well, in fact, I prefer that it be so!" he cried. "I am safer here than at home, amid all their plots. And, since you are going to keep me here, M. le Lieutenant, you will have the kindness not to refuse to answer a few respectful questions on my part. I fancy that you are not quite as fully informed of matters as you think you are, and that I may find means to prove to you my loyalty and good faith by some useful revelations."

"Hum! I doubt it," said M. de Braguelonne.

"In the first place, what do you know of the last assemblies of the Huguenots, monseigneur?" asked the lawyer.

"Do you speak of that at Nantes?" said the lieutenant of police.

"Ah, you know that? Well, then, yes, the assembly at Nantes. What took place there?"

"Do you allude to the conspiracy formed there?" returned M. de Braguelonne.

"Alas! yes, and I see I cannot add much to your knowledge on the subject," said Des Avenelles. "That conspiracy—"

"Is to carry off the king from Blois, violently install the princes instead of M. de Guise, convoke the States-General, etc. All that is ancient history, my dear M. des Avenelles, as ancient, in fact, as the 5th of February."

"And the conspirators believed themselves so sure of secrecy!" cried the lawyer. "They are lost; and I also. For undoubtedly you know the leaders of the plot?"

"The secret leaders and the acknowledged leaders. The secret leaders are the Prince de Condé and the admiral. The acknowledged leaders are La Renaudie, Castelnau, Mazères. But the enumeration would be too long. Stay; here is the list of their names and the provinces they are to excite to revolt."

"Great Heaven! how clever the police are, and what' madmen are the conspirators!" exclaimed Des Avenelles a second time. "Have I then nothing to tell you at all? Do you know where the prince and La Renaudie are?"

"At Paris, together."

"This is frightful! and I can only recommend my soul to God. Still, another word, if you please. Where are they at Paris?"

M. de Braguelonne did not answer at once, but, with

his clear, penetrating gaze, seemed to be sounding the
eyes and soul of Des Avenelles.

The latter, scarcely breathing, repeated his question.
"Do you know where the prince and La Renaudie
are?"

"We shall find them without any trouble," replied
M. de Braguelonne.

"But you have not found them yet!" cried Des Avenelles, in an ecstasy. "Ah, God be praised! I can still
gain my pardon. I know where they are, monseigneur."

The eye of Démocharès sparkled, but the lieutenant of
police dissembled his joy.

"Where are they, then?" said he, in the most indifferent tone possible.

"At my house, gentlemen, at my house!" said the lawyer, proudly.

"I knew it," replied M. de Braguelonne, quietly.

"What! how? you knew that too?" cried Des Avenelles, turning pale.

"Undoubtedly. But I wanted to try you, to see if you
were sincere. It is all right now, and I am satisfied with
you. But your case was serious indeed. To think of har-
boring such great criminals!"

"You have rendered yourself as great a criminal as
they," said Démocharès, sententiously.

"Oh, don't talk about that, monseigneur," returned Des
Avenelles. "I have long suspected the dangers I was running. So ever since I have been aware of the dangerous
designs of my two guests, I have scarcely lived. But I have
only known them for three days, I swear to you. You must
know that I was not at the assembly at Nantes. When
the Prince de Condé and La Renaudie arrived at my house
at the beginning of this week, I believed I was entertaining
Reformers, and not conspirators. I have a horror of conspirators and conspiracies. They said nothing to me about
the matter at first, and that is what excites my indignation.
To expose a poor man who had never done them anything

but good to such peril! It was very bad. But these great personages never act otherwise."

"Eh?" said M. de Braguelonne, who regarded himself as a great personage indeed.

"I speak of the great personages of the Reform," the lawyer answered hurriedly. "Then they have begun by hiding everything from me. But they were whispering together all the day, and writing day and night, and receiving visits every minute. I watched and listened. In short, I guessed that they were beginning to plot, so that they were forced to tell me at last all about their Nantes assembly and their grand conspiracy—all, in fact, that you know of and which they believed so well concealed. But ever since that revelation I neither sleep nor eat, indeed, I no longer live. Every time people enter my house—and God knows how often they do enter it!—I imagine they are coming to drag me before the judges. At night, during my rare intervals of slumber, I dream of nothing but tribunals and scaffolds and executioners, and I awake, bathed in a cold sweat, to calculate and foresee and measure the risks I was running."

"The risks you were running?" said M. de Braguelonne.

"Why, first, the jail."

"Then, the torture," continued Démocharès.

"Next, hanging probably," added the lieutenant.

"Perhaps burning," pursued the grand inquisitor.

"Considering the nature of the crime, very likely the wheel," said M. de Braguelonne, to clap the climax.

"Imprisoned! tortured! hanged! broken on the wheel!" echoed Master des Avenelles at every word, as if he was actually undergoing the punishments enumerated.

" 'Sdeath, man! you are a lawyer; you know the law," retorted M. de Braguelonne.

"I know it only too well!" cried Des Avenelles. "And so, after three days of anguish, I could no longer restrain myself. I felt such a secret was a burden too heavy to bear, and I have come to place myself in your hands, M. le Lieutenant de Police.''

''It was your safest course,'' replied M. de Braguelonne; ''and, although your revelations are not of much us to us, as you see, we will have some regard to your good intentions.''

He conversed for some moments in an undertone with M. de Mouchy, who appeared to be persuading him, not without difficulty, to adopt a certain course of action.

''Above all, I implore of you as a great favor,'' said Des Avenelles, beseechingly, ''not to betray my defection from my old accomplices; for, alas! those who massacred President Minard would not be unlikely to do me an ill turn also.''

''We intend keeping your secret,'' replied the lieutenant of police.

''But you will keep me prisoner also, will you not?'' said the prisoner, timidly and humbly.

''No; you can return home freely this very moment,'' answered M. de Braguelonne.

''Really?'' said the lawyer. ''Then I see it is my guests and not myself you are going to lay hold of.''

''Not at all. They will be as free as you are.''

''How is that?'' asked Des Avenelles, astounded.

''Listen to me,'' answered M. de Braguelonne, authoritatively, ''and pay close attention to my words. You will return home at once, for fear a too long absence might excite suspicion. You will not utter a single word to your guests either as to your fears or their secrets. You will act and let them act as if you had never been in this cabinet. Are you sure you understand me? Do not hinder anything, and do not be surprised at anything. Let matters take their course.''

''That's easy,'' said Des Avenelles.

''But,'' added the lieutenant, ''if we need any information, we shall send to you for it, or we shall summon you here, and you will always hold yourself at our service. If it is judged necessary to visit your house, you will render every assistance to the officers."

"Since I have done so much as a beginning, I will complete the work," said Des Avenelles, with a sigh.

"That is right. One word more. If things pass in such a manner as to indicate that you have complied with these very simple instructions, you shall have your pardon. If we have reason to suspect the least indiscretion on your part, you will be the first to suffer, and that in the most grievous way."

"You shall be burned at a slow fire, by Our Lady!" said Démocharès, in his deep, lugubrious voice.

"However—" the lawyer was beginning with a shudder.

"Enough," said De Braguelonne. "You have heard. Remember. *Au revoir.*"

He made an imperious gesture. The too prudent advocate retired, at once relieved and crushed.

After his departure there was a moment's silence between the lieutenant of police and the grand inquisitor.

"You would have it so, and I have yielded," said the former. "But I confess I have my doubts as to the wisdom of this course."

"No; everything is for the best," answered Démocharès. "It is necessary, I tell you, that this affair should have a free course, and therefore the conspirators must not be alarmed. Let them think they are undiscovered, and let them act. They fancy they are advancing forward in the dark, and we are watching every one of their movements in broad daylight. It is glorious! Such a chance of dealing a fatal blow to heresy may not exist for the next twenty years. Besides, I know what the ideas of the Cardinal de Lorraine are on the subject."

"Better than I do, I am aware," said the lieutenant. "But the question now is what is to be done."

"You," returned Démocharès, "will remain at Paris, and keep an eye, by means of Lignières and Des Avenelles, on the two leaders of the conspiracy. I shall start in an hour for Blois and warn the Guises. The cardinal will at first be a little afraid; but the Balafré is there to reassure him, and on reflection he will be enchanted. It will be their business to surround the king in a fortnight, as quietly as possible, with all the forces they can dispose of. Our Huguenots will suspect nothing. They will fall into the snare, either in a body, or one by one, the blind gulls, and they are ours! We have them in our clutches, and then—a general slaughter."

The grand inquisitor strode up and down the room joyfully, rubbing his hands.

"God grant," said M. de Braguelonne, "that no unforeseen accident may bring this magnificent scheme to naught!"

"Impossible!" returned Démocharès. "A general slaughter! We have them. Pray summon Lignières, and let him bring his disclosures to a finish; I must report them all to the Cardinal de Lorraine. But I consider heresy dead already. A general slaughter!"

CHAPTER XXXIII

GIRL QUEEN AND BOY KING.

IF WE allow our imagination to take a leap over forty leagues in two days, we shall be, on the 27th of February, at the splendid chateau of Blois, where the court was for the time staying.

There had been, on the evening before, high festival and joyous celebrations at the chateau, under the direction of Antoine de Baïf the poet, with jousts, ballets, and allegories.

So, on the next morning, the young king and the little queen awoke later than usual, and still rather tired on account of the fete that had been given in their honor.

Fortunately, they were not forced to hold a reception on that day, and, as a relaxation, could chat about the fine things they had admired.

"For my part," said Mary Stuart, "I thought these festivities the finest and strangest in the world."

"Yes," returned Francis; "the ballets and the scenes that were acted, especially. But I confess the sonnets and madrigals seemed to me just a little too long."

"What!" protested Mary; "they were very gay and sparkling, I assure you."

"Yes; but you must agree, my darling, that the laudation was a little overdone. To hear one's self praised hour after hour is anything but amusing; and I had a fancy yesterday evening that the good God must be sometimes weary of this sort of thing in His paradise. Besides, Messieurs de Baïf and de Maisonfleur scatter such a number of Latin

words through their discourses that I do not always understand.''

"But that gives a work quite a distinguished flavor,
and shows that the author is a learned man and has fine
taste.''

"Ah, what a scholar you are!'' said the young king,
sighing. "You make verses and understand Latin, which
is all Greek to me!''

"But learning is the lot and recreation of us women, just
as action and command belong to you men and princes.''

"All the same,'' returned Francis, "I should like, if
only to be your equal in something, to know as much as
my brother Charles.''

"Speaking of Charles, by the way, did you notice him
yesterday in the part he took in the allegory of 'Religion
Defended by the Three Theological Virtues'?''

"Yes; he was one of the knights who represented the
Virtues—Charity, I think.''

"Perfectly correct. Well, did you notice with what fury
he struck the head of Heresy?''

"Yes; when it advanced into the middle of the flames
with the body of a serpent, Charles seemed really beside
himself.''

"And say, gentle sire, did this head strike you as resembling any one?''

"In fact, though I thought I was mistaken, it seemed to
me not unlike the head of Coligny—was I right?''

"Say, rather, that it was M. l'Amiral in every feature.''

"And all those devils who carried him off!'' said the
king.

"And the delight of our uncle the cardinal!'' returned
Mary.

"And my mother's smile.''

"It was almost frightful,'' said the young queen. "No
matter! Francis, your mother was very beautiful yesterday
evening, with her dress of shimmering gold and her tan-
colored veil—a magnificent costume.''

"Yes, darling; and so I have sent for a similar one to Constantinople by M. de Grandchamp, and you shall also have a veil of Roman gauze like my mother's."

"Oh, thanks, gentle king! thanks. I do not envy the lot of our sister Elizabeth of Spain, who is said never to wear the same dress twice. Yet I should not like that any woman in France, even your mother, should look, to you especially, better dressed than I."

"After all, what does it matter to you?" said the king. "Will you not always be the most beautiful?"

"It hardly appeared so yesterday," returned Mary, with a little pout; "for, after the torch dance in which I took part, you did not say a single word to me. I can only believe it did not please you."

"It did really!" cried Francis. "But, good Heaven! what could I say among all those wits of the court who were complimenting you in prose and verse? Dubellay insisted that you had no need of a torch, and that your two eyes were sufficient. Maisonfleur was frightened at the danger of the hall being set on fire by sparks from those two bright luminaries. Next, Ronsard declared that the same eyes were stars giving light during the darkness of the night and outshining the sun by day. Was I then to come, after all this poetry, and simply tell you that I thought yourself and your dance both charming?"

"Why not?" returned Mary. "Those simple words from you would have given me more pleasure than all their insipid nonsense."

"Well, I say these words this morning, darling, and with all my heart; for this dance was quite perfect, and made me almost forget the *pavane d'Espagne*, which I used to like so much, and the *pazzemeni d'Italie*, which you and poor Elizabeth danced so divinely. The reason is that everything you do is better done than anything done by others. For you are the fairest of the fair, and other women look like chambermaids beside you. Yes; in royal cos-tume, or simple *déshabillé* as you are now, you are always my queen and my love. I see only you; I love only you."

"My own darling!"

"My adored one!"

"My life!"

"My supreme happiness! Stay! though you had but a peasant's hood, I would still love you better than all the queens in the world!"

"And you alone should have my heart, though you were but a simple page."

"Oh," cried Francis, "how I love to pass my fingers through your silky, fair hair, to sport with it and tangle it! I can well fancy that your women should often ask to kiss that neck, so round and white, and those arms, plump and rounded. But do not let them, Mary."

"And why?"

"I am jealous of them!" said the king.

"Child!" answered Mary, with a child's adorable gesture.

"Ah!" cried Francis, passionately, "if the choice lay between renouncing my crown and Mary, the choice would soon be made."

"What folly!" returned the young queen. "Just as if you could renounce the crown of France, the fairest of all after that of heaven."

"I might do so because it weighs so heavily upon my forehead," said Francis, with a smile half gay, half melancholy.

"What do you mean?" asked Mary. "But I was forgetting that we have a matter to arrange—an affair of the greatest importance referred to us by my uncle of Lorraine."

"Oho!" cried the king; "he doesn't do that very often."

"He requires us," said Mary, gravely, "to decide upon the colors of the uniform of our Swiss Guards."

"It is a mark of confidence that does us honor. Let us deliberate on the subject at once. What are your Majesty's views upon this important question?"

"Oh, I speak only after you, sire."

"Well, I think the style of the dress should remain the same—broad doublet with wide sleeves, slashed in three colors. Am I not right?"

"Yes, sire; but the colors? That is the question."

"Not so easy by any means. But you do not help me, fair counsellor mine. The first color?"

"White, most assuredly, the color of France."

"Then the second must be that of Scotland, blue."

"And the third?"

"What if it were yellow?"

"Oh, no! it is the color of Spain. Green rather."

"It is the color of the Guises," said the king.

"Suppose so, monsieur; is that a reason for excluding it?"

"No. But do these colors harmonize?"

"I have an idea!" cried Mary Stuart. "Let us take red, the color of Switzerland; it will at least remind these poor people a little of their country."

"An idea as excellent as your heart, Mary!" returned the king. "So now this difficult affair is brought to a glorious termination. *Ouf!* we have had enough of trouble with it. Luckily, we are not asked to concern ourselves with more serious matters. Your dear uncles take the burden of them on their own shoulders. It is delightful! I have only to sign, sometimes without reading. If I took a fancy to travel, the crown over my royal seat would do very well in my place."

"But you know well, sire, that my uncles have at heart solely your interest and that of France?"

"Why should I not know that? They repeat it to me too often for it to be possible for me to forget it. Oh, by the way, the council meets to-day. We shall see M. le Cardinal de Lorraine arrive, with his humble demeanor and exaggerated respect—they don't always amuse me, I confess; and we shall hear him say, in his soft voice, as he bows at every word: 'Sire, the proposal I submit to your Majesty has nothing in view but the honor of your crown. Your

Majesty cannot doubt our zeal for the glory of your reign and the good of your people. Sire, the splendor of the throne and the church is the sole aim,' etc."

"How well you imitate him!" cried Mary, laughing and clapping her hands.

But, in a more serious tone, she resumed—

"It is well to be indulgent and generous, Francis. Do you think, then, that your mother, Madame Catherine de Médicis, is very agreeable to me when, with her severe, pale face, she gives me everlasting lectures on my dress, my servants, and my household? Can you not hear her saying to me, with her pinched lips: 'Daughter, you are the queen. I am to-day only the second woman in the realm; but if I were in your place I should insist on your women never missing Mass, or vespers, or sermon, either. If I were in your place I would never wear crimson velvet, because it is a color anything but sober. If I were in your place I would have my silver-gray dress *à la bourbonnaise* made over, because it is far too *décolletée*. If I were in your place I would never dance myself, but rest content with seeing others dance. If I were in your place—' "

"Oh," cried Francis, roaring with laughter, "it is my mother herself! But, after all, darling, she is my mother, and I have already offended her grievously enough by excluding her from State affairs, which are now managed by your uncles alone. You must therefore give way in some things and bear her rebukes submissively. For my part, I resign myself to the gentle sway of the Cardinal de Lorraine solely because you are his niece—do you understand?"

"Thanks, sire; thanks for this sacrifice," said Mary, kissing him.

"But really there are moments when I am tempted to abandon the title of king, as I have already abandoned the power."

"Oh, why do you say that?" protested Mary.

"I say it because I feel it, Mary. Ah! if I could be

your husband without being King of France! Just think of it! I have nothing but the weariness and restraints of royalty. The meanest of our subjects is freer than I. Why, if I had not asserted myself in a rather angry fashion, we should have had each a separate apartment! Why? Because we were told it was the usage of the kings and queens of France."

"How absurd they are with their usages!" returned Mary. "Well, we have changed their usage and established a new one, which, thank God! is quite as good as the other."

"Certainly, Mary. But do you know what has been my secret wish for some time past?"

"No, really."

"To escape; to fly away; to give up for a time the cares of a throne, Paris, Blois, even France, and go—where? I do not know; but at least far from here! to breathe a little at my ease like ordinary men. Say, Mary, would not a journey of six months or a year give you pleasure?"

"I should be delighted, dear sire, especially for your sake," answered Mary, "as your health of late has given me some uneasiness: you suffer too much from these nasty headaches. The change of air, the novelty of different scenes, would distract you and do you good. Yes, let us go; let us go! Oh, but would the cardinal and queen-mother allow it?"

"Oh, after all, I am the king; I am the master," said Francis the Second. "The kingdom is calm and tranquil; and, since they can so well dispense with my will in the government, they can very well dispense with my presence. We will start before winter, Mary, like the swallows. See, where should you like to go, Mary? What if we were to visit our realm of Scotland?"

"What! pass the sea!" said Mary. "Go among those fogs that might do such mischief to your delicate chest, my darling! No! I much prefer our smiling Touraine and this pleasant chateau of Blois. Why not go to Spain and pay a visit to our sister Elizabeth?"

"The air of Madrid is not good for the Kings of France, Mary."

"Well, then, Italy," returned Mary. "It is always warm there. A blue sky and a blue sea! orange-trees in flower, music and fetes!"

"Then, let it be Italy!" cried the king, gayly. "We will see the holy Catholic religion in all its glory, the fine churches, and the holy relics."

"And the paintings of Raphael," said Mary; "and St. Peter's and the Vatican!"

"We will ask the Holy Father for his blessing, and bring back plenty of indulgences."

"It will be charming!" said the queen; "and to realize this sweet dream together, side by side, loving and loved, to have the azure of heaven in our hearts as well as over our heads—"

"Paradise!" exclaimed Francis, with enthusiasm.

But, while he was thus giving vent to the emotions conjured up by these delightful hopes, the door suddenly opened, and the Cardinal de Lorraine, thrusting aside the usher-in-waiting, who had not even time to announce him, entered pale and breathless into the royal chamber.

The Duke de Guise, calmer, but quite as serious, followed his brother at a short distance, and his measured tread was already heard in the antechamber, through the open door.

CHAPTER XXXIV

END OF THE JOURNEY TO ITALY

"WHAT! M. le Cardinal," said the young king, quickly, "can I not have a moment of leisure and freedom even in this place?"

"Sire," answered Charles de Lorraine, "I regret to have infringed your Majesty's orders; but the business that brings my brother and me here does not admit of delay."

At this moment the Duke de Guise gravely entered, saluted the king and queen silently, and stood behind his brother, mute, impassive, and serious.

"Well, I am listening. Speak, monsieur," said Francis to the cardinal.

"Sire," replied the latter, "a conspiracy against your Majesty has just been discovered. Your life is no longer safe in the chateau of Blois; you must leave it immediately."

"A conspiracy! leave Blois!" cried the king; "what does this mean?"

"It means, sire, that wicked men are aiming at your life and crown."

"What!" said Francis, "they wish to harm me!—me who am so young; seated but yesterday on the throne, and who never, at least knowingly and voluntarily, have done evil to any one! Who are those wicked men, then, M. le Cardinal?"

"And who could they be," returned the cardinal, "except the accursed Huguenots and heretics?"

"Heretics again!" cried the king. "Are you sure, M. le Cardinal, that you are not allowing yourself to be carried away by suspicions without foundation?"

"Alas!" said Charles de Lorraine, "there is no room left for doubt on the present occasion!"

The young king, so unseasonably interrupted in his joyous dreams by this disagreeable reality, seemed terribly disturbed; Mary was greatly troubled by his ill-humor, and the cardinal by the news he brought. The Balafré alone, serene, and master of himself, awaited the issue of all these words impassively.

"What have I done to my people that they do not love me?" continued Francis, bitterly.

"I have told your Majesty that the rebels are only Huguenots," rejoined the Cardinal de Lorraine.

"They are not the less Frenchmen," said the king. "M. le Cardinal, I confided all my authority to you in the hope that you would cause it to be blessed; and I see nothing around me but troubles and complaints and discontent."

"Oh, sire! sire!" said Mary Stuart, reproachfully.

The Cardinal de Lorraine retorted a little dryly—

"It would not be just, sire, to render us responsible for the misfortunes of the times."

"Nevertheless, monsieur," continued the young king, "I should like to get at the bottom of things for once; and to have you away from me for a time, so that I might learn which of us two is the object of this hostility—"

"Oh, your Majesty!" cried Mary again, deeply affected.

Francis paused, reproaching himself with having already gone too far. The Duke de Guise did not show the slightest annoyance. Charles de Lorraine, after an icy silence, assumed the constrained and dignified attitude of a man unjustly offended.

"Sire, since we have the misfortune to see our efforts misunderstood or useless, nothing remains for us, as your loyal subjects and devoted relatives, but to retire and give way to others more successful and more worthy—"

The king, embarrassed, said nothing; and the cardinal, after a pause, continued—

"Your Majesty has only to say, therefore, into whose hands we are to surrender our offices. As far as I am concerned, nothing will be more easy, doubtless, than to replace me; and your Majesty can select either M. le Chancelier Olivier, M. le Cardinal Tournon, or M. de L'Hôpital—"

Mary Stuart, utterly hopeless, covered her face with her hands, and the repentant Francis would have asked nothing better than to do away with the results of his childish anger; but the haughty silence of the great Balafré intimidated him.

"However," went on Charles de Lorraine, "the office of Grand Master and the direction of military affairs require such rare talents and the possession of such lofty fame that, after my brother, I scarcely can find two men worthy of such a position. M. de Brissac, perhaps—"

"Oh! Brissac, always scolding and always in a temper," said the young king. "It is impossible!"

"And, in the second place," resumed the cardinal, "M. de Montmorency, who, if he lack the talents, has at least the renown."

"Ah!" said Francis, "M. le Connétable is too old for me, and formerly treated the dauphin too slightingly to have much respect for the king now. But, M. le Cardinal, why do you omit my other relatives—the princes of the blood, the Prince de Condé, for example?"

"Sire," returned the cardinal, "I regret to have to tell your Majesty that among the names of the secret leaders of the conspiracy just discovered, the first is that of the Prince de Condé."

"Is that possible?" said the young king, astounded.

"Sire, it is certain."

"Why, then, this plot against the State must be quite grave, must it not?" asked Francis.

"It is almost a rebellion, sire," replied the cardinal,

"and, since your Majesty relieves me and my brother from a responsibility more terrible than any ever imposed upon us, my duty bids me to pray you to name our successors as soon as possible; for in a few days the Reformers will be under the walls of Blois."

"What is this you are saying, uncle?" cried Mary, in terror.

"The truth, madame."

"Are the rebels numerous?" inquired the king.

"It is said, sire, they amount to two thousand. Rumors which I could not believe until I received special information from M. de Mouchy, who is at Paris, imply that their vanguard is already near La Carrelière— We retire, then, M. de Guise, and I—"

"What!" said Francis, quickly, "it is while I am in such danger that you both abandon me?"

"But I thought such was your Majesty's wish," answered Charles de Lorraine.

"What would you have?" said the king. "It saddens me when I think that you have made me—or that I have so many enemies! But stay, let us speak no more of that, fair uncle; rather give me some details as to the insolent attempt of the rebels. What do you intend doing to prevent it?"

"Excuse me, sire," said the cardinal, still offended; "after what I have heard from your Majesty, it seems to me that others than we—"

"Oh, fair uncle, I pray you, dismiss my hasty words from your mind; I regret them," said Francis the Second. "What can I say more? Must I ask your pardon?"

"Oh, sire," returned Charles de Lorraine, "the moment your Majesty restores to us your precious confidence—"

"Entirely, and with all my heart," added the king, offering him his hand.

"We are losing much time!" said the Duke de Guise, gravely.

They were the first words he had uttered since the beginning of the interview.

Thereupon, he marched to the front, as if what had passed until then had been only insignificant preliminaries —a tiresome prologue in which he had left the principal part to the Cardinal de Lorraine. But, these childish dis-cussions being at an end, he proudly assumed the right to speak and take the initiative.

"Sire," said he to the king, "here is how matters are: two thousand rebels, commanded by Baron de La Renaudie, and supported secretly by the Prince de Condé, are about to descend one of these days from Poitou, Béarn, and other provinces, and attempt to surprise Blois and carry off your Majesty—"

Francis made a gesture of surprise and indignation.

"To carry off the king!" cried Mary Stuart.

"And you with him, madame," continued the Balafré. "Do not be alarmed, however; we are watching over your Majesties."

"What measures will you adopt?" asked the king.

"We have only been warned of this an hour ago," an-swered the Duke de Guise. "But the first thing to do, sire, is to make sure of the safety of your sacred person. You must therefore leave this open city of Blois and its defence-less chateau to-day, and retire to Amboise, whose fortified chateau shelters you from any surprise."

"What!" said the queen; "shut ourselves up in that ugly chateau of Amboise, perched up so high, and so gloomy and sad!"

"Child!" his severe eyes, if not his lips, said to his niece.

But he only answered—

"Madame, it is necessary."

"But then we shall be flying before these rebels!" said the young king, quivering with fury.

"Sire," replied the duke, "you do not fly before an enemy who has not yet attacked you; who has not even proclaimed war against you. We are supposed to be igno-rant of the designs of these seditious persons."

"But we know them, notwithstanding," said Francis.

"Would your Majesty deign to accept my opinion as to questions of honor?" replied Francis de Lorraine. "We avoid the combat only to change the field of battle. And I hope the rebels may be kind enough to follow us as far as Amboise."

"Why do you say you hope so, monsieur?" asked the king.

"Why?" said the Balafré, with his superb smile. "Because it will give us the opportunity of making an end, once for all, of heretics and heresy; because it is time to strike them in some other way than by fictions and allegories; because I would have given two fingers of my hand—of my left hand—to bring about, without any injustice on our side, the decisive struggle which these rash men invite for our triumph."

"Alas!" exclaimed the king, "for all that, this struggle is not the less civil war."

"Let us accept it, then, in order to end it forever," replied the duke. "Briefly this is my plan. Your Majesty must remember that we are dealing with rebels. After this retreat from Blois, which I hope will not alarm them too much, we must feign the most perfect security and the most entire ignorance as far as they are concerned. And when they advance as traitors to surprise us, it is they who will be surprised and caught in their own snare. No appearance, therefore, of fear or of flight; I recommend this to you especially, madame," he said, addressing Mary Stuart. "My orders will then be given and your people notified, but secretly. Let no one have any suspicion as to our preparations and apprehensions, and I answer for everything."

"And what is the hour fixed for our departure?" asked Francis, with an air of dejected resignation.

"Three in the afternoon, sire," said the Duke de Guise; "I have hurried forward the necessary arrangements."

"What! hurried them forward?"

"Yes, sire," returned the Balafré, firmly; "for I knew

beforehand that your Majesty would act in accordance with reason and honor.''

"Be it so!" said the king, now reduced to submission, in a feeble voice. "We will be ready at three, monsieur; we have entire confidence in you."

"Sire," rejoined the duke, "I thank you for this confidence; I will be worthy of it. But will your Majesty deign to excuse me? In such circumstances, we cannot waste a moment; and I have twenty letters to write, a hundred commissions to give. Permit us, then, sire, to humbly take our leave of your Majesty."

After a rather brief salutation to the king and queen, he and the cardinal withdrew.

Mary and Francis regarded each other piteously.

"So, *ma mie*, what is to become of our fine journey to Rome?"

"It has turned into a flight to Amboise," returned Mary, sighing.

At this moment entered Madame Dayelle, the queen's first lady.

"Is what they say true, madame?" she asked, after the usual salutations. "Are we to break up house at once, and quit Blois for Amboise?"

"It is only too true, my poor Dayelle," answered Mary.

"But do you know, madame, that there is nothing in that chateau; not even a decent mirror?"

"Then everything must be brought from here, Dayelle. Write down at once a list of such things as are indispensable. I will dictate. First, my new dress of crimson damask with gold lace trimmings—"

And, turning to the king, who was standing in a recess of one of the windows, pensive and sad—

"Is not the audacity of these Reformers inconceivable, sire? But, excuse me, you ought also to think about what you may need yonder, so that you may not find yourself unprovided."

"No," answered Francis, "I leave all that to Aubert, my *valet-de-chambre*. As for me, I can think of nothing but my mortification."

"Do you think that mine is less keen?" said Mary. "Madame Dayelle, write down my farthingale, covered with violet camlet embroidered in gold and my white damask dress with silver trimmings.—It is one's duty to be reasonable," she added, addressing the king, "and not incur the danger of being without things of paramount importance.—Madame Dayelle, be sure to remember my *manteau de nuit*, of cloth of gold, lined with lynx fur.—Is it not some centuries ago, sire, since the chateau d'Amboise has been inhabited by the court?"

"Since the time of Charles the Eighth, I do not believe a French king has stayed there more than two or three days," answered Francis.

"And we may have to stay there a whole month!" cried Mary. "Oh, those abominable Huguenots!—Do you think the bedchamber is not too scantily furnished?"

"The safest plan," was the reply, "would be to act as if there was nothing there."

"Then write down this gold-framed mirror, this casket in violet velvet, and the shaggy carpet to put round the bed.—But was such a thing ever seen, sire," she added, turning again to the king, "as for subjects to march in this fashion against their master and, so to speak, hunt him from his home?"

"Never, Mary, I believe," answered Francis, sadly. "Ruffians have sometimes resisted the orders of the king, as was done fifteen years ago at Mérindol and La Cabrière; but to attack the king's person—I could never have imagined it, I confess."

"Oh!" said Mary, "my uncle of Guise is then right. We cannot take too many precautions against these mad rebels.—Madame Dayelle, add a dozen pairs of shoes, the same number of pillows and sheets. Is that all? I really think I shall go out of my senses. Stay a moment, my dear—this velvet pincushion, this gold candlestick, this bodkin, this gilt needle-case.—That's all, I think."

"Is madame taking her two jewel-cases with her?" said Madame Dayelle.

"Yes, indeed; I should think so!" cried Mary, quickly. "What! leave them here to fall into the hands of these miscreants! I should say I'll take them! Am I not right, sire?"

"It is a wise precaution," said Francis, with a feeble smile.

"There is nothing more of importance, I fancy, Dayelle, is there?" said Mary, looking anxiously around.

"Madame has not forgotten her prayer-books, I hope," replied the lady-in-waiting, with a slightly sanctimonious air.

"Ah! I was near forgetting," said Mary, naively. "Bring the most beautiful ones with you, especially those given me by my uncle the cardinal, and the one in scarlet velvet faced with gold. Madame Dayelle, I recommend all this to your attention: for you see that neither the king nor I can give our minds to anything but the grievous necessity which renders our departure necessary."

"Madame has no need to stimulate my zeal," said the duenna. "How many chests and trunks will be required to carry off everything? Five will be enough, I fancy."

"Six, surely," answered the queen. "We must not be short-taken in the deplorable extremity to which we are reduced. Six, without reckoning those of my ladies, of course. They must make their own arrangements. I have certainly not the heart to meddle with them.—In fact, I am like yourself, Francis; I can think of nothing but these Huguenots.—Alas! You can now retire, Dayelle."

"No orders as to the lackeys and coachmen, madame?"

"Let them put on their cloth clothes only. Go, my dear Dayelle; go at once."

Dayelle bowed, and took three or four steps toward the door.

"Dayelle!" cried Mary, calling her back, "when I said our people were to put on their cloth clothes, it was for the journey, remember. They must be careful to take with them their violet velvet capes and their violet mantles lined with yellow velvet; you hear?"

"Yes, madame. Has your Majesty any further orders?"

"No; there is no more, I think. But see that everything is executed as soon as possible. We have only till three o'clock; and mind, don't forget about the mantles of the lackeys."

This time Dayelle left for good.

Turning to the king, Mary said:

"You agree with me as to those mantles for our people, do you not, sire? Messieurs the Reformers will allow us surely to dress our household decently. Royalty must not be too deeply humiliated in presence of these rebels! I even hope, sire, we may find means to give a little fete, in spite of their teeth, in this frightful Amboise of ours!"

Francis sadly shook his head.

"Oh, do not frown down my idea," returned Mary. "It will frighten the rebels more than you think, by showing we are not afraid of them. A ball in present circumstances, I have no fear in asserting, would be sound statesmanship; your mother, who poses as a great politician, could not find anything better. No matter! For all that, my heart is rent with anguish, my poor dear sire. Ah, these wretched Huguenots!"

CHAPTER XXXV

TWO APPEALS

SINCE the fatal tournament of the 10th of July, Gabriel had led a calm, retired, and gloomy life. This man of action, movement and energy, whose days had once been so full of passionate endeavor, took pleasure now in solitude and oblivion.

He never showed himself at court; he never saw a friend. He hardly left the hotel, where his days slipped by in dreamy, sombre revery, passed in the society of his nurse Aloyse and his page André, who had returned to him when Diana de Castro suddenly took refuge in the convent of the Benedictines of St. Quentin.

Gabriel, young in years, was old in sorrow. He remembered; he no longer hoped.

How often during these months—months longer than years—did he not regret that he was not dead! How often did he ask himself why the Duke de Guise and Mary Stuart had been placed between him and the wrath of Catherine de Médicis, and imposed upon him the bitter gift of life! What, in fact, was he doing in this world? What was he good for? Was the tomb more sterile than the existence he led?—if it could be called existence!

There were, however, moments when his youth and strength rose in protest against himself.

Then he stretched his arm, raised his head, and looked at his sword.

And he had a vague feeling that his life was not ended;

that there was a future for him still, and that the warm hours of struggle, and perhaps of victory, would sooner or later become again part of his destiny.

Nevertheless, considering everything, he saw only two chances that could restore him to his real life—to action —a foreign war or religious persecution.

If France and the king should happen to be engaged in some new war, should attempt a conquest, or repel an invasion, Count de Montgommery said to himself that his juvenile ardor would flame up again without difficulty, and it would be sweet to die as he had lived, fighting.

And then he would love to pay the involuntary debt in this fashion, contracted toward the king and the Duke de Guise.

He also thought it would be fine to give his life in testimony of the new truths he had embraced in these latter days. The cause of Reform was, in his eyes, the cause of justice and liberty, and was doubtless a holy and noble cause.

The young count read all the books of controversy that then abounded. He grew passionately attached to the great principles revealed in magnificent words by Luther, Melanchthon and Calvin and many others. The books of all these freethinkers had seduced, convinced and enthralled him. He would be proud and happy to sign with his blood the attestation of his faith.

It was always the noble instinct of this noble heart to devote his life to some one or to some cause.

Lately he had a hundred times risked it to save or avenge his father or his beloved Diana. (O eternally bleeding memories in that wounded soul!) Now that these cherished beings were no more, he would defend sacred ideas.

His country instead of his father, his religion instead of his love.

Alas, alas! it is useless speaking; they are not the same things, and enthusiasm for abstractions can never equal, in its pains and its pleasures, our affection for human beings.

No matter! For one or other of these causes, for France or for the Reform, Gabriel would still have been content to sacrifice himself; and it was on one of these sacrifices he counted for the wished-for termination of his career.

On a rainy morning of the 6th of March, Gabriel was leaning back in his chair at a corner of the fireplace meditating on those thoughts that had now become habitual to him, when Aloyse showed in a messenger, booted and spurred and covered with mud, after a long journey.

This courier had come from Amboise with a strong escort, bearing several letters from M. de Guise, Lieutenant-General of the Kingdom.

One of the letters was addressed to Gabriel, and this is what it contained:

My dear and good Comrade—I write to you in haste, and have neither leisure nor power to explain myself. You told the king and me that you were devoted to us, and when we had need of this devotion we had only to call you.

We call you to-day.

Start immediately for Amboise, where the king and queen intend staying for some weeks. I will tell you on your arrival in what manner you can serve him.

It is well understood, nevertheless, that you remain free to act or not to act. Your zeal is too invaluable to me for me to wish either to abuse or compromise it. But, whether you are with us or remain neutral, if I failed to show my confidence in you, I should fail in my duty.

Come, then, with all speed, and you will be, as always, welcome. Your affectionate

FRANCIS OF LORRAINE

Amboise, this 4th day of February, 1560.

P. S.—I inclose a safe-conduct in case you should be questioned by any royal troop on the way.

The messenger had departed to fulfil his other commissions when Gabriel finished the letter.

The ardent young man rose at once and said to Aloyse—

"My good Aloyse, summon André and tell him to saddle my dapple-gray and prepare my travelling-bag."

"You are setting out again?" asked the worthy woman.

"Yes, nurse, in two hours, for Amboise."

There could be no reply, and Aloyse left sadly, but silently, to execute her master's orders.

But during the preparations another messenger came, asking to see M. de Montgommery in private.

He did not make any noise and had no escort. He entered silently and modestly, and, without uttering a word, handed Gabriel a letter.

Gabriel started. He recognized in the man before him the person who had formerly brought him the invitation to attend the Protestant conventicle in the Place Maubert.

It was indeed the same man, and the letter bore the same signature.

This letter said:

FRIEND AND BROTHER—I did not wish to leave Paris without seeing you, but I lacked time, and events have crowded upon me, and are hurrying me on; I must leave you without either grasping your hand or telling you of our plans and hopes.

But we know you are with us, and I know what kind of a man you are.

With men like you, there is no need of preparations, assemblies and discourses. A word is enough.

Here is the word: We need you. Come.

Be at Noizai, near Amboise, on the 10th or 12th of March.

You will find there our brave and noble friend, Castelnau. He will tell you what is contemplated. I dare not confide it to paper.

It is agreed that you are by no means pledged; that you have the right to stand apart; and that you can always do so without incurring the slightest suspicion or reproach.

But, for all that, come to Noizai. I will find you there, and, if we do not have your help, we will at least claim your advice.

Besides, can anything be accomplished in the party without your being informed of it?

Au revoir, then, with the hope that we may meet soon at Noizai. We count on your presence in any case.

L. R.

P.S.—If any of our soldiers meet you on the way, our password is again *Geneva*, and our countersign *Glory of God!*

"I start in an hour," said the count to the taciturn messenger, who bowed and passed out.

"What does all this mean?" asked Gabriel of himself when he was alone; "and what mean these two appeals from parties so antagonistic giving me a rendezvous almost at the same place? It does not matter. Toward the omnipotent duke as well as to my oppressed fellow-believers my obligations are equally undoubted. My first duty is to start. Let what will happen after. However difficult my position may become, my conscience tells me I shall never be a traitor."

And an hour afterward, Gabriel was on his way, accompanied by André alone.

But he did not foresee the strange and terrible dilemma which his very loyalty had to encounter.

CHAPTER XXXVI

A DANGEROUS CONFIDENCE

WITHIN an apartment of the Duke de Guise in the chateau of Amboise, the Balafré himself was engaged in questioning a tall, nervous, and vigorous man, with strongly marked features, lofty and fearless demeanor, and wearing the uniform of a captain of arquebusiers.

"Marshal de Brissac has assured me, Captain Richelieu, that I might have full confidence in you," said the duke.

"M. le Maréchal is very kind," answered Richelieu.

"It seems you are ambitious, monsieur," returned the Balafré.

"I am so far ambitious as not to like remaining captain of arquebusiers all my life. Although sprung from a rather good stock—for there were lords of Plessis at Bovines—I am the fifth of six brothers, and therefore need to add a little to my resources and not encroach too much on my patrimony."

"Good!" said the duke, with satisfaction. "You can render me some services here, monsieur, of which you shall not repent."

"Monseigneur, I am, as you see, ready to do anything to satisfy you," said Richelieu.

"To begin," returned the Balafré: "I have ordered the charge of the principal gate of the chateau to be given to you."

"And I promise to give a good account of it, monseigneur."

"It is not because I think the Reformers are so badly advised as to attack a side where they will have to carry seven gates in succession; but, as nothing ought to enter or leave by that gate henceforth, the post is of special importance. Do not, therefore, let any one pass, either from within or without, except on an express order signed by my hand."

"It shall be done, monseigneur. However, a young gentleman, named Count de Montgommery, presented himself just now, without any special order, but with a safe-conduct signed by you. He comes, he says, from Paris. Am I to introduce him to you, monseigneur?"

"Yes, yes! at once!" said the duke, quickly. "But wait; I have not given you all my instructions. To-day, at noon, the Prince de Condé will appear before the gate of which you have charge. We have sent for him, in order to have the reputed leader of the rebels in our power, and, I answer for it, he will not venture to excite suspicion by inattention to our summons. You will open the gate, but to him alone, and not to those he brings with him. You will be careful to fill all the recesses and casements that are under the arch with your soldiers; and as soon as he arrives, all, under pretence of doing him the honors, will parade, arquebuse in hand and matches lighted."

"It shall be done in accordance with your orders, monseigneur," said Richelieu.

"Moreover," resumed the duke, "when the Reformers begin the attack, keep a close eye upon our man yourself; and, you understand me, if he budges a step, if he shows any sign of uniting with the assailants, or even if he hesitates to draw his sword against them, as his duty commands him to do, do not hesitate—strike him down."

"I should see no difficulty, monseigneur," said Richelieu, with simplicity, "except that my rank as a mere captain of arquebusiers may not render it easy for me, perhaps, to be always as near him as I ought."

The Balafré reflected a minute and said—

"M. le Grand Prieur and the Duke d'Aumale, who will never leave the reputed traitor a moment, will give you the signal, and you will obey them."

"I will obey, monseigneur," replied Richelieu.

"Good!" said the duke. "I have no other order to give you, captain. If the splendor of your house began with Philip Augustus, it may well begin again with the Duke de Guise. I count on you; count on me also. Go, please, and introduce M. de Montgommery to me immediately."

Captain Richelieu bowed profoundly and retired.

Some minutes after, Gabriel was announced.

He was sad and pale, and the cordial reception of the Duke de Guise did not render him less so.

In effect, by comparing his own conjectures with some words the guards had let drop without scruple in presence of a gentleman bearing a safe-conduct from the Duke de Guise, the young Calvinist had been able to guess the truth pretty closely.

The king who had pardoned him, and the party to which he had devoted himself, were at open war, and his loyalty was compromised in the conflict.

"Well, Gabriel," said the duke, "you must know now why I called you?"

"I suspect, but do not know precisely," replied Gabriel.

"The Reformers are in open revolt," returned the Balafré. "They are in arms, and about to attack the chateau of Amboise. That is the news."

"It is a painful and terrible extremity," said Gabriel, thinking of his own situation.

"My friend, it is a magnificent opportunity," replied the Duke de Guise.

"What do you mean, monseigneur?" asked Gabriel.

"I mean that the Huguenots think they are surprising us, and we are awaiting them. I mean that their plans are discovered, their designs betrayed. It is fair war, since they have been the first to draw the sword; but our enemies are about to deliver themselves into our hands. They are lost, I tell you."

"Is it possible?" cried Count de Montgommery.

"Judge for yourself," continued the Balafré—"judge for yourself how clearly we know all the details of their mad enterprise. On the 16th of March they are to assemble before the city at noon and attack us. They have accomplices among the king's guards; this guard has been changed. Their friends are to open for them the Western Gate; this gate is walled up. In fine, their detachments were to arrive here secretly by certain paths in the forest of Chateau-Regnault; the royal troops will fall unexpectedly on these detachments as soon as they appear, and will not allow the half of their forces to reach Amboise. We are exactly informed and admirably on our guard, I hope."

"Admirably!" repeated Gabriel, in dismay. "But," he added, in his confusion, and not knowing very well what he said—"but who can have informed you?"

"Ah!" returned the Balafré; "two have betrayed all their designs—one for money, and one through fear. Two traitors, I confess—the one a paid spy, the other a terrified alarmist. The spy, whom you perhaps know—alas! we have many of the sort among ourselves, and have to be on our guard against them—is the Marquis of—"

"Do not tell me!" cried Gabriel, quickly; "do not mention these names! I asked for them without thinking; you have told me more than enough already. But for a man of honor the most difficult thing of all is not to betray traitors."

"Oh!" said the duke, with some surprise, "we all have the most boundless confidence in you, Gabriel. We were speaking of you only yesterday evening with the young queen. I told her I had sent for you, and she congratulated me on doing so."

"And why did you send for me, monseigneur? You have not yet told me that."

"Why?" said the Balafré. "The king has only a small

number of sure and devoted servants; you are one of them; you will command a detachment against the rebels."

"Against the rebels? Impossible," said Gabriel.

"Impossible! and why?" asked the Balafré. "I have not been accustomed to hear that word from you, Gabriel."

"Monseigneur," said Gabriel, "I am also of the religion."

The Duke de Guise started up suddenly and regarded the count with a surprise in which there was something of dismay.

"The case is this," rejoined Gabriel, smiling sadly. "Whenever you are pleased, monseigneur, to confront me with Spaniards or Englishmen, you know that I will not recoil, and that I will offer you my life with more than devotion, with joy. But in a civil war, in a religious war, against my countrymen, against my brethren, I am obliged, monseigneur, to reserve the liberty you were good enough to guarantee me."

"You a Huguenot!" at last the duke was able to say.

"A sincere Huguenot, monseigneur," said Gabriel; "it is my crime, but it is also my excuse. I have faith in the new ideas; I have given them my soul."

"And your sword at the same time, doubtless?" said the Balafré, with a little bitterness.

"No, monseigneur," was the grave answer of Gabriel.

"Oh, nonsense!" retorted the Balafré; "are you going to make me believe that you were ignorant of the plot formed against the king by your brethren, as you call them, and that these same brethren are willing to renounce cheerfully the aid of such an intrepid ally as you?"

"They must do so," said the young count, more gravely than ever.

"Then you will desert them," returned the duke; "for your new faith places you between two breaches of faith, that is all."

"Oh, monsieur!" cried Gabriel, reproachfully.

"How can it be otherwise?" said the Balafré, flinging his cap almost angrily on the chair he had just left.

"How can it be otherwise?" rejoined Gabriel, coldly and severely. "The thing is simple. My opinion is that the falser the position a man has taken, the sincerer he ought to be. When I became a Protestant, I firmly and loyally declared to the Huguenot leaders that certain sacred obligations toward the king, queen, and the Duke de Guise would always prevent me, during the entire duration of this reign, from fighting in the ranks of the Protestants, if there was fighting. They know that for me the Reform is a religion, and not a party. I have stipulated with them as with you, monseigneur, for the most absolute freedom. I have the right to refuse my assistance to them as well as to you. In this sad conflict between gratitude and belief, my heart will bleed at every blow that is struck, but my arm will not strike any. And that is why, monseigneur, you misunderstand me, and why, by remaining neutral, I hope to remain honorable and honored."

Gabriel spoke with pride and animation. The Balafré, who had gradually recovered his serenity, could not help admiring the frank and noble nature of his late companion.

"You are a strange man, Gabriel!" he said pensively.

"Why strange, monseigneur? Is it because I say what I do, and do what I say? I was ignorant of this conspiracy of the Protestants, I swear to you. Nevertheless, I confess I received, at the same time I received your letter, a letter from one of them at Paris. But this letter, like yours, did not explain anything, and only said, 'Come'; I saw the hard alternative I had to confront, and still I have come in response to this double summons, monseigneur. I have come in order not to abandon any one of my duties. I have come to say to you: I cannot fight against those whose belief I share. I have come to say to them: I cannot fight against those who spared my life."

The Duke de Guise offered his hand to the young Count de Montgommery.

"I was wrong," said he, cordially. "Attribute my

slight vexation to the real sorrow I felt on finding you, upon whom I relied so much, among my enemies."

"Enemy!" cried Gabriel. "Oh, I am not your enemy, monseigneur, and never can be your enemy. Because I am more frank than they, am I more your enemy than M. de Coligny or the Prince de Condé, who are, like me, Protestants, yet not in arms against you?"

"Yes, but they are in arms against me," replied the Balafré. "I know it well; I know everything. Only they hide their arms. But it is certain that if we met, I should dissemble as they do, I should call them friends, and, at need, warrant officially for their loyalty. A comedy, it is true; but the comedy is necessary."

"Well, monseigneur," said Gabriel, "since you have been kind enough to dispense with these conventional necessities in my regard, be kind enough also to tell me that, outside of politics, you believe in my devotion and honor, though I am a Huguenot, and, particularly, that if any foreign war should break out anew, you would always do me the favor to claim the fulfilment of my pledge, and send me where I can die for king and country."

"Yes, Gabriel," said the Duke de Guise; "while deploring the difference that now separates us, I trust and shall always trust you; and as proof of this and to redeem my momentary suspicion, which I regret, take this, and make what use you like of it."

He went to a table and wrote a few words, which he signed and handed to Gabriel.

"It is an order to let you pass from Amboise and go to any place you choose," said he. "With this paper you are free. And I assure you I would not give such a mark of esteem and confidence to the Prince de Condé, whom you mentioned just now, and who, as soon as he sets foot in this chateau, will be watched as an enemy and silently guarded as a prisoner."

"I refuse this mark of confidence and esteem, monseigneur," said Gabriel.

"Why?" asked the Duke de Guise, in astonishment.

"Monseigneur, do you know where I should go, after leaving the chateau of Amboise?"

"That is your concern, and I do not ask."

"But, on the other hand, I will tell you. After leaving you, I intend going where my duty calls me, among the rebels at Noizai."

"Noizai? Castelnau commands there."

"Yes; oh, you are well informed, monseigneur."

"And what do you propose doing at Noizai, unhappy man?"

"Ah! what do I propose doing at Noizai? Say to them: 'You have summoned me and I am here, but I can do nothing for you;' and, if they question me on what I might have remarked or heard on the road, I must be silent; I could not warn them of the snare you have set for them. Your confidence deprives me of that right. Therefore, monseigneur, I ask a favor of you—"

"What is it?"

"Detain me as a prisoner, and save me thus from a cruel perplexity; for, if you allow me to depart, I must at least show my presence among those who are lost, and if I go there, I am not free to save them."

"Gabriel," returned the duke, after a few moments' reflection, "I cannot show such distrust in you as that would imply. I have disclosed to you my whole plan of battle; you are going among friends to whom it is a matter of pre-eminent importance to know that plan; and yet—here is your passport."

"Then, monseigneur," returned Gabriel, dejectedly, "grant me at least one last favor. I implore you in the name of all I have been able to do for your glory at Metz, in Italy, and at Calais, in the name of all I have suffered since; and I have suffered much!"

"What is your request, my friend? If I can grant it, you may be sure I will."

"It is in your power, monseigneur, and perhaps it is

your duty to grant it; for those against whom you are about to fight are Frenchmen. Give me leave to try to make them abandon their fatal purpose, not by revealing to them the certain result, but by prayers, by advice, by entreaty."

"Gabriel, take care!" said the Duke de Guise, solemnly. "If a word as to our plans escape you, the rebels will simply modify their dispositions, but persist in the execution of them, and then it is the king, Mary Stuart, and I who are destroyed. Weigh this well. Do you pledge your honor, therefore, as a gentleman, that you will not let them guess or suspect, by word, allusion, or gesture, anything that is passing here?"

"Yes, on my honor as a gentleman."

"Go, then, and get them to renounce their criminal project, and I will joyfully renounce my easy victory, thinking that, by doing so, I am sparing the blood of Frenchmen. But, if the last reports do not lie, and I think they do not, their confidence in their enterprise is so blind and stubborn that you will fail, Gabriel. No matter. Go and make this last effort. For their sake, and still more for yours, I do not wish to refuse."

"On their part and mine, I thank you, monseigneur."

A quarter of an hour later, he was on the road to Noizai.

CHAPTER XXXVII

LOYALTY ROOTED IN DISLOYALTY

BARON DE CASTELNAU was a valiant and high-spirited young man, to whom the Protestants had not assigned the least difficult post when they sent him to take possession of the chateau of Noizai, the general rendezvous of their detachments, on the 16th of March.

He was required to make his presence known to the Protestants, while keeping clear of the Catholics, and this delicate situation demanded equal coolness and courage.

Thanks to the password in La Renaudie's letter, Gabriel reached the Baron de Castelnau with little difficulty.

This occurred on the afternoon of the 15th.

In eighteen hours, the Protestants would all be at Noizai; before twenty-four, they would attack the chateau of Amboise.

If they were to be turned from their purpose, then, there was no time to lose.

Baron de Castelnau was well acquainted with Count de Montgommery; he had often met him at the Louvre, and had heard the leaders of the party speak of him several times.

He went to meet him, and received him as an ally and friend.

"So here you are, M. de Montgommery," said he when they were alone. "In truth, I hoped for you, but did not expect you. The admiral blamed La Renaudie for having written you that letter. He said: 'M. de Montgommery should have been informed of our enterprise, but not called to share it. He could then do as he wished. Has he not told you that as long as Francis the Second reigned, his sword belonged neither to himself nor us?' To this La Renaudie replied that his letter pledged you to nothing, and left you your entire independence.''

''That is true,'' answered Gabriel.

''Nevertheless, we thought you would come,'' said Castelnau; ''for the missive of that hare-brained baron told you nothing of the undertaking in hand, and I am charged to make you acquainted with our plans and hopes.''

''I am listening,'' said Count de Montgommery.

Castelnau thereupon repeated to Gabriel all he had already learned from the Duke de Guise.

Gabriel saw with dismay how accurately the duke was informed of everything. Not a single detail brought him by the informers was incorrect; not a single circumstance had been omitted by them. The conspirators were really lost.

''Now you know everything,'' said Castelnau to his despairing auditor, ''and I have only to address a question to you, to which I foresee the response, however. You cannot join us, can you?''

''No,'' answered Gabriel, sadly shaking his head.

''Well, we shall not be the less friends on that account,'' rejoined Castelnau. ''I am aware it was stipulated by you beforehand that you were not to be called upon to take part in the combat; and you are more than ever entitled to claim this reserved right of yours now, for we are absolutely certain of victory.''

''Are you so absolutely certain, then?'' asked Gabriel, meaningly.

''Oh, yes, perfectly,'' replied the baron; ''the enemy suspects nothing, and will be taken by surprise. We were for a moment alarmed when the royal family removed from the open city of Blois to the fortified chateau of Amboise. Evidently they had some suspicions.''

''Nothing can be clearer than that,'' said Gabriel.

"Yes," said Castelnau; "but our hesitation quickly ceased. In fact, this unexpected change of residence, far from injuring our plans, is of the utmost service to them. The Duke de Guise now sleeps in false security; and, just fancy, my dear count, we have actually friends in the place. The Western Gate will be opened to us as soon as we show ourselves. Oh, success is certain, I tell you, and so you can, with a clear conscience, abstain from the fight."

"The result sometimes deceives the most magnificent expectations," returned Gabriel, gravely.

"But here we have not a single chance against us; not one!" repeated Castelnau, joyously rubbing his hands. "To-morrow will see the triumph of our party and the fall of the Guises."

"And what about treachery?" said Gabriel, with an effort, heart-broken to see such youthful courage rushing blindly to destruction.

"Treason is impossible," returned Castelnau, imperturbably. "The leaders alone are in the secret, and none of them are capable of— Now, hold there, M. de Montgommery," he added, interrupting himself, "on the word of a gentleman, I believe you are jealous of us; and you augur ill of our enterprise, because you are wild to take part in it. Oh, what an envious person you are, my friend!"

"Yes, envious indeed!" said Gabriel, gloomily.

"There, I was sure of it!" cried the young baron, laughing.

"Look here, M. de Castelnau," rejoined Gabriel; "you have, I believe, some confidence in me?"

"A blind confidence, if we are to speak seriously."

"Well, will you listen to a good advice, to a friendly counsel?"

"What is it?"

"Renounce your scheme of taking Amboise to-morrow. Send messengers to all our people who are to join you to-night cr to-morrow at once, telling them the project has failed or must at least be deferred."

"But why? why?" exclaimed Castelnau, beginning to be alarmed. "You have surely some grave reason for speaking thus?"

"Good heavens, no!" returned Gabriel, with a constraint that tortured him.

"Surely you do not advise me to abandon and persuade our brethren to abandon a scheme that looks so auspicious without some good reason?"

"Doubtless I have a reason, but I cannot tell you what it is. Will you and can you believe me upon my word? I have already gone further in this matter than I have a right to do. Do me the favor of believing me on my word."

"Listen," answered Castelnau, seriously; "if I resolve in this strange fashion to turn rein at the last moment, I shall be responsible to La Renaudie and the other leaders. Can I at least refer them to you?"

"Yes," replied Gabriel.

"And you will tell them the reasons that have dictated your advice?"

"Alas! I have not the right to do so."

"How do you expect, then, that I could yield to your request? Should I not be reproached with having cruelly annihilated hopes that were certainties? With all our confidence in you, M. de Montgommery, a man is but a man, and may be mistaken, with the best intentions in the world. If you allow no one to examine and approve your reasons, you surely cannot expect us to be guided by them."

"Then beware!" returned Gabriel, severely. "You in your turn accept the responsibility of any misfortune that may happen."

Castelnau was struck by the tone in which these words were uttered.

"M. de Montgommery!" said he, suddenly enlightened, "I think I have a glimpse of the truth. You have had a secret confided to you, or you have surprised it, which you cannot reveal. You have some serious knowledge as to the probable issue of this enterprise; you know, perhaps, that we have been betrayed—is that not so?"

"I have not said so," said Gabriel, quickly.

"Either," continued Castelnau, "you saw the duke on your way hither—he is your friend, and, not knowing that you are one of us, perhaps he has allowed you to get at the bottom of things—"

"I have said nothing to lead you to suppose so," protested Gabriel.

"—or," went on Castelnau, "when passing through Amboise, you have noticed certain preparations, obtained certain disclosures. In fine, our plot is discovered."

"Have I, then, given you any reason to believe this?" cried Gabriel, in dismay.

"No, M. le Comte; for you are pledged to secrecy, I see. So I do not ask you for a positive assurance, not even for a word. But if I am mistaken, a gesture, a look, even your silence may suffice to enlighten me."

Gabriel, however, full of anxiety, was trying to recall the very words of the terrible pledge he had given to the Duke de Guise. He had bound himself on his honor as a gentleman not to allow what was passing at Amboise to be guessed or suspected by a word, sign, or allusion.

After a prolonged silence, the Baron de Castelnau said, with his eyes riveted on his face—

"You do not speak. I understand you, and shall act accordingly."

"And what are you going to do?" asked Gabriel, quickly.

"What you advised me at first: to warn La Renaudie and the other leaders to bring the movement to a halt and declare to those of our brethren who arrive here that some one in whom we have confidence has informed us that treachery is probable—"

"But such is not the case!" interrupted Count de Montgommery, quickly. "I have not given you any information, M. de Castelnau."

"Count," answered Castelnau, pressing Gabriel's hand meaningly, "is not your very reticence a warning and our salvation? And once put on our guard, then—"

"Then?" repeated Gabriel.

"Everything will turn out well for us and badly for them. We lay aside our enterprise until more propitious times; we discover at any cost the informers, if there are any, among us; we redouble our precautions, hide our plans in greater mystery than ever, and one fine day, when everything is prepared, and we are absolutely certain of success, we renew our attempt, and, thanks to you, instead of failing, triumph."

"Ah, but that is just what I wanted to avoid!" cried Gabriel, who saw with terror that he was hurried to the very brink of an involuntary treason. "Now, M. de Castelnau, the true source of my warning and advice is, really and truly, your criminal and dangerous enterprise. By attacking the Catholics, you put yourselves entirely in the wrong. You justify all their reprisals. You were oppressed subjects; you become rebels. Must you avenge on the young king your grievances against his ministers? Ah, I feel the very anguish of death in thinking of all this. You must renounce this impious struggle for good and all. Let your principles fight in your behalf, I say. Let the truth not be bespattered with blood. This is what I wanted to tell you. This is why I implore you and all our brethren to have nothing to do with these fatal civil wars which can only retard the progress of our cause."

"Is that really the only motive of your discourse?"

"The only one," answered Gabriel, in a hollow voice.

"Then I thank you for your good intentions, M. le Comte," returned Castelnau, with some coldness; "but they cannot hinder me from acting in accordance with the instructions of my leaders. I can easily understand that it must be painful to a gentleman like you to see others fight without you. Still, you can hardly be allowed to trammel and paralyze the movements of a whole army."

"So," said Gabriel, pale and gloomy, "you will continue your fatal enterprise and let others do so also?"

"Yes, M. le Comte," returned Castelnau, with a firmness that did not admit of reply; "and if you allow me, I will now give the necessary orders for to-morrow's attack."

He bowed to Gabriel, and passed out without waiting for an answer.

CHAPTER XXXVIII

THE BEGINNING OF THE END

G ABRIEL, however, did not leave the chateau of Noizai, but resolved to spend the night there. His presence would give the Reformers a pledge of his good faith in case they should be attacked, and moreover he hoped to be able to convince, in the morning, some other leader less obstinately blinded than Castelnau. If La Renaudie could only come!

Castelnau left him entirely free, and seemed to be rather scornfully inattentive to him.

Gabriel met him several times that evening in the halls and corridors of the chateau, going and coming, giving orders for reconnoissances and supplies.

But these two brave young men, each equally high-souled and noble, did not exchange a word.

During the long hours of that night of anguish, Count de Montgommery, too anxious to be able to sleep, remained on the ramparts, listening, meditating, praying.

At daylight, the troops of the Reformers began to arrive in little separate bands.

At eight, they had come in large numbers, and at eleven Castelnau expected no more of them. But Gabriel did not know one of their commanders. La Renaudie had sent word that he and his troop would reach Amboise by way of the forest of Chateau-Regnault. Everything was ready for departure. Mazères and Raunai, the captains commanding the vanguard, had already descended to the terrace of the chateau to form their detachments in marching order. Castelnau was triumphant.

"Well?" said he to Gabriel, on meeting him, passing over in his joy the conversation of the evening before, "well, you see, M. le Comte, you were wrong, and that all goes well."

"Wait!" replied Gabriel, shaking his head.

"But what can we do to inspire you with faith, O thou incredulous one?" retorted Castelnau, with a smile. "Every one of our men has kept his engagements. They have all arrived at the appointed hour, with more men than they had promised. They have traversed their provinces without being interfered with, and still better, without interfering with others. Is not that an unusual piece of good fortune?"

The baron was interrupted by a noise of trumpets and arms and by a great tumult outside.

But, in the intoxication of his confidence, he was not alarmed, and could only believe in something lucky having occurred.

"Stay," said he to Gabriel; "I wager these are new reinforcements that were not expected. Doubtless, Lamothe and Deschamps with the conspirators from Picardy. They were not to have arrived until to-morrow; but they made a forced march, my brave comrades, to share in the battle and the victory! These are friends to have."

"Yes; but are they friends?" asked Gabriel, who had turned pale on hearing the sound of the trumpets.

"What else?" answered Castelnau. "Come into this gallery. You can see the terrace from which the noise is proceeding through the battlements."

He drew Gabriel after him; but when he reached the edge of the wall, he uttered a loud cry, raised his arms, and stood like one petrified.

It was not the troops of the Reformers, but a body of royal troops that had occasioned the tumult. It was not Lamothe that commanded the new arrivals, but Jacques de Savois, Duke de Nemours.

Taking advantage of the woods surrounding Noizai, the

royal cavalry had been able to reach, almost without being perceived, the open terrace, on which the vanguard of the rebels was forming in battle array.

There was not even a struggle, for the first thing the Duke de Nemours did was to seize the stacks of arms.

Mazères and Raunai had been forced to surrender without striking a blow; and at the moment Castelnau looked from the top of the wall, his men, conquered without even fighting, were surrendering their swords to the conquerors. Where he believed he should see his soldiers, he saw only prisoners.

He could not trust his eyes. He stood a moment motionless, dazed and speechless. Such an event was so remote from his anticipations that he failed to account for it. Gabriel, less surprised by this sudden attack, was no less overwhelmed.

As they were regarding each other, both equally pale and disheartened, an ensign entered hurriedly in search of Castelnau.

"What is the state of affairs?" said he, his very anxiety giving him back his voice.

"M. le Baron," replied the ensign, "they have seized the drawbridge and the first gate; we had only just time to close the second. But it will not resist long, and in a quarter of an hour they will be in the court. Are we to fight or send a flag of truce? We await your orders."

"I will descend," said Castelnau, "as soon as I have put on my armor."

He hurriedly entered the next hall to buckle on his cuirass and sword. Gabriel followed him.

"What are you going to do, my friend?" he said sadly.

"I do not know; I do not know," replied Castelnau, bewildered. "One can always die."

"Alas!" said Gabriel, "why did you not believe me yesterday?"

"Yes, I see you were right," returned the baron. "You foresaw what happened. You knew it beforehand, perhaps?"

"Perhaps," said Gabriel. "It is my greatest torture. But, Castelnau, there are in life strange and terrible complications of destiny. What if I was not at liberty to dissuade you by giving the real reasons that were upon my lips? What if I pledged my word of honor as a gentleman not to lead you to suspect the truth, either directly or indirectly?"

"Then you did well to be silent. I should have acted like you in your place. It is I, madman that I was, who ought to have understood you; it is I that ought to have known that a brave man, such as you are, would not have dissuaded us from battle, except for some powerful reason. But I will expiate my fault: I will die."

"And I with you," said Gabriel, calmly.

"You! and why?" exclaimed Castelnau. "Fighting is the one thing you are bound to abstain from."

"I shall not fight, therefore," said Gabriel; "I cannot. But my life is a burden to me. The seemingly double part I am playing is odious to me. I shall go to battle unarmed. I will not slay, but be slain. I will throw myself between some deadly stroke and you. If I cannot be a sword, I may be a shield."

"No," rejoined Castelnau; "remain. I ought not and will not drag you with me to destruction."

"Ah!" said Gabriel, "but you will drag to destruction, without any advantage, all those of our party shut up with you in this chateau. My life is much more useless than theirs."

"Can I do otherwise, for the glory of our party, than ask this sacrifice of them? Martyrs are more useful and glorious than conquerors."

"Yes; but is not your first duty to try to save the forces intrusted to you? Time enough to die at their head when their safety cannot be reconciled with honor."

"Then, you advise——"

"To try peaceful methods. If you resist, you cannot avoid defeat and massacre. If you yield to necessity, they have not, it seems to me, the right to punish those who have planned, but not executed an enterprise. Simple intentions cannot be prejudged, still less chastised. You disarm your enemies by disarming yourselves."

"I feel so much repentance for not having heeded your first warning that I should like to obey you now. Still, I confess I hesitate. I do not like the idea of retreating."

"To retreat, you must have advanced. Now what is there to prove your rebellion so far? Only by drawing the sword can you show yourself criminal. Stay; my presence may, thank God, be good for something, after all. I could not save you yesterday; will you let me try to do so to-day?"

"What would you do?"

"Nothing unworthy of you, you may be sure. I will go to the Duke de Nemours, who commands the royal troops; I will announce to him that there will be no resistance, that the gates will be thrown open and you will surrender on parole. I will ask him to pledge his ducal honor that no harm shall happen to you or your gentlemen, and that, after conducting you before the king to explain your wants and grievances, you shall be set at liberty."

"And if he refuses?" asked Castelnau.

"If he refuses," returned Gabriel, "his will be the wrong. He will have rejected a fair and honorable capitulation, and all the responsibility for the blood that is shed will rest on his shoulders. If he refuses, Castelnau, I will return and die by your side."

"Would La Renaudie, think you, consent to such an arrangement in my place?"

"On my soul, I think any reasonable man would do so."

"Do as you have advised. Our despair will only render us the more formidable, if your mission to the duke
fail, as I fear it will."

"Thanks," said Gabriel; "I hope, with God's help, to
succeed, and thereby be the means of saving so many noble
and valiant lives."

He descended to the terrace running, had the door of
the court opened, and, with a flag of truce in his hand,
approached the Duke de Nemours, who, in the midst of
his troops, awaited the issue of peace or war.

"I do not know whether monseigneur recognizes me,"
said Gabriel. "I am Count de Montgommery."

"Yes; I recognize you, M. de Montgommery," replied Jacques de Savoie. "M. de Guise told me I
should find you here, but added that you were here
with his permission, and that I must treat you as a
friend."

"A precaution that might do me harm in the opinion
of other unfortunate friends," said Gabriel, shaking his
head sadly. "But, monseigneur, might I ask the favor
of a few words with you?"

"I am at your service," was the reply.

Castelnau, who, through a grated window of the chateau,
was following with agony every movement of the duke and
Gabriel, saw them retire apart and converse with much
animation. Then Jacques de Savoie demanded paper, and
wrote rapidly on a drumhead a note which he handed
to Count de Montgommery, who seemed to thank him
warmly.

There was some hope, therefore. Gabriel, in effect,
hastened speedily to the chateau, and a moment after
placed, voiceless and almost breathless, the following
declaration in the hands of the baron:

M. de Castelnau and his companions in the chateau of
Noizai having consented to lay down their arms on my
arrival and to surrender, I, the undersigned, Jacques de

Savoie, do pledge my princely word, my honor, and hopes
of salvation, that they shall not have any harm, and that
I will dismiss them safe and sound—fifteen among them
with the Sieur de Castelnau only, to go with me to Amboise, and there present to the king, our sovereign lord,
their peaceful remonstrances.

Given at the chateau of Noizai, this 16th day of
March, 1560.   JACQUES DE SAVOIE.

"Thanks, my friend," said Castelnau to Gabriel, after
reading. "You have saved our lives, and more than our
lives—our honor. On these conditions, I am ready to follow M. de Nemours to Amboise. We shall at least not
arrive there as prisoners before their conqueror, but
as oppressed subjects before their king. Once more,
thanks."

But, while grasping the hand of his liberator, Castelnau perceived that Gabriel had become as sad as
before.

"What is the matter with you, pray?" he asked.

"I am thinking of La Renaudie and the others who
are to attack Amboise to-night," answered Gabriel. "It
is, alas! too late to save them. Still, if I tried? Was
not La Renaudie to come through the forest of Chateau-
Regnault?"

"Yes," said Castelnau, eagerly; "and you might find
him, perhaps, and save him as you have saved us."

"I will at least try," said Gabriel. "The Duke de
Nemours will leave me free, I think. Adieu, then, my
friend. I go to continue, if I can, my work of concilia-
tion. *Au revoir* at Amboise."

"*Au revoir!*" replied Castelnau.

As Gabriel had foreseen, the Duke de Nemours made
no objection to his leaving Noizai and the royal detachment.

The ardent and devoted young man was thus enabled
to gallop at full speed in the direction of the forest of
Chateau-Regnault.

As for Castelnau and the fifteen gentlemen with him, they followed confidently Jacques de Savoie to Amboise.

But, on their arrival, they were immediately led to prison. They were to remain there, they were told, until the affray was over, and there was no longer any danger in introducing them to the presence of the king.

CHAPTER XXXIX

THE FOREST OF CHÂTEAU-REGNAULT

L UCKILY, the forest of Château-Regnault was not more than a league and a half from Noizai. Gabriel rode thither at full speed; but when he got there, he was more than an hour before meeting with any body of troops, friendly or hostile.

At last, he thought he heard, at the turn of an alley, the measured tramp of cavalry. But these could not be Huguenots, for the latter had it too much at heart to conceal their movements not to observe the most perfect silence.

No matter! Gabriel turned in their direction, and soon descried the red scarfs of the royal troops.

As he advanced toward their leader he recognized him, and was recognized in turn.

It was Baron de Pardaillan, a young and valiant officer, who had fought with him under M. de Guise in Italy.

"Ah! it is Count de Montgommery," cried Pardaillan. "I thought you were at Noizai, count."

"I have just come from there," said Gabriel.

"And what has passed? Ride with us a short distance and tell us the news."

Gabriel related the sudden arrival of the Duke de Nemours, the surprise of the terrace and drawbridge, his own intervention, and the peaceful submission which was the happy result of it.

"*Pardieu!*" exclaimed Pardaillan; "hasn't M. de Ne-

mours luck? I wish I had as much! Do you know,
M. de Montgommery, against whom I am marching at
this moment?"

"Against La Renaudie, doubtless?" said Gabriel.

"Right. And do you know what La Renaudie is
to me?"

"Your cousin, if I remember right."

"Yes, my cousin, and more than my cousin, my
friend, my brother-in-arms. Do you know it is hard
to fight against one who has fought by your side?"

"Yes, indeed," answered Gabriel; "but you are not
sure of meeting him."

"Oh, but I am sure! My instructions are only too
precise; and the reports of those who have betrayed him
only too faithful. Listen: in a quarter of an hour I must
meet La Renaudie face to face, in the second alley on
the left."

"But supposing you took another alley?"

"I should fail in my honor and duty as a soldier,"
returned Pardaillan. "Even if I would, I could not. My
two lieutenants have received the same orders from M. de
Guise as I have, and would not let me infringe them.
My sole hope is that La Renaudie may consent to surrender. A very uncertain hope that, for several reasons—he
is proud and fearless; being in the open country, he will
not be surprised, like Castelnau; we are not very superior
to him in numbers. But you will help me, M. de Montgommery, in persuading him to come to terms?"

"Surely," said Gabriel, "I will do my best."

"To the devil with these civil wars!" said Pardaillan,
in conclusion.

They rode in silence for nearly ten minutes.

"We must be near him," said Pardaillan. "My heart
is beating fast. For the first time in my life, I think, devil
take me if I am not afraid!"

The royal troopers were no longer laughing or chatting,
but advanced slowly and cautiously.

They had not proceeded two hundred yards when, through a clump of trees, they thought they could see the gleam of arms upon a path running parallel with the highway.

They had not long to doubt, besides, for a firm voice cried out almost immediately—

"Halt! who goes there?"

"It is La Renaudie's voice," said Pardaillan to Gabriel. And his reply to the summons was—

"Valois and Lorraine!"

La Renaudie immediately issued out of the by-path, followed by his band. He then ordered his soldiers to halt, and advanced a few paces.

Pardaillan imitated him, ordered his soldiers to halt, and also advanced a few paces.

They looked more like two friends eager to embrace after a long absence than two enemies about to fight.

"I should have answered you according to the dictates of my duty," said La Renaudie, already approaching, "if I had not believed I recognized the voice of a friend. Either I am mistaken, or that visor conceals the face of my dear Pardaillan."

"Yes; it is I, my dear La Renaudie," answered Pardaillan. "And if I may give you a brother's advice, renounce your enterprise, my friend, and lay down your arms."

"Oh, yes! a brother's advice, truly!" said La Renaudie, somewhat ironically.

"Yes, M. de La Renaudie," added Gabriel, showing himself; "it is the advice of a loyal friend, I swear. Castelnau surrendered to M. de Nemours this morning; and, if you do not imitate him, you are lost."

"Oho! M. de Montgommery!" retorted La Renaudie; "so you, too, are on the side of these people?"

"Neither with them nor with you," said Gabriel, gravely and sadly; "I am between you."

"Oh, excuse me, M. le Comte," returned La Renaudie,

moved by the noble and dignified accent of Gabriel. "I did not wish to offend you; and I should sooner doubt my own honor than yours."

"Then trust me," said Gabriel, "and do not risk a useless and fatal engagement. Surrender."

"Impossible!" answered La Renaudie.

"But understand, pray," said Pardaillan, "that I have here only a feeble advance-guard."

"And do you believe that my whole force consists of the men you see here?" replied the Reformed leader.

"I warn you," returned Pardaillan, "that you have traitors in your ranks."

"They are now in yours," said La Renaudie.

"I undertake to obtain your pardon from the Duke de Guise," said Pardaillan, in despair.

"My pardon!" cried La Renaudie. "I hope to be soon in a condition to grant pardons rather than receive them!"

"La Renaudie! La Renaudie! you will not force me to draw my sword against you, Godefroy, my old comrade, my childhood's friend!"

"I fear you must do so, Pardaillan; you know me too well to believe I am likely to give way before you."

"M. de La Renaudie," cried Gabriel, "I tell you once more that you are in the wrong!"

But he was roughly interrupted.

The horsemen on both sides, who, though at a distance, were in sight of each other, could not understand this singular parleying of their leaders, and were burning to come to close quarters.

"What the devil are they saying there at such length?" murmured the soldiers of Pardaillan.

"Ah!" on the other hand, the Huguenots were grumbling, "do they think we have come hither to listen to them chattering about their private affairs?"

"Wait!" said one among the band of Protestants, in

which every soldier was a leader; "I'll shorten their conversation!"

And, at the very moment Gabriel was beginning to speak, he fired a pistol at the troops of Pardaillan.

"You see!" cried Pardaillan, sorrowfully, "your men have fired the first shot."

"Without my leave!" said La Renaudie, quickly. "But, since the die is cast, so much the worse. Forward! my friends; forward!"

He turned toward his people; Pardaillan did the same, and also shouted—

"Forward!"

The firing began.

Gabriel, however, remained motionless between the reds and the whites, the Royalists and Reformers. He hardly moved his horse aside, and received the fire of both parties.

At the first volley, the plume of his helmet was pierced by a ball, and his horse shot under him.

He freed himself from the stirrups, and continued to stand, pensive and impassive, in the midst of this terrible affray.

The powder ran out; the two bands rushed upon each other, and continued the combat with the sword.

Gabriel never stirred amid the clash of arms; and, without even touching the hilt of his sword, he was contented to look on, as steel met steel in furious conflict, sad and somber—an image of France stationed among her children while engaged in slaying one another.

The Reformers, inferior in number and discipline, were beginning to give way.

La Renaudie, in the tumult, had come upon Pardaillan.

"Fall to!" he cried out to him. "Let me at least die by your hand!"

"Ah!" said Pardaillan; "he who shall kill the other will be the more generous!"

And they attacked each other vigorously. The strokes

resounded on their armor like hammers on the anvil. La Renaudie rode round Pardaillan, who had a firm seat in his saddle, and parried and thrust with unflagging strength. Two rivals athirst with vengeance could not have been more furious.

At last La Renaudie plunged his sword in the breast of Pardaillan, who fell.

A cry was heard, not from Pardaillan, but from La Renaudie.

Happily for the conqueror, he had not even time to gaze upon his victim.

Montigny, Pardaillan's page, fired at him with his arquebuse, and he fell, mortally wounded.

Nevertheless, before dying, he had strength enough left to kill the page with a backward stroke of his sword.

Around these three bodies the conflict waged more furiously than ever.

But the Huguenots had clearly the worst of it, and after their leader was slain were soon in full flight.

Most of them were killed; a few escaped, and a few were taken prisoners.

This fierce and bloody combat did not last ten minutes.

The royal troopers prepared to return to Amboise. The bodies of Pardaillan and La Renaudie were laid upon the same horse.

Gabriel, who, despite his ardent wish, had not received a scratch, being, no doubt, spared by both sides, gazed sadly on these two bodies, still alive but a few moments before—bodies containing hearts the noblest he had perhaps ever known.

"Which of the two was the braver?" he said to himself. "Which of the two best loved the other? Which of the two was the greater loss to his country?"

CHAPTER XL

THE POLITICS OF THE SIXTEENTH CENTURY

EVERYTHING, however, did not end with the surrender of the chateau of Noizai and the skirmish in the forest of Chateau-Regnault.

Most of the Nantes conspirators had not been notified of the two checks experienced by their party, and continued their march on Amboise, ready to assault the place that night.

But we know that, thanks to the precise reports of Lignières, they were expected.

So the young king did not care to retire to rest, but, with feverish anxiety, kept walking up and down the vast, unfurnished hall, which had been reserved as a chamber for his use.

Mary Stuart, the Duke de Guise, and the Cardinal de Lorraine were with him, watching and waiting also.

"What an everlasting night!" exclaimed Francis the Second. "I am in pain; my head is on fire, and these insupportable earaches torture me. What a night! what a night!"

"My poor, dear sire," answered Mary, gently, "do not excite yourself, I implore you. You only thus increase your bodily and mental sufferings. Will you not take a few moments' rest—for my sake?"

"Ah! Mary, how can I rest," said the king—"how can I remain tranquil when my people are in arms and rebellion against me? Ah! all these troubles are sure to shorten the little life that God has granted me!"

Mary did not answer; but the tears flowed down her lovely cheeks.

"Your Majesty must not be so deeply affected," said the Balafré. "I already have had the honor to assure you that our measures were taken and that victory was certain. I answer for your safety, sire."

"Have we not begun well?" added the Cardinal de Lorraine. "Castelnau a prisoner, La Renaudie slain— are not these happy auguries for the issue of this affair?"

"Very happy, indeed!" said Francis, bitterly.

"To-morrow all will be over; the other rebel chiefs will be in our power," continued the cardinal, "and we can, by a terrible example, frighten those who would try to imitate them. It is necessary, sire," he said, in reply to a gesture of repugnance on the part of the king. "A solemn act of faith, as they say in Spain, is essential to the outraged glory of religion and the threatened security of the throne. To begin with, Castelnau must die. M. de Nemours has taken it upon himself to promise him his life; but that does not concern us, and we have promised nothing. La Renaudie has escaped his just punishment by death; I have given orders, however, that his head be exposed at daybreak to-morrow on the bridge of Amboise, with this inscription: Leader of the rebels."

"Leader of the rebels!" repeated the young king. "But you said yourself he was not the leader, and that the confessions and correspondence prove that the real mover of the enterprise was the Prince de Condé alone."

"In the name of Heaven! do not speak so loud, I entreat you, sire," interrupted the cardinal. "Yes, it is quite true; the prince has conducted and directed everything from a distance. These wretches named him the *dumb captain;* and after the first success he was to declare himself. But as this success has not taken place, he has not declared himself, and will not declare himself. Let us not, therefore, drive him to any dangerous extremity. Let us not openly recognize him as the powerful head of the rebellion. Let us pretend not to see him, in order to avoid the necessity of pointing him out as such publicly."

"Still, M. de Condé is not the less a genuine rebel for that!" retorted Francis, whose youthful impatience was little in accord with these governmental fictions, as they have since been styled.

"Yes, sire," answered the Balafré; "but the prince, far from confessing his schemes, denies them. Let us feign to believe him on his word. The prince has come to-day to Amboise, where he is kept in sight; but in the same way he has conspired—at a distance. Let us pretend to receive him as an ally; it is less perilous than to have him as an enemy. The prince, in fine, will, if required, strike his accomplices this night along with us, and be present at their execution to-morrow. Is not the necessity to which he has to submit, then, a thousand times more painful than any imposed upon us?"

"Yes," said the king; "but will he do that? And if he does, can it be possible that he is guilty?"

"Sire," said the cardinal, "we have in our hands, and will place in those of your Majesty, if you desire, all the proofs of the secret complicity of M. de Condé. But the more flagrant these proofs are, the more we must dissemble; and I regret keenly myself some words that have escaped me, and that, if reported to the prince, might offend him."

"To fear offending a criminal!" cried Francis. "But what is that noise outside? Good heavens! would it be the rebels already?"

"I will run and see," said the Balafré.

But before he had crossed the threshold of the door, Richelieu, the captain of the arquebusiers, entered, and said quickly to the king—

"Pardon me, sire; M. de Condé believes he has heard certain words impugning his honor, and he demands eagerly permission to clear himself publicly, once for all, in presence of your Majesty, from these insulting suspicions."

The king would have refused perhaps to receive the prince; but the Duke de Guise had already made a sign. The arquebusiers of Captain Richelieu moved aside, and M. de Condé entered, with haughty mien and flushed cheeks.

He was followed by a few gentlemen and a number of the canons of St. Florentin—ordinary denizens of the chateau of Amboise, whom the cardinal had for this night transformed into soldiers, in order to assist in the defence, and who, as was common enough at the time, carried the arquebuse along with the rosary, and wore the helmet under the hood.

"Sire, you will excuse my boldness," he said, after bowing to the king; "but this boldness is justified perhaps by the audacious nature of the accusations which my enemies bring against my loyalty in the dark, and which I wish to force them to bring in the daylight, so that I may refute and brand them as they deserve."

"To what do you allude, my cousin?" asked the king, gravely.

"Sire," answered the prince, "certain persons have dared to say that I am the real chief of the rebels whose mad and impious attempt has thrown the realm into confusion, and alarmed your Majesty."

"Ah! they have said this. And who, pray, have said it?" inquired Francis.

"Sire, I have heard these odious calumnies from the lips of these reverend brothers of St. Florentin, who, doubtless believing themselves in security, have not hesitated to repeat aloud what has been whispered to them by others."

"And do you accuse those who have repeated or those who have whispered the offensive words?" said Francis.

"I accuse both, sire," replied the prince; "but especially the instigators of those cowardly slanders."

Having said this, he looked the cardinal full in the face, who concealed his embarrassment behind his brother as best he could.

"Well, my cousin," said the king, "we permit you to refute the slanders and the slanderers. Do so."

"Refute the slanders, sire!" repeated the Prince de Condé. "Do not my acts do so better than any words of mine? Have I not come, on the first summons, into this chateau, to take my place among the defenders of your Majesty? Is that the act of a criminal? I ask your Majesty yourself."

"Then accuse the slanderers!" said Francis, who did not wish to answer differently.

"I will do so, not by words, but by deeds, sire," said Condé. "If they have any courage, let them accuse me themselves openly. I here publicly fling my glove in the presence of God and the king. Let the man, be his quality or rank what it may, come forward and maintain that I am the author of this conspiracy! I offer to do battle with him when and how he wills; and, should he not be my equal, to accept him as my equal for this combat."

When the Prince de Condé finished, he threw his glove at his feet. His glance was a sufficient commentary on the meaning of his challenge; it was haughtily fixed on the face of the Duke de Guise, who did not move a muscle.

There was a moment of silence, every one doubtless meditating on this queer exhibition of mendacity given by a prince of the blood to the entire court, in which there was not a page who did not know him guilty, twenty times over, of the very crime from which he was exculpating himself with well-affected indignation.

But, to tell the truth, the young king was the only one, perhaps, artless enough to be astonished at it, and nobody suspected the virtue or the valor of the prince on this account.

The ideas of the Italian courts on politics, imported by Catherine de Médicis and her Florentines, were then fashionable in France. He who best deceived was reputed cleverest. To conceal one's thoughts and disguise one's deeds was the great art. Sincerity would have passed for folly.

The noblest and purest characters of the time—Coligny, Condé, and Chancellor Olivier—were tainted with this leprosy.

Consequently, the Duke de Guise did not despise the Prince de Condé; he admired him.

But he said to himself, with a smile, that he was at least quite as clever as he was.

Advancing a step forward, he slowly took off his glove, and dropped it beside that of the prince.

There was a moment of surprise; and it was at first thought he was going to accept the insolent challenge of M. de Condé.

But he would not have thus shown himself the great statesman he flattered himself he was.

In a loud and firm voice—a voice almost of sincerity, really!—he said—

"I uphold and approve the words of M. le Prince de Condé; and I am so much his servant, having the honor of being his relative, that I myself here offer myself as his second, and I will take arms against all comers to assist him in so just a defence."

And he gazed around boldly and inquiringly upon those who were about him.

The Prince de Condé had to lower his eyes, abashed.

He felt more thoroughly beaten than if he had been conquered in the lists.

"Does nobody," said the Duke de Guise, "raise the Prince de Condé's glove or mine?"

In fact, no one stirred, as may be easily imagined.

"My cousin," observed Francis the Second, with a melancholy smile, "you are now, it seems, cleansed from all suspicion of felony as you desired."

"Yes, sire," returned the *dumb captain*, with naïve impudence; "and I thank your Majesty for having aided me—"

He turned with some effort to the Balafré, and added—

"I thank my good ally and relative, M. de Guise. I hope to prove to him and to prove to all again, by fighting the rebels to-night, if I am allowed to do so, that he did not act wrong in defending me."

Thereupon, the Prince de Condé and the Duke de Guise exchanged the most profound and courteous salutations.

Then the prince, being well and duly justified, and having nothing further to do, bowed to the king and withdrew, followed by the spectators who had accompanied him on his entrance.

There only remained in the royal chamber the four personages whose tedious waiting and fears had been for a moment distracted by this singular comedy.

But this chivalrous scene discloses the fact that high politics dates from the sixteenth century, at least.

CHAPTER XLI

THE TUMULT OF AMBOISE

AFTER the departure of Condé, neither the king nor Mary Stuart nor the two brothers of Lorraine dwelt on the event that had just occurred. They seemed by a tacit and common accord to avoid this dangerous subject. Minutes and hours slipped by in the impatient and gloomy silence of their wearisome waiting.

Francis the Second often raised his hand to his burning head. Mary, seated apart, was gazing sadly upon the pallid, thin face of her young husband, and, from time to time, wiped away a tear. The Cardinal de Lorraine was listening with absorbed attention to the sounds from outside. As to the Balafré, who had no orders to give, and whose rank and office kept him near the king, he appeared to suffer cruelly from his forced inaction, and sometimes quivered and stamped the floor, like some brave war steed gnawing at the bit that restrains him.

However, the night was advancing. The clocks of the chateau, and afterward that of St. Florentin, had struck six, and then half-past six. Day was beginning to dawn, and no noise of attack, no signal from the sentinels, had troubled the quiet night.

"Do you know, M. le Cardinal," said the king, breathing with relief, "I am beginning to think that this Lignières has deceived your Eminence, or else the Huguenots have changed their mind?"

"So much the worse!" said Charles de Lorraine; "for we were sure of crushing the rebellion.

"Oh, no! so much the better!" rejoined Francis; "for the conflict itself would have been a defeat for royalty—"

But the king had not finished speaking when two arquebuse shots, the alarm signal agreed on, were fired, and the cry of, "To arms! to arms! to arms!" was heard on the ramparts, and repeated from post to post.

"There can no longer be any doubt; it is the enemy!" cried the cardinal, turning pale in spite of himself.

The Duke de Guise rose almost joyously, and, saluting the king, said simply—

"Sire, we shall soon meet again; rely upon me."

And he left hurriedly. His powerful voice was heard in the antechamber, when a new arquebusade resounded.

"You see, sire," said the cardinal, perhaps hoping to dispel his alarm by the sound of his own voice—"you see that Lignières was well informed, and that he only made a mistake of a couple of hours."

But the king was not listening; and, while biting angrily his pale lips, was attending only to the growing noise of artillery and arquebuses.

"I can hardly believe in such audacity!" he murmured. "Such an affront to the crown!"

"Will turn into shame for these wretches, sire," said the cardinal.

"Well, to judge by the noise they make," returned the king, "these Huguenot gentlemen are very numerous and not at all afraid."

"All that will be extinguished immediately, like a fire of straw," said Charles de Lorraine.

"It does not seem so, for the noise draws nearer," answered Francis; "and the fire, instead of being extinguished, is burning brighter, I believe."

"Great heavens!" cried Mary Stuart, in dismay, "do you hear the bullets ringing against the walls?"

"It seems to me, nevertheless, madame—" stammered the cardinal. "I really believe, your Majesty— As for myself, I do not hear any increase of noise—"

He was interrupted by a terrific explosion.

"There is an answer for you!" said the king, with a bitter smile, "even though your pale and frightened face did not contradict you."

"I smell powder already," returned Mary; "and now there are tumultuous cries!"

"Better and better!" said Francis. "Then these gentlemen must have carried the town, and are about to lay siege to us in form in the chateau."

"Sire," said the cardinal, trembling, "would it not be better, under the circumstances, for your Majesty to retire to the donjon? We may be sure at least that they will not get possession of that."

"What! I hide myself from my subjects!" cried the king—"from heretics! Let them come even here, my good uncle. I shall be very glad to learn to what extent their audacity reaches. They will, I have no doubt, insist on our singing psalms with them in French, and on turning our chapel of St. Florentin into a Protestant conventicle."

"Sire, for God's sake have a little prudence!" said Mary.

"No," returned the king, "I will see the end of this; I will await my trusty subjects here, and, by my royal name, the first who fails in the respect he owes me shall see whether this dagger by my side is worn for show only."

The minutes slipped by, and the arquebuse firing became more and more lively. The poor Cardinal de Lorraine had no longer strength to utter a word. The young king wrung his hands in anger.

"What!" cried Mary Stuart; "nobody brings us any news! Is the danger so great, then, that no one dares to leave his post for a moment even?"

"Ah!" said the king, at last quite beside himself, "this waiting is unendurable; and anything would be better than it, I am sure! But I know one way of learning how matters are, and that is to join in the conflict. Doubtless M. le Lieutenant-Général will not refuse to receive me as a volunteer."

Francis took two or three steps in the direction of the door. Mary threw herself before him.

"Sire, you cannot think of such a thing? And you so ill!" she cried.

"I no longer feel ill," he answered. "Indignation has banished pain."

"A moment, sire!" said the cardinal; "it seems to me that this time the noise is growing more distant. Yes, and the discharges are fewer. Ah! here is a page with news, no doubt."

"Sire," said the page, "M. le Duc de Guise charges me to inform your Majesty that the rebels have broken ranks and are in full retreat."

"At last!" cried the king. "That is fortunate!"

"As soon as M. le Lieutenant-Général believes he can safely quit the walls," continued the page, "he will come and make his report to the king."

The page passed out.

"Well, sire!" said the Cardinal de Lorraine, triumphantly, "did I not foretell that the whole thing would be a mere trifle, and that my illustrious and valiant brother would make short work of these psalm-singers?"

"Ah, fair uncle," retorted the king, "how suddenly you have regained your courage!"

But at this moment an explosion more terrible than anything before occurred.

"What means that noise?" cried the king.

"In fact—it is singular," said the cardinal, trembling again.

Happily, the terror was not of long duration. Richelieu, the captain of the arquebusiers, entered at the same time, his face black with powder, and a dinted sword in his hand.

"Sire," said he to the king, "the rebels are utterly beaten. They scarcely had time to explode a quantity of powder, which they had placed near one of the gates, and which has not done us the slightest harm. Those who have not been killed or taken have crossed the bridge and barricaded themselves in one of the houses in the Faubourg du Vendomois, where we shall make short work of them. Your Majesty can see from this window how we deal with them."

The king went quickly to the window, followed by the cardinal, and more slowly by the queen.

"Yes," said he; "I see they are besieged in their turn. But what a smoke there is from yonder house!"

"Sire, it has been set on fire," returned the captain.

"Splendid!" cried the cardinal. "Do you see them jumping through the window, sire? Two—three—four— You can hear their cries from here."

"Oh, the poor people!" cried Mary, clasping her hands.

"It seems to me," observed the king, "that I notice the plume and scarf of our cousin of Condé at the head of our soldiers—am I right, captain?"

"Yes, your Majesty," answered Richelieu. "He has been with us throughout, always beside M. de Guise, sword in hand."

"Well, M. le Cardinal," said Francis, "you see that he did not require much pressing."

"He had to do it, sire," replied Charles de Lorraine. "M. de Condé would have risked too much by acting otherwise."

"But," cried Mary, at once attracted and repelled by the horrible spectacle outside, "the flames are more intense than ever! the house is going to fall on the poor creatures!"

"It is falling!" said the king.

"Hurrah! all is over!" exclaimed the cardinal.

"Oh, leave this place, sire! it makes me ill," said Mary, drawing the king away.

"Yes," answered Francis, "now is the time for pity."

And he withdrew from the window, where the cardinal stayed alone, quite delighted.

But he soon turned back, on hearing the voice of the Duke de Guise.

The Balafré entered, calm and haughty, accompanied by the Prince de Condé, who did his best not to appear sad and downcast.

"Sire, all is finished," said the duke to the king; "and the rebels have paid the penalty of their crime. I thank God for having delivered your Majesty from this peril; for, after what I have seen, I know it to have been greater than I at first imagined. There were traitors among us."

"Is it possible?" exclaimed the cardinal.

"Yes," rejoined the Balafré; "at the first attack the Reformers were seconded by the men-at-arms brought by Lamothe, and we were charged in flank by them. For a time they were masters of the town."

"This is frightful!" said Mary, pressing close to the king.

"It would have been still worse, madame," continued the duke, "if the rebels had been supported by Chaudieu, the brother of the minister, as they expected to be, who was to have made an attack upon the Porte des Bons-Hommes."

"The attack failed?" asked the king.

"It did not take place, sire," answered the duke. "Thank God! Captain Chaudieu was late, and did not arrive until all his friends were crushed. He may now attack at his ease! He will find us prepared both within and without the walls. And to give him time for reflection I have ordered twenty or thirty of his accomplices to be hanged from the battlements of Amboise. This spectacle will be ample enough warning for him, I fancy."

"A wise precaution," said the cardinal.

"I thank you, my cousin," said the king to the Balafré. "But I see that the protection of God has been specially manifested in this dangerous crisis, since He alone has permitted the confusion that has led to the discomfiture of our enemies. Let us then proceed to the chapel and render Him thanks."

"Next," said the cardinal, "we must see to the punish-

ment of the surviving criminals. You will be present at
their execution, with the queen and queen-mother, will you
not, sire?"

"But—will that be necessary?" said the young king,
walking to the door, and much disturbed.

"Sire," returned the cardinal, following him, "it is indispensable. The glorious King Francis the First, your
illustrious grandsire, never failed to be present at the
burning of heretics. As to the King of Spain, sire—"

"Other kings may do as they please," said Francis, still
walking; "and I intend doing as I like also."

"I must also inform your Majesty that the nuncio of the
Pope also counts on your presence at the first 'act of faith'
of your reign," added the pitiless cardinal. "When every
one is present, even the Prince de Condé, does it become
your Majesty to be absent?"

"Oh, we can speak of that another time," returned
Francis. "The prisoners are not yet even sentenced."

"Oh, yes, but they are!" rejoined Charles de Lorraine,
emphatically.

"Very well," answered Francis; "you can impose this
terrible burden on my weakness at the proper time and
place. But at present, M. le Cardinal, let us go, as I have
said to you already, and kneel before the altar, and there
thank God, who has deigned to save us from the perils of
this conspiracy."

"Sire," said the Duke de Guise, "we ought not to am-
plify those matters and give them greater importance than
they warrant. Will your Majesty be good enough not to
call this movement a conspiracy? It was, in truth, a
tumult."

CHAPTER XLII

AN ACT OF FAITH

ALTHOUGH the conspirators had inserted in the manifesto discovered among the papers of La Renaudie a declaration "not to attempt anything against the king's majesty, or the princes of the blood, or the good of the realm," they had, for all that, been in open rebellion, and could only look forward to the fate of those vanquished in civil wars.

The manner in which the Calvinists had been treated when they were peaceful and submissive subjects left them little hope of pardon.

In fact, the Cardinal de Lorraine urged on their trial with a passion which, if ecclesiastical, was hardly Christian. He confided the trial of the noblemen implicated in this fatal affair to the parliament of Paris and Chancellor Olivier. Consequently, matters proceeded without any delay. The interrogations were hurried through rapidly, and the sentences pronounced more rapidly still.

These vain formalities were dispensed with in the case of humbler culprits, who were broken on the wheel or hanged daily without giving any trouble to the parliament. The honors and expense of a trial were only granted to persons of a certain rank and reputation.

At last, thanks to the pious zeal of Charles de Lorraine, everything was finished at the end of three days, as far as the latter were concerned.

The 15th of April was fixed for the public execution

With a flag of truce in his hand, he approached the Duke de Nemours, who, in the midst of his troops, awaited the issue of peace or war.

The Two Dianas, II
—p. 329

of twenty-seven barons, eleven counts, and seven marquises—in all, forty-five gentlemen and leaders of the Huguenots.

Nothing was neglected to give this singular religious ceremony all the pomp and splendor desirable. Immense preparations were made. From Paris to Nantes public curiosity was stimulated by the methods in use at the period for such a purpose; that is to say, the execution was announced by the preachers and curés in their churches.

On the appointed day three elegant galleries, the central and most magnificent of which was reserved for the royal family, were erected on the platform of the chateau at whose foot the bloody tragedy was to be enacted.

Around the square, benches rising one above the other were occupied by all the faithful of the neighborhood who could be brought thither by fear or favor. The bourgeoisie and rustics, who might have had some dislike for this spectacle, were constrained by force or corruption to be present. Some were promised that their taxes would be remitted; others were threatened with the loss of their places, their franchises, or their privileges. All these motives, joined to the curiosity of this one and the fanaticism of that one, brought such a multitude to Amboise that, on the evening of the fatal day, more than ten thousand persons had to encamp in the fields.

From an early hour the roofs of the houses in the town were crowded, and the casements overlooking the square fetched as much as ten crowns apiece—an enormous sum for the period.

A vast scaffold, covered with black cloth, was erected in the centre of the inclosure. On it was placed the *chouquet*, the block upon which each of the condemned was to lay his head in turn, after kneeling. An armchair near by, draped in black, was reserved for the registrar, whose duty it was to call by name the several gentlemen in succession, and read out their sentence.

The square was guarded by the Scotch company and the gendarmes of the king's household.

After a solemn Mass heard in the chapel of St. Florentin, the condemned were led to the foot of the scaffold. Many of them had already suffered torture. Monks supported them, and tried to make them renounce their religious principles. But all refused, and declined to answer the monks, whom they suspected of being spies of the Cardinal de Lorraine.

However, the galleries of the court were filled, except the central one. The king and queen, whose consent to be present had been forced from them, were permitted to stay away, at least until the end, when the principal leaders would be executed. But they would be there, and that was all the cardinal asked. Poor young sovereigns! poor crowned slaves! they, too, like many of the humble spectators, feared for their places and privileges.

The execution began at noon.

When the first of the Reformers climbed the scaffold, his companions intoned a psalm translated by Clement Marot, as much for the purpose of sending a last consolation to the one about to be executed as to mark their firmness in the presence of their foes and of death.

They sang, then, at the foot of the scaffold:

> May God to us benignant be
> And graciously His gifts bestow;
> And, oh, His brightness may we see,
> In that blest kingdom where we go!

A verse was sung as each head fell; and each head that fell made a voice less in the chorus.

At one, there were only twelve left—the principal leaders of the conspiracy.

There was then a pause; the two executioners were tired, and the king was present.

He was more than pale—he was livid. Mary Stuart placed herself on his right, and Catherine de Médicis on his left.

The Cardinal de Lorraine was beside the queen-mother and the Prince de Condé beside the queen.

When the prince appeared on the platform, almost as pale as the young king, the twelve condemned men saluted him.

He gravely returned the salutation.

"I always bow in the presence of death," he said aloud.

The king, moreover, was received with less respect, so to speak, than the Prince de Condé. No acclamation greeted his arrival. He remarked it, and, frowning, said—

"Ah! M. le Cardinal, I am angry with you for having brought me here!"

However, Charles de Lorraine raised his hand to give the signal for a display of loyal devotion; and a few scattered voices in the crowd cried—

"Long live the king!"

"You hear, sire?" he cried.

"Yes," answered Francis, sadly shaking his head; "I hear a few awkward fellows who make the general silence more marked."

Meanwhile, the rest of the royal gallery was being filled; the king's brothers, the papal nuncio, and the Duchess de Guise entered one after the other.

Then came the Duke de Nemours, quite dejected, and, as it were, shaken by remorse. Finally, two men appeared at the back, whose presence at such a time and in such a place was not less strange than that of the Prince de Condé.

These two men were Ambroise Paré and the Count de Montgommery.

A different duty had brought them both hither.

Ambroise Paré had been summoned, some days before, by the Duke de Guise, who was alarmed about the health of his royal nephew; and Mary Stuart, not less disturbed than her uncle at seeing Francis rendered so despondent by the mere thought of the "act of faith," begged the surgeon to be at hand in case the king fainted.

As for Gabriel, he came to make a last effort to save at least one of the condemned, who was to be the last beheaded, and whom he reproached himself with having brought to this extremity by his advice; namely, the young and brave Castelnau des Chalosses.

Castelnau, it will be remembered, surrendered only on the written and signed pledge of the Duke de Nemours, guaranteeing him liberty and life.

Now, ever since his arrival in Amboise, he had been in prison, and was to be the last beheaded, as being the guiltiest.

Justice must, however, be done to the Duke de Nemours. When he saw his word as a gentleman compromised, he was beside himself with despair and anger, and for three weeks was constantly running from the Cardinal de Lorraine to the Duke de Guise, and from Mary Stuart to the king, soliciting and imploring the release of him for whom he was bound in honor to obtain deliverance. But Chancellor Olivier, to whom the matter was referred, declared, according to M. de Vieilleville, that "A king is by no means bound to keep faith with a rebellious subject, no matter what promise may have been given in his name"—which caused great anguish to the Duke de Nemours, "who," adds the chronicler, naïvely, "was tormented about his signature only; for, as for his word, he would always have given the lie to any one who dared to reproach him with it, his Majesty alone excepted, so valiant and generous a prince was he!"

Like Gabriel, the Duke de Nemours was led to the place of execution, more terrible for him than for any one else, by the secret hope that he might, even at the last moment, save Castelnau.

However, the Duke de Guise, on horseback at the foot of the gallery with his captains, made a sign to the executioners; and the bloody work, as well as the psalm-singing, which had been for an instant interrupted, continued.

In less than a quarter of an hour, eight heads fell. The young queen was near fainting.

There were only four left at the foot of the scaffold.

The registrar read, in a loud voice:

"Albert Edouard Roger, Count de Mazères, guilty of heresy, high treason, and an attack in arms on the person of the king."

"It is false!" cried Mazères on the scaffold.

Then, showing the people his blackened arms and his breast bruised by the torture—

"See," he cried, "the state to which I have been brought in the king's name. But I know he is unaware of it, and I do not the less on that account cry: *Vive le roi!*"

The last three Reformers who were awaiting their turn at the foot of the scaffold repeated the first verse of the psalm:

> May God to us benignant be,
> And graciously His gifts bestow;
> And, oh, His brightness may we see
> In that blest kingdom where we go!

The registrar continued—

"Jean Louis Albéric, Baron de Raunai, guilty of heresy, high treason, and an attack in arms on the person of the king."

"You lie like two clowns, you and your cardinal," said Raunai; "it was against him and his brother alone that we took up arms. I wish they may both die as tranquil and as pure as I do."

Then he laid his head on the block.

The last two condemned men sang:

> O Lord, Thou hast our spirits tried
> And sounded deeply every heart,
> And, like the gold that's purified,
> In fire Thou cleansest every part.

Again the clerk read his bloody summons—

"Robert Jean René Briquemant, Count de Villemongis, guilty of heresy, high treason, and an attack in arms on his Majesty."

Villemongis steeped his hands in the blood of Raunai, and, raising them to heaven—

"Eternal Father!" said he, "Thou beholdest the blood of thy children; Thou wilt avenge it!"

And he fell struck to death.

Castelnau alone remained. He sang:

> For us the foe has laid his snare,
> And Thou hast let us fall therein;
> In vain the binding net we tear;
> Thou hast enmeshed us for our sin.

In the hope of saving Castelnau, the Duke de Nemours had been liberal with his money. The registrar, the executioners even, had an interest in pardon. The first executioner said he was exhausted; the second took his place. There was, therefore, an interval of delay.

Gabriel profited by it to excite the duke to new efforts.

Jacques de Savoie leaned over the Duchess de Guise, with whom, it was said, he was a favorite, and whispered a word in her ear.

The duchess had great influence with the young queen.

She rose at once, as if she could no longer endure the spectacle, and said loud enough to be heard by Mary—

"Ah, it is too frightful for women! Look, the queen is going to faint. Let us retire."

But the Cardinal de Lorraine fixed a severe look upon his sister-in-law.

"A little more firmness, madame!" he said sternly. "Remember you are of the blood of Este, and the wife of the Duke de Guise."

"Ah, that is what agitates me!" replied the duchess. "Never had a mother greater cause for anxiety than I have. All this blood and all this hatred will fall upon the heads of our children."

"Women are timid," murmured the cardinal, who was a coward.

"But," returned the Duke de Nemours, "there is no need to be a woman to be moved by this dismal spectacle. Are not you yourself, M. de Condé, moved by it?" he added to the prince.

"Oh," said the cardinal, "the prince is a soldier accustomed to the presence of death on the field of battle."

"Yes," replied the prince, courageously, "but not in cold blood on the scaffold."

"Has a prince of the blood, then, so much compassion for rebels?" said Charles de Lorraine again.

"I have compassion for brave officers," rejoined the prince, "who have always worthily served the king and France."

What could the Prince de Condé do more in his position —he who was suspected himself? The Duke de Nemours understood, and turned to the queen-mother.

"Look, madame; there is only one," said he. "Could you not save him?"

"I can do nothing," answered Catherine, turning away her head.

But the unfortunate Castelnau was climbing the steps of the stairs, singing—

> May God to *me* benignant be,
> And graciously His gifts bestow;
> And, oh, His brightness may *I* see
> In that blest kingdom where *I* go!

The people, deeply affected, forgot their dread of spies and *mouchards*, and cried, all with one voice—

"Pardon! pardon!"

The Duke de Nemours was at this moment trying to move the Duke d'Orléans.

"Monseigneur," he was saying to him, "have you forgotten that it was in this very town of Amboise that Castel nau saved the life of the late Duke d'Orléans in a riot in which it was imperilled?"

"I will do whatever my mother decides on," answered the Duke d'Orléans.

"But," said Nemours, beseechingly, "what if you were to address the king? A single word from you—"

"I repeat," replied the young prince, dryly, "I await the orders of my mother."

"Ah, prince!" cried the duke, reproachfully. And he made a sign to Gabriel of discouragement and despair.

The registrar then read slowly—

"Michel Jean Louis, Baron de Castelnau-Chalosses, accused and convicted of the crime of high treason, heresy, and attacking the person of the king."

"I call my judges themselves to witness that the declaration is false, unless it be a crime of high treason to have opposed the tyranny of the Guises with all my might. And if that is treason, then the Guises ought to have been declared kings long ago. Perhaps it will come to that in the end; but it concerns those who survive me." And, addressing the executioner, he added in a firm voice, "Now do your office."

But the executioner, who noticed some excitement in the galleries, pretended to be attending to his axe, so as to gain time.

"This axe is blunt, M. le Baron," he whispered, "and you have a right to die at a single stroke at least. And who knows but another moment might— It seems to me that something in your favor is taking place yonder."

The entire people cried anew—

"Pardon! pardon!"

Gabriel, losing all self-restraint at this supreme moment, cried aloud to Mary Stuart—

"Pardon! Madame la reine!"

Mary turned round, saw his heartrending look, understood his desperate cry, and, kneeling before the king—

"Sire," said she, "at least pardon this one; I ask it on my knees."

"Sire," said the Duke de Nemours in turn, "has not enough blood been shed? And yet you know the proverb, 'The king's face bringeth grace.'"

Francis, who was trembling in every limb, appeared struck by these words. He seized Mary's hand.

"Remember, sire," said the nuncio to him, to recall him to severity, "remember that you are the Most Christian King."

"Yes, I remember it," returned Francis, firmly. "Let a pardon," he added, "be granted to the Baron de Castelnau."

But the Cardinal de Lorraine, feigning to misunderstand the meaning of the first phrase of the king, had made an imperative sign to the executioner.

At the moment that Francis the Second uttered the word pardon, the head of Castelnau rolled on the scaffold.

On the next day the Prince de Condé set out for Navarre.

CHAPTER XLIII

ANOTHER SKETCH OF POLITICS

EVER since that fatal execution the health of Francis the Second had grown worse.

Six months after (toward the end of November, 1560), the court being at Orléans, where the States-General had been summoned by the Duke de Guise, the poor young king was obliged to take to bed.

Beside that bed of pain, where Mary Stuart prayed and watched and wept, a most thrilling drama waited its dénouement in the life or death of the son of Henry the Second.

The question, although many others were interested in it, lay entirely between a pale woman and a sinister man, seated side by side on the night of the 4th of December, some feet from the patient sufferer, who was asleep, and from Mary, in tears by his pillow.

The man was Charles de Lorraine, and the woman Catherine de Médicis.

The vindictive queen-mother, who gave no sign of life for some time after the accession of her son, had been quite awake for the last eight months, ever since the tumult of Amboise, in fact. Here is what she had done, because of her ever-increasing animosity toward the Duke de Guise.

She had secretly allied herself with the Prince de Condé and Antony of Bourbon; she had secretly become reconciled to the old Constable de Montmorency. Only hatred could make her forget hatred.

Her new and singular friends, urged by her, had fomented rebellions in various provinces, had stirred up Dauphiné under Montbrun, Provence under the brothers Mouvans, and made, through Coligny, an attempt on Lyons.

The Guises, on their side, were not asleep. They had convoked the States-General at Orléans, and had a devoted majority in that body.

Then they had summoned to this States-General the King of Navarre and the Prince de Condé, who had a right to be there.

Catherine sent warning after warning to the princes to dissuade them from placing themselves in the hands of their enemies; but they replied their duty called them, the Cardinal de Lorraine gave them the king's word as a pledge of their safety.

They came to Orléans then.

On the very day of their arrival, the Prince de Condé was cast into prison, and Antony of Navarre was consigned to a house in the city, where he was constantly kept in sight. Then an extraordinary commission, inspired by the Guises, tried and condemned to death at Orléans the man for whose innocence the Duke de Guise had pledged his faith upon his sword at Amboise.

All that was required for the execution of the sentence was one or two signatures delayed by the Chancellor d'Hôpital.

Such was the state of affairs on this evening of the 4th of December—a state of affairs of supreme importance to the party of the Guises, of which the duke was the arm, and the cardinal the head, and to the party of the Bourbons, of which Catherine de Médicis was the secret soul.

Everything depended, for either side, on the expiring breath of a crowned boy.

If Francis could only live a few days, the Prince de Condé might be executed, the King of Navarre killed in some riot or other, and Catherine de Médicis exiled to Florence. Through the States-General, the Guises were masters, and, if need be, kings.

If, on the contrary, the young king died before the Guises were masters of their enemies, the struggle had to begin again, with the chances against them rather than in their favor.

Therefore, what Catherine and Charles de Lorraine were expecting and watching for with such anguish, on this cold night of the 4th of December, was not the life or death of this royal son and nephew so much as for the triumph or defeat of their party.

Mary Stuart alone watched by the bedside of her young husband without dreaming that death might snatch him from her arms.

It must not, however, be imagined for a moment that the secret antagonism of the cardinal and queen-mother showed itself externally, either in language or manner. On the contrary, never had they shown more mutual trust and affection.

At this moment, profiting by the slumber of Francis, they were conversing in a low voice, and in the most amicable way possible, about their most secret interests and most intimate thoughts.

For, in harmony with that Italian policy of which we have already given a sketch, Catherine always dissembled her secret designs, and Charles de Lorraine constantly feigned not to perceive them.

So they had never ceased to speak as friends and allies. They were like two gamblers, each loyally cheating for his own side and openly using loaded dice against the other.

"Yes, madame," said the cardinal; "this obstinate L'Hôpital stubbornly refuses to sign the decree for the execution of the prince. Ah, you were right, madame, in your opposition to his succeeding Olivier six months ago! If I had only *understood* you then!"

"What! is there no way of overcoming his resistance?" asked Catherine, who was at the bottom of this very resistance.

"I have tried caresses, madame, and I have tried threats, and I have found him inflexible," returned the cardinal.

"What if M. de Guise were also to try?"

"Nothing could move this Auvergne mule. Besides, my brother declares he does not wish to have anything to do with this affair."

"Why, the thing is becoming embarrassing," returned Catherine, enchanted.

"There is, nevertheless, a plan by the aid of which we can manage without any chancellor," said the cardinal.

"Pray, what might it be?" anxiously inquired the queen-mother.

"We could get the decree signed by the king."

"By the king!" repeated Catherine. "How can that be? Has the king this right?"

"Yes," said the cardinal. "This, in fact, has been our manner of proceeding so far in this very affair, and that by the advice of the best jurists, who have affirmed that he might be tried and sentenced, notwithstanding his refusal to answer."

"But what will the chancellor say to this?" asked Catherine, now really alarmed.

"He will grumble as usual," replied Charles de Lorraine, quietly; "he will threaten to surrender the seals."

"And, in fact, will do so."

"A double advantage. We shall be delivered from an inconvenient censor."

"And when would you have this decree signed?" said Catherine, after a pause.

"This night, madame."

"And executed?"

"To-morrow."

The suddenness of the blow sent a shudder through the queen-mother.

"This night! to-morrow! are you not dreaming?" said she. "The king is too ill and feeble, and is not clear-minded enough even to comprehend what you would ask of him."

"No need of his comprehending, provided he signs."

"But his hand is too weak to hold the pen."

"It can be guided," said the cardinal, delighted at the terror he saw painted on the face of his dear enemy.

"Listen," said Catherine, seriously. "I give you a warning and advice. The end of my poor son is nearer than you think. Do you know what Chapelain, the first physician, has told me? He does not think the king can be alive to-morrow evening except by a miracle."

"The greater reason to make haste," said the cardinal, coldly.

"Yes, but," returned Catherine, "if Francis the Second is not alive to-morrow, Charles the Ninth reigns, and the King of Navarre is perhaps regent. What a terrible account will he not demand from you of the infamous death of his brother? Will not you, in your turn, be tried and condemned?"

"Oh, madame, he who risks nothing loses all?" cried the cardinal, hotly. "Besides, who proves that Antony of Navarre will be regent? Who proves that Chapelain is not mistaken? In fine, the king is still alive!"

"Not so loud, uncle!" said Mary Stuart, rising in alarm. "You will waken the king. Stay; you have wakened him."

"Mary, where are you?" said Francis, in a weak voice.

"Here, near you always, sweet sire," answered Mary.

"Oh, how I suffer! my head is on fire!" returned the king. "This pain in my ear is like one continual dagger-thrust; and I suffer asleep as much as awake. Ah, it is all over with me! all is over!"

"Do not say that! do not say that!" said Mary, keeping back the tears.

"My memory is failing," answered Francis. "Have I received the Last Sacraments? I wish to receive them as soon as possible."

"All your duties shall be fulfilled, sire; do not torment yourself about them."

"I wish to see my confessor, M. de Brichanteau."

"He will be with you in a moment," said Mary.

"Are they at least saying prayers for me?"

"I have been doing so nearly all the morning."

"Poor dear Mary! and where is Chapelain?"

"There, at your call, in the next room. Your mother and my uncle, the cardinal, are there also. Do you want to see them, sire?"

"No, no; only you, Mary!" said the dying young king. "Turn a little this way—there—that I may see you once again at least."

"Courage!" returned Mary. "God is so good, and I have prayed to Him so earnestly."

"I am in pain, Mary; I no longer hear; your hand, Mary, where is it?"

"There! lean upon me," said Mary, supporting the pale little head of her husband upon her shoulder.

"My soul to God! my heart to thee, Mary! Always! Alas, alas, to die at seventeen!"

"No, no; you shall not die! What have we done to Heaven that it should punish us thus?"

"Do not weep, Mary. We shall meet above," answered the king. "All I regret in this world is you. If I could take you with me, I should be happy to die. The journey to heaven is finer than that to Italy; and then it seems to me that you will have no joy in living without me. They will make you suffer. You will be cold and desolate. They will kill you, poor soul! The thought of this afflicts me even more than death."

The king, exhausted, fell back on his pillow and maintained a gloomy silence.

"But you shall not die! you shall not die, sire!" cried Mary. "Listen; I have a great hope. One chance in which I have faith remains for us."

"What is that you say?" interrupted Catherine de Médicis, drawing near in surprise.

"Yes," answered Mary; "the king may still be saved,

and shall be saved. Something cries in my heart that all the doctors who surround and weary him are blind and ignorant. But there is one skilful man, a man of learning and fame, who saved my uncle at Calais."

"Master Ambroise Paré?" said the cardinal.

"Master Ambroise Paré!" repeated Mary. "They say this man ought not and does not wish to have the king's life in his hands, that he is a heretic and accursed, and that, though he were to accept the responsibility of such a case, it ought not to be confided to him."

"That is quite certain," said the queen-mother, scornfully.

"Well, what if I confide it to him!" cried Mary. "Can a man of genius be a traitor? A great man, madame, is always a good man."

"But," said the cardinal, "my brother did not wait until to-day to consult M. Paré. He has been already sounded."

"And who has been sent to him?" returned Mary. "His enemies, perhaps, or those who were indifferent. But I have sent a sure friend of his, and he will come."

"It will take time for him to come from Paris," said Catherine.

"He is on the way; he must have even arrived," returned Mary. "The friend of whom I spoke promised to bring him this very day."

"And who is this friend, pray?" asked the queen-mother.

"Count Gabriel de Montgommery."

Before Catherine could utter a syllable, Dayelle, Mary's first waiting-woman, entered and said to her mistress—

"Count de Montgommery is here and awaits your commands, madame."

"Oh, let him enter! let him enter!" said Mary, quickly.

CHAPTER XLIV

A GLIMMER OF HOPE

"A MOMENT!" said Catherine de Médicis, dryly and coldly. "Before this man enters, madame, wait at least until I leave. If it please you to intrust the life of the son to him who has cut short the days of the father, it does not please me to see and hear once more the murderer of my spouse. I protest against his presence in this place, and withdraw at his approach."

And she passed out, without giving a dying son a mother's farewell.

Was it because the abhorred name of Gabriel de Montgommery recalled the first offence she had been compelled to endure from the king? It may be. At all events, she did not dread as much as she feigned the aspect and voice of Gabriel, for she was careful to leave the hangings half open, on withdrawing into her own apartment next the royal chamber; and no sooner had she closed the door opening on a corridor deserted at this late hour of the night than she applied eye and ear in turn to the lock, in order to see and hear what took place after her abrupt departure.

Gabriel entered, conducted by Dayelle, knelt and kissed the hand of the queen, and bowed profoundly to the cardinal.

"Well?" asked Mary Stuart, impatiently.

"Well, madame, I have at last prevailed with Master Ambroise Paré," answered Gabriel; "he is here."

"Oh, thanks, my faithful friend!" cried Mary.

"Is the king worse, then, madame?" said Gabriel, in a whisper, after looking anxiously at the bed upon which Francis lay stretched, without color or motion.

"Alas! he does not improve, and I needed to see you badly," said the queen. "Did Master Ambroise make a great difficulty about coming?"

"No, madame," answered Gabriel. "He was asked before, indeed, but in such a way as to provoke a refusal. He was called upon to pledge himself, on his life and honor, to save the king before he had seen him. He was told that, being a Protestant, he was suspected of desiring the death of a persecutor of the Protestants. In fact, such was the insulting distrust with which he was treated, such were the hard conditions required of him, that, except he was without spirit or prudence, he must necessarily have kept away. This he has, to his great regret, done, and from that time he was pressed no further by those sent to him."

"Can Master Paré have so misinterpreted our meaning?" said the Cardinal de Lorraine, quickly. "Yet my brother and I sent for him two or three times. We have been told in return of his obstinate refusals and strange suspicions. And we thought we could rely upon those we despatched for him!"

"But could you really do so, monseigneur?" asked Gabriel. "Master Paré believes the contrary, now that I have told him of your true sentiments in his regard and of the kind words of the queen. He is persuaded that, without your knowledge, an attempt has been made to keep him from the bedside of the king, and that with a guilty object."

"There can be no doubt of that now," answered Charles de Lorraine. "I recognize," he murmured, "the hand of the queen-mother in this. She has, in fact, every interest in her son dying. But is she going to corrupt all upon whose devotion we count? This is on a par with the nomination of her L'Hôpital. How she does trick us!"

However Mary Stuart, leaving the cardinal to his reflections upon the past and his anxieties about the future, said to Gabriel—

"But Master Paré has followed you, has he not?"

"At my first request," answered Gabriel.

"And he is here?"

"Awaiting your gracious permission to enter, madame."

"At once! Let him come at once!" cried Mary Stuart.

Gabriel went on the moment to the door by which he entered, and returned with the surgeon.

Catherine de Médicis watched behind her door, more attentive than ever.

Mary Stuart ran to meet Ambroise, took his hand, led him to the bed of her dear sufferer, and, as if to cut short all compliments, said, walking all the time—

"Thanks for coming, master; I count on your zeal as I count on your science. Come to the king's bed, the king's bed!"

Ambroise Paré, obedient to the impatience of the queen, which did not allow him to utter a word, was soon standing by the bed where Francis the Second, vanquished by pain, had only strength to moan feebly and almost imperceptibly.

The great surgeon paused a moment to contemplate that little, drawn, and almost skeleton face.

Then he leaned over his king, who for him was but a patient, and touched and examined the painful swelling in the right ear with a hand as light and gentle as Mary's.

The king felt instinctively that a physician was near him, and endured his touch without even opening his heavy eyes.

"Oh, how I suffer! how I suffer!" he only murmured, in a voice of agony. "Can you not relieve me?"

The light being too far away from Ambroise, he beckoned to Gabriel to bring it nearer. But Mary Stuart had seized it before him and held it for the surgeon, while he made a long and careful examination of the seat of the disease.

This silent, minute study lasted about ten minutes. Then Ambroise Paré rose gravely, absorbed in his meditation on what he had seen, and let the curtain of the bed drop.

Mary Stuart, whose heart beat rapidly, did not dare to question him, for fear of disturbing his thoughts, but scanned his features with anguish. What sentence would he pronounce?

The illustrious physician shook his head sorrowfully, and it seemed to the despairing queen as if he had pronounced a decree of death.

"What!" said she, incapable any longer of controlling her emotion; "is there no chance of saving him?"

"There is but one, madame," answered Ambroise Paré.

"But there is one!" cried the queen.

"Yes; and although it is not a certain one, alas! yet it exists, and I should have every hope of curing him, if he were not—"

"What?"

"A king, madame."

"Oh," cried Mary Stuart, "treat him as if he were the meanest of his subjects!"

"But if I fail? For, after all, God is alone the master," said Ambroise at length. "Shall not I, a Huguenot, be held accountable for his death? Will not this heavy and fearful responsibility be enough of itself to enfeeble and unnerve my hand, at the very moment I need all my calmness and assurance?"

"Listen," said Mary. "If he live, I will bless you my whole life, and if, if—he die, I will defend you to the death. Therefore try, oh, try to save him, I implore, I beseech you! Since you say it is the last and only chance, for God's sake, do not take it from us! that would be a crime."

"You are right, madame, and I will try—if I am permitted to do so, if you permit me; for I do not conceal from you, madame, that the means to which I shall have recourse is extreme, unusual, and in appearance, at least, violent and dangerous.''

"Really?" said Mary, trembling, "and you have no other?"

"No other, madame. Moreover, it must be employed at once. In twenty-four hours certainly, and in twelve, perhaps, it would be too late. An abscess has formed in the king's head, and, unless discharged by a very speedy operation, it will overflow the brain and cause death.''

"Do you wish to operate on the king at once, then?' said the cardinal. "I do not care to take the responsibility on myself alone.''

"Ah, now you doubt already!" said Ambroise. "No; I have need of daylight, and I require the rest of the night to meditate on the subject, to train my hand, and make one or two experiments. But I can be here to-morrow morning at nine. Do you be present, madame, and you, monseigneur; let M. le Lieutenant-Général and all those whose devotion to the king has been well tested be present also; but no others, and as few doctors as possible. I will then explain what I propose to do, and if you all authorize me, with God's help, I will try the only chance that God leaves us.''

"And is there no danger until to-morrow?" asked the queen.

"None, madame," said Master Paré. "But it is essential that the king rest and gain all the strength he can for what he must undergo. I will drop two drops of this elixir into the harmless beverage I see on that table," he added, suiting the action to the words. "Let the king take this immediately, madame, and you will see him fall into a calmer and deeper sleep. Watch yourself, after this has taken place, that he be not disturbed.''

"Be tranquil on that point," said Mary Stuart. "I will answer for it. I shall not leave this place to-night.''

"It is very important," said Ambroise Paré. "For the

present, I have nothing more to do here, and I will ask your permission to withdraw, madame, in order to devote myself to the king still, and prepare for my great task."

"Go, master, go!" answered Mary, "and accept my thanks and blessings in advance. Until to-morrow."

"Until to-morrow then, madame," returned Ambroise, "hope."

"I shall pray always!" said Mary Stuart.

"I thank you, too, M. le Comte," she continued, addressing Gabriel. "You are one of those whom Master Paré speaks of, whose devotion the king has tried. Be here to-morrow, then, and support your illustrious friend by your presence."

"I will, madame," said Gabriel, retiring with the surgeon, after saluting the cardinal and queen.

"And I too will be there," said Catherine de Médicis to herself behind the door where she was watching. "Yes, I will be there; for that Paré is quite capable of saving the king, clever fellow that he is! and destroying his own party, the prince, and myself, the fool! But I will be there."

CHAPTER XLV

SLEEP WELL GUARDED

CATHERINE DE MEDICIS continued in her occupation of spying for some time, although the only persons in the royal chamber were Mary Stuart and the cardinal. But she did not see or hear anything further of interest. The queen administered the sleeping potion to Francis, and, as Ambroise Paré had promised, he appeared to sleep more tranquilly. Everything then subsided into silence. The cardinal sat and thought; Mary knelt and prayed. The queen-mother quietly retired to her bedchamber to think, like the cardinal.

If she had remained for some moments more, however, she would have been present at a scene worthy of herself.

Mary Stuart, rising after a fervent prayer, said to the cardinal—

"Nothing forces you to keep watch with me, uncle, and I intend staying here until the king awakes. Dayelle, the physicians, and the people in attendance will suffice, if anything is wanted. You can, therefore, go and take a little rest. Should it be necessary, I will warn you."

"No," said the cardinal; "the Duke de Guise, who has been detained by a number of urgent matters until now, told me he intended to inquire about the king's condition before retiring, and I promised to wait for him here. And listen, madame; is not that his step I hear?"

"Oh, let him make no noise!" cried Mary, hastening to the door to warn the Balafré.

The Duke de Guise entered, very pale and very much agitated. He saluted the queen, but was so absorbed that he forgot to inquire about the king, and went straight to his brother, whom he took aside into the recess of a window.

"Terrible news! a real thunderbolt!" he began.

"What is the matter?" asked Charles de Lorraine.

"The Constable de Montmorency has quitted Chantilly, with fifteen hundred gentlemen," said the Duke de Guise. "The better to hide his movements, he has avoided Paris, coming by way of Ecouen and Corbeil to Pithiviers along the valley of Essonne. He will be at the gates of Orléans with his company to-morrow. I have just received notice of his approach."

"It is indeed terrible," replied the cardinal. "The old rascal wishes to save the head of his nephew. I wager it is the queen-mother who has sent for him. And not to be able to do anything against that woman!"

"This is not the time to act against her, but to act for ourselves. What ought we to do?"

"Go and meet the constable at once with your forces."

"Do you answer for the maintenance of order in Orléans when I am gone?"

"Alas, I cannot!" answered Charles de Lorraine. "All these Orléans people are bad, Huguenots and Bourbons at heart. But at least we have the States on our side."

"And L'Hôpital against us, brother! Ah, our position is very disagreeable. How goes the king?" said the duke, danger recalling to him his last resource.

"The king is going on badly," replied Charles de Lorraine; "but Ambroise Paré, who has come to Orléans on the invitation of the queen—I will explain this to you later —hopes to save him to-morrow morning by a hazardous but necessary operation, which may have the best results. Be here at nine, then, brother, to support Ambroise, if necessary."

"Certainly," said the Balafré; "for there lies our only hope. Our authority dies with the king. And yet it might be a good thing to frighten and perhaps drive back the constable by welcoming him with the head of his fair nephew as a present."

"Yes; it would be a very eloquent greeting, in my opinion," said the cardinal, thoughtfully.

"But this confounded L'Hopital stops everything!" returned the duke.

"If we got the king's signature to the sentence of the prince, instead of L'Hopital's, we might proceed, might we not, brother? And could not the execution take place tomorrow morning before the arrival of Montmorency, before the operation of Master Paré?"

"It would not be very legal, but it would be possible," answered the Balafré.

"Well, then," said Charles de Lorraine, earnestly, "leave me here, brother; you have nothing to do this night, and you must need rest. The town clock has just struck two; you must husband your strength for to-morrow. Retire and leave me. I, too, wish to try some desperate remedy for our fortunes."

"What do you intend doing?" asked the Duke de Guise. "Do nothing definitive until you have consulted me, fair brother."

"Do not be alarmed; if I get what I want, I will wake you before daybreak to deliberate in common."

"Well and good!" rejoined the Balafré. "On this assurance I withdraw. It is true I am exhausted. But, prudence!"

He addressed a few words of condolence to Mary Stuart, and passed out as noiselessly as possible, on her recommendation.

In the meantime, the cardinal had sat down before a table, and wrote a copy of the sentence of the commission, the original of which lay in front of him. This finished, he rose and walked to the bedside of the king.

But Mary Stuart threw herself in front of him, and stopped him with a gesture.

"Where are you going?" she said, in a voice low but firm, and already showing anger.

"Madame," said the cardinal, "it is important, it is indispensable, that the king should sign this paper."

"What is above all important and indispensable is that the king should not be disturbed."

"His name at the bottom of this document, madame, and I will not trouble him further."

"But you will awake him," returned the queen, "and I cannot allow it. Besides, he is incapable at this moment of holding a pen."

"I will hold it for him," said Charles de Lorraine.

"I have told you I do not wish it," said Mary Stuart, authoritatively.

The cardinal paused for a moment, surprised by an obstacle of which he had not dreamed.

Then he resumed, in an insinuating tone—

"Hear me, madame. My dear niece, hear me. I am going to tell you what is at stake. You understand that I would respect the repose of the king, were I not constrained by the gravest necessity. It is our fortune and yours, our safety and yours, that are in jeopardy. Understand me well. This paper must be signed by the king before daybreak, or we are ruined! ruined, I repeat!"

"That does not concern me," returned Mary, quietly.

"Indeed it does! our ruin is your ruin, child that you are!"

"Well, what does that matter to me?" said the queen. "Do I care for your ambitions? My ambition is to save him whom I love; to preserve his life, if I can, and, at any rate, his precious repose. Master Paré has bid me guard the king's slumbers. I forbid you to disturb them, monsieur. Understand me well in your turn. I forbid you! With the death of the king royalty dies! I care nothing for that! But as long as a breath of life remains, I will protect that last breath against the odious exigencies of your courtly intrigues. I have contributed, more than I ought, perhaps, to strengthen your hands and your power, my uncle, when my Francis was well and strong; but I revoke all that power as soon as there is question of respecting the last hours of peace that God may perhaps grant him in this life. The king, says Master Paré, will have need of all the strength left him to-morrow. No person in the world, on any pretext whatever, shall rob him even of a moment of this refreshing slumber."

"But when the motive is so grave and urgent—" said the cardinal.

"Under no pretext must any one wake the king," answered Mary.

"Ah! but some one must!" retorted Charles de Lorraine, ashamed at last of being so long withstood by the mere resistance of a child, his own niece. "The interests of the State, madame, do not harmonize with these sentimental motives. I require the signature of the king immediately, and I must have it."

"You shall not, M. le Cardinal," said Mary.

The cardinal took a step toward the bed of the king.

But Mary again threw herself before him, and barred his passage.

The queen and the minister looked each other in the face for a moment, both equally excited and angry.

"I will pass," said Charles de Lorraine, curtly.

"Do you dare to lay your hand upon me, monsieur?"

"My niece!"

"No longer your niece, but your queen!"

This was said in a tone so firm, dignified, and royal that the cardinal recoiled, speechless.

"Yes, your queen!" returned Mary; "and if you take another step toward the king, I will go to that door; I will summon those who are watching there; and, though you are my uncle, though you are minister and cardinal, I will order you—I, the queen—to be arrested upon a charge of high treason."

"Such a scandal!" murmured the cardinal, thoroughly scared.

"Which of us has caused it, monsieur?"

The sparkling eyes, the quivering nostrils, the heaving bosom of the young queen—all told plainly enough that she would execute her menace.

And then she was so beautiful, so high-spirited, and at the same time so touching that even the marble-hearted priest was moved and vanquished.

The man yielded to the child; and reasons of State gave way to the cry of nature.

"Well, then," said the cardinal, with a deep sigh, "I will wait until the king awakens."

"Thanks!" said Mary, in the sad and sweet tone which had become habitual to her since the illness of her husband.

"But, at least," returned Charles de Lorraine, "as soon as he awakes—"

"If he is in a condition to hear and satisfy you, uncle, I will raise no objection."

The cardinal saw he had to be content with this promise. He returned to his table, and Mary to her *prie-Dieu*—he waiting, she hoping.

But the slow hours of that night of watching passed away, and Francis the Second did not awake. The promise of Ambroise Paré had not been ineffectual; it was many nights since the king had enjoyed a sleep so long and profound.

From time to time he stirred slightly, or uttered a feeble moan, or pronounced a word, a name, particularly that of Mary.

But he would then fall back again into his deep slumber. And the cardinal, who had arisen hastily, would return to his place, disappointed.

He rubbed in his hand impatiently that useless sentence, that fatal sentence, which, without the king's signature, might perhaps be meted out to himself.

He saw in this manner the tapers gradually burn out and grow pale, and the cold dawn of December whiten the panes.

At last, when it struck eight, the king moved, opened his eyes, and called—

"Mary! are you there, Mary?"

"Always," said Mary Stuart.

Charles de Lorraine darted forward, with the paper in his hand. It was still time, perhaps! A scaffold is soon erected!

But, at the same moment, Catherine de Médicis entered the royal chamber by the door leading to her own.

"Too late!" said the cardinal to himself. "Ah! fortune abandons us! and if Ambroise does not save the king, we are lost!"

CHAPTER XLVI

THE DEATH-BED OF KINGS

D URING the night the queen-mother had not lost her time. She had despatched her creature, Cardinal de Tournon, to the King of Navarre, and had made a written agreement with the Bourbons. Then, before daybreak, she had received Chancellor Olivier, who informed her of the near arrival of her ally, the constable, at Orléans. L'Hôpital promised her to be, at nine o'clock, in the great hall of the bailiwick, in front of the king's chamber, and to bring thither as many partisans of Catherine as he could find. Finally, the queen-mother summoned Chapelain and two or three other royal physicians, whose mediocrity was the natural-born enemy of the genius of Ambroise Paré, to meet her at half-past eight.

Her precautions thus taken, she was the first, as we have seen, to enter the chamber of the king, who had just awoke.

She went first to the bed of her son, gazed on him for some moments, with bent head, like a sorrowful mother, placed a kiss on his unheeding hand, and, after wiping away a tear or two, sat down so as to have him always in view.

She, too, like Mary Stuart, would henceforth watch over that agony on which so much depended.

The Duke de Guise entered almost immediately after. After exchanging a few words with Mary, he went to his brother.

"You have done nothing, then?" he asked.

"Alas! I have not been able to do anything," answered the cardinal.

"Then luck is against us," replied the Balafré. "There was a crowd this morning in the ante-chamber of Antony de Navarre. And have you any news of Montmorency?"

"None. I have waited for some in vain. He must not have taken the direct road. He is now perhaps at the gates of the city. If Ambroise Paré fails in his operation, good-by to our fortune!" said Charles de Lorraine, in consternation.

The doctors, summoned by Catherine, arrived at this moment.

The queen-mother conducted them to the bed of the king, whose sufferings and groans had begun anew.

The doctors examined their royal patient in turn, then gathered in a corner to consult. Chapelain proposed a cataplasm to draw out the foreign matter; but the two others pronounced for the injection of a certain medicated water into the ear.

They had decided on this last method, when Ambroise Paré entered, accompanied by Gabriel.

After examining the condition of the king, he joined his brethren.

Ambroise Paré, surgeon to the Duke de Guise, whose scientific renown was already established, was now an authority with which it was necessary to reckon. The doctors therefore informed him of the resolution they had just come to.

"I affirm that the remedy is insufficient," said Ambroise Paré, in a loud voice; "but we must make haste, for the brain will fill much sooner than I expected."

"Oh, hasten, in the name of Heaven!" cried Mary Stuart, who had heard him.

The queen-mother and the two Guises drew near the physicians, and mingled with them.

"Have you, then, Master Paré," asked Chapelain, "a better and surer method than ours?"

"Yes," said Paré.

"What is it?"

"It would be necessary to trepan the king," said Ambroise Paré.

"Trepan the king!" cried the three doctors, with horror.

"And what is the nature of this operation?" asked the Duke de Guise.

"It is little known yet, monseigneur," said the surgeon. "It is an operation with an instrument invented by myself, and which I call a trepan, making on the top of the head, or rather on the lateral part of the brain, an opening the width of an angelot."

"God of mercy!" cried Catherine de Médicis, indignantly. "Pierce the king's head! And you would dare it!"

"Yes, madame," replied Ambroise, simply.

"But it would be an assassination!" returned Catherine.

"What! madame," said Ambroise, "is not the boring of a hole in the head, with every scientific precaution against danger, to do what is daily done on the field of battle by the blind and violent sword? Yet how many wounds do we not cure?"

"But, Master Ambroise, do you answer for the life of the king?" asked the Cardinal de Lorraine.

"God alone has the life and death of men in His hands, you know that better than I do, M. le Cardinal. All I can assure you of is that this is the last and only chance of saving the king—yes, the only chance! but it is a chance."

"You say that your operation may succeed, do you not, Ambroise?" said the Balafré. "Tell us now whether you have ever practiced it successfully?"

"Yes, monseigneur," replied Ambroise; "some time ago, on M. de La Bretesche, Rue de la Harpe, at the Rose Rouge; and, to speak of matters with which monseigneur is very well acquainted, I performed the opera-

ion at the siege of Calais, on M. de Pienne, who was
wounded in the breach.''

It was not perhaps without an object that Ambroise
Paré recalled the memory of Calais. At all events, he
was successful, and the duke appeared deeply impressed.

"In fact, I remember that," said he. "Then I hesitate
no longer; I consent to the operation.''

"And I also," said Mary Stuart, doubtless enlightened
by her love.

"But not I!" cried Catherine.

"But, madame," returned Mary, "since you know it is
our only chance!''

"Who says so?" rejoined the queen-mother. "Master
Ambroise Paré, a heretic. But it is not the opinion of
the physicians.''

"No, madame," said Chapelain; "and these gentlemen
as well as I protest against the method of Master Paré.''

"Ah! you see now!" cried Catherine, triumphantly.

The Balafré, who was beside himself with anxiety,
went to the queen-mother and led her into the recess
of a window.

"Madame," said he, in a low tone, and with clinched
teeth, "listen to me. You wish your son to die, and the
Prince de Condé to live— You have formed an alliance
with the Montmorencys and Bourbons! The bargain is
concluded; the spoils are divided in advance! I know
everything. Take care! I know everything, I tell you!''

But Catherine de Médicis was not a woman easily frightened, and the Duke de Guise had blundered. His words
only made her comprehend better the necessity of boldness,
since her enemy had thrown off his mask. She darted a
withering glance at him; and, escaping from his grasp by
a sudden movement, she ran to the door, which she flung
wide open herself.

"M. le Chancelier!" she cried.

L'Hopital, in accordance with the instructions he had
received, was in the grand hall, waiting to be called; and

with him were all the partisans of the queen-mother and the princes he had been able to gather.

At the summons of Catherine he advanced hastily, and the group of lords pressed curiously toward the open door.

"M. le Chancelier," continued Catherine, in a loud voice, so as to be well heard, "it is proposed to authorize a violent and desperate operation on the person of the king. Master Paré wants to pierce his head with an instrument. I, his mother, protest, with the three doctors here present, against this crime. M. le Chancelier, register my protest."

"Close that door!" cried the Duke de Guise.

In spite of the murmurs of the gentlemen gathered in the great hall, Gabriel did as the duke ordered.

The chancellor alone remained in the chamber of the king.

"Now, M. le Chancelier," said the Balafré, "this operation of which you have heard is necessary, and the queen and I, the Lieutenant-General of the Kingdom, answer, if not for the operation, at least for the surgeon."

"And I," cried Ambroise Paré, "accept at this supreme moment all the responsibilities you wish to lay upon me. Yes; you may take my life if I do not succeed in saving that of the king. But, alas! it is full time! See there! look at the king!"

And, in fact, Francis the Second was livid, motionless, with lifeless eyes. He seemed no longer to see nor hear; nay, even to exist. He no longer responded to the caresses and appeals of Mary.

"Yes; hasten!" said the latter to Ambroise; "hasten in Christ's name! Only try to save the life of the king; I will protect yours."

"I have not the right to prevent anything," said the impassive chancellor; "but my duty is to take the protest of the queen-mother."

"M. l'Hopital, you are no longer chancellor," coldly rejoined the Duke de Guise. "Go on, Ambroise," he said to the surgeon.

"We retire," said Chapelain, "in the name of the physicians."

"Be it so," replied Ambroise. "I need the most absolute quiet around me. Leave me, then, if you please, gentlemen. Let me be the sole master for the time, as I am solely responsible."

For some time Catherine de Médicis had not uttered a word or made a gesture. She had withdrawn to the window, and was looking into the court of the bailiwick, where a great tumult was heard. But, in this critical conjuncture, nobody except herself had paid any attention to the noise outside.

All, even the chancellor, had their eyes riveted upon Ambroise Paré, who had regained all his self-possession as a great surgeon, and was now looking to his instruments.

But at the very moment when he was bending over Francis the Second, the commotion approached nearer, even into the next hall. A bitter and joyous smile flickered over the pale lips of Catherine. The door opened violently, and the Constable de Montmorency, armed as if for battle, appeared menacingly upon the threshold.

"I arrive in season!" cried the constable.

"What does this mean?" cried the Duke de Guise, laying his hand on his dagger.

Ambroise Paré was compelled to stop. Twenty gentlemen accompanied Montmorency, and poured even into the chamber. At his side were Antony de Bourbon and the Prince de Condé. Moreover, the queen-mother and the Chancellor Olivier came and stood beside him. There was no need for them to employ force to be masters in the royal chamber.

"I also," said Ambroise Paré, in despair, "retire."

"Master Paré," cried Mary Stuart, "I, the queen, order you to continue the operation!"

"Ah! madame, I have told you the greatest quietness was necessary," answered the surgeon. "And you see!"

He pointed to the constable and his suite.

"M. Chapelain," said he to the first physician, "try your injection."

"It will be the affair of an instant," said Chapelain, eagerly; "all is prepared."

With the aid of two assistants, he injected his preparation into the king's ear.

Mary Stuart, the Guises, Gabriel, and Ambroise made no opposition, and were silent, crushed, and, as it were, turned to stone.

The constable alone babbled foolishly.

"Well and good!" said he, pleased with the forced docility of Master Paré. "When I think that but for me you would have opened the head of the king in that fashion! Kings of France are only so treated on the field of battle, look you! The steel of the enemy alone can touch them; but a surgeon's steel, never!"

And, enjoying the dejection of the Duke de Guise, he continued—

"I arrived in time, thank God! Ah, messieurs, you wanted, I have been told, to cut off the head of my dear and gallant nephew, the Prince de Condé! But you have aroused the old lion in his den, and here I am! I have delivered the prince; I have spoken to the States, which you oppress. I have, as constable, dismissed the sentinels you placed at the gates of Orléans. Since when has it been customary to thus guard the king, as if he were not in safety in the midst of his subjects?"

"Of what king do you speak?" asked Ambroise Paré. "There will soon be no other king except King Charles the Ninth; for you see, gentlemen," he said to the doctors, "in spite of your injection, the brain is affected, and is beginning to be filled."

Catherine de Médicis saw clearly from the despondent air of Ambroise Paré that all hope was lost.

"Your reign is coming to an end, monseigneur," she could not help saying to the Balafré.

Francis the Second at this moment raised himself with

a sudden movement, opened wide his frightened eyes, stirred his lips as if to stammer a name, then fell back heavily on his pillow.

He was dead.

Ambroise Paré, with a sorrowful gesture, announced the fact to the spectators.

"Ah, madame, madame! you have slain your child!" cried Mary Stuart, leaping toward Catherine in her bewilderment and despair.

The queen-mother darted a cold and venomous glance at her daughter-in-law—a glance big with the hidden hatred of eighteen months.

"My dear," said she, "you have no longer the right to speak thus, understand; for you are no longer queen. Ah, yes, indeed! queen in Scotland. And we shall send you back as soon as possible to reign over your foggy realm."

Mary, by a reaction inevitable after this first outburst of sorrow, fell on her knees, weak and sobbing, at the foot of the bed on which the king was stretched.

"Madame de Fiesque," continued Catherine, tranquilly, "go immediately for the Duke d'Orléans."

"Messieurs," she went on, looking at the Duke de Guise and the cardinal, "the States-General, which were, perhaps, devoted to you a quarter of an hour ago, are now, as you may very well suspect, devoted to us. It has been agreed between M. de Bourbon and myself that I shall be regent and he Lieutenant-General of the Kingdom. But, M. de Guise, you are *still* Grand Master. Fulfil, therefore, the duties of your charge; announce the death of King Francis the Second."

"The king is dead!" said the Balafré, in a deep, hoarse voice.

The king-at-arms repeated, in a loud voice, on the threshold of the grand hall, according to the customary ceremonial—"The king is dead! the king is dead! the king is dead! Pray to God for the salvation of his soul."

And the first gentleman cried immediately after—

"Long live the king!"

At the same moment, Madame de Fiesque led the Duke d'Orléans to the queen-mother, who took him by the hand and passed out with him in order to show him to the courtiers, all of whom were shouting—

"Long live our good King Charles the Ninth."

"Our fortunes are ruined now!" said the cardinal, sadly, to his brother, who alone had remained behind with him.

"Ours, perhaps, but not that of our house," answered the ambitious warrior. "We must bethink ourselves of clearing a path for my son."

"Is there any way of renewing our alliance with the queen-mother?" asked Charles de Lorraine, musingly.

"Leave her to quarrel with her Bourbons and her Huguenots," said the Balafré.

They left the chamber by a secret door, all the time talking.

"Alas! alas!" murmured Mary Stuart, kissing the ice-cold hand of Francis the Second, "there is none left to weep for him but me—the poor darling who loved me so much!"

"And me, madame," said Gabriel de Montgommery (who had stood apart until now), advancing, with tears in his eyes.

"Oh, thanks!" said Mary Stuart, with a look into which she put her whole soul.

"I will do more than weep," he continued, in an undertone, as he followed with angry eyes the figure of Montmorency strutting beside Catherine de Médicis. "Yes, I shall avenge him, perhaps, by resuming the interrupted work of my own vengeance. Since the constable has become powerful, the struggle between us is not over!"

Gabriel, too, alas! kept his personal grievances alive in the presence of the dead.

Decidedly, Regnier La Planche was right when he said, "It is a wretched thing to be king only to die."

And he was doubtless right also when he added—

"During this reign of Francis the Second, France was a theatre in which the most terrible tragedies were enacted—tragedies which posterity will both wonder at and abhor."

CHAPTER XLVII

GOOD-BY, FRANCE!

EIGHT months after the death of Francis the Second, on the 15th of August, 1561, Mary Stuart was about to embark at Calais for her kingdom of Scotland. During these eight months she had struggled day by day, and, so to speak, hour by hour, with Catherine de Médicis, and even with her uncles, who were anxious, for various reasons, to see her leave France. But Mary could not make up her mind to separate from that sweet land where she had been so happy and beloved a queen. Even in the sorrowful memories which recalled her premature widowhood, the dear places where she dwelt had for her a charm and a poetry from which she could not tear herself.

Not only did Mary Stuart feel this poetry, she gave it expression also. She not only wept over the death of Francis the Second as a wife, she sang it as a muse. Brantome, on account of his admiration, has preserved that sweet complaint which she made on the occasion, and which may be compared to the most noteworthy poetry of this epoch:

> Ah! the dolorous plaint
> Of a heart rent with anguish!
> With my misery faint,
> In dull sorrow I languish,
>   And, with gloom overcast,
>   All my young years have passed.
>
> Has grim fate ever dealt
> Such a blow of disaster?

Or great queen ever felt
A calamity vaster
　　Than was mine when my sweet
　　Lay there, dead, at my feet ?

In the bloom of my youth,
When hope's flower is in blossom,
Pangs that know not of ruth
Make their home in my bosom,
　　And no hopes quench the fire
　　Of regret and desire.

What once gave me delight
Now but heightens my sorrow;
From the day that is bright
Naught of brightness I borrow;
　　All things blissful and fair
　　Feed my lonely despair.

For, wherever my way,
Be it forest or meadow,
In the noontide of day
Or in evening's gray shadow,
　　I am longing for One—
　　For the saint that is gone!

If betimes to the skies
I look up in my dreaming,
The soft glance of his eyes
Through the cloud-rifts seems gleaming
　　And the depths of the sea
　　Cannot hide him from me!

When a respite from woe
On my couch I am questing,
His dear voice, soft and low,
Speaks, unceasing, unresting—
　　Through the night, through the day
　　He is with me alway!

End, my song, this sad strain
Of thy grievous lamenting,
Whose despairing refrain
Tells of pangs unrelenting!
　　Nor can absence abate
　　A love stronger than fate!

It was at Rheims, where she had first retired with her uncle of Lorraine, that Mary Stuart uttered this melodious and moving lament. She remained until the end of the spring in Champagne. Then the religious troubles which had broken out in Scotland demanded her presence in that country. Besides, the almost passionate admiration of Charles the Ninth, even while yet a child, for his fair sister-in-law, whenever he spoke of her, alarmed the suspicious regent Catherine.

Mary Stuart had therefore to resign herself to depart.

She came to St. Germain in the month of July, to take leave of the court. The tokens of devotion and of adoration almost which she received there augmented, if it were possible, her bitter regrets.

Her dowry, charged on Touraine and Poitou, brought her an income of twenty thousand livres; she was also carrying with her some rich jewels into Scotland; and this rich booty might tempt some sea-rover. Moreover, violence was feared from Elizabeth of England, who saw in the young queen of Scotland a rival. A number of gentlemen offered to escort Mary to her own dominions; and, when she arrived at Calais, she had around her not only her uncles, but Brantome, Damville, and the best part of that elegant and chivalrous court.

Mary found two galleys awaiting her in the harbor of Calais, ready to sail whenever she ordered them. But she remained six days at Calais—so hard did those who had accompanied her to this fatal place of separation find it to part from her!

At last, as we have said, the 15th of August was fixed for her departure. The weather on that day was gloomy and threatening; but there was no wind or rain.

On the shore, before putting her foot on the vessel that was to carry her away, Mary, in order to thank those who had escorted her to the utmost limit of their country, wished to give each her hand to kiss as a last farewell.

All came, sad and respectful, knelt down, and pressed with their lips that adored hand.

The last of all was a gentleman who had followed Mary ever since she quitted St. Germain, but who, during the journey, had always remained in the background, concealed by his cloak and his hat. He had not shown himself nor spoken to any one.

But when he came in his turn to kneel before the queen, Mary recognized Gabriel de Montgommery.

"What! it is you, count!" said she. "Ah! I am happy to see you again, my faithful friend—you who have wept with me by the bier of my dead king. But since you were among these noble gentlemen, why did you not appear?"

"I wanted to see you, madame, and yet not be seen," answered Gabriel. "In my isolation I could the better dwell upon my memories and enjoy more keenly the satisfaction I felt in performing so pleasing a duty."

"Thanks once more for this last proof of your attachment, M. le Comte," said Mary Stuart. "Would I could prove my gratitude to you better than by words! But I can no longer do anything; and, unless it should please you to follow me into my poor Scotland with Messieurs de Damville and Brantome—"

"Ah! it would have been my most ardent wish, madame!" cried Gabriel; "but another duty detains me in France. A person who is very dear and sacred to me, and whom I have not seen for two years, is waiting for me at this very hour—"

"Do you mean Diana de Castro?" asked Mary, quickly.

"Yes, madame," said Gabriel; "I received a letter in Paris from her, asking me to come to St. Quentin on to-day, the 15th of August. I cannot be there until to-morrow. But, whatever be her reason for sending for me, she will pardon me, I am sure, when she learns that I did not wish to leave you until the moment you were leaving France."

"Dear Diana!" murmured Mary, pensively. "Yes; she

too loved me, and was a sister to me. Stay, M. de Montgommery; give her this ring in memory of me, and go to
her at once. She needs you, perhaps; and if there is
question of her welfare, I would not detain you. Adieu,
adieu, my friends; adieu, all. They are waiting for me.
I must part with you; alas! I must part."

She tore herself away from those who still wished her
to stay a while longer, entered the boat, and was rowed to
the galley of M. de Mévillon, followed by the envied lords
who were to accompany her to Scotland.

But, just as Scotland could not console Mary for France,
those who came with her could not make her forget those
she had left; and it was the latter she seemed to love the
most.

Standing on the prow of her galley, she continued to
wave the handkerchief with which she wiped away her
tears to the friends and relatives that remained on the
shore as long as the vessel was in sight.

At last she was in the open sea; and her eyes, in spite
of herself, were drawn toward a ship about to enter the
port she had just quitted. She was gazing earnestly upon
it, envying it its destiny, when suddenly the vessel leaned
over, as if it had received some submarine shock, and,
trembling from stem to stern, began, amid the cries of
her crew, to sink into the ocean. It disappeared before
the boat despatched by M. Mévillon to its relief could
reach it. For a moment some black points might be
seen floating here and there on the surface of the water
in the place where the ship had gone down, then vanish-
ing, one after another, before the boat could come up with
them, although the rowers exerted themselves vigorously.
The boat returned without having rescued a single one of
these poor shipwrecked creatures.

"O God!" cried Mary, "what an omen for my voyage
is this!"

Meanwhile, the wind freshened and the sails of the galley were beginning to be filled, so that the crew were able

to rest for a while. Mary, seeing that she was so swiftly being borne away from land, leaned against the bulwarks, her eyes turned toward the port—eyes that were darkened by big tears—and never ceased repeating—

"Adieu, France! adieu, France!"

She remained thus nearly five hours—that is to say, until nightfall; and she would never have thought of retiring, perhaps, had not Brantome come to tell her that they were waiting for her at supper.

Then, weeping and sobbing more bitterly than ever, she said—

"It is now, indeed, dear France, that I really lose you, since night, jealous of my last happiness, drops its black veil before my eyes to bereave me of the pleasure of beholding thee. Adieu, then, dear France; I shall never see thee more!"

Then, making a sign to Brantome that she would go down after him, she took her tablets, sat down on a bench, and wrote with a pencil, by the fading light, these well-known lines:

> A last farewell! sweet France, a last!
>   Ah! land than all lands nearer
>   To this fond heart and dearer!
> Land where my happy childhood passed
> In joys I may again feel never!
> The bark that bears me from thee fast
> The links that bind us cannot sever!
> One part of me bides with thee still,
> So that thy loving heart may fill
> With memories of the other ever!

At last she descended, and, approaching her shipmates, who were awaiting her, said—

"I am acting quite differently from Dido; for, when Æneas abandoned the Queen of Carthage, she could not keep her eyes away from the ocean, while I cannot keep mine away from the land."

She was invited to sit down to supper, but she could eat

Gabriel, on turning round his head, perceived the other Diana, Madame de Poitiers. She laughed, as demons must laugh.

But Gabriel, with contemptuous carelessness, turned away from her and again fixed his eyes and all his thoughts on Sister Bénie.

"My sister!" he repeated ardently and sadly.

Thereupon Diana de Poitiers coldly answered—

"It is, no doubt, your sister in Jesus Christ, monsieur, whom you salute by that title, and who was yesterday called Madame de Castro."

"What do you mean, madame? Great God! what do you mean?" cried Gabriel, rising and quivering in every member.

Diana de Poitiers did not answer him, but addressed her daughter.

"My child," said she, "it is now time, I think, to reveal to you the secret of which I spoke yesterday, and which my duty forbids me to keep longer from you."

"Oh, what is it?" cried Gabriel, bewildered.

"My child," continued Madame de Poitiers, tranquilly, "it was not to bless you only that I left the retreat where I have lived, thanks to M. de Montgommery, for nearly two years. Do not regard my words as ironical," she said mockingly, in answer to a gesture of Gabriel. "I am really grateful to you for having torn me, violently or not, from an impious and corrupting world. I am happy now; grace has touched me, and the love of God fills my heart. To thank you in return, I wish to spare you a sin, a crime, perhaps."

"Oh, what is it?" asked Sister Bénie, in turn, her heart throbbing wildly.

"My child," went on Diana de Poitiers, with her infernal coolness, "I fancy that on yesterday I could, by a word, have arrested on your lips the sacred vows you were about to pronounce. But was it for me, a poor sinner, so happy to be delivered from earthly chains, to rob God of a soul so freely given to him in freedom and chastity? No, I was silent."

"I dare not guess; I dare not!" murmured Gabriel.

"To-day, my child, I break my silence, because I see," resumed the ex-favorite, "by the grief and ardor of M. de Montgommery, that you still engross all his thoughts. Now he must forget you; he must really. Nevertheless, if he was always deluded by the fancy that you were his sister, the daughter of Count de Montgommery, he might let his memory dwell upon you without remorse. It would be a crime! And I, who have been converted, yesterday, cannot be the accomplice of that crime. Know then, Diana, that you are not the sister of M. de Montgommery, but really and truly the daughter of King Henry the Second, whom M. le Comte so unfortunately struck in that fatal tournament."

"Horrible!" cried Sister Bénie, hiding her face in her hands.

"You lie, madame!" cried Gabriel, violently; "you must lie. Where is the proof that you do not lie?"

"Here it is," answered Madame de Poitiers, quietly, handing him a paper which she took from her bosom.

Gabriel seized the paper with a trembling hand and read greedily.

"It is," said Madame de Poitiers, "a letter from your father, written some days before his death, as you see. He complains of my cruelty, as you see also. But he resigns himself, as you may see as well, with the reflection that I shall soon be his wife, and that I have reserved for him a purer and fuller happiness than any he has hitherto enjoyed. Oh, the terms of that letter, signed and dated, are by no means equivocal! Is not that your opinion? You see then, M. de Montgommery, that it would have been criminal for you to think of Sister Bénie; for no tie of blood unites you to her who is now the bride of Christ. And, in sparing you such a sacrilege, I hope that I have acquitted myself of the debt I owed you, and paid you, over and above, for the happiness I have gained through you in my solitude.''

During this sarcastic discourse, Gabriel had completed the perusal of the fatal but sacred letter. It left no doubt, in fact. It was for Gabriel the voice of his father issuing from the tomb to attest the truth.

When the unhappy young man raised his haggard eyes, he saw Madame de Castro fainting at the foot of a *prie-Dieu*.

He rushed instinctively toward her. The thick bars of the grating stopped him.

Turning round, he beheld Diana de Poitiers, on whose lips flickered a smile of placid satisfaction.

Beside himself with grief, he took two steps toward her, his hand raised.

But he stopped, frightened at himself, and, striking his forehead like a madman, only cried, ''Adieu, Diana! adieu!'' and took flight.

If he had stayed a minute longer, he could not have helped crushing this impious mother as though she were a viper.

Jean Peuquoy was anxiously awaiting him outside the convent.

''Do not question me! ask nothing!'' Gabriel shouted, in a kind of frenzy.

And as the brave Peuquoy looked at him in astonishment—

''Pardon me,'' said Gabriel, more gently. ''I am afraid I am nearly mad. I do not wish to think, you see; and to escape from my thoughts, I must leave, I must fly to Paris. Accompany me, if you kindly wish to do so, my friend, as far as the gate of the city where I have left my horse. But, for God's sake, do not speak of me! speak of yourself.''

The worthy weaver, as much from a desire to distract Gabriel as to obey him, related how marvellously well Babette was; how she had lately made him the father of a young Peuquoy—a wonderful child that! how his brother

Pierre was about to set up as armorer in St. Quentin; how, in fine, he had lately had news of Martin Guerre, through a reiter returning home from Picardy, and how happy Martin was with his Bertrande, now as sweet as honey.

But it must be confessed that Gabriel, dazed with grief, did not hear, or heard very imperfectly, this tale of joy.

However, when he reached the Paris gate, he shook the weaver's hand cordially.

"Adieu, my friend," said he. "Thanks for your affection. Remember me to all those you love. I am happy to know you happy; do you who prosper think sometimes of him who suffers."

And without waiting for other reply than the tears that shone in Jean Peuquoy's eyes, Gabriel mounted his horse and galloped away.

On his arrival at Paris, as if fate wished to overwhelm him with every sort of misfortune at the same time, he found his good nurse Aloyse dead, after a short sickness, without seeing him again.

The next day, he visited Admiral de Coligny.

"M. l'Amiral," said he, "I know that the persecutions and the religious wars will soon begin again, in spite of so many efforts to prevent them. I have to tell you that henceforward I can offer to the cause of Reform, not only my heart, but my sword also. My life is good for nothing but to serve you. Take it, and do not spare it. Besides, in your ranks I can best defend myself against one of my enemies and chastise another."

Gabriel was thinking of the queen-regent and the constable.

There is no need to say that Coligny received with enthusiasm this priceless auxiliary, whose bravery and energy he had so often tested.

The history of the count from that moment was the history of the religious wars which left so many bloody marks on the reign of Charles the Ninth.

Gabriel de Montgommery played a terrible part in these

wars; and at every great event his name caused the cheeks of Catherine de Médicis to turn pale.

When, after the massacre of Vassy in 1562, Rouen and all Normandy declared for the Huguenots, Count de Montgommery was known to be the principal author of this revolt.

He was, the same year, at the siege of Dreux, where he performed prodigies of valor.

He was said to have wounded with a pistol-shot Constable de Montmorency, who commanded on that occasion, and he would have killed him if Prince de Porcien had not sheltered and received the constable as prisoner.

Every one knows how the Balafré, a month after the battle in which he had plucked victory from the unskilful hands of the constable, was treacherously slain by the fanatic Poltrot before Orléans.

Montmorency, rid of his rival, but deprived of his ally, was even more unsuccessful at the battle of St. Denis in 1567 than he had been in that of Dreux.

The Scotchman Robert Stuart summoned him to surrender. His answer was to strike his face with the hilt of his sword. Some one fired a pistol at him, hiting him in the side, and he fell mortally wounded.

Through the cloud of blood that spread over his eyes, he thought he recognized the features of Gabriel.

The constable expired the next day.

Though he had no longer any direct enemies, Gabriel did not on that account relax the force of his blows.

When Catherine de Médicis asked who had reduced Béarn to submission to the Queen of Navarre, and who had caused the Prince de Béarn to be recognized as generalissimo of the Huguenot armies, the answer was: Count de Montgommery.

When, on the day after St. Bartholomew (1572), the queen-mother, impatient for vengeance, inquired for the names of those who had escaped, not of those who had perished, the first name she heard was—Montgommery.

Montgommery threw himself into La Rochelle with La-noue. Rochelle sustained nine terrible assaults, and cost the royal army forty thousand men. It kept its liberty while capitulating, and Gabriel could leave it, safe and sound.

He next threw himself into Sancerre, besieged by the Duke de Berri. He knew a good deal, it may be imagined, about the defence of places. A handful of Sancerrois, without other weapons than iron-shod clubs, resisted a body of six thousand soldiers for six months. When they capitulated, they obtained, like the people of La Rochelle, liberty of conscience and a pledge of personal safety.

Catherine de Médicis saw, with ever-increasing fury, her old and invincible enemy constantly eluding her grasp.

Montgommery left Poitou, which was on fire, and returned to stir up Normandy, which was being pacified.

After leaving St. Lô, he took Carentan in three days, and stripped Valognes bare of all its supplies. The whole Norman nobility ranged itself under his banner.

Catherine de Médicis and the king immediately set on foot three armies, and published the ban and arrière-ban in La Perche and Le Mans. The leader of the royal troops was the Duke de Matignon.

This time, Montgommery no longer fought. Lost in the ranks of his co-religionists, he made head directly and personally against Charles the Ninth, and had his army, as the king had his.

He combined an admirable plan which ought to have assured him a brilliant victory.

He let Matignon besiege St. Lô with all his forces, secretly left the city, and went to Domfront. There, Francis du Hallot was to join him with all the cavalry from Bretagne, Anjou, and Caux. With these troops, he was to fall unexpectedly upon the royal army before St. Lô, which, taken between two fires, would be exterminated.

But treason vanquished the man hitherto invincible. An ensign warned Matignon of the secret departure of

Montgommery for Domfront, accompanied only by forty horsemen.

Matignon was much less anxious to take St. Lô than to take Montgommery. He left the siege to one of his lieutenants, and ran to Domfront with two regiments, six hundred cavalry, and a powerful artillery.

Any one except Gabriel would have surrendered without attempting a useless resistance. But with his forty men he held out against a whole army. The story of this incredible siege ought to be read in the history of De Thou.

Domfront resisted twelve days. Count de Montgommery made seven furious sorties during that time. At last, when the walls of the town, riddled and tottering, were as it were in the hands of the enemy, Gabriel abandoned them, but only to withdraw into the Tower of Guillaume de Bellême and renew the struggle.

He had now but thirty men left.

Matignon ordered for the assault a battery of five pieces of heavy artillery, a hundred cuirassiers, seven hundred musketeers, and a hundred pikemen.

The attack lasted five hours, and six hundred cannon-shot were fired at the old keep.

In the evening, Montgommery had but sixteen men, but he still held out. He spent the night in repairing the breach, like a simple workman.

The assault was renewed with the dawn. Matignon had received fresh reinforcements during the night. There were then around the keep of Bellême and its seventeen defenders fifteen thousand soldiers and eighteen pieces of cannon.

It was not courage the besieged lacked, but powder.

Montgommery, in order not to fall alive into the hands of his enemies, resolved to pass his sword through his body. But Matignon sent him a flag of truce, the bearer of which swore in the name of his chief "that his life should be safe and he should be at liberty to depart."

Montgommery surrendered on the faith of this oath. He might, however, have remembered Castelnau.

On the same day, he was sent, bound hand and foot, to Paris; Catherine de Médicis had him at last. It was by treachery; but what did it matter? Charles the Ninth had just died; until the return of Henry the Third from Poland, she was queen-regent and all-powerful.

Montgommery was tried before the parliament and condemned to death on the 26th of June, 1574.

He had been fighting the wife and sons of Henry the Second for fourteen years.

On the 27th of June, Count de Montgommery, to whom, by a refinement of cruelty, the extraordinary torture had been applied, was carried to the scaffold and beheaded. His body was then drawn and quartered.

Catherine de Médicis was present at the execution.

Thus ended the career of this extraordinary man—one of the strongest and finest souls the sixteenth century has seen. He had never risen above the second rank, but he had always proved himself worthy of the first.

His death accomplished to the very letter the prediction of Nostradamus—

> Enfin, l'aimera, puis las! le tuera
> Dame du roy.

Diana de Castro was not alive at the time of his death. Sister Bénie had died the preceding year in the convent of the Benedictines of St. Quentin, of which she was abbess.

END OF PART TWO OF "THE TWO DIANAS"